About the Authors

Barbara Wallace can't remember when she wasn't dreaming up love stories in her head, so writing romances for Mills & Boon is a dream come true. Happily married to her own Prince Charming, she lives in New England with a house full of empty-nest animals. Readers can catch up with Barbara through her newsletter. Sign up at www.barbarawallace.com

After completing a degree in journalism, then working in advertising and mothering her kids, **Robin Gianna** had what she calls her 'awakening'. She decided she wanted to write the romance novels she'd loved since her teens, and now enjoys pushing her characters toward their own happily-ever-afters. When she's not writing, Robin's life is filled with a happily messy kitchen, a needy garden, a wonderful husband, three great kids, a drooling bulldog and one grouchy Siamese cat.

Kate Hardy has been a bookworm since she was a toddler. When she isn't writing Kate enjoys reading, theatre, live music, ballet and the gym. She lives with her husband, student children and their spaniel in Norwich, England. You can contact her via her website: www.katehardy.com

Romantic Escapes

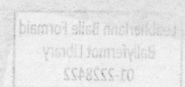

Romantic Escapes:
Paris

BARBARA WALLACE

ROBIN GIANNA

KATE HARDY

MILLS & BOON

First Published in Great Britain 2022
by Mills & Boon, an imprint of HarperCollins*Publishers* Ltd,
1 London Bridge Street, London, SE1 9GF

www.harpercollins.co.uk

HarperCollins*Publishers*
1st Floor, Watermarque Building,
Ringsend Road, Dublin 4, Ireland

ROMANTIC ESCAPES: PARIS © 2022 Harlequin Books S.A.

Beauty & Her Billionaire Boss © 2015 Barbara Wallace
It Happened in Paris... © 2015 Robin Gianakopoulos
Holiday with the Best Man © 2016 Pamela Brooks

ISBN: 978-0-263-30422-0

MIX
Paper from
responsible sources
FSC® C007454

This book is produced from independently certified FSC™ paper to ensure responsible forest management.

For more information visit: www.harpercollins.co.uk/green

Printed and Bound in Spain using 100% Renewable electricity at CPI Black Print, Barcelona

BEAUTY & HER BILLIONAIRE BOSS

BARBARA WALLACE

To Pete—your patience and support are a gift for which I can never say thank you enough.

And to M.G.—for giving someone that dose of common sense when we most needed it.

CHAPTER ONE

THERE SHOULD BE a law against a man looking so good in a tuxedo. Staring at the man asleep in the chair, Piper felt an appreciative shiver. Monsieur Frederic Lafontaine had shed his jacket and untied his tie, yet he still looked like a million dollars, what with the way his shirt pulled taut across his linebacker-sized shoulders. She had to start using his dry cleaner. The guy must have been sprawled here for hours, and yet his clothes didn't have a single wrinkle. Piper's uniform wouldn't last five minutes. In fact—she ran a hand down the front of her black skirt—it hadn't.

Then again, she didn't have cheekbones that could cut glass or thick brown hair that begged to be touched, either. Maybe perfection came in bundles.

Taking a deep breath, she touched his shoulder and tried not to think about the broad muscles beneath her fingers. Eight months of working for the man, and she still hadn't shaken her attraction. "Monsieur? You need to wake up. It's after seven o'clock."

When he didn't respond, she shook his shoulder again, this time a little more aggressively. The motion did the trick. Slowly, his eyes opened, and he blinked unseeingly. "You fell asleep in the chair," she told him.

"Oh." His voice was thick with sleep, making it deeper and rougher than usual. "What—what time is it?"

"Seven fifteen."

"What?" He bolted to his feet, arms akimbo, his right hand connecting with the cup of coffee Piper set on the end table only seconds before. The cup took flight, sending coffee over everything.

"Dammit!" he hollered as the hot liquid splashed his shirt. He immediately started pulling at the cloth, lifting it from his skin. "How many times have I told you, you must tell me when you put something within reach? You know I can't see anything put to the side."

It was hard to say much of anything seeing as how he jumped up before she had a chance to open her mouth. "I'll get you a towel."

"Don't bother." He'd already yanked the shirt free from his waistband. "Clean up the rest of the spill before it stains the carpet. I'm going to take a shower." He turned to head upstairs.

"Wait," Piper called.

Moving this time before he could speak, she scooped up the cup from where it had fallen on the carpet, half an inch from the toe of his shoe. "You were going to crush it," she said, holding the china teacup in front of his face.

If he appreciated her heads-up behavior, he didn't say so. "Tell Michel when he arrives that I will be ready shortly. And make sure my briefcase is by the front door. *On the left*," he added with emphasis.

As if she would leave it somewhere else. Piper bit back the sarcastic response. She learned a long time ago that some fights weren't meant to be won. Arguing with a man who was wearing hot coffee on his stomach was definitely one of those fights. Instead, she waited until he'd stalked his way upstairs, then treated herself to a glare in his direction. It would serve him right if she moved his bag to the right just to spite him. Because goodness knows the world might end if the briefcase was on the wrong side of the doorway.

Not that she would actually move the thing. Put out or not, she wasn't so petty that she'd pick on a blind man—or half-blind man as the case may be. Truth was, nitpicky as they were, monsieur's "rules" served a purpose. When she took this job, it was made very clear his limited field of vision required everything in the house to be just so. Chief on the list was that nothing should be set to the side without his knowledge. His lack of peripheral vision might cause a mishap, he'd explained. Most of the time, the system worked. There were times in fact, such as when he crossed the room with his slow, purposeful strides, that Piper forgot the man had trouble seeing.

After double-checking on the briefcase—which was on the left as always—she headed for the utility closet. "So goes another fun-filled day in Paris," she said as she marched into the kitchen for her cleaning supplies. Naturally, the coffee had fallen on the handmade Persian carpet. That meant instead of using the nice handy carpet-cleaning machine in the closet, she had to get the stain up with water and a vinegar paste.

This was not how she expected her year abroad to go. Her year here was supposed to signal the start of a new and exciting life. The wonderful moment when she stopped being dumpy Piper Rush and became Piper Rush, chef extraordinaire who dazzled the culinary institute with her skills and enthralled French men with her American wit. In short, the complete opposite of her life in East Boston.

She should have known better.

Didn't take long for her to realize that Paris was exactly the same as Boston, only in French. Which actually made it worse than Boston. Despite spending hours shoulder to shoulder with a dozen other people, she hadn't made a single close friend. Everyone was too busy trying to impress Chef Despelteau. In a way, you'd think the fact that she couldn't impress the man if she tried would help her cause, but no. Yesterday, after she didn't use enough confit to brown her chicken, he declared her cassoulet flavorless and spent ten minutes lecturing her on the importance of taste, even when making "peasant food." All her classmates did was snicker. City of Lights, her foot. More like the City of the Unfriendly.

Even Frederic barely paid attention to her, unless there was an errand to run, or she needed to wake him up. He was too busy lecturing at the university or heading off to some fancy social event.

The perpetual loneliness she fought to keep under wraps threatened to wedge free. She had to swallow to keep it from rising up and choking her. God, what she wouldn't give for someone to talk to. *Or to go home.*

Out of habit, her hand reached for the cell phone

tucked in her apron only to leave it behind. It was still the middle of the night in Boston. Her sister, Patience, would still be asleep. Patience—the only reason she was sticking things out to completion. Her sister was convinced Piper was living the dream, and considering how much Patience had sacrificed so Piper could actually have a dream, she didn't dare disturb the fantasy. Besides, her sister had issues of her own. She and her boss's nephew were doing some kind of back-and-forth that had Patience on edge. The last thing she needed right now was a whiny baby sister burning up the data package complaining because her year abroad wasn't all sunshine and roses.

She carried her supplies into the salon, pausing when she reached the front window. A few blocks away, the Eiffel Tower loomed tall, reminding her she really had no right complaining. She might be lonely, but she was a lonely person living in luxury. Instead of monsieur's mansion, she could be living in some ratty apartment battling roaches for breakfast. Or worse, living on the streets. Been there, done both. She didn't feel like doing either again.

If only she had someone to share Paris with, then things wouldn't be so bad. It wasn't going to happen, though. If she hadn't found a kindred spirit yet, she wasn't going to. She was simply going to have to suck things up, the way she always did.

Speaking of sucking, she had a carpet to clean. Staring at the stain darkening the beige carpet, she sighed. This better not be a sign of how the rest of her day was going to go.

* * *

Frederic winced as he peeled the wet shirt from his body. Not because the liquid stung his skin, although it did, but because he was appalled at his behavior. Yelling at his housekeeper that way. Like a child throwing a tantrum. Didn't he swear he would never be that way? Become one of those angry invalids who took their bad moods out on others? Yet the first time he spills a drink, he lashes out. Embarrassment was no excuse.

What did he expect, falling asleep in the salon like that? It was the last glass of Bordeaux. Knowing the way alcohol went to his head and made him overly pensive, he never should have indulged. Last night found him sitting for hours, watching the tower's twinkling lights, his mind a sea of morose thoughts.

The dampness from his shirt found its way to his palms. Resisting the urge to hurl the garment across the room, he draped it on top of the duvet for Piper to find later. He stripped off the rest of his tuxedo as well, making sure he returned the suit and his shoes to their assigned places in the closet. Oh, but for those days when undressing meant toeing off your shoes wherever you stood and tossing your clothes in a heap.

Obviously, last night's moroseness hadn't subsided. Why else would he be bemoaning a past that he couldn't get back? After all, he'd come to terms with his failing eyesight long before it started to steal his peripheral vision. From the moment the doctors first told him his retina was degenerating, in fact. He knew full well that one day the tunnel through which he viewed the world would close completely, leaving him blind. He'd accepted his fate and framed his life in anticipation. And when the time came, he would shoulder the burden alone, the way a person should. He wouldn't drag others down with him. A promise that, until this morning, he'd done a very good job of keeping.

He owed his housekeeper a very large apology.

When the employment agency first recommended the American culinary student, he thought the idea ridiculous. A temporary resident? She'd be too distracted by studies and sightseeing. But as it turned out, Piper was nothing short of exemplary. Today aside, she did her job quietly and unobtrusively. In fact, the two of them could go days without crossing paths. Precisely the kind of help Frederic preferred.

Today's mistake with the coffee was as much his fault as hers. She no doubt set down the cup to wake him, not expecting him to stand up so quickly.

He would definitely apologize.

Unfortunately, there wasn't time right now. Leaning in close, he read the time on his nightstand clock. With luck, he could shower and make his first class in plenty of time. Whether or not his morning began poorly didn't matter to his superiors at the university. They expected him to deliver his lectures on time, regardless. This evening, then. Before the symphony. He would find Piper and explain that he overreacted. Then they would both forget this morning ever happened.

Staining the carpet turned out to be the high point of the day.

First, cleaning the rug took longer than planned. In

addition to the major stain, there were a dozen or so tiny spots that needed blotting. It took her forever to find them all, so by the time Piper finished, she was running late. Chef Despelteau was less than thrilled to see her slip through the door five minutes into his lecture.

Now this.

"Uninspired," Chef Despelteau pronounced. "Your spices, they do not dance, they plod. I expect my students to produce magic in the kitchen, not…" He dropped his fork back onto the plate with an expression that was usually reserved for walking around landfills. Shaking his head, he moved on, his silence letting everyone know Piper wasn't worth more of his time.

"…so pathetic. Why is she even here?"

The whispered comment drifted from the stovetop across the aisle. Apparently whoever said it didn't care if anyone heard him. Why should he, when the whole class was thinking the same thing?

Keeping her shoulders square, Piper stared straight ahead and pretended she didn't hear a thing. That was the number one rule. Never let them think they were getting to you. Never lose control. Never let them see you cry. Crying only gave the bullies power. Let them whisper behind her back all they wanted; she would not give them the satisfaction of seeing so much as a twitch.

She succeeded, too. All through Chef Despelteau's final remarks, through the Métro ride home, and even into the house. She managed to last until she saw the living room carpet and the faint brown ring reminding her she'd failed that task, too. Letting out the coarsest obscenity she knew, she broke down.

Screw cooking school. Tossing her bag in the chair, she stomped into the kitchen. Screw monsieur, too. Him and his impossible-to-clean carpeting. Screw Paris with its beautiful buildings and sidewalk cafés and shops she couldn't afford. She hated them all.

Carbs. She needed carbs. Yanking open the refrigerator door, she grabbed a wedge of cheddar cheese and an onion. Creamy, gooey macaroni and cheese, that's what this pity party needed. *How's that for peasant food, Chef Despelteau?*

Now if she would only stop crying. Sniffing back a fresh batch of tears, she grabbed the cheese grater and took to demolishing the cheddar to a shredded pulp.

"There you—"

"What now?" she snarled. What else could she add to her list of mistakes today?

Frederic blinked in shock. Great. Yelling at her boss. That's what she could add. Because, of course.

Horrified, she turned back to the cheese. "I mean, about this mor—morn…" The tears were back. She scrunched her face trying to stop them.

A paper towel floated in front of her face.

"Is everything all right?"

Why'd he have to sound nice, too? It made things worse. "Fine." Taking the paper towel, she wiped her cheeks and blew her nose.

"You don't look fine."

"The cheese is making my eyes water."

"I see. It must be quite pungent."

Piper ignored the comment, choosing to wipe her nose again instead. "Did you need something, monsieur?"

A tentative smile worked its way across his features. Afraid to set her off again, probably. "I wanted to apologize for losing my temper this morning. The coffee, it was not your fault."

No, it wasn't, she wanted to say. She didn't. Since he apologized, the least she could do was be gracious in return. "I should have known better than to put a cup where you couldn't see it."

"And I should know better than to behave like a brat," he countered, one-upping her. "It's rude to blame others for my shortcomings."

Piper wasn't sure she'd call partial blindness a shortcoming, but she accepted the apology anyway. If she didn't, the two of them might spend all night exchanging regrets. "Thank you," she said with a sniff. The man would never know that his "I'm sorry" had just beat out the coffee stain as the day's bright spot.

"Do you need another paper towel? I would offer you something nicer, but I'm not a handkerchief person. A napkin perhaps?"

That made her smile, picturing him retrieving a napkin from the linen closet. "Thanks, but I'm okay now." There remained a slight pressure behind her eyes trying to push out tears, but she could keep that under control. A quick splash of water and she'd be fine.

"Are—" She took one last swipe at her nose. "Are you in for the evening?" As if she didn't already know the answer. Frederic was seldom "in." His evenings were one big social engagement. How one person could squeeze so much activity into a week, she didn't know.

Just as she expected, Frederic shook his head. "I

have tickets for the symphony. I came home to change my shirt is all."

Meaning he would be home late, as usual. "I'll make sure to leave the foyer light on before I turn in."

"Thank you." He turned to leave only to pause. "Why don't you take the evening off as well? Some time with friends might make you feel better."

Sure it would, if she had friends to go out with. "I…" Thankfully, the *beep* of an incoming message on her cell phone saved her from having to make up some embarrassing lie.

"Sounds like your friends have the same idea," Frederic said.

She reached into her pocket, smiling when she read the message on her screen. "It's my sister," she told him. Why she felt she needed to tell him that, she didn't know.

"You have a sister."

A question as much as a statement. Surely he knew. Then again, he might not. This was the longest conversation they'd ever had.

"She works as a housekeeper back in Boston."

"Ah, so cleaning is a family business."

"More like a family situation we both fell into." From his expression, she could tell he didn't get the joke. No surprise. It wasn't very clear, or funny. "She wants to video chat."

"Sounds like you've got something to look forward to."

"Yeah." Piper smiled. Talking to Patience would definitely make her feel better.

"I'm glad." And for the first time she could remember, he gave her a warm, genuine smile. "I'll leave you alone so you can talk. Good night."

"Good night." To her horror, she almost said "Don't go" instead. Her loneliness was out of control if a smile could make her slip up like that.

Piper waited until she heard the front door shut before going to get her computer. Her apartment sat at the back of the house. Technically, it was more like a suite of rooms—bedroom, bathroom and sitting room—but they were still nicer than anything she could afford on her own. They also came with kitchen privileges and monsieur's kitchen was a dream come true even for an *uninspired* cook like her.

It was into the kitchen that Piper carried her laptop. Patience specifically said video chat, which meant she was planning on a nice long conversation. By putting the laptop on the counter, Piper could cook while they talked. It would be almost like home.

Almost.

A few keystrokes later, Patience Rush's face appeared on screen. Took the older woman about two seconds to frown. "Your eyes are all red and puffy," she said. "Is everything okay?"

Wow, was that the question of the night or what? Maybe she should have looked in a mirror to see how awful she actually looked. "I was chopping onions," Piper replied. At least it was more believable than blaming the cheese.

Too bad her sister didn't let the lie slide as easily as her boss had. "Onions, huh? You sure?"

"Yes, I'm sure."

Patience arched a brow. Her form of mother guilt. It worked every time.

"Okay," Piper admitted, "*maybe* I was thinking about home a little bit too."

"Oh, sweetie, I miss you, too. But hey, a couple more months and you'll be back in Boston bragging to everyone you know how you're a fancy French chef. Do you have any idea how proud I am of you?"

"I do," Piper replied, the familiar knot starting to twist in her stomach. She got the heavy unsettled feeling every time Patience started gushing about her great Paris adventure.

"So what is it that has you video chatting me in the middle of your day?" she asked, changing the topic. Her sister seemed especially bubbly today. A big difference from the last few phone calls. Her image on the screen glowed and not from computer glare either.

"What? A girl can't miss her baby sister?"

"A girl can definitely miss her baby sister." Same way the baby sister could miss her. Piper blinked back some fresh tears. "But usually you text. I know you've got a lot on your plate."

"Never too much for you."

"Awww." Sweet as the sentiment was, Piper wasn't buying. Not with the way her sister's eyes were sparkling. "Seriously, what do you want?"

"I have a favor to ask."

"I knew you wanted something." Although what kind of favor could Piper do from halfway around the world? Send someone a souvenir? "What do you need?"

"I need you to pay a visit to someone there in Paris."

"Who?"

Piper listened as her sister explained. The favor was for Piper to visit the sister of a dead artist named Nigel Rougeau.

"Hey, isn't your boss's cat named Nigel?" she interrupted. Patience was always telling stories about the big Maine coon cat.

"The cat's a namesake," Patience replied. "Nigel was Ana's lover in the seventies." Ana being the little old lady Patience worked for.

Her sister went on to explain a very tragic story involving Ana and the painter. "There's a small chance that one of the paintings Ana posed for still exists," she said.

"And you want me to talk with Nigel's sister and find out for you."

"If anyone knows if one of Nigel's paintings survived, it would be someone in his family."

True enough. Especially if Nigel and his sister were as close as she and Patience were.

"I think she'd find talking to you a lot less intimidating than a private detective."

"I am definitely unintimidating," Piper replied. More often than not, she was the one intimidated.

"So you'll do it?"

"Of course." A couple hours of her time was nothing. In fact, it would break up the monotony. "I'll call her tomorrow and see if she'll meet with me. Maybe you'll luck out and there'll be a big old painting of Ana hanging in her house."

"Wouldn't that be something," Patience said with a

laugh. "Stuart and I will be glad for any information you can find out."

"Stuart, huh?" That was a new development. Until recently, Patience's descriptions of Stuart Duchenko leaned more toward the suspicious jerk variety. Putting down her knife, she leaned close to the screen. "How are things going with the two of you? Is he still cool with, you know, the club?"

"Seems to be," Patience replied.

"See? I told you he'd understand. It's not like you went to work in that place because you liked dancing naked on tables." It was the same reasoning Piper used on herself whenever the teasing at school got to be too much to bear. Of course, she never told Patience about what the kids used to say. Her sister was embarrassed enough.

Case in point, the wince crossing Patience's face right now. "Of course I didn't, and you were right. Stuart says he understands."

"Wait—what do you mean 'says he understands'? Don't you believe him?" There was a note of reluctance in the comment Piper didn't like.

"No, I believe him. Stuart's been great."

"Then what's wrong?"

"Nothing." Patience shook her head.

Nothing came with a very dreamy sigh. No way was Piper letting the reaction go by unnoticed. "Patience? What aren't you telling me?"

"Um…"

Son of a gun, her sister was red as a tomato. There was only one thing that would make her blush that deeply. "Oh my God! Is something going on between you and your boss?"

"He's not my boss," Patience said quickly. "He's my boss's nephew."

She was splitting hairs and they both knew it, which was why Piper asked, "What exactly is the difference?"

"About the same as between you dating *your* boss and you dating his next-door neighbor."

"Pul—leeze." Like that was a good example. "The only neighbor I've met is an eleven-year-old boy, and my boss doesn't even…"

"Doesn't even what?"

Notice I'm here. That's what Piper was going to say, anyway. Only he had noticed tonight. Absently, she ran a knuckle down her cheek as she remembered his kind gesture.

"Piper?"

"Sorry," she said, shaking off the memory. "I lost track of what I was about to say. And *you* still haven't answered my question. Are you dating Stuart Duchenko?"

There was a definite darkening to her sister's blush. "For now, yes."

A different kind of heaviness took up space in Piper's stomach. The same uncomfortable feeling she used to get as a kid when waiting to be picked for dodgeball. She was always left for last.

Ignoring the sensation, she pushed her lips into a smile. "No way! That's great! I'm so happy for you." She was, childish reaction aside. She had no reason to feel anything *but* happy, really. It was just her pity party making its reappearance.

"Don't go making a big deal," her sister was saying. "The two of us are having fun together, that's all. It's nothing serious."

The sparkle in Patience's eyes said otherwise, but Piper kept the thought to herself. Patience would admit the truth soon enough.

The two of them talked and joked while Piper worked and for a little while, her loneliness receded.

"Why aren't you making some fancy French dish?" Patience asked as she was putting the casserole in the oven.

"Because I felt like macaroni and cheese. Would you feel better if I called it *macaroni au fromage*?"

"A little." From her chair on the other side of the world, her sister frowned again. "Are you sure you're all right? You mentioned your boss earlier. Is he still treating you okay?"

Once again, a paper towel and a smile flashed before Piper's eyes. "He's treating me fine."

"That sounded weird."

"What do you mean?"

"The way you said 'fine' with a long sigh."

Piper rolled her eyes. As if her sigh could be any longer or dreamier-sounding than the ones her sister made. "How should I say it? He treats me fine. We hardly see each other." Today's encounters notwithstanding. "Not everyone socializes with their boss, you know. I meant Ana," she added quickly before Patience got the wrong idea.

"So long as he isn't giving you a hard time."

"I swear, he isn't."

They talked a little longer, mostly about silly stuff. Patience told a few stories about Nigel the cat and about how things were going with Stuart. Piper lied about how well school was going. By the time they said goodbye, she'd cooked and eaten her casserole. She would have said that the night was exactly what she needed, except that as soon as she turned off the computer, her melancholy returned stronger than ever.

"It's Hollywood's fault," she said to the Eiffel Tower a little while later. "All those movies making Paris look so wonderful. Leading a woman to hope life might be more magical under French skies."

There was a smudge on the glass. Breathing some fog on the pane, she wiped at it with her sleeve. Patience would be horrified by her casualness. Her sister took cleaning very seriously.

Maybe if she tried a little harder. Gave more effort in class, learned to appreciate her surroundings more. Maybe then she could work up the enthusiasm she was supposed to feel for this adventure. Right now, she only felt tired. The carbohydrates were kicking in. Merging with her sad mood and killing what was left of her cleaning ambitions.

Discarding her plans to dig out the cleaning supplies, she sank into a nearby chair. The same one she found Frederic sleeping in this morning, she realized. Outside, the tower twinkled mockingly. Leaning her head back, she watched the lights dance. They were beautiful, weren't they?

"Easy chair to fall asleep in, no?"

The voice close to her ear was deep and rough. Piper jumped to her feet. Grabbing the first thing she could find, she whirled around ready to attack.

Frederic raised his hands in mock surrender. "I'm sorry. I didn't mean to scare you."

"You didn't…" Considering she was wielding a pillow as a weapon, she gave up the argument. "I wasn't expecting you home so early, is all." It was early, right? *Please say it was early.*

"My date wasn't feeling well, so we left the concert at intermission." His eyes narrowed, as if zooming in on her. Too late, Piper realized she still wore her chef's jacket instead of her uniform. "You were working hard?"

"No. I mean, I planned to but I…"

"I am joking."

"Oh." Thank goodness the lights were dim and he couldn't see how red her cheeks were.

"If I recall, I suggested you take the night off to relax. I'm glad you did." He crossed to the window. Hands clasped behind his back, he stood looking out at the tower.

One of the things Piper had noticed while working for Frederic was the way he concentrated so intently on whatever he was doing. Walking. Looking out the window. Some of the focus she attributed to his bad eyes, but lousy vision didn't explain the power behind his movements. He moved with such deliberation. As though nothing could deter him from the action at hand. The guy could give Chef Despelteau a run for his money when it came to laser glares, that's for sure. She could only imagine what it was like to be one of his students.

Or one of his dates, for that matter.

All of a sudden she realized those slate-colored eyes were looking at her. He'd said something, and she missed it. Again, she thanked the dim lighting for protecting her from bigger embarrassment. "I'm sorry, what did you say?"

"I asked if you were enjoying your year in Paris so far."

You mean her crying jag earlier didn't give him a clue? "It's a beautiful city."

"That it is. Have you done much sightseeing?"

"A little." When she first arrived and was still in her starry-eyed phase. After a couple weeks, however, solo sightseeing lost its luster. "Between class and work, I haven't had much time."

"That is too bad. You should make sure you see as much as possible. You never know when you'll have another chance."

"I'll try to remember that." For some reason, Piper felt as though he was talking about more than sightseeing. Or maybe fatigue was making her read too deeply between the lines. For all she knew, this was his normal way of making conversation. He approached everything else with intensity; why wouldn't he approach talking the same way?

Regardless of the reason, the exchange left a hum in the air that made her antsy. Piper couldn't help thinking how crisp and elegant he looked in his summer suit.

Meanwhile, she was growing more aware of her wrinkled jacket by the second. Not to mention the smell of onion and cheddar cheese clinging to her fingers.

Suddenly, she needed some space. Setting down her pillow, she announced, "I'm going to finish cleaning the kitchen." The kitchen was spotless, but she needed some kind of excuse. Then, whether because of the thickened atmosphere or something else, she added, "I'm really sorry, too, about my meltdown earlier."

"Already forgotten, Piper. I hope whatever caused your distress is gone by tomorrow."

"I hope so, too." Not very likely, but a girl could hope. She went to say good-night, but Frederic had already turned his back to the room, his attention once again on the scene outside his window.

Must have been a trick of the shadows. Standing there with his hands behind his back, he suddenly looked alone and far away. *Maybe I'm not the only lonely person in Paris.* The thought was in her head before Piper could stop it.

Frederic Lafontaine, lonely. Sure. Now she knew she was tired.

CHAPTER TWO

THE NEXT MORNING, Piper called Marie Rougeau-Montpelier and introduced herself. To her surprise, the elderly woman said she would be thrilled to meet with her, especially once Piper mentioned her brother's artwork. She invited Piper to visit after lunch. The appointment meant skipping a day of class, but Piper didn't really mind. A day off, in fact, might do her some good. Help her get her head back into the game.

Marie's address, which turned out to be a luxury tower near La Défense, the business district just outside the city, was easier to find than she expected. Not wanting to ring the woman's bell before she was expected, Piper found herself wandering around La Grande Arche, the city's twentieth-century version of the Arc de Triomphe. It was the perfect summer's day. Not too hot, not too cold. Being lunchtime, the square was filled with people. Business executives sat on nearby steps soaking up the sun while tourists and others lounged on the grass in the nearby park. Piper strolled the perimeter and watched as they laughed and chatted with each other. Was this what Frederic meant when he told her to see as much of the city as possible?

Thinking of her boss made her insides sag. He was nowhere to be found when she woke up this morning. That didn't surprise her, he was nowhere to be found most of the time, but Piper sort of hoped that after last night, the routine might have changed. She still couldn't shake the image of him staring out his salon window. Looking so solitary and distant. So *alone*.

There's a word for what you're doing, you know. Projecting or connecting, something like that. Whatever the word, she needed to stop. Just because she was in another sad mood didn't mean her boss was too.

Her feet hurt, protesting having to wear sandals after months of wearing sturdy shoes. She looked around for a café where she could give them a break. There was one on the corner with a maroon-and-white awning that wasn't overly crowded. Helping herself to one of the empty rattan chairs that lined the sidewalk, she had just pulled out her cell phone when she heard a familiar-sounding voice ordering an espresso.

No way. She looked to her left. Even with aviator sunglasses covering his face, she recognized Frederic's profile instantly.

He was alone. At least the chair across from him was empty, and judging from the way his long legs were stretched out to claim the table's real estate, he wasn't expecting a guest to arrive anytime soon. Piper's eyes traveled their length, from his wingtips to the muscular thighs that disappeared beneath the tablecloth.

In contrast to last night, today he looked the picture of ease.

Must be nice to feel so confident instead of having to fake it all the time. And to be that good-looking. Patience was always saying that being beautiful wasn't all it was cracked up to be. Piper wouldn't know. She was never someone people thought of as beautiful. When the guys in high school made fun of Patience's job, they did so with a glaze of lust in their eyes. No one's eyes ever glazed for Piper.

Just then, as though sensing her stare, Frederic turned in her direction. Piper started to shrink back into the shadows, then caught herself and waved instead. He didn't wave back.

She was about to take offense when she realized she wasn't in his field of vision. Smoothing her skirt, she walked toward his table.

"Bonjour, monsieur," she greeted with a smile.

The sound of an American accent jarred Frederic from his thoughts. He knew of only one person who spoke French with an accent like that. Blinking out of his fog, he found a whirl of yellow and red in his line of sight. Lifting his eyes, he saw a familiar brunette head. "Piper? Where did you come from?"

"Two tables over. I waved, but you weren't paying attention."

She was being polite. They both knew he didn't wave because she wasn't sitting in his field of view.

"Lost in thought," he replied, continuing the pretense.

"I'm not bothering you, am I?" Piper's question brought him back.

"Not at all. I'm killing time after an appointment is all." Yet another pointless meeting with his ophthalmologist. He went every few months simply to hear that his eyes were still diseased.

"And you?"

"Killing time before an appointment, actually."

Sitting back in his chair, Frederic found himself wishing he'd been paying attention when she approached. Whenever he saw Piper at the apartment, she wore either her chef's jacket or that awful maid uniform that was the antithesis of every French maid fantasy ever written. This sundress, however... The bright colors definitely suited her better. Plus, there was an expanse of flesh around her shoulders he didn't normally get to enjoy.

"Are you meeting a classmate?" he asked. A date would certainly explain the dress. Why he was suddenly intrigued by her social life, Frederic wasn't sure, except that the memory of her crying by the kitchen counter refused to leave him. He found it odd, an attractive American—and she was attractive as that expanse of skin attested—spending her evenings in Paris alone.

"I'm supposed to meet with someone at the Rose d'Arms," she said. "It's a retirement home a block or so from here."

"Looking for a surrogate grandmother?"

"Hardly," she said with a laugh. A very pleasant-sounding laugh, too. Like bells. "I'm doing a favor for my sister."

"At a retirement home?"

"It's a long story. I won't bore you with the details. I really just stopped by to say hello. I'll let you get back to whatever it was you were…"

"Please. Stay. We can kill time together."

"Are you sure?"

There was hesitancy in her voice. Frederic couldn't blame her. Eight months of hardly talking, and now here they were on their third conversation in two days. "I wouldn't have offered if I wasn't sure," he told her. "There is no reason for the two of us to sit at separate tables when we are both by ourselves. Besides, you have me intrigued."

The café had arranged the tables as so many cafés in the city did, with the seats side by side so that patrons could enjoy the view. As Piper slipped into the seat beside his, Frederic was struck by an aroma of vanilla and spices that made his mouth water. "Did you bake today?" he asked.

"No. I skipped class. Why?"

"No reason." Who knew a person could smell delicious? "Tell me this long story of yours."

Piper took a deep breath. "Apparently, Ana, my sister's boss, lived with an artist here in Paris in the seventies and posed for a bunch of paintings. Her great-nephew, Stuart, is hoping to surprise her with one as a gift, so Patience asked me if I would talk to the artist's sister to see if any of his paintings survived."

"Doesn't your sister realize there are easier ways to track down an artist's work? If he is well-known…"

"This is where it gets complicated."

She paused while the waitress brought his espresso and she placed her order.

"Complicated how?"

"The artist died in an accident a long time ago. According to Ana, he would have been huge—like Picasso huge—but then Theodore Duchenko went and bought up…"

"Wait…" Frederic needed to go back a step. "Did you say Theodore *Duchenko*?"

Piper nodded. "That's right. Patience works for his sister, Ana Duchenko."

Unbelievable. Duchenko Silver was world renowned. Frederic knew curators who gushed over adding a piece of the famed Russian silver to their collections. As for the late Theodore Duchenko, the man had been considered one of the most ruthless tycoons of the twentieth century. "You're saying that you're trying to track down a portrait of Ana Duchenko."

"Not just a portrait. A nude," Piper replied. "Nigel painted a bunch, and they were supposedly pretty racy, which is why…"

"Duchenko wanted them destroyed," he finished for her. "This is astounding. The Duchenko name, it is… well, let us say that if a portrait still exists, the significance in terms of pop culture alone would be immeasurable."

"I don't think Stuart cares if the painting has any kind of value—he just wants to give his aunt back a piece of her history. The way my sister tells it, Ana truly loved the man."

The waitress returned with her café au lait. "It's all very tragic, really," Piper said, taking a sip.

Tragic but exciting. Frederic found his curiosity piqued in a way he hadn't felt in years. Not since his university days. "There is nothing like the thrill of discovering a new artist," he told her. "The euphoria, it hits you like a…" The sexual metaphor was too crude to share with a woman. He settled for saying "There are few pleasures like it. I envy you."

"The whole thing is probably a long shot."

"Perhaps," he said, reaching for his drink. It quite probably was, in fact. "But long shot or not, the chase is always exciting."

"Want to come with me?"

Frederic set his cup down with a *clink* so he could focus his gaze on her. "Pardon?"

"You just said you envied my going on the hunt. Besides, I don't know anything about art. What if there's a giant painting of Ana hanging on this woman's wall? How will I know if it's worth Stuart's money?"

And she thought *he* was the best person to evaluate? "You just said the painting wasn't about value."

"It isn't." There was silence as she shifted in her chair. When she spoke again, Frederic heard a change in her voice. It became lower, with less spark. "Never mind. It was only a suggestion."

"No, I'd love to join you." Unsettled by the sadness he thought he heard in her voice, he spoke without thinking.

The smile worked its way back into her voice. "Awesome! I'll finish my coffee and we'll go."

A visit to a retirement home, Frederic said to himself as he sipped his espresso. *To meet with an old woman. No harm in that.*

Why, then, did he feel as if he was getting involved in something more?

There wasn't, of course, an undiscovered painting hanging in Marie's apartment. Only a very tall, pinched-looking woman wearing a velvet tracksuit. She greeted the two of them with a wide smile. "A professor. How exciting," she gushed, squeezing his hand. "Please come in."

"I knew you'd be a hit," Piper murmured as she stepped inside.

Frederic grinned in response. His insides were feeling the thrill of the hunt.

While he still wasn't entirely sure why Piper had asked him to come along, he'd decided to embrace the opportunity. Who knew when another chance would cross his path? Or, for that matter, come with such an attractive package. Piper was far enough into the room that he could finally see her figure. She had curves a sculpture would love. Soft and supple. The kind meant to be traced by a person's hands.

That's it. He was getting rid of the maid's uniform.

"What period do you study, Professor?" Marie was asking. The older woman was already limping across the sitting room en route to the bookcase.

"Medieval. Pre-Romanesque mostly."

"Nigel would have called you stuck in the past, but

then he prided himself on being antiestablishment. We all did back then. Please, have a seat."

She gestured to a sofa barely large enough to deserve the label. Feeling overly large, he perched on the edge of the seat and wondered how a woman Marie's height could ever sit comfortably. The cushion dipped and Piper sat beside him. Vanilla and spice teased his nostrils again. It was like walking into the most pleasant bakery on earth every time the woman sat down.

"He had such promise, my brother. My mother used to brag he knew how to paint before he could walk. An exaggeration, I'm sure. Come to think of it, though, I can't remember a time when he wasn't drawing or painting or something."

Reaching up, she pulled out what looked like a large plastic binder and opened it up. "This is him here," she said. "Five years old and he'd already won his first competition."

She set the album on Frederic's lap. The old photo was too small and blurry for him to focus much on, but he leaned forward and pretended all the same. Piper leaned in as well, her left knee knocking against his as she shifted angles. Frederic sucked in his breath at the awareness shooting up his thigh. Even with two layers of material, he felt every bump and bone pressed against him.

"Impressive," he murmured. Although he wasn't sure if he meant Nigel's childhood art or Piper's knee.

"He could have done so much," Marie said. "We all told him to stop riding that motorbike, but he was stubborn." A crack worked its way into the end of her voice.

"I'm sorry," she said, pressing a fist to her lips. "It's been a long time since I've talked about Nigel at all."

"We're sorry if we're bringing up bad memories," Piper remarked.

"That's all right. They aren't all bad. In some ways, I think Nigel wanted to die young. He once told me that art only reached the masses once you were gone."

"I could name a few living painters who might disagree," Frederic replied.

Her resulting smile was watery, but strong. "I never said his theory made sense. In the end, it didn't matter anyway, because his work never reached anyone."

Because Theodore Duchenko ordered it destroyed.

"That is why we're here," Piper said. "My sister works for Ana Duchenko."

Every ounce of humor disappeared from Marie's face. "That family destroyed my brother," she said, stiffening. "I was only a child, but I remember how my parents cursed Theodore Duchenko and the rest of them."

To her credit, Piper didn't stiffen in return. He always thought how a person reacted when challenged said a lot about them. His housekeeper, it appeared, knew how to stand tall. "From what I hear, Theodore Duchenko deserved cursing," she said. "What he did was awful."

"It was an outrage. Ruining my brother's life, decimating his art all because he was afraid his family would be embarrassed." The rest of her rant disappeared in a soft mutter.

"For what it's worth, Ana never spoke to her brother again because of what he did."

Marie stopped muttering. "She didn't?"

"No. My sister says Ana blames her brother for Nigel's death as much as you do. She never married, either."

"Because of Nigel?"

"She loved your brother very much."

This was the part of the story that made Frederic uncomfortable. Love stealing a young heiress's future. The idea of a life stolen out from under you struck a little too close to home.

Marie was back at the bookcase, a long purple silhouette whose head was cut off in darkness. "I only met her once," she was saying. "Nigel brought her to Sunday dinner and told us all she was his muse. My parents were not happy. I remember my father whispering that Ana 'looked expensive.'" Frederic could picture the scene. Nigel, their starving artist son, walking in with his wealthy seventeen-year-old lover.

"I know that Theodore tried to destroy all of Nigel's paintings." Piper's knee brushed Frederic's again as she shifted in her seat. His entire leg felt the contact this time. "We're hoping, though, he might have missed one or two."

"If one existed, don't you think my family would have kept it?"

"Perhaps there was a sale he made before Theodore arrived in France," Frederic suggested. "Or a gift he gave to a friend."

Marie shook her head. "I have no idea. The only paintings left of Nigel's that we have are a couple small landscapes he did for my mother while he was in art school."

"It's all right," Piper replied. "We figured it was a long shot."

Perhaps, thought Frederic, but she had clearly hoped. Her disappointment was palpable.

Whenever one of his students felt let down, he made a point of reminding them life was full of disappointments.

Right now with Piper, all he wanted was to squeeze her hand. Reassure rather than remind. It was definitely not like him.

Marie was still talking. "To be honest, even if a portrait of Ana did survive, I'm not sure my parents would have kept it. They didn't want anything to do with the Duchenkos."

"No," Piper said. "I don't suppose they would."

"My brother did have a friend who might know. He owned an art gallery in the Marais. A very successful one, I believe. His name was Gaspard."

Frederic looked up. "You don't mean Gaspard Theroux?"

"Yes, that's him."

"You know him?" Piper asked.

"Galerie Gaspard Theroux is one of the most respected galleries in Paris."

"Gaspard and Nigel were very close. If he is still alive, he might know whether any of Nigel's early Ana studies sold."

"I'll tell you one thing," Frederic said as they were walking across the square a short while later. "If Gaspard represented Nigel's work, he must have been very talented. The gallery is known for discovering the best rising talent in Europe. I've bought a couple pieces from Gaspard's son, Bernard. He doesn't have quite the same eye as his father, but he does well."

Piper didn't care how good an eye the guy had. All she cared about was that her search hadn't reached a dead end. It took her by surprise just how disappointed she was when Marie first said the paintings were gone. The repeated stories of Ana and Nigel's love affair had gotten to her.

She turned so she could get a better view of the man walking beside her. Inviting Frederic to join her was a total impulse. He sounded so animated when he was talking about Nigel's work being a significant discovery. Plus, she liked the idea of his company in case Marie wasn't as friendly as she had sounded on the phone. There wasn't a woman of any age who wouldn't like seeing a man who looked like Frederic on her doorstep.

Now as it turned out, he turned out to be an invaluable resource. "I don't suppose you know if Gaspard Theroux is still alive, do you?"

"He is, but he has had health problems the past few years. His mind…" Frederic gestured with his hands as to say he didn't know.

That's what Piper was afraid of. She combed her fingers through her hair with a sigh. At least she had a place to start. "Maybe his son knows something. What did you say his name was?"

"Bernard."

"I'll give him a call tomorrow." Maybe his father kept records from those days.

"Good luck. Bernard is not the easiest person to reach. He tends to ignore people who aren't serious collectors. Even his gallery is open by appointment only."

Great. How was she going to get an appointment? Make a pest of herself until he called back?

Or... An idea struck her. "He returns your phone calls, doesn't he?"

"Of course. We've done business for years. Are you asking me to call Bernard for you?"

"Would you? It might make him more willing to talk with me. Then, if the painting gets discovered, you can take partial credit."

Frederic laughed.

"What?" Piper had heard him laugh before, but never with such a teasing tone. In spite of his sunglasses, the smile lit up his face. She liked how he threw his head back, too, as if tossing the laugh toward the sky. "You don't want credit?"

"On the contrary, recognition is always welcome."

"Then what's so funny?"

"Nothing."

Something amused him. Was it her? If so, why didn't she feel a knot in her stomach, the way she usually did when people laughed at her? Instead, she had a warm squishy feeling running all through her.

"Will you call Bernard?"

"Yes, I will. As soon as I get back to the university."

"Thank you! You're awesome." She was so glad she asked him along today. Finally a good day in Paris. She threw her arms around his neck and hugged him.

It didn't dawn on her what she had done until she

felt the corner of his belt buckle against her rib cage. With heat shooting to her toes, she released her grip, and prayed her face wasn't as flushed as it felt.

"Um…thank you," she stammered.

"My pleasure," he replied. Piper thought she saw a hint of a smile as he spoke, but double-checking meant looking into his face. Considering her skin was on fire, staring at the cell phone he was now dialing seemed a safer bet. "As enjoyable as this afternoon has been," she heard him say, "I have a faculty meeting I need to attend. Should I have Michel drop you off at the house?"

Meaning sit with him in the backseat of his car? "That's all right, I'll take the Métro." Another safe bet. "I want to stop at the farmers' market, anyway."

"Suit yourself. I'll let you know what Bernard says."

Piper watched as he headed to the same café where their afternoon started, moving with his usual careful, deliberate grace. Clearly, her hug affected only one of them. But then, did she really expect otherwise?

CHAPTER THREE

WHEN SHE RETURNED from class the following day, Frederic was waiting in the main salon. "We've got a meeting with Bernard in half an hour," he said. "The car is on the way."

"We?" she repeated, making sure she heard correctly. This was the first they'd spoken since she rushed off last night, and considering her overreaction to his hug, there was a good chance she misheard. "You're coming?"

"I have to. I'm invested in the search now. Plus, Bernard has a painting he thinks I might be interested in."

"Oh." So she hadn't heard wrong. Her stomach gave a tiny bounce at the discovery. "I'll go get ready."

She rushed through the kitchen, unbuttoning her jacket as she went. Frederic worked fast. Sure, he said he would call yesterday, but she fully expected to be dropped in priority when he got to his meeting. *He did say he was invested*, she reminded herself. Still, the idea that her errand stayed atop his to-do list left her strangely flattered.

Yesterday's yellow dress was on the back of her chair.

Her one good summer outfit. She'd foolishly assumed she'd be shopping in Paris.

Better than jeans and a T-shirt, she reminded herself while slipping the dress over her head. The skirt was wrinkled from yesterday, but serviceable. Only Frederic would know she was wearing the same outfit. Assuming he even paid attention to what she wore. Grabbing her sandals, she hurried back to the salon.

"That was fast," Frederic remarked when he saw her. He, she noticed, looked as crisp and perfect as ever in his linen blazer.

"You said to hurry."

"I'm not used to people understanding what that means. You forget, I spend my day with university students. They have a different view of time."

He opened the front door and gestured for her to step outside. "Shall we?"

Like many of Paris's art galleries, the Galerie Gaspard Theroux was in the Marais, the historic district, near the Place des Vosges. Piper stepped into the sunshine with a silent sigh of relief.

"I have to admit," Piper said as she stepped out of the cab, "I like this section of the city much better." The business district was beautiful but modern. But here… This was the Paris she dreamed about. "The statues in the middle of the street and the cobblestones…it's all so…"

"Romantic?"

His drily spoken answer made her blush. "I know, typical American, right?"

"Yes, but also no. This is my favorite part of the

city, too. As impressive as skyscrapers are, you cannot top classic French design. Did you know this square is one of the first examples of urban planning? Henri IV was ahead of his time." He swept his arm wide in an animated arc. "It was also one of the few times all the building fronts were designed the same way. See the arcades lining the perimeter?"

He went on, talking about the different sections of the building, architectural and historical details Piper wished she could appreciate. She was far more entertained by the expression on his face. His enthusiasm was obvious, despite the sunglasses masking his eyes. The way he spoke was reverent. So much lighter than his usual tone, which was so serious it bordered on short, she could have listened to him go on forever. Good thing Chef Despelteau didn't have such a voice. She'd be so distracted by the way the words dripped off his tongue she'd never get any recipe right.

"For an art history expert, you sure know a lot about architecture," she teased.

There was no mistaking the pink spots peering out beneath the rims of his aviators. "In my opinion, architecture is its own form of art," he told her. "The gargoyles of Notre Dame, for example. Or Louis the thirteenth's statue in the park. I appreciate the effort that goes into creating beauty. When I think of this section of the city, especially, and the disasters and wars it has survived, I cannot help but be impressed.

"Come," he said, taking her elbow, "Bernard's gallery is on the western side." Taking her by the elbow, he led her toward the shaded walkway on the far end of the plaza.

Art galleries and antiques stores lined the sidewalk beneath the arch. As they walked, Piper tried to appreciate the various pieces in the windows, but she was too distracted by the lingering sensation on her elbow. Twice she needed to check, even though Frederic released her seconds after touching her.

"Bernard's gallery is number thirty-three," Frederic said. "He often keeps the door locked. We might have to ring the bell."

"A locked store and visits by appointment. You're right, he is selective about his customers."

"He can afford to be."

"Must be nice. Hopefully I make the cut."

"You will," Frederic said with a smile. "You are with me."

Piper spotted the gallery before he did. A quick tug showed the door to be unlocked. As Frederic opened it wide, a bell tinkled overhead.

"Bonjour!" Bernard Theroux appeared from the back of the gallery. He was a tall, slender man with a wispy gray mustache and thinning gray hair that he wore combed back. The moment he saw Frederic, his porcelain features broke into a grin and he began speaking in rapid French, far too fast for Piper to keep up.

"I'm sorry," he said, switching to perfect English. "I was lecturing someone about being a stranger."

"And I was explaining how busy work has been."

"I can vouch for that," Piper remarked. "He's hardly ever home." The comment made her sound like a dis-

gruntled wife. "I mean, he works a lot." That didn't
sound much better.

Thankfully, the gallery owner was more interested in
dragging Frederic toward one of the paintings. "Like I
told you on the phone, you are going to love this piece.
He's a new artist out of Prague—I discovered him on my
last trip. Wait until you see what he does with shadow."

"I'm sure it's spectacular," Frederic said. "But before
I look at anything, Piper had some questions she wanted
to ask. About a friend of your father's."

Although his sigh said he'd rather talk about the
painter from Prague, Bernard turned to Piper. "Of
course. Although like I told Frederic, my father had a
lot of painter friends over the years. If it was before I
was born, I doubt I can help you."

"He wasn't only a friend—he was possibly a client,"
Piper replied. "His sister thinks your father sold one or
two of his paintings."

She reached into her purse for her cell phone. Patience had emailed her a snapshot that featured one of
the paintings. "I'm hoping that a record of the sale still
exists. The artist's name was Nigel Rougeau. The painting would have looked like this one."

She held out her phone so he could see the image.
Instantly, Bernard's eyes became saucers.

"Dear God, I don't believe it. This is the painting
you're looking for? This nude?"

"Yes?" Although she suddenly wasn't sure she should
say so. The gleam in Bernard's eyes made her nervous.
"Why?"

"I grew up looking at that woman."

"You—you did?"

"Yes, she hung in our dining room."

No way. Piper couldn't believe her good luck. She'd been prepared to strike out, and here the man was saying he'd seen the painting. "Does your father still have the painting?"

Bernard shook his head. "I'm afraid not. I sold most of the collection when we closed down his house. To pay his expenses. The nude was sold with the others."

She should have known the search wouldn't end easily. Still, there was hope. "You wouldn't know the name of the man who bought it, would you?" she asked.

"I keep records for every painting," Bernard replied with a sniff.

"Could we get the name?" Frederic asked. Piper started. She had assumed he was studying the painting, and so his deep voice caught her off guard.

"Yes, but it will take me a few minutes to pull up the record on the computer."

"Thank you," Piper said, speaking as much to Frederic as to Bernard. "I truly appreciate the help."

"I'll be back with the information as soon as I can. In the meantime, you now have plenty of time to study the Biskup. It's called *Zoufalstvi*." His smile was smug as he gestured toward the painting. "I know you're going to be as impressed with his style as I am."

Piper walked up to the painting. It was contemporary art, a mash-up of black, white and red, which she assumed had some kind of meaning. She understood the price well enough. She paid less for the entire year of culinary school.

"What do you think?" she asked, looking over her shoulder.

Frederic stood where she left him, taking in the painting from a distance. "Interesting," was all he said.

"Your friend isn't really expecting you to buy it today, is he?"

"Oh, he is. Bernard never jokes when it comes to artwork. If he says the painting is a good investment, then I'm sure it is."

"And you would what? Just write a check if you liked it?"

"If I liked it."

She shook her head. The idea of writing a check for an amount that took her months upon months to save— and that was with pinching every single penny—boggled her mind. Here Frederic talked about dropping that amount like he was buying a new shirt. "Do you like it?" she had to ask.

"Do you?" he asked back.

"Honest opinion?" He nodded. "I'm not sure what I'm looking at. It all looks like a bunch of colors to me."

She squinted, trying to make sense of the image. In a way, it was similar to the other paintings in Frederic's house. They too were modern, but warmer and with brighter colors. This painting was definitely not warm. It did conjure up emotion, a weirdly familiar feeling in the pit of her stomach, but she wouldn't call the sensation pleasant. Nor would she want to feel it every day.

"It's a very sad-looking painting," she said.

"I should hope so." Footsteps sounded on the

wood floor, and suddenly Frederic was at her elbow. "*Zoufalstvi* is Czech for *desperation*."

No wonder it left her feeling empty. "I don't see why anyone would want to buy such a depressing picture. But then, I'm not much of an artist."

"Really? I thought chefs considered cooking an art form."

"Great cooking, sure. All the best chefs are artists." As Chef Despelteau reminded them so often. "But I was talking about *art* art. You know, paintings and stuff." She turned her attention to a different piece. "Growing up, the fanciest thing on our walls was a framed poster of Monet's *Water Lilies*. I'm going to go out on a limb and say Bernard doesn't sell posters."

"No, he does not."

"Too bad." They stood quietly in front of the painting. This second one had prettier colors, but the image wasn't nearly as powerful to look at.

That was it, Piper realized suddenly. Why the Biskup painting seemed so familiar. The image reminded her of Frederic. He, too, was forceful and compelling. Where did the sadness come in, though? Her boss could hardly be described as sad.

He was solitary, though. For all his activity, the man was alone much of the time. If there were family and friends in his life, they certainly didn't visit the house.

"I hope you don't buy the painting," she said aloud.

He turned at that moment and looked into her face, his eyes grayer than usual. "Why not?"

"Because I—" What was she supposed to say? Because it made her think sad thoughts about him? Like she told herself yesterday, she was pushing her thoughts onto him. Solitary didn't mean lonely. For all she knew, Frederic was simply a man who liked his privacy.

Her answer didn't matter anyway, because the moment she met his eyes, any explanation she might have come up with disappeared. All this time, she'd thought his eyes were gray, but they were really far softer. Like feathers or a fluffy cloud of smoke. She could almost feel the haze in the air, surrounding her like a warm plume.

A shock of hair had fallen over one eyebrow, knocked loose when he took his sunglasses off. The dark strands begged to be brushed aside.

"Piper?" she heard him ask.

Oh, good Lord, she was staring at him with her jaw half open like an idiot.

"What I meant," she said, tucking imaginary hair behind her ear, "was that I don't like the idea you might have to buy something on my account."

"You're afraid I won't know how to say no?"

"Of—of course you can. Say no, that is. I just don't want…"

"Don't worry," he said, saving her from making a bigger fool of herself than she already had. "I stopped acquiring pieces a while ago. Bernard forgets I no longer have the eye for detail I once had."

Piper's heart gave a little twist at the wistful shadow that flickered over his features. Bernard wasn't the only one who'd forgotten. The man was so capable and self-assured. *Who wouldn't forget?*

"I'll take that as a compliment," Frederic said with a chuckle.

Meaning she'd spoken her thoughts aloud. The floor could swallow her up any time now.

"So, what do you think? Do you not love the expressive way he plays light on shadow?" Bernard came around the corner, saving her. "I am predicting this artist will be very popular. Already, several serious collectors have put him on their watch lists. This would be your chance to acquire a piece before his popularity drives the price up."

"Don't you mean while you still have him on a string?" Frederic replied. The teasing retort caught Piper by surprise. "Bernard only pushes this hard when he's personally involved," he explained to her. "Isn't that right, Bernard?"

The gallery owner's cheeks turned crimson. "I do predict big things for him. You know I only push if they have talent."

"Yes, I know. Did you find the address?"

"I did." He turned to Piper. "The painting is called *Ana Reclining*. I'm ashamed that I didn't remember. It was purchased by a man named John Allen. Whether or not he still owns the piece, I do not know."

Piper took the slip of paper. This was fantastic. They had a real live name. Wait until she told Patience. "Gloucestershire," she read. "England?"

"Northwest of London," Frederic replied.

There was no way of knowing if the address and phone were current, either. Still, it was a start. A very good start.

"Two days ago, we didn't know if a painting even existed," she remarked when she and Frederic stepped outside. "And now here I am with a name. I feel like Piper Rush, art detective."

"It's always exciting when a lost work is discovered. Did you know they once discovered a seventeenth-century Le Brun hanging in a suite at the Ritz-Carlton?"

"I wouldn't put this painting on the same level. But Ana's nephew will be excited." She had no idea who Le Brun was, but seventeenth-century sounded important. "Lucky for him that Bernard's father decided to keep one of the paintings for himself."

"Indeed." Although they were standing in the shade, he lowered his sunglasses in place anyway. As the dark lenses slid over his features, Piper felt a flutter in her stomach. Relief that she'd been saved from whatever that strange sensation was when she looked into his eyes before. As it was, the moment had left her with this restless, jumbly sensation, as if her insides drank too much caffeine.

"So what is your next move, Madame Detective?" he asked her.

"Give the information to Patience so they can track John Allen down, I suppose."

"You don't sound very excited about the prospect."

In a strange way, she wasn't. "I'll miss playing detective," she said. "The past couple days have been a nice break in my routine." That included the unexpected time she spent with him. Having finished her favor for Patience, life would go back to normal. Normal and lonely.

"You don't have to stop."

She laughed. "You know another piece of art that needs to be tracked down?"

"No, but the search for this one is not complete."

True. Bernard's information could be woefully out of date. "Guess I should make a phone call or two to make sure my lead pans out." She added the detective lingo on purpose, just because it was fun to use.

"And if need be, travel to England to inspect the canvas."

"Now that might be going a little too far." Piper could see herself now, knocking on John Allen's door and asking if she could inspect his nude portrait.

"Why? Do you not want a chance to see the painting up close?"

"Sure, but… Would you?"

"For a chance to discover a lost painting, I'd go anywhere. I've traveled farther for far less."

"Well, if you don't mind, I'll start with a few phone calls," Piper replied.

Just then, the car arrived, pulling to the curb with the soft *beep* of the horn. "Sorry to keep you waiting," Michel said as he hurried to open the passenger door.

The switch from bright sunlight to the car's interior temporary plunged Piper into darkness, making her blink several times before she could properly see her surroundings. Today was the first time she'd ever ridden in a limousine, and while she told herself the experience was no different from riding in a cab, it was. For one thing, cabs didn't have supple seats that molded to your body. And they definitely didn't smell like leather and spicy aftershave. Yesterday's decision to ride the Métro had definitely been the right one. In fact, she inhaled deeply, she wondered if she shouldn't have made the same decision this afternoon.

The car itself was not nearly as fancy as she expected. On TV, the limousines always had skylights and crystal decanters. Frederic went for a sleek simplicity. All the more impressive, really. Reminded her of how quality food didn't need a lot of trimmings to taste impressive. Frederic didn't need trimmings, either.

If only she didn't feel so jittery. She'd love to blame the feeling on being out of her element, but that wouldn't explain why the sensation didn't fully grip her until she lost herself in Frederic's gray eyes. Or why the quiet determination in his voice just now turned her insides upside down.

Frederic slipped into the seat beside her and the driver shut the door, sealing them together in the dimness. If only he weren't so tall and broad-shouldered. A smaller man would take up less space. His body heat wouldn't cross the distance to buffet her body. It turned the air thick.

Piper smoothed her skirt. The yellow was suddenly way too bright for the space. "Thank you again for arranging the meeting with Bernard," she said.

"You already thanked me twice on the trip here. There's no need to do it again."

"I'm excited the trip was successful, is all." Not to mention talking eased her tension and thank you was the only thing she could think of. "I feel like I owe you something. After all, you did give up part of your afternoon to help me. You could have let me deal with Bernard on my own."

He laughed, teeth white in the shadows. "If I had, you would still be leaving messages on his machine."

True enough. Bernard was a character. "We have a name for guys like him back home."

"There are names for guys like him everywhere," Frederic replied. "And again, I was glad to help. I'm as intrigued by this painting as you are. It's been a while since I've played art detective myself. If this painting is as good as Bernard believes, it will be quite the discovery."

Piper thought of his comment from earlier, about traveling farther for less. "Do you miss it? Tracking down art?"

"Yes, but what can you do?" He shrugged. "Life is what it is. It's not as though I can change anything, is it?"

"I guess not." Remembering his wistful expression at the gallery, Piper couldn't help wondering if he was as Zen about his circumstances as he sounded. If she were losing her sight, she would be railing against the universe. She certainly wouldn't talk about it as matter-of-factly as he did.

She turned to steal a look at him, only to find he was looking back at her with that unnaturally intense gaze of his.

"I'm glad helping me didn't keep you from anything important," she said, jumping back to the original conversation. Her attention returned to her lap and the imaginary wrinkles she needed to smooth away.

Leather crinkled as Frederic shifted, too.

"Definitely not," he replied. "The only thing on my schedule is tonight's meeting of the Société pour la Conservation Artistique. We have a speaker coming to discuss new methods of varnish repair."

"Really." Piper didn't have a clue what that meant. "Sounds…"

"Tedious? Sleep-inducing?" He chuckled, cutting off any chance of her arguing otherwise. "I understand. I'm sure I would feel the same way about a lecture on flaky pastry. What about you? What are your plans for the evening?"

"You mean other than looking up John Allen on the internet? Nothing unusual. Do the cleaning I missed today, stream a little American television on my computer…"

"You should go out."

Piper shook her head. Clearly he was only saying that to be polite. They both knew she had no social life. The suggestion was as silly as her suggesting he stick around the house more. "I don't think so."

"Why not? Surely your culinary school friends…"

It was instinctive. As soon as he mentioned the word *friends*, she stiffened. "Culinary school isn't the kind of place where you make friends," she said. No sense hiding the reaction. "It's too competitive."

"You're surprised?"

"No. And yes." She struggled to explain. If the never-ending competition was the only problem, school wouldn't be so bad. "I guess I hoped that even with the competition, people would be friendlier. Supportive.

"Naive, I know," she added before he could say it. "I should have realized, school is school. Some things don't change."

"I don't understand. What does being at school have to do with anything?"

Of course he wouldn't understand. How could he?

"Were you popular in school?" she asked.

She watched as he contemplated the question. That he had to stop and think was almost an answer in itself. "I never paid attention to whether I was or not."

Bet he was, then. People who were well-liked never paid attention.

"And you were not popular?"

"I was chubby, poor and being raised by my sister." *Who stripped for a living*, she added silently. "Plus I caught lice in fifth grade. You can guess where that put me on the popularity scale."

"Where were your parents?"

"My mom died when I was little."

"I'm sorry."

"Happens."

Piper hated the sympathy in his voice. Pity parties were one thing, but to have others feeling pity for her... that only made her pathetic. "Needless to say, I was always a bit of an outsider."

Frederic nodded, attention on the space in front of him. "Personally, I always found being on my own to be the easier path," he said. "Being involved only means more drama."

"Oh, there was drama anyway." She didn't mean to say anything aloud, the words just came out, so when he frowned, she did her best to play the comment off. "I mean, you know how kids can get."

She should have known he wouldn't let her get away with it. "What did they do?" he asked.

"Do? Nothing really. They mostly said stuff." *Hey,*

Piper, I got twenty bucks. Think your sister will give me a lap dance? She winced at the memory. "That's how school works. Once you get a reputation, you're stuck with it. I learned to suck it up over time."

"Suck it up?"

"Cope," she said, translating the slang.

"Ah. I know what that is like."

Of course he would. He had his own issues, and they were far more serious than being teased in school. In a way it was funny, how they were both more alone than not. Piper wasn't sure why, but that made her like him all the more.

A very dangerous feeling.

"I'm making it sound worse than it was," she told him, hoping to break the spell. "To be honest, I don't know why I brought high school up in the first place. We were talking about culinary school, which is supposed to be competitive, right? People are fighting for their livelihoods.

"Besides..." She went back to examining imaginary wrinkles. "It's not like I came to Paris to make friends."

Frederic leaned forward and knocked on the glass that divided them from the driver. "Michel," he said. "Would you pull over at the next stoplight?"

"Are you getting out?" They must have arrived at his meeting. That she knew he had a prior engagement didn't stop her stomach from dropping with insecurity.

"No," Frederic replied, "*we* are."

CHAPTER FOUR

THAT WAS POSSIBLY one of the weakest lies Frederic had ever heard, and Frederic had heard a lot of them. *Did not come here to make friends, indeed.*

He slid his hand along the door panel until his fingers curved around the handle. Blasted poor lighting made seeing details difficult. "We are going to see Paris," he said, letting daylight in.

"What are you talking about?"

"This is the second time you've mentioned Paris disappointing you. I refuse to let you think my city is cold and unfriendly."

Stepping onto the sidewalk, he motioned for her to do the same before scanning his surroundings to determine his location. Took only a moment before he managed to spy the Louvre's familiar Pyramide to his left. Perfect.

"We're going to walk a bit," he told Michel. "I will call you when we're ready to go home."

"What about your meeting?" Piper had joined him on the sidewalk. Her dress was ridiculously bright, much like the sun-filled sidewalk. The color filled his view every time he looked in her direction. He liked it. It was like looking into sunlight. It was not a color that should be lonely.

He stepped back so he could see more of her face. "The society will live without me. Defending our city's honor is far more important."

"You really don't have to do this."

"Don't I?" He started down the sidewalk, forcing her to catch up.

"But I thought you said Americans have unrealistic expectations about Paris."

"Yes, but that was before."

"Before what?"

Before he heard her trying so hard to sound casual about her loneliness. Perhaps it was the resignation in her voice, as though she didn't expect to have better. A tone that sounded suspiciously like the voices from his childhood. *Don't complain. Don't need.* The lessons he'd learned hurt when he heard them applied to someone else.

Or perhaps it was simply because he himself had only so long to appreciate his surroundings. Either way, he was suddenly gripped with the urge to show her more.

"Before I realized you spent your evenings inside streaming American television," he told her.

"I watch French shows, too."

He shot her a look. "Paris is a city meant to be experienced, not watched from the sidelines like a spectator. No wonder you have been disappointed. I bet you took one of those double-decker tour buses as well."

"What's wrong with that? You get to see all the important landmarks in one trip."

"Would you enjoy a gourmet meal in one bite?"

Her resulting silence told him she didn't have a counterargument. Smiling to himself, Frederic continued walking, his focus on the sidewalk unfolding in front of him. The *click-clack* of Piper's heels on the concrete made a pleasant rhythm for counting out steps.

"If we're going to the Louvre, I've already been," she said when they passed a street sign. "The bus stopped there. I even went in and waited in line to see the *Mona Lisa.*"

It was amusing, the way she insisted on defending her tour. "I'm glad. I hope you saw some of the other great works as well. We are not going to the Louvre, however."

"Where are we going, then?"

"You will see."

Based on her exasperated sigh, Frederic could only imagine her expression. She probably rolled her eyes dramatically the way one of his students might.

"Don't you like surprises?" he asked.

"Only when I know what they are."

"Well, this time you'll simply have to trust me."

Having reached a cross street, he turned his head. They stood too close for him to see her entire face, but in scanning, he saw that she was worrying her bottom lip. The pink flesh was pinched tight beneath her teeth.

"It's nothing bad, I promise," he told her. Then, because he could not stand to see that lip gnawed red, he reached out and cupped her cheek. Instantly, her lips parted with a tiny gasp of surprise. He lifted his eyes to meet hers. "Trust me."

"I—I do."

Frederic could feel curve of her earlobe teasing his fingertips. Without thinking, he brushed his little finger along the patch behind her ear. The skin beneath his hand was still cool from the car's air-conditioning and smooth as satin.

Her jaw muscle pulsed against his palm, making him realize what he was doing. "Good," he said, pulling his hand back. "Because we're almost there."

Resisting a suddenly inexplicable urge to grab her hand, he started across the street.

There turned out to be the Musée de l'Orangerie in the Jardin des Tuileries, a smaller museum a block away from the Louvre. Piper gasped as she stepped through the vestibule. The room she entered was all white, with soft light that turned the color smooth as cream. A beautiful canvas of a room created specifically for one purpose. To display the panels that covered its walls.

"Monet's *Nymphéas*," Frederic said. "As it was meant to be displayed."

The water lilies. Piper stepped toward the center of the room. A sea of color surrounded her. Blues, greens, purples. She was swimming in them.

"This is way better than a poster," she whispered. The room called for sounds no louder.

"I had a feeling you would like it."

"Like it? It's amazing."

"I'm glad you think so."

His breath tickled her ear, causing Piper to brush at the sensation. In doing so, her fingers accidently traced the same spot Frederic had touched when he cupped her cheek. Goose bumps danced across her skin. She rubbed her arms, chasing them away.

"I read about this museum when I was planning my trip." She forgot about it, though, once she realized visiting museums on her own wasn't much fun.

"It's one of my favorite places," Frederic told her.

Piper went back to studying the panels filling the room. They were larger than the painting she'd seen in Boston. These paintings loomed over her, dwarfing their surroundings with their magnitude.

"That's because they are murals," Frederic replied when she said as much. "This building was built specifically to house them."

"They're immense. I wonder how long it took to paint each panel?"

"I am guessing a very long time."

"Is that your expert opinion?"

"It is indeed." His grin was warm and endearing. If they were different people, Piper might think he was flirting.

Being late afternoon, most of the tourists had already filed through, leaving the two of them with the room to themselves. Frederic took a seat on the benches in the center of the room. "Monet has always been my favorite of the Impressionists," he said. "Did you know he painted over two hundred and fifty versions of his lily pond? Many of them he painted while he had cataracts. You can tell which ones because they have red in them."

"Is that why you like him?"

"You mean, do I feel some sort of affinity for him

because we both have bad eyes?" He shrugged. "Never thought much about it. But now that you ask, I suppose I do have a unique appreciation for what he accomplished."

Piper joined him on the bench, her legs stretched in the opposite direction from his. "Did you ever think of becoming an artist?" All the art talk the past couple days had made her curious. His interest in art history had to start somewhere. Was it the backup for a different goal? It would be nice to know if someone else stumbled while chasing a dream.

It was hard to picture Frederic failing at anything, though...

"I dabbled a little when I was younger. I'm not sure you'd call the results art."

"Worse than the painting Bernard tried to sell you?"

God, she liked his laugh. It sounded so rich and throaty, even when soft. "Don't let Bernard hear you say that," he said. "And yes, it was worse. For the record, the Biskup was not a bad painting."

"No, just depressing."

"Some people like depressing art. As for my abilities... I'm afraid the artistic gene stopped with my mother."

"So your mother was an artist. Do you have any of her paintings?" The floral one in the salon, she bet.

"Unfortunately, no. She had to give up her work."

"Why?"

His gaze dropped to the floor. "She just did."

Not by choice, either, she'd say, based on the sorrow in his voice. What happened? She wanted to ask, but it was obvious Frederic didn't want to share and who was she to push? After all, there were things in her life she wasn't ready to share either. She settled for giving his shoulder a nudge to draw him back to the moment. "So your lack of an art gene... Is that why you became a teacher? Because those who can't, teach?"

If ever a comment didn't fit a person. Fortunately, Frederic got the joke and nudged her shoulder in return. "Professor, thank you very much. There's a second set of panels in the next room. Then I want to take you upstairs to see another favorite of mine. If you're a good girl, we can stop at the gift shop and buy you a new poster as well."

"Don't let Bernard hear you say that," Piper shot back with a smirk. She was holding him to that promise, though.

Piper assumed that once they finished at L'Orangerie, Frederic would call for the car so they could return to the house, but he did not. Instead, he asked her for the time.

"Almost half past six," Piper replied.

"Good. We have plenty of time."

"Plenty of time for what?"

"To walk along the river, of course. We'll walk until we get hungry, and then we'll find a place to eat."

"You don't have to take me to dinner," she told him.

"Why not? You can tell me if the food holds up to your culinary school standards."

"Because..." Because she hadn't forgotten that she was talking about her sad, friendless state just before he stopped the car, which made her fear this adventure was nothing more than a very romantic pity trip. "I've already taken up too much of your day as it is." Along with half of yesterday too. "I'm sure you've got other things you'd rather do."

"I already told you, I do not. What I do want is to enjoy this beautiful summer night."

Taking her by the elbow, he stepped off the curb only to jump back when a car horn blared loudly.

"Perhaps we should wait until the light changes." He spoke with a smile, but Piper saw a pair of pink spots peering out beneath the rims of his aviators nonetheless. "I'm usually quite good about checking traffic, but sometimes I get distracted."

"I didn't look, either," she pointed out. "We both deserved the horn in this case."

Even so, the incident must have bothered Frederic more than he let on, because once they were across the street, he fell quiet.

Once again, Piper didn't push. People needed to work out their embarrassment their own way, even people like Frederic, who didn't get embarrassed all that often. As they walked in silence, she contented herself with studying the riverbank. The bag carrying her posters from L'Orangerie slapped against her thigh, and she imagined the sound was the water lapping the river's edge.

The view was a familiar one. Over the past eight months, Piper had walked the river dozens of times. After school. On errands. In all four seasons. Yesterday, if someone had asked her, she would have said the

path didn't live up to the billing… Today, though…
Today, it was as though she was seeing the riverbanks
for the first time. Probably because she wasn't walking alone.

More than that. For the first time in months, she
didn't *feel* alone.

Looking over at Frederic, she wondered how many
of the people passing them envied her his company.
A man who so obviously could have his pick of any
woman in Paris. Her insides toppled end over end that
she was the one he picked. So what if today was a pity
date? Tomorrow's routine would return soon enough.
Today she would take his pity, and enjoy the break.

"My mother."

Frederic's voice was soft and unexpected. Yanked
from her thoughts, Piper nearly stumbled.

"You asked me why I studied art history," he said.
"My mother was the one who taught me to appreciate art."

Strange that he would choose now to address a re-
mark made at the museum. Here she thought he'd been
dwelling on their near miss with the car. Unless the two
were related.

"Sounds like you got part of the art gene after all,"
she said.

"More likely she wanted to make sure I was exposed
to as many beautiful things as possible."

There, Piper realized sadly, was the link. She had this
image of Frederic's mother exposing him to sight after
sight. How young had he been when his eyes started to
fail? "It's funny," she heard herself saying, "but some-

times I forget you have trouble seeing. You certainly wouldn't know it at home."

"That is because I work hard to make sure I function without assistance. I made up my mind very early in life that blindness wouldn't leave me helpless."

"You're not blind, though."

"Yet."

Her stomach sank. In the back of her mind, she'd known what his response would be, but she'd hoped otherwise. "I'm sorry."

"Don't be," he said cutting her off. "I accepted my fate a long time ago. Someday, I will wake up and my eyesight will be gone. Perhaps not so drastically, but it will happen."

"What will you do then?" Piper wasn't sure she wanted to know. There was a resignation to his voice that made her sad.

Frederic stopped so he could turn to face her. The sunglasses masked his eyes, but the rest of his face was resolute. "I will deal."

A fair enough answer. Why then did it make her want to throw her arms around him and hold on tight?

"If my sister were here, she'd add, 'then figure out a way to fix the situation'."

His mouth curved into a smile. "Somehow I doubt she was referring to degenerative eye disease."

"No, although she definitely got us out of some dark times."

"Dark?"

Probably not the best word to use. Giving a shrug, she started to do what she always did and play off the comment, but then changed her mind. "Things weren't always great when I was growing up. Patience always did her best to make them better. I owe her everything." A small wedge of guilt worked its way into her throat, the way it always did when talking about her sister.

"Sounds like your sister is a special woman."

"I always thought so," she said.

"Must run in the family."

Was he talking about her? Piper shook her head. "I don't think…"

He pressed a finger to her lips. "Never turn down a compliment, Piper."

What was it with Frederic touching her and walking away? Twice now his fingers had stroked her face. She traced the spot on her lips, convinced his fingers left a part of himself behind. Why else would they continue to tingle?

"Piper?" Ahead a few feet, Frederic had stopped and was looking for her.

"Sorry, I was think— Do I hear music?"

She did. The soft sound of violins and accordians could be heard in the distance.

"It's coming from around the bend," Frederic said.

"A concert?" It sounded like too many instruments to be a regular sidewalk performance. A dinner cruise maybe. She tried to remember if there was a dock ahead.

Meanwhile, Frederic was trying very hard to hide a smile. "You know what it is, don't you?"

"Perhaps," he replied.

Oh, he definitely knew. He was holding out on her, just like he did with the Monet exhibit. Question was, what was he hiding? A thrill of anticipation passed through her, strengthened by her still-tingling lips. They rounded the corner, and she spied a large crowd surrounding the amphitheaters. "It *is* a concert."

"Is it? You might want to look closer." He flashed another one of those mysterious smiles, making Piper think her insides might melt.

Drawing closer, she saw that the crowd was watching a swirl of movement. "Oh my God, are they dancing?"

"Ballroom dancing at dusk," Frederic murmured in her ear. "A summer tradition."

It was a beautiful sight to see. Dozens of couples twirling to the music.

Piper pointed to a graceful blonde woman moving between the dance groups. "The woman in the red shirt. Is she a judge or something?"

"Instructor, more likely. Here to help the less-skilled dancers learn the steps."

Didn't look as if anyone needed lessons. The pairs moved in graceful synchronicity to the slow, pulsing beat. "Do you know what dance they are performing?"

"Based on the music, I would say the tango."

She should have known. The air was ripe with sensuality. You could literally feel the passion as the more experienced dancers stalked the dance floor. Piper felt her breath quickening in response. Behind her, Frederic breathed quickly as well, his chest brushing against her back with each rise and fall of his lungs. A dinner boat passed, its bow lights creating a fairy-tale background just as the music peaked.

"Wow," she whispered when the song had ended. She

looked over her shoulder. "I've never really seen ball-room dancing up close before. It's beautiful to watch."

A new song began to play. Piper recognized the strands of "La Vie en Rose."

"The dancing is open to everyone," Frederic said. "Would you like to join them?"

"Out there? I'm no ballroom dancer."

"You don't have to be. The only requirement is to enjoy moving to the music."

More couples were making their way to the dance floor, made brave by the familiar music. Piper couldn't help noticing that several of the pairings barely moved. They were content to simply hold each other and sway to the beat.

She imagined Frederic's arms holding her and grew warm all over. Before she could say a word, a hand molded to the small of her back and she was propelled forward.

"Stay by the edge, where there isn't too much of a crowd," he said. Piper really wished his breath wouldn't tease her skin the way it did.

He led her to an open space near where they were standing. "I hope you can do this without stepping on anyone's toes, because I can't," she said.

His arm slipped around her waist and pulled her tight. "Moving to the music is the easy part," he told her. "It's the crowds that are the problem."

The crowds, she repeated to herself. The crowds were why he was holding her so close. Another inch or so, and her cheek would be flush with his shoulder. The music's familiar three-beat rhythm echoed in her ear. Head bobbing in time, Piper counted her steps. "Relax," he said. His chest rumbled against her cheek as he spoke. "Let the music guide your feet."

"I think my feet might be tone-deaf."

"Nonsense. You're in Paris. Everyone is graceful in Paris." He tightened his grip, his cheek pressing against her temple. "Let yourself go and enjoy."

Why not? When would she ever have this opportunity again? The sun was setting, the breeze was warm and the spires of Notre Dame were keeping watch. What could be more magical? Piper closed her eyes and let the music take control. It couldn't have been more perfect.

"See?" Frederic said. "I told you that you could dance."

Truthfully, they weren't so much dancing as swaying in time, but Frederic didn't mind. The crowd made more complex moves difficult for him. Holding Piper's hand against his chest, he contented himself with inhaling the scent drifting off her skin. How was it a woman could smell so good without perfume?

Piper had her head nestled against his shoulder, the crown of her head tucked near his chin. He wondered if she realized how much like an embrace their dance had become. Not that he was averse to the position. It had been a while since he held a beautiful woman so close. And he couldn't remember the last time he actually danced with a woman.

"Hold me close and hold me fast," Piper was singing under her breath. "The magic spell you cast."

"This is *la vie en rose*," he finished.

She lifted her head and they were close enough that he could see the dreamy expression in her eyes. The soft glow brought his awareness to life.

"I always loved this song," she told him. "Before I came here, I used to imagine the city with accordion players on all the streets playing this song, just so people could walk around to it."

She really did have a romantic's view of his city. Shame on those other students for destroying that dream. "I'm sorry we let you down."

"It's okay," she said, putting her head back on his shoulder. "This works, too."

They walked the rest of the way home. He would probably regret using his eyes so much, but at the moment, listening to Piper hum "La Vie en Rose" under her breath, he thought it worth the sacrifice.

Ahead, the Eiffel Tower blinked in all its lit-up glory. Frederic couldn't help but stop. "Beautiful, isn't it?" he said.

"Yeah, it is," she said, craning her neck to get a better view. "No matter how cranky I get about life in Paris, I can never hate the tower."

Neither could he. He didn't know why, but he found himself feeling very open and poetic tonight. Wasn't like him. As a rule, he preferred to keep the world at arm's length. He never wanted to get to a point where someone felt obligated to him because they shared a closeness. He knew only too well what obligation led to. Far easier—and safer—to stay charming and superficial. Tonight, though, it seemed he was destined to break that rule.

"I told myself a long time ago that I would never take

the tower for granted," he told Piper. "Ever since then, I've made a point of looking at her every day."

Because you never know when you'll have the chance to see it again.

He heard a soft cough. Turning his head, he saw Piper smiling at him. "Thank you," she said. "For this afternoon. For showing me the Paris I've always dreamed of. I'll never forget it."

Frederic didn't know what to say. He still wasn't 100 percent sure why she compelled him to be so whimsical. Inexplicable as his decision was, however, he had to admit that she wasn't the only one who'd enjoyed the day. "I'm glad," he said. "I had a good time, too."

She was smiling, and he could make out a sparkle shimmering in her eyes. Their sheen was luminescent. So was her skin, he thought, letting his eyes take in as much as they were able. The smell of vanilla and spices wafted toward him, like a siren's call. Then suddenly, she was closer, and her lips brushed his cheek in a shy kiss.

The feel of her lips on him stayed long after Piper disappeared into her rooms. Not yet ready to head upstairs, Frederic sat in the dark and studied his tower. Today was not what he expected. Piper wasn't what he expected.

Whether or not that was a good thing, he didn't know.

CHAPTER FIVE

IT WAS OFFICIAL. Piper hated Chef Despelteau as much as he hated her. There was no way her culinary skills were that far below the rest of the class. Honestly, she was beginning to think the man would have a problem with Julia Child's French cooking.

Wonder what Chef Despelteau would think if he knew she didn't like half the foods they were preparing? They were all so froufrou.

Feeling rebellious, she stopped at the grocery on her way home and bought a roast and potatoes. She'd like to see Chef Despelteau make a Yankee pot roast as well as she could.

Might as well face it, babe, you're a common food girl at heart. A common girl, period.

Maybe so, but she was also a girl who had waltzed under the Paris moon. How many people back home could say that? No sooner did the thought enter her head than the memory washed over her. Piper smiled. If she concentrated, she could remember every detail, right down to the smell of Frederic's skin.

So many of the guys she knew used slow dancing as

an excuse to cop a feel. They'd rest their hands on your rear or plaster their bodies so tightly against yours that the two of you might as well be sleeping together. Frederic held a woman like a man who had nothing to prove. Of course, it didn't matter how he held her. It wasn't as if last night was like some magic spell that changed them from boss and employee into something else.

Still, he'd given her a great memory. Now if anyone asked, she wouldn't have to lie about having spent time with a handsome Frenchman.

She arrived at the house to find her handsome Frenchman stretched out in his chair again. Amazing how he could make something as simple as sprawling in a chair look elegant. He had one arm flung over his eyes while the other rested gently on his stomach. Piper's gaze fell to the long fingers that were curled ever so slightly against his shirt. As though it remembered their touch, her skin began to tingle.

"I know you're standing there," he said, stirring.

Piper winced at getting caught. Thank goodness she was behind the chair so he couldn't see how red her cheeks were.

"I thought I might have to wake you up again," she said. "You looked dead to the world."

"Only resting. My meeting for tonight had been canceled, so I decided to rest my eyes for a moment. They tend to get tired this time of day."

"Sorry I disturbed you then." It never occurred to her, what with his limited field of vision, how much energy it must take for him to focus. Making yesterday's adventure all the more special.

"No worries. Are you carrying something?" She held up the brightly colored bag she used for errands. "Ahh, I thought I saw a pink handle."

"Groceries. I decided to make a pot roast." Piper paused. If his meeting was canceled, did that mean he would be home for dinner?

"Will that be a problem?" Frederic asked when she checked.

Before today, she would have said no. While Frederic's schedule kept him out of the house most nights, there were times when he stayed home and expected her to cook. All those nights happened before they'd danced together, however. Those few minutes in his arms had colored their relationship. An ordinary activity such as cooking now had a more intimate flavor.

But the inability to separate last night and today was her problem, wasn't it? When push came to shove, Frederic was still her boss and she still his housekeeper.

Offering a smile, she replied in as casual a voice as she could muster. "Why would it be a problem? Cooking is part of my job, isn't it? I mean, the title is house-keeper-slash-cook."

"Yes, but when I mentioned staying in, your voice sounded a little...off. Made me concerned."

"I was calculating cooking times in my head is all. To make sure I don't serve you too late." *Please don't ask what time I consider late because I'm totally making things up.*

"You don't have to worry about the time. I'll eat whenever the meal is ready."

"Well, I better go change uniforms and get started.

Oh, by the way," she said, remembering. "I called the carpet cleaning company. They're closed for vacation. I made a note to call them next week."

"That's not necessary, you know."

"It is if you want to get rid of the coffee stain."

"No, I mean, changing. You don't have to switch uniforms on my account."

"You might change your mind when you realize how badly this jacket smells like today's seafood lesson."

"I meant you don't have to wear a uniform. Put on your regular clothes."

But she always wore a uniform. The employment agency insisted. *To maintain a barrier between staff and the house* or something like that.

"I've been thinking about it for a couple days. There is no reason you should have to keep changing from one uniform to another and back every day. You should be comfortable."

Comfortable while cooking for him. Yeah, that wouldn't feel domestic at all. "Thanks," she told him. "I'll do that."

A short while later, the kitchen smelled like beef and onions. Piper breathed in the familiar scents to calm her nerves. *Get a grip*, she told herself. It's no different from any other night. In fact, this was a good reminder to keep her head on straight. As her little stare-fest in the living room proved, she was crossing the line from attractive boss to being attracted to her boss—something neither of them needed.

Her attention shifted to the phone on the counter.

Odd. She had two missed calls. She must have been so engrossed in chopping vegetables she didn't notice the phone vibrating. Both were from Patience. Wanting to know how the painting search was going, no doubt. Piper wasn't going to have much to tell her. John Allen hadn't returned her phone call yet.

Only, Patience's voice mail wasn't about the painting. It was about her and Stuart Duchenko. She replayed the message twice to make sure she heard her sister correctly. Difficult, since Patience was sniffling throughout.

Oh, Patience. Sick to her stomach, she dropped into one of the kitchen chairs and stared at the call screen. You'd think after everything else, her sister would catch a break.

"I can smell dinner from up in my office. It smells delicious."

"Thanks," she replied, attention stuck on the phone. She didn't even bother to look up when Frederic joined her.

"Something has upset you." His arm reached across the table and brushed the top of her wrist, drawing her attention. "Is it about the painting? Did Monsieur Allen have bad news?"

"No, I'm still waiting to hear from him. My sister left her job." Her thumb wavered between texting and calling direct. Video chatting would be best, but she didn't know if Patience had her laptop.

Frederic drew up a chair and sat down. "She is no longer working for Ana Duchenko? Why not? I was under the impression she cared about the woman."

"She does. Problem is she cares about Stuart Duchenko more."

"The nephew who is searching for the painting. I didn't realize they were…friends."

Piper had to smile at his use of euphemisms. "According to her voice mail, they aren't 'friends' any longer. They had a fight about something in her past. She was crying, so I couldn't understand the whole message. I'll find out more when I call her back."

Piper's eyes dropped back to her phone screen. "And here I thought after everything she'd been through, she'd finally found happiness."

"Everything she'd been through? I don't understand. Yesterday you said you both suffered through tough times."

"We did. But Patience suffered more, or at least I think so."

"What do you mean?"

Piper exhaled. She hadn't planned on sharing the story with him, but now that she opened the door, she might as well walk all the way through. After all, Frederic opened up about his eyesight, right?

"Do you remember when I told you that no matter how tough life got for us, Patience found a way to make it better?"

"Yes."

"Well, life got real tough. Like the two of us living in a car tough."

She tried not to cringe at his sudden sharp breath. "You—you were homeless?"

"Only for a week or so." Yesterday's sympathy had

returned to his voice. Hearing it left a sour taste in her mouth and so she rushed to erase it as quickly as possible. "It was right after my mom died. Soon as we could afford to, we found a cheap motel room and then later an apartment."

"Must have been terrifying."

"I was more scared someone would find out and take me away. Patience promised we would stay together."

"She kept her promise."

"Yes, she did. She took the only job she could find to pay the bills."

"Working for Ana Duchenko as a housekeeper."

"The job with Ana came later, after I moved here. When I was a kid, she was a dancer in a club. A club where women were paid to dance."

There was a pause as the full meaning of her answer sank in. "I see," he said finally.

"She didn't have a choice." The defense came automatically, before he could say anything judgmental. "I told you, it was the first job she could find."

Twirling her phone end over end, she thought about those dark days. Remembering how she sat shivering in a blanket in the backseat, crying because the only thing she'd eaten that day were the free saltines they swiped from the local convenience store. "For most of my life it's been just me and Patience. Couldn't have been easy being stuck raising a kid right out of high school."

"I would think it was hard for both of you."

He spoke frankly, exactly the way Piper preferred. Bluntness was so much better than pity or sarcasm.

"When she first got the job I was too young to understand what she was doing," she told him. "Then when I was old enough…" Hopefully, her shrug filled in the blanks. When she was old enough, she sucked it up, for Patience's sake.

"The argument your sister and the Duchenko nephew had? This is the information he discovered?"

"I think he learned a few of the more sordid details. From the sound of it, there were things I didn't even know about."

It made her wonder how many more difficulties her sister bore alone for Piper's sake. The guilt she carried on her shoulders pressed heavier.

Meanwhile, Frederic sat stiffly in his chair, drawing patterns on the table with his index finger. "Sounds as if both of you were very brave. I've known people who weren't half as brave when life kicked them."

Who? Certainly not him.

"If your sister is as strong as she sounds," he continued, "then I am sure she will weather this storm as well. Did you not just say she always found a way to fix a bad situation?"

"You're right. She did." Patience was a survivor. A fact Piper needed to remember. "Being over five thousand miles away has got me on edge. I'm sure that once I have a chance to talk with her, I'll feel better."

In fact, her spirits were already beginning to lift, in large part because of the man across from her. "Who knows? Maybe once he's had a chance to get over the shock, Stuart will realize Patience's past is no big deal."

After all, life has a way of doing a one-eighty on you. Last week she would have been sitting here dealing with Patience's message on her own.

"Thank you," she said.

"For what?"

"Listening. It was nice having a shoulder for a change." Reaching across the table, she covered his hand with hers. It was a simple gesture, meant to be an expression of gratitude, but it sent warmth coiling through Piper in unexpected ways. She looked up, wondering if Frederic noticed her reaction, and saw that his eyes were dark with an unreadable emotion. Her pulse skipped.

"I should go call her back," she said, standing. Her hand didn't seem to want to separate from his; she had to force the command down her arm to make it move. "I'll try to be quick."

"Take as much time as you'd like," Frederic told her. His attention was on the hand she had just released, his voice distracted.

Piper didn't want to think about it. Pushing the moment from her thoughts, she headed toward her suite, her finger hitting redial before she reached it. Patience's phone went straight to voice mail. "You can't call me crying, then not answer your phone," she said. "Call me back ASAP. Everything will be okay," she added in a gentle voice.

Barely two seconds went by before a message appeared on her screen.

Doing better. Checking into a motel. Will call u later.

Soon, OK? Piper typed back. Love you.

Her sister would bounce back, Piper reminded herself as she tucked the phone in her back pocket. Frederic was right about her being a survivor. It still sucked though that Patience couldn't seem to catch any happiness.

Maybe it wasn't in the Rush girl DNA. What with them being common girls and all that, maybe they weren't meant to be anything more. She tapped the phone against her lips. At least Piper was here making sure some of her sister's sacrifices were worthwhile.

A thought came to her. There was one more thing she could do. She could talk to Stuart herself. Piper opened her email.

Frederic was moving about the kitchen when she returned a short time later. Whatever the thickness was that had been in the atmosphere before she left had eased. "Did you talk to your sister?" he asked.

"No, but she texted me. Said she's feeling better."

"You seem to be, as well."

Yeah, she was. "That's because after I heard from Patience, I decided to take a page from her playbook and do something to fix the situation. I decided to contact Stuart to see if I could make him see how backed in a corner Patience was back then."

"Good thinking."

"Unnecessary too. When I logged on, I found an email from him asking how he could make things right."

Might not be perfect, but it was a start.

"There you go. He's already over whatever news he learned. I'm sure that means they will talk things out."

"I really hope so."

All of sudden she saw that Frederic was setting the kitchen table. With two place settings.

"I thought we'd be more comfortable in here," he said when he noticed her staring.

"We're eating together?" All the other times she'd served him, he'd eaten in the dining room.

"Foolish for us to eat in separate rooms, is it not? Especially now that we are friends."

Friends. Apparently, he forgot that he used the same term to describe Patience's and Stuart's relationship.

She watched as he moved from cupboard to table. She never noticed before, but he looked at the space in sections, presumably until the object he was seeking came into view. Methodical, but subtle and graceful at the same time. To the unknowing eye, he was simply a man in supreme control. Heck, he looked that way to her *knowing* eye. She couldn't imagine him being anything but in control.

What was it she was supposed to remember about finding him attractive and being attracted?

"…going?"

He was looking in her direction waiting for an answer. "Should I assume from your lack of response that class did not go well again today?"

Right, he was talking about school. Piper shook her head. "No, but school never does go well, so it's no big deal."

"I am sorry." His voice lifted at the end, as if he wasn't sure he should offer condolences or not.

"Hey, like I said yesterday, great cooking is an art. Don't all artists suffer?"

"Some do."

"Well, so do some chefs. I'm telling myself that in the end, the hassle is making me a better chef.

"In the meantime," she said, reaching for the cornstarch, "I'm learning a whole bunch of new ways to insult a person's dinner. Today's word was *mundane*. My sauce was mundane. I like to think it's a step up from earlier this week when my food was uninspired."

"I see your teacher is one of those instructors."

"What do you mean, 'one of those'?" she asked as she mixed thickener for the gravy.

"I mean the type who believes insulting their students makes for good motivation."

"Assuming he is trying to motivate and not simply telling the truth."

"The aromas in this kitchen suggest otherwise."

It felt so good to have someone compliment her cooking, Piper decided to not worry about whether he was being polite and smiled instead. "Pot roast is one of my specialties. I've always been wicked good when it comes to New England cooking. Your country…" She waved her hand back and forth. "Not so much. I should have realized after I tried to make vichyssoise." Good Lord, she hadn't thought about that in ages. The memory made her laugh. "I think I was seven."

"And attempting French cooking?"

"What can I say? I was a prodigy." She left out the

part about how if she didn't cook, she didn't eat. "Anyway, someone mentioned cold potato soup on TV. I figured it couldn't be that hard to make, so I tried it. Ended up serving Patience a can of condensed potato soup straight out of the cupboard. No water or anything." She could imagine what Chef Despelteau would say.

"I'm glad your skills improved."

"Me, too. And for the record, I know how to make a kick-ass vichyssoise now. Patience refuses to eat it, though. Can't really blame her. Too many canned soup dinners burned her out."

Piper stared at the cloudy liquid in front of her. "She's the reason I'm here, you know. In Paris. She never stopped encouraging me. Telling me I could do anything I wanted."

"Like a good parent should."

"She'd laugh if she heard you say that, but yeah, exactly like a parent. I remember when I got my acceptance letter. She was more excited than I was." There was no way Piper couldn't fulfill their dream after that.

Distracted by memories, Piper forgot she was supposed to be stirring the thickener. The bowl slipped from her hands, bounced off the counter edge and landed on the floor.

Shoot. Cornstarch splattered the cabinets. That's what she got for not paying attention. She reached for the paper towels only to collide with Frederic as he did the same. Their fingers linked together.

Just like that, the thickness returned to the atmosphere. Piper felt it pressing around them, like energy waiting to hum. She looked at their interlocked fingers and wondered why neither of them had pulled away.

"Guess this is the week for spills," she joked.

"This is the week for a lot of broken rules," he said, a strangely serious response to what was meant as a tension breaker. She'd been looking for something to distract from the pull of attraction gathering strength in her belly. Piper didn't have to look up to know Frederic felt similarly. They were both breathing faster. Out of the corner of her eye, she saw his head dip closer, intentions clear. If she said no, he would stop.

She met him halfway.

Their mouths slid together as easily as their hands. Piper sighed at how well they fit. Frederic kissed like he moved, each caress of his lips deliberate and sure. His hand still gripping hers, he wrapped his other arm around her waist and pulled her close. *Just like dancing,* she thought as her eyes fluttered shut.

A moment later, Frederic broke away. Shaking and out of breath, Piper leaned her forehead against his. Holy cow! Never in a million years did she think a kiss could feel like that.

Frederic looked shell-shocked himself. She took pleasure in seeing his hand shake as he swiped a thumb across her lower lip. "Your phone is ringing," he said in a tight voice.

Phone? Piper blinked. Sure enough, she heard the sound of computerized jazz coming from her pocket. "Th-that's probably Patience."

"You should answer."

Yes, she should. Balling the hand Frederic had been

holding into a fist, she reached for the phone with her other.

Not Patience. The number on her call screen was unfamiliar. She didn't know if they had telemarketers in France, but if this was one, she was not going to hang up politely.

"Hello!" a cheery voice replied. "Am I speaking with Piper Rush? This is John Allen. I understand you're interested in a painting of mine."

While Piper spoke to John Allen, Frederic moved across the room. He needed to put some space between them before he took his housekeeper on the kitchen floor. It wasn't that he was against making love in the kitchen; he simply wasn't sure he should make love to Piper. As she was quickly proving, Piper was no ordinary housekeeper. She was soft and sweet in ways he wasn't used to. There was an essence about her that demanded connection, compelling him to reach out to her. She made him want to comfort her.

She... God, she tasted like vanilla. She made him want to taste her again. But was that a good idea?

Just then, Piper laughed, a sweet sound that reminded him of tinkling crystal, and he thought, perhaps it was a very good idea.

"Are you sure?" he heard her ask. "That would be great. Miss Duchenko would be thrilled."

Thrilled at what? Curiosity overrode his desire. Did this mean Allen had the painting? That they had tracked down the work so easily was almost comical. Experts searched lifetimes for paintings and sculptures and here his houskeeper locates one in three days? Amazing.

He was surprised at his investment in the search. Naturally, he would have a passing interest in tracking down a lost painting of any kind, even a scandalous portrait by a no-name artist like this one. The fact that his interest ran deeper he attributed to his frighteningly intriguing housekeeper.

"Looks like I'm going to England on an art hunt after all," Piper announced when she hung up. "Mr. Allen has invited me to see *Ana Reclining* in person."

"Congratulations." Her smile was contagious. "Does his invitation mean he is willing to part with the painting?"

"He said he would have to think about whether he was willing to sell. The painting is one of his favorite pieces."

But of course it was. As anyone hoping to net a good price would say.

"However, he did offer to let me inspect the painting's condition and to take a photograph of the work for Ana. If he doesn't sell, she will at least have proof one of her portraits survived."

Explaining why Miss Duchenko would be thrilled.

"I thought I would go this weekend. Mr. Allen's leaving on a business trip next week and wasn't sure how long he'd be gone. I figured I could take the train out tomorrow. That is, if you can spare me for a few days."

"I can," he replied. But did he want to? It was clear from the excited energy in her voice that the rest of tonight would be absorbed by itineraries and trip planning. To then have to wait an entire weekend before having the chance to kiss her again?

The words were out of his mouth before he had a chance to think them through. "Actually, I thought I would go with you."

"You did?"

"Why not? I've been part of your search for the last two days. Surely you didn't expect me to stay home when you got to the best part?"

"Do you really want to?" he heard her ask. "Go to England?"

"Yes, Piper, I do."

He could see her fidgeting as she tried to decide. After the kiss they just shared, there could be no doubt as to what traveling together to England might lead to. Frederic stayed quiet; he wouldn't push her one way or the other. No matter how tempting the thought of kissing her into agreement.

From her spot across the room, Piper nodded. "What time do you want to leave?"

CHAPTER SIX

PIPER WASN'T AN IDIOT. She knew perfectly well what could happen if Frederic accompanied her to England. Especially after the kiss they shared.

What she hadn't known was that kissing Frederic would leave her with some kind of ultra-hyper responsiveness that would fade. Every move, every sound Frederic made—right down to the crinkle of his shirt when he bent his elbow—sent a rush of awareness running through her. You'd think it was her first kiss. In a way, it was. It was certainly the first kiss that made her insides feel as though they were being kissed, too. If one short kiss could make her feel this way, she hated to think what would happen if he kissed without interruption.

The only thing that kept her from throwing herself at him to find out was, ironically enough, arranging their trip.

They caught the first train the next morning.

Piper took out the map of England she'd bought at the station and located the town where John Allen lived. "Have you been to this place before?" she asked Frederic.

"The town? No. I've been to the Cotswolds several times, though."

As he answered, he shifted in his seat, causing his jeans leg to brush hers. Impossibly the contact managed to reach through the layers to leave goose bumps.

The hyperawareness was as strong as ever.

Piper shifted in her seat as well, hoping she could add a little space between their legs. Otherwise, it would be a very long tunnel ride. "I read about the Cotswolds online last night." Mainly because she needed to do something to calm the hyperawareness. Turned out reading up on the trip you were taking with the man who kissed you senseless wasn't a relaxing solution. "It looked gorgeous in the pictures." Not to mention romantic. Another reason she had trouble sleeping.

She suddenly wondered what kind of visits Frederic's other trips to the Cotswolds were. "Did you go there on vacation?"

"There's an abbey not far from Chipping Campden that has the most unique ninth-century mural of Saint Michael. I wrote a journal paper on it." There was nostalgia in his smile. "I heard they restored it a few years ago. I wonder how it turned out."

"Why don't we go see it while we're in the area?" As far as she was concerned, anything that put such a smile on his face had to be worth a visit.

"I was already planning to," he replied. "Did you know that for centuries, no one knew this mural was there? At some point, it was covered by a second layer of stone. It was discovered when a lightning strike knocked a piece of the outer wall loose."

"Do they know why it was covered up?"

"No one knows for sure. My personal theory is that it was hidden during the Reformation so as not to anger Henry VIII." He launched into an explanation about the monks and allegiance to the king only to stop suddenly with a blush. "Sorry. I'm afraid I get carried away."

"It's okay—I don't mind," Piper replied. She'd been only half listening anyway. Too busy enjoying the sparkle in his eyes. "I have to be honest," she told him. "It's hard to imagine you poring over books in a research library." Today, for example, in his jeans and silk T-shirt, he looked more like a vacationing playboy or professional soccer player.

"Sit in one of my classes sometime. My students will say I must spend all my time there. That is why my lectures are so boring."

"They are not." She could listen to him talk all day.

"You are in a rarefied group then. Sometimes I think it's a good thing my lecture hall has low lighting. Keeps me from seeing how many of my students have fallen asleep. It's difficult enough when I call on them and they can't repeat what I mentioned five minutes earlier."

He was exaggerating. Piper honestly couldn't see him as boring, no matter how dry the topic. Distracting, however, was a far different story. If she were a college student, she could see herself spending class time fantasizing about the professor. "Your classes wouldn't be mostly female, would they?"

"About a seventy to thirty percent ratio. Why?"

"Trust me, those girls aren't sleeping."

The blush creeping over his cheeks was as captivating as the rest of him. "Is that your way of suggesting they're captivated by my looks?"

Piper joined him in blushing. "Is that your way of fishing for a compliment?"

"Perhaps." He traced a pattern across the map with his index finger. Piper followed with her eyes, and wondered if he was drawing a route or tracing aimless lines.

"I could say the same for you as well," he murmured without looking up.

"That I'm fishing for compliments?"

"That it's easy to be distracted by your good looks."

"Says the man who can't see." Realizing what she said, Piper started to cringe, only to stop when Frederic let out a laugh.

"Even through a pinhole, a man can see a diamond."

"Now I know you're exaggerating."

"Only a little." He moved his tracing from the map to her arm, his finger following the same lazy, loopy path across her skin. "You are a beautiful woman."

Piper pushed back a shiver. "I bet you say that to all your housekeepers."

"Only the American ones."

"Let me guess, you only hire Americans."

"No. You are the first." His finger took one last trip down her arm and disappeared. "I don't make a habit of kissing the help."

"Then why...?" What made her so different? She wasn't used to being singled out as special.

"I don't know," Frederic replied. He looked past her for a moment as if trying to figure out the answer himself before smiling at her again. "Why don't we enjoy it for what it is?"

"What is it?"

"Today? It is a road trip."

"And tomorrow?"

"Why don't we take things as they come? Stay in the present."

In other words, no strings attached.

"When I was a little kid, living in the present meant we were sure we'd have enough rent money." It was meant to be a joke, but the catch in her voice killed the effect.

Frederic shifted so they were face-to-face and took her hand. "I don't believe in giving false expectations," he told her. "Especially when it comes to relationships. It wouldn't be fair."

For whom? The other day he said being involved only meant more drama. Was that what he feared? That she might grow too attached? If so, maybe he should work on being a little less charming and attractive.

"Maybe I'm old-fashioned, but I like to know what I'm getting into," she said, only to realize that he had told her in very clear terms. No strings.

"You're thinking too much. Let us take one moment at a time, all right? Whatever happens, happens. There is no pressure."

Piper nodded. No pressure she could do.

Hopefully.

There was a car and driver waiting for them when they arrived at Saint Pancras station. A girl could get pretty spoiled by this kind of travel, Piper decided as she slid into the backseat. Definitely beat struggling to drive on the wrong side of the road with a rented stick shift. Which is what she'd be doing if Frederic weren't with her.

Best not to get too spoiled, though. At some point this whole Cinderella experience was going to end. There would be no limousines driving her around Boston. No guarantee she would have limousines driving her around Paris much, either. Taking things moment to moment could mean going back to being a housekeeper on Monday.

One good thing did come out of Frederic's "no pressure" comment, though. She managed to put the lid back on her over-boiling senses, meaning she could actually sit in the backseat without too much awareness. The only time she had real problems was when Frederic leaned into her space, sending a hint of his spicy wood aftershave in her direction. Then she would get a most unwelcome flutter below the waist. Fortunately, he didn't lean toward her too often.

"How long a drive is it to the Cotswolds?" she asked the driver.

"Ninety minutes or so. Little less maybe depending on traffic."

She reached into her bag to see if she missed any calls while underground. Nothing. "Patience still hasn't checked in."

"Perhaps she's been too busy."

"That's what I'm hoping." Too busy working out her problems with Stuart. "Do you know I still haven't told her about John Allen?"

"That could be for the best, since you haven't seen the painting yet. After you have met with Monsieur Allen, you will be able to give her much more information."

Like whether the collector would be willing to sell. "Do you think his position will change once he hears the painting's history?"

"It could. Or it could sway him the other way. Knowing the painting is attached to a world-renowned silver dynasty makes it—"

"Worth more, I know."

"Notoriety often does. Regardless, I'm sure no matter what the outcome of our meeting, Stuart Duchenko will spare no effort in trying to get his aunt's portrait returned."

"You are?"

"I know if it was something I wanted badly, I'd be relentless," he replied. The promise in his voice turned her insides upside down.

The English countryside was even more beautiful than the photos she saw online. Piper couldn't stop snapping pictures of the rolling green landscape.

"We have beautiful countryside in France as well," Frederic said, when she commented on a passing sheep farm.

"Yes, but that's French countryside. This is England," Piper countered. Spying a flock of grazing sheep, she took another photo.

"So?"

He almost sounded pouty. "You make it sound like it's a competition."

"It's always a competition when England is concerned."

"Well, at least it's easier to read the roadside signs here," she replied. Competition indeed. Both countries were better than any place she'd been before.

"Is there a place you can pull over so I can get a really good shot?" she asked the driver.

"The dozen or so you have already taken are not enough?" Frederic asked.

"I've got one more I want to take." And a moving car wouldn't do the subject justice.

"Will the shoulder ahead do?" He pointed to a particularly beautiful piece of scenery. A large checkerboard field in shades of green sprawled from the road to the horizon.

"Perfect."

The car slowed to a stop. "You have to get out, too," Piper told Frederic when he opened the door.

"Why?"

"Because I want you in the picture, that's why."

"A photograph of me standing on the side of the road."

"Actually, standing in front of that tree," she replied, pointing to a shrub-like tree a football field away.

From behind his sunglasses, Frederic was focusing in on her in his concentrated way. She tried to figure out his thoughts based on the rest of his expression, but it was impossible.

"Please?" she said, "I didn't think to take photos yesterday." Leaving her with zero visual evidence the magic day even happened. "I don't want to forget again this weekend." And be left with nothing.

"Only for you would I do this," he said.

"Thank you. Go stand by the tree and I'll be as quick as possible. Watch your step!" she added when he stepped down into a gulley.

"You're supposed to warn a person before they stumble," he said. Piper grinned. Hard to take the admonition seriously when he was grinning, too.

Not wanting to push her luck too much, she snapped three pictures in rapid succession. Her only regret was in forgetting to ask him to take off his sunglasses. She would have liked a picture with his eyes showing.

Maybe another time. "All done," she called to him. "You can get back into the car."

"Not yet. Gregory," he called to the driver, "Will you take mademoiselle's phone?"

"Yes, sir."

"You made us stop to take these photos. It is only fair you pose as well."

"Oh, no." Piper shook her head. "I hate having my picture taken."

"Gregory…"

The driver held out his hand expectantly.

"Watch out for the dip," Frederic said.

"Fine." Would be nice to have a photograph of her and Frederic for a memory. Giving her hair a quick fluff with her fingers, she stepped into the field.

Frederic met her under the tree. "Stand right here," he told her. Piper did as she was told, figuring they would pose side by side. Therefore she was caught off guard when Frederic moved behind her and wrapped his arms around her waist. "Smile for the camera," he murmured before pressing his cheek to Piper's temple.

"Got it," Gregory called.

Piper went to step forward, only to find herself held tight against Frederic's torso.

"Hold on," he said.

Keeping one arm around her waist, he caught her chin with the other, turned her head sideways and kissed her. Hard and thorough. "Now we can go."

Piper nearly forgot how to breathe. "What happened to no pressure?"

"No pressure, yes. I never said I wouldn't try to convince you, though, did I?" He held out a hand. "Shall we? Gregory is waiting."

"This is the inn John Allen recommended," Frederic said.

"It certainly is something," Piper replied.

It was a quintessential romantic country inn. A crooked building made of stone and quirky angles that sat at the top of the main street, while the rest of the village spread below. The whole thing was a postcard come to life. Thatched-roof buildings surrounded by rolling green hills and woodland. A local farmer driving his sheep down the road was all it needed to complete the picture.

It looked like the kind of place lovers went to hide. Precisely the kind of place a man would take a woman like Piper.

Why that thought left Frederic antsy, he wasn't sure.

The proprietress, a Mrs. Lester, met them at the

front door. "You must be the people who called last night." She smiled widely. "You are lucky. We don't usually have rooms this time of year, but we had a family cancel at the last minute, leaving us with two rooms open."

He almost chuckled at Piper's relieved breath.

While Piper went in search of a Wi-Fi signal so she could contact her sister, Frederic made arrangements with Gregory for the next day, then went upstairs to lie down. His head ached. He was not used to traveling outside Paris anymore. Navigating unfamiliar locations and crowds took extra concentration. Especially Saint Pancras station, where he had the additional strain of translating signage.

He'd been pushing himself harder than usual the past couple days. Piper was having such a good time; he wasn't about to spoil her happiness by asking that they slow down. Besides, the truth was, he didn't want to slow down, either. He was having a good time, too. No knowing how many more days like these he would have.

He was breaking his own rule about taking things day by day. Something about Piper made him reflective.

As his head sank against the pillows, he turned his focus to a more pleasant thought: the kiss he stole earlier. He'd been craving a second kiss since their first one ended, and after three hours of forced proximity —where her vanilla scent surrounded him like a cloud—he could no longer wait. She tasted as sweet as he remembered. There was a delicious innocence to her kisses. Then, there was an innocence to her, too.

As rocky as her childhood was, she still saw beauty in the world. She was the type of woman for whom fairy tales could exist. Look at how she was with her sister, going so far as to email Stuart Duchenko to salvage the sister's romance. She no doubt thought this portrait she was chasing represented a wonderfully tragic grand passion. It was infectious, this spirit of hers. Why else would he stand stupidly under a tree on the side of an English highway?

It was also why he made sure she understood from the start that whatever was between them would be a very finite fairy tale that would end when she returned to America.

Until then, though, he would show her a romantic time. And while he would not pressure her into his bed—he would never pressure any woman—he would do his best to convince her that his bed was where she wanted to be.

He must have fallen asleep, because the next thing he knew there was a soft knock on the door.

"I'm sorry," Piper said when he opened it. "Were you sleeping?"

"Dozing. Happens when I rest my eyes." He ran a finger through his hair, tugging the roots to clear the cobwebs. "Did you reach your sister?"

"I did. We had a good talk. I'm actually very hopeful for her and Stuart."

"That's good." He stepped aside to let her come in, only for her to start and stop. The way she toyed with the neckline of her jersey suggested she wasn't entirely sure what she wanted to do. Her hesitancy fit with all the other innocent facets of her personality.

It was utterly charming.

"I thought I'd take a walk through the village. See if any of those eight buildings was a gift shop. I was going to ask if you wanted to join me, but if you're not feeling well…"

"My eyes are tired is all," he replied.

"Do you want to rest?"

Hardly. "If I stayed behind every time my eyes weren't one hundred percent, I would never leave my house." And he would not be that person in a million years. "I would love to walk the village with you."

"You believe in pushing yourself, don't you?" she asked when they were downstairs. "I mean, you're on the go all the time."

"I don't believe in holding others back." An understatement if ever he made one. "And I believe in making the most of every moment."

"We've certainly crammed a lot of stuff into the past couple days, that's for certain."

He leaned close and said in a voice only she could hear, "The weekend is still young. Who knows what interesting activities we will discover." He didn't need peripheral vision to know he'd made her blush. So adorable.

Based on the village center, Frederic guessed this was not one of the Cotswold villages that catered to weekend travelers. They found a wine shop, a real estate business and a law firm. The only shop was an apothecary, where Piper bought a handful of postcards and two bottles of English lavender bath salts.

"What do you think?" she asked as she held the bottle under his nose. "Will it make a nice souvenir?"

"Very nice." Although her own scent was much nicer.

They contented themselves with walking the sidewalks after that. Piper was enchanted with the houses and hidden walkways. "I feel we walked onto a Hollywood set," she said, stopping to smell a hedge of blackberries. "If I were going to make a movie about an English country village, this is what it would look like."

Frederic had to admit, the gardens and brambles were beautiful. He liked the quiet. Moreover, he liked the comfortable silence the two of them shared. He noticed the other day that there wasn't a pressure to fill the space with noise the way there was with some of the women he spent time with. He was able to focus on navigating the uneven sidewalks without distraction. Well, almost without distraction, he thought, as his companion stopped to admire another garden. While he had been resting earlier, she pulled her hair into a ponytail. He liked when she wore her hair back; he could see her features better.

Because he could, he curled a stray hair behind her ear. She immediately ducked her head. "I don't know about you, but I'm getting hungry. I haven't eaten since the train," she said. Did she know her fingers were retracing the path he just made? "The man at the store told me there's a pub about a half mile to the north. The Hen & Chick or something like that. Should we try it out?"

"I don't think we have much choice. There seems to be an equal number of inns and restaurants."

"True," she said, smiling. "Considering how nice the rest of the town is, I don't see how the pub could be bad. And you did say to take things as they come…"

The subtext of her comment sent a thrill through him. "Good to see you're getting into the spirit."

"As far as dinner is concerned, anyway." She ducked her head again, but he caught the tiny smile she was trying to hide nonetheless.

"Dinner's always a good start," he told her.

They started walking again. "I wonder what the chances are that this place has a traditional pub menu. I've always wanted to try steak and kidney pie. And steamed pudding. Like spotted dick or treacle."

Frederic had to laugh at her enthusiasm over her potential menu. "I'm beginning to understand why you became a chef. You clearly love food."

"Good food," she corrected. "I'll try anything once, but to be honest, some of the froufrou stuff I can do without."

"Froufrou?" He didn't understand.

"Overly fancy. I'm not a fan of when chefs try too hard with food. I mean, don't get me wrong. I'm all for mixing things up, but sometimes a steak is best when you leave it a plain old steak." She let out a soft laugh. "Guess that explains why Chef Despelteau hates me. He's the king of froufrou."

"I'm sure you're exaggerating, and he doesn't *hate* you."

"Don't be so sure. I know you think he's pushing me

to be better, but I think he just doesn't groove on the way I cook. Hasn't since day one."

They were passing under an oak tree. She reached up and plucked one of the leaves. "You know, the other day when you found me crying in the kitchen, I was thinking of quitting," she told him.

"Really?" He knew she was upset, but thought she simply had a bad day. If she had quit, they wouldn't be walking this sidewalk. "What made you change your mind?"

"We worked too hard to get me to Paris. It'd be wrong not to see things through."

We. Meaning her sister and her. Frederic wasn't sure why, but talk of her sister and culinary school together unsettled him. There was an element of obligation to the way she talked about the combination that he didn't like.

"Surely if you are unhappy, your sister would not want you to continue." At least not the sister she'd described to him. "She'd want you to be happy."

"Oh, she does," Piper replied. "She would tell me to come home in a second, but like I said, quitting doesn't feel right.

"Besides," she added, "I'm not unhappy. Not right now, anyway."

"I'll take that as a compliment." His satisfaction almost outweighed the uneasiness he was feeling on her behalf. "So you finish your coursework. What then? What will you do when you go back to Boston?"

"Get a job at one of the local restaurants and work my way up the chain," she said. "Isn't that what one does with a culinary certificate?"

Yes, but one usually sounded more enthusiastic about the prospect. Then again, most students enjoyed school as well. This was one of those times when he wished he could walk and focus on his companion at the same time. To be able to see what she was thinking.

"You could open your own restaurant. Café du Piper."

She laughed. "Someday, maybe. A little bistro where I could design my own menu. Patience and I used to talk about my doing that."

Again, Patience. The woman was beginning to bother him, she was so ubiquitous. "Are all your dreams tied to your sister?" he asked, sharply.

"No." But her voice was too defensive to be convincing. "I have plenty of my own dreams."

"Like what?" Suddenly, very interested in hearing what she wanted, Frederic stopped walking and positioned himself so he could look her in the eye. "If you could do anything you wanted, what would it be?"

"Cooking, of course."

"Is that all? Just cooking? Tell me, what is Piper's passion?"

He was glad he stopped if for no other reason than he was gifted with the sight of her lashes sweeping downward like a thick black curtain. "You'll think it's silly."

"No, I won't." There was nothing about her he'd ever find silly. "I'd truly like to know."

"All right, but I'll warn you, it's not all that fancy."

"No one said it had to be."

She took a deep breath. "If I could do anything in the world, I would spend my time cooking wonderful meals for the people who matter to me. Food was there for me when I needed a friend. I would like to give people the same gift.

"Told you it was silly," she said, turning her head.

"Not silly at all. It's a lovely sentiment." One that fit her perfectly. How lucky those people would be.

Leaning close, he kissed her cheek. "I hope you get your dream," he whispered.

Don't let it die for your sister's sake, he added silently.

The pub was called the Hen & Rooster, and while the plaque next to the front door said it was established in 1666, Piper was pretty sure it had been modernized many times. The blast of comfortable, clean-smelling air that greeted them upon entering was her clue.

Aesthetically, the inside looked exactly like a seventeenth-century tavern. So much so, in fact, that Piper almost expected the bartender to be wearing period clothing and a leather apron. The floors were slanted. The walls were uneven. As they were walking into the dining room, Frederic clipped the top of his head.

"Must not have had too many people taller than six foot," she teased.

"More like five. There should be a sign warning people. Or padding on the cross beams."

"Poor baby. Does this help?" She massaged the top of his head, where he had tapped the beam.

"Much better," he replied. She couldn't see his eyes for the sunglasses, but she could feel their stare on her skin nonetheless. Felt as if he was concentrating all his attention on her face. Her mouth, to be precise. Taking her hand in his, he brought it to his lips. "Thank you."

She slipped her hand free and fought the urge to run it nervously across the back of her neck. Amazing how the air between them shifted so quickly, easy one moment, humming with awareness the next.

Of course, the fact that he'd kissed her twice in ten minutes probably helped that cause along.

Other than a pair of men at the bar, the restaurant was empty. That didn't stop the hostess from placing them at a table in the corner near an unused fireplace. Intimate and romantic. What a surprise. Maybe there was a competition between France and England, after all. To see which one could make her fall under Frederic's spell the fastest.

She could have told them they needn't work so hard. Frederic was doing fine without their help. Desperate for a distraction, she studied the single-sheet menu the hostess handed her.

"Do they have your pie?" Frederic asked.

"Afraid not. Looks like the chef prefers more continental than traditional British. Unless quinoa is an English staple I didn't know about."

"I'm sorry."

"Me too," she said, giving an exaggerated sigh. More to best him in the dramatics department than anything. "I'll simply have to make do with roasted guinea fowl."

"Poor baby." Just like that, the mood went back to being easy. If only they'd struck up a friendship earlier in her employment. The year could have been so much nicer. In the back of her mind, she sent up a silent thank-you to Ana. Without her portrait, they would still be virtual strangers.

"Good evening. Can I take your order?" The bartender appeared at their table with a pad in his hand. Piper gave her order.

"The same, along with a bottle of sauvignon blanc," Frederic said when she was finished.

"Did you even look at the menu?" She saw him fingering the paper, but the sheet never actually left his plate.

"I trust your judgment. Plus, I left my magnifying glass in my overnight bag."

"Ahh, the truth comes out. Now it's my turn to hope you aren't disappointed."

"I haven't been so far."

A flutter danced through her. *Better be careful.* She already liked him more than she should.

Now that they were seated, he'd removed his sunglasses, giving her the chance to study him straight-on. What she saw left her feeling guilty. There were lines around his eyes and mouth. The kind that came with fatigue. He was rubbing his thumb and middle finger across his eyebrows, massaging the skin underneath.

She waited while the bartender served the wine, then asked him, "Eyes still tired?"

"A little."

She had a feeling the two of them had different definitions of the term. "You didn't have to come with me, you know. I could have gone sightseeing on my own."

Wouldn't have been as enjoyable, but she would have endured.

"Absolutely not. I told you before, I am not going to sit in my room acting like an invalid because of a little eyestrain." The fierceness with which he spoke startled her. Way more than you'd expect for a simple suggestion.

He must have realized how sharp he sounded, too, because when he spoke again, his voice was softer and more in control. "I thought we settled this back at the inn."

"We did. But then I started thinking about how tired you looked. I feel bad that I didn't think about your needs."

Apparently, she said something wrong, because he immediate stiffened. "My need is for you not to accommodate me," he said, glaring over his wineglass.

"I only meant…"

"I know what you meant." Again, he corrected his voice, clearly trying to cover whatever nerve she'd touched with her comment. "I'm sorry," he said. "I don't mean to be sharp. Let us say I have done my share of accommodating people's needs in the past and it wasn't pleasant."

Clearly. "Would it help if I told you I won't be one of those women?" It was the only thing she could imagine had happened. That a former girlfriend had been overly demanding.

"It wasn't a woman."

Who, then? Piper watched as he rolled the stem of his glass back and forth between his fingers. His eyes were focused on the contents, but she had a feeling he wasn't really looking at the wine. Rather he was debating what kind of answer to give.

She wasn't sure why, but she expected some kind of clever deflection. Thus it surprised her when he said, "The problem with accommodating is that it is very easy for a person to turn someone else into their servant."

A harsh way of thinking. Whoever this person was must have really been demanding. "All I said was I could have gone to the drugstore alone. It's not like I offered to cut your meat or anything. Although technically you could order me to do that since I am your servant."

That should have earned a laugh, but it didn't. Frederic simply went back to rotating his wineglass. His features had grown stormy; in the dim light, his eyes were like thunderclouds.

"My mother did everything for my father," he said.

"Some women are traditional that way." Even as she spoke, however, the words sounded flat.

"This had nothing to do with traditional. My father was incapable of doing anything without help. He needed my mother constantly. She had no life of her own. Everything revolved around him."

"You don't have to explain." She hoped he would—there was so much she wanted to know about him—but from his sudden hoarseness she could tell the subject was a painful one.

"What about all the things she did with you? You said the other day she exposed you to art…"

"I said she made sure I was exposed. The nanny would take me, and when I came home, she and I would talk about what I saw." He looked down at his wine again. "To be fair, if she had a choice she would have taken me herself."

Piper knew all about not having choices. "Why was he so…" She wanted to say *selfish*, but it didn't seem her place.

"He was blind."

Piper blinked. "How?" It explained a lot.

"Retinitis pigmentosa is hereditary."

And Frederic, as the lucky heir, was doing his best to handle the disease differently than his father, was that it? Was that why he flew off the handle at what was a minor gesture of kindness? "I'm—" With a shake of her head, she cut the apology off. No way Frederic would want to hear her tell him she was sorry. Not now. So she said nothing.

"Let's talk about something else," Frederic said, breaking her thoughts. "I don't want to spoil the evening being maudlin. Tell me what you think about the wine."

Not wanting to spoil the evening either, Piper complied.

CHAPTER SEVEN

FREDERIC LISTENED AS Piper talked about how she could never tell the difference between an oak sauvignon blanc and a dry sauvignon blanc. "You'd think I could, being a cook and all, but wine is a whole different science," she said.

For the second time this week, he appreciated how she knew when not to push. Perhaps because of her own touchy childhood subjects, she understood when a conversation stepped too close to a nerve. Whatever the reason, he was grateful she decided to let the news about his father's blindness go by without comment.

Why he brought up the subject in the first place was beyond him. He certainly didn't intend to. His childhood was something he *never* discussed. Sharing the past—sharing anything personal—implied intimacy, which could lead a person to believe the relationship had a future. The last thing he wanted to do was mislead someone like Piper.

But then, he thought about all the secrets she'd shared about her childhood, and he started to feel as if he owed her some measure of equality. A secret for a secret. And so he shared his.

Now he wished he hadn't, because the memory was alive in his head. His father's voice, broken and slurred, the ice in his tumbler rattling. *I need you. I can't do it on my own.* "It" being so many things. Generations of being waited on by servants left their mark. His father had been left incapable of doing for himself. As a result, his neediness knew no bounds.

Frederic, on the other hand… He might have inherited his father's fortune, but his life taught him how not to need. And so he forced the conversation back to superficial, happy conversation, and Piper, bless her heart, played along.

It helped that dinner turned out to be delicious. "See?" he said, setting his fork down. "I was right to trust your judgment. I enjoyed my fowl."

"It wasn't bad," she replied. "Though I would have cut back on the thyme."

"Would that make the dish thyme-less?"

The tinkle of her laugh left him wanting to hear more. It was disturbing how easy he found her company. She was fun, she was smart. And, her kisses aroused him in a way he hadn't felt since his teenage years.

A hollow feeling started to spread behind his breastbone, causing him to squeeze his hand into a fist. Ninety-nine days out of one hundred, he accepted his future without complaint. Every so often, however, he would feel the ache for what he would miss. Unless he decided to be as selfish as his father…

I need you, Patrice. His father's constant mantra.

Frederic would not need. Would never need.

He could, however, *want*, and at the moment, he wanted the woman seated across from him very much.

Piper gave a soft cough. She knew he was studying her. "I was cursing the poor lighting," he said. "I want to be able to see you better." Her cheeks were no doubt turning as crimson as the roses they passed on their walk. Would the color spread to other parts of her body?

He reached across the table for her hand, feeling a victorious thrill when she met him halfway. "Do you still want your pudding?" he asked, playing with her fingers.

"I didn't see it listed on the menu."

"What a shame. I would hate for you to miss out on dessert."

"I'm sure I'll find something that will tempt me." She leaned closer and added, "On the menu."

The little minx. Two could play that game. "You should know," he said, leaning as well, "that when we're finished here, I plan to kiss you senseless. Then I'm going to kiss you again."

He might not be able to see her face clearly in the shadows, but he definitely heard her breathing quicken.

"Now that I think about it," she said, "I don't have to have the cheesecake."

"Good." Not bothering to signal for the bill, he took out his wallet and tossed down a stack of notes thick enough to cover ten dinners and grabbed her hand. "Let's go."

Amazingly, he made it the entire walk back without pulling her into his arms. Safety first, he reasoned. Kissing her would obliterate his concentration.

He also took masochistic pleasure in pushing the anticipation to its peak. He tortured himself by holding only her hand on the walk, and when they climbed the stairs to their rooms, he walked a step behind so that her that her vanilla scent filled his nostrils.

When they reached the top of the staircase, he finally broke and put his hands on her waist. From the trembling beneath his fingers, he knew he was not the only one who had been tortured. "I believe I promised you something," he said, turning her around.

Cupping her cheeks, Frederic focused all his attention on her lips. Last night was but an appetizer. Tonight, he would take his time. Savor. He kissed one corner of her mouth, then the other. Her quickened breath was his reward. When he finally lowered his mouth to hers, she let out a whimper. Relief.

"My room or yours?" he whispered when they broke to breathe.

"Doesn't matter."

She was right. It didn't. He reached for a door.

"There you are. I've been knocking on your door for ten minutes."

Piper looked up from the French press she'd been timing. Frederic stood barefoot in the dining room doorway, his shirt untucked and buttoned incorrectly. He looked the picture of a man who had just rolled out of bed. Which, of course, he had. Piper knew because up until an hour ago, she'd been in bed with him.

Thinking about what they did there made her flush.

"Mrs. Lester and I were talking about breakfast recipes," she replied, her voice overly bright. Could she sound any more like she was trying to be in control? "I gave her the recipe for huevos rancheros and she's going to give me hers for bangers and mash."

"The least I can do after all your help," Mrs. Lester replied. The innkeeper swiped back an errant red curl. "Guests aren't supposed to be allowed in the kitchen, but hard to say no to a real chef."

"I might have done a little of the prep work while we were talking," Piper added, sheepishly. She needed something to burn off her nervous energy. Speaking of…she checked to see if the grounds had brewed long enough. "Would you like some coffee?"

"I'm surprised you're awake so early," Frederic said. Leaning forward, he added in a voice only she could hear, "I wasn't expecting to find your side of the bed empty."

Piper shivered as his voice tickled her ear. "You were asleep," she told him. "I didn't want to wake you."

And okay, maybe she might have wanted to avoid any potential morning-after awkwardness. Last night had been amazing, with a capital *A*, but she knew as well as anyone that night and morning were two vastly different times of day, and what seemed like a good idea after a couple glasses of wine might look like a disaster in the daylight. She was afraid to face the regret in Frederic's eyes.

It wasn't regret she was seeing right now, however. The expression looking down on her was as predatory as ever. "My ego is hurt," he said. "Usually when I am with a woman, it's the other way around. I must be losing my touch."

No, he definitely wasn't losing that. Piper's insides melted from simply thinking about the things his hands could do. She looked over her shoulder to see if Mrs. Lester had heard. The innkeeper had her head in the oven, checking on pans of bread dough.

"I'm sorry. I started thinking about this morning's meeting and couldn't fall back asleep." It wasn't a complete lie. She did think about the meeting in passing. "I decided to come down here for a cup of coffee, and that's when I ran into Mrs. Lester."

"Who put you to work making your huevos ranchos. Come back to bed."

"Huevos *rancheros*," she corrected automatically, "and I wasn't just giving her the recipe. I was making breakfast potatoes."

"Come back to bed." His lips moved to her ear again despite Mrs. Lester being a room away. "I want to show you what you missed by leaving early."

Piper's knees buckled. "Is—is it all right if we take the coffee upstairs?" she asked Mrs. Lester.

"Sure thing," Mrs. Lester replied. "Leave the press in your room, and I'll have the cleaning girl bring it down. Thank you, too, for your help this morning. First time I ever have had a guest who made breakfast potatoes better than me."

"That's sweet of you to say. We'll be back down—" Frederic was pushing her toward the stairwell. "You didn't let me finish," she said to him.

"I don't care," he replied. "Do you have any idea how many downstairs rooms I looked in before I found you?"

"There are only three."

"Three too many. Now, back to our room with you, young lady. The door is unlocked."

Our room. The words gave Piper as big a thrill as Frederic's intentions. With his hands holding her waist, Piper climbed the stairs.

A couple hours later, they were back in the dining room, showered and ready for the day.

Mrs. Lester greeted them with a knowing smile that had Piper blushing again. "Sit anywhere you'd like. You're the last ones for the day.

"By the way," she added, "Your driver arrived while you were upstairs." Gregory sat at a corner table reading the paper. He too gave them a smile and a nod.

"The whole room knows what we were doing," she whispered to Frederic.

"You mean Gregory, and I don't think he's surprised. If anything, he is jealous. I know I would be in his shoes."

All it took was a trace of his finger running down her forearm and Piper melted again.

"Do you do this often?" she asked him.

"Steal away to England with a beautiful woman?" When she didn't take the bait, he grew more serious. "My bedpost doesn't have too many notches, if that is what you're asking."

That was exactly what she was asking. Now that he had answered, Piper realized that he rarely stayed away all night. He had guests in his house even less. Off the top of her head, she remembered one, possibly two, and they had both gone home before breakfast.

"I'm glad." Based on the way his eyes widened, her honesty surprised him. "No woman wants to think she is one in a long line." Knowing there were but a few women made her less mundane, to steal one of Chef Despelteau's words. More in keeping with what Frederic meant to her.

Mrs. Lester appeared, pot of coffee in hand, to end the conversation. "Piper tells me you're meetin' with John Allen this morning. About a painting."

"We are," Frederic replied. "Do you know him?"

"A bit. Comes in here for tea now and again. A queer little fella, he is—I don't mean that in the politically insensitive way or nothing. He's just quirky."

"Quirky, how?" Piper asked. They were heading to the man's house. If he was a crazy person, she'd like to know.

"Little things really. Like he always insists on bringing his own pastries when he comes here. Richest man in town and he won't pay for a bloody scone, but then leaves a one hundred and fifty percent tip."

"Sounds like he's very particular," Frederic said over his coffee cup.

"*Particular* is a good word for it. I've got one last basket of breads. Do you folks want it?"

"Yes, please," Piper replied. Once Mrs. Lester was out of earshot, she looked back in Frederic's direction. "Is *particular* good or bad, do you think?" It sounded suspiciously like Bernard's selectivity, if you asked her.

The Frenchman shrugged. "Hard to say. Art collectors are a bit like snowflakes. No two are the same."

"Maybe I'll get lucky, and Ana's story will break his heart to the point he wants her to have the painting."

"Or your friend Stuart will write enough zeroes that he can't refuse."

"He's not my friend—he's Ana's great-nephew. And hopefully Patience's—"

"Friend?" he finished with a smirk to rival Mrs. Lester's. He dragged the word out, long and with plenty of subtext.

"When you say it that way, Stuart is definitely not my friend." Piper reached for her coffee. She wasn't forgetting that *friend* was also how he described their relationship.

His lips were wet with coffee as he smiled from across the table. "I'm glad. I don't like sharing."

He didn't like to share and he didn't like to think about tomorrow. Kind of put her in limbo, didn't it?

John Allen's house was at the end of a long road tucked between two giant lavender fields. With nothing marking the turn, they drove past the place twice before locating the winding dirt road. Considering Allen was supposed to be a wealthy patron of the arts, Piper had been expecting someplace more upscale and artsy, or at the very least, someplace large, not this crooked cottage with a thatched roof. But then, maybe this was what passed for artsy and upscale out here. They were in the middle of nowhere. She looked for a car, but the only item with wheels was a bicycle propped by the garden shed.

"Are you sure we have the right address?" she asked Gregory.

"GPS says we do."

"Perhaps he is trying to discourage thieves," Frederic said.

That was one theory. Stepping out of the car, she was greeted by the smell of flowers and freshly tilled dirt.

"It appears Monsieur Allen does not believe in landscaping," Frederic remarked as he joined her. He had a point. Time and rain had cut deep ruts into the dirt driveway, turning the already-rough surface into a bumpy hazard. There were primroses that lined the walk leading to the door, and a container of annuals, but other than that, the outside of the cottage was bare. "Maybe he figures the lavender fields were enough."

"Perhaps." Frederic took a deep breath. "The aroma certainly is pervasive."

"The better to hide bodies. A joke," she said when he turned with a frown. She slipped her hand into his, stealing comfort from his grip. "I'm glad you are here."

Something she couldn't read flickered across his face. "Thank you," he said, squeezing her fingers. He looked about to say more when the cottage door flew open.

"Helloo!" the newcomer greeted. "You must be Piper. It's good to see you. I was worried you'd gone and got yourself lost." With his thick accent, the last word sounded more like "loost." "And you brought a friend. Hullo." He smiled widely in Frederic's direction.

Mrs. Lester's description suddenly made sense. Dressed from head to toe in white linen, John Allen looked like a miniature version of a 1920s English gentleman. The crown of his silver head barely reached Piper's nose. How on earth could Bernard not remember meeting him?

Piper introduced them, and he shook Frederic's hand enthusiastically. "Call me John, please. Both of you."

"Thank you for meeting with us," Piper said.

"Well, I must admit you have me curious. I had no idea my impulse purchase had such notoriety."

Frederic caught her attention and pointed a finger upward, letting her know where the price would be heading.

Unlike the outside, which looked ignored, the inside was a modern showplace. John had knocked down several walls to open one large room with vaulted ceilings. There was a kitchen that could rival Frederic's. Piper was half tempted to chuck looking at art so she could explore the appliances. Out of the corner of her eye, she saw Frederic doing his best to take in details.

Their host noticed as well. "Bought the place on the cheap at auction a few years ago, I did," he replied when Frederic complimented him. "Had to completely gut the place, though. Didn't hold up in the wet and got a bad case of rot. Place is climate-controlled now. Wouldn't hang the canvases until it was installed."

"Sound thinking," said Frederic.

"I thought so. Seemed daft to spend a fortune and not see to it properly. The main collection is on the back wall."

"How many pieces do you have?" Piper asked.

"Right now? Fifteen. A couple of the larger works are on loan in New York. Haven't got the space here."

She could see why. The large back wall had half a dozen paintings already. Frederic was squinting at a watercolor of a woman tilling a garden. "Bergdahl?" he asked.

"Good eye, Professor. Bought it from a gallery in New York around twenty years ago."

"His pieces seldom come on the market now."

"I heard a rumor one of his seascapes might be going up for sale next month. I've already let my man know I'm interested. Ana's back here, in my dining room. Help yourself to tea and scones, by the way. I baked them myself."

Piper tugged on Frederic's sleeve. "I hate to sound tacky, but how much would you pay for that painting? It was barely the size of a piece of copy paper."

"Trust me, you do not want to know."

John was waiting in the dining room doorway. "And here she is. *Ana Reclining.*"

"Wow" was all Piper could say. Hard to believe the woman reclining on the settee was the same little old woman who popped in to say hello during one of their video chats.

"Beautiful, isn't she?" John said.

"Breathtaking."

"I fell in love the moment I saw her. I love how he made her skin so luminous-looking. And her lips. The way he caught them in mid sigh? Doesn't she look like a woman who'd just been—"

"Right," Piper said. This was her sister's elderly boss

they were talking about. Some images were best left to the imagination.

Unfortunately, John was right. The painting dripped with sensuality. It wasn't the sexiness that caught your attention, though. At least not as far as Piper was concerned. It was Ana's expression. She was looking at the artist with nothing short of adoration. They weren't looking at a seventeen-year-old girl draped naked across a sofa. They were looking at a woman in love. Piper wondered if that wasn't the reason Theodore Duchenko wanted all the paintings destroyed.

She tried to imagine how it would feel, to be that deeply in love and have it ripped away from you.

"Are you all right?" John asked.

"Fine. I was thinking about poor Ana Duchenko is all. She's going to be so happy to know this painting survived." She reached into her bag for her cell phone. "You said I could take a few photographs?"

"Yes, yes. Be my guest. Just make sure the flash is off, if you don't mind. I don't want the colors to fade."

"Thank you." Whether he sold Stuart the painting or not, Ana needed to see proof her love for Nigel still existed on canvas.

While she clicked away, John maneuvered his way around the dining room table to pour tea. Frederic, meanwhile, had moved to the opposite of the room to study the painting. Piper caught the telltale movement of his head that said he was looking at it in sections.

"You said on the phone, you were trying to locate the painting for the real Ana?" John handed her a teacup, then offered one to Frederic.

"Ana Duchenko," Piper replied. She proceeded to tell him the story. As the details poured out, she realized she was destroying any chance Stuart had at buying the painting cheaply, but that didn't matter. It was more important John Allen understand that the painting was more than "notorious."

"Fascinating," John said. "So as far as you know, this is the only painting left that Nigel Rougeau painted."

"Unless someone has one hidden in their basement, yes." Frederic gave a soft cough, a warning that she ignored. "Nigel died shortly after Ana went back to the States."

John gave an odd sigh. "Such a tragic story. I knew that painting had to be a work of love the first time I saw it. You can see the emotion in her eyes."

So he did understand. "You know, Ana never married."

"She didn't?"

Piper shook her head. She felt as if she were gossiping about some old Hollywood romance the way her host was hanging on every word. "She lives in Boston with her cat, Nigel."

"The cat is named Nigel?" John clutched his chest. "I think I might cry."

"So you can see why her nephew wants to buy the painting. He wants to return the portrait to her while she's still alive."

"That's such an amazing story," John said. "To think, poor Nigel, robbed of his potential greatness. Can you imagine what he could have achieved if Theodore Duchenko hadn't destroyed his work?" He looked to Frederic, as if waiting for confirmation.

"A genuine loss," Frederic replied.

"Not to mention a great inspiration," Piper added. She snapped a few more pictures to be safe. She'd already made a mental note to send Nigel's sister a copy as well. "I think Ana really was his muse."

"I think so, too. I see why her nephew wanted to track the work down."

"The question is…" For the first time since they'd sat down, Frederic addressed the elephant in the room. "Would you be willing to sell her?"

"Well…" John drew out the word for several beats. Never a good sign. "I'll be glad to talk with Mr. Duchenko, of course, but like I said, she is one of my favorite pieces. I love looking at her while I eat."

That was an image Piper could do without.

They spent another hour or so looking at the rest of the collection, the older man thrilled to show his paintings to someone who "appreciated them." When they were finished, Piper once again urged him to consider selling *Ana Reclining*.

"I promise I'll think about it," he said. "I do have a soft spot for star-crossed lovers."

"Thank you." Looking at Ana's portrait one last time, she crossed her fingers that the painting would be heading to Boston soon.

"Mrs. Lester was right," she said when they were on the way to the car. "He is quirky."

"Quirky but savvy. His collection is amazing. The Bergdahl alone was worth the trip.

"Congratulations, by the way." With his arm around her shoulders, Frederic kissed her temple. "Your treasure hunt was a success."

Yeah, it was. Still, Piper frowned.

"Is something wrong?"

"I don't know. I thought I'd be more excited, but…"

"You're sad because your hunt is over. That is not unusual."

It was more than the end of the hunt. She was reminded all of a sudden that looking for Ana's painting was what kept Frederic in her orbit. Now that the search was over, would she be enough to make him stay around? Or would their affair be over when they returned to Paris?

She really stank at this taking-things-as-they-come stuff.

"These last couple days of adventure have spoiled me." In more ways than one.

"The day is not over. We can still have adventures."

"Like what?" she asked, as if she couldn't guess already.

Frederic stopped walking and stared at her with a focus Piper had never seen before. Part desire, part… confusion? Whatever the emotions behind his eyes, it set off a slow burn in the pit of her stomach.

"May I show you something?" he asked, running his thumb across her lower lip.

"Of course," she replied. When he looked at her like that, he could show her anything.

CHAPTER EIGHT

It HAD TO be the ugliest painting Piper had ever seen. Not depressing ugly like the painting in Bernard's gallery, but ugly-ugly. From what she could tell, the mural had been a group effort. Different sections reflected different styles. In the center of the mess, Saint Michael wrestled a fire-breathing dragon. At least the description said it was a dragon. Piper thought it looked more like a winged cow. The army of angels behind him was one giant block of white and gold, on which black lines had been painted to represent limbs while the villagers on the ground…she wasn't quite sure what the artist was thinking when he painted them. As for poor Saint Michael, he was rewarded with a protruding nose and lips so large he looked as if the dragon had slammed his face into a rock.

To her right, Frederic beamed at the work like a man looking at his child. "Saint Michael vanquishing evil," he said, reverence in his voice. "What do you think?"

"Umm, it's different."

"Have you ever seen anything so ugly? It's even worse than I remembered."

Oh, good. She was afraid she was going to have to pretend something way beyond her acting skills.

They were in the chamber by themselves, the abbey ruins not being one of the area's more popular attractions. Piper could see why. Ugly mural aside, there wasn't much else to see. Much of the monastery had fallen into ruin. Only the room they were in survived.

She turned back to the painting. "You wrote a paper on this piece?" After all the beautiful things he'd shown her the past couple of days, it was a bit of a letdown.

And yet Frederic seemed thoroughly enchanted. "Yes, I did."

"Why?" She had to be missing something. Maybe there was some historical connection she didn't understand.

Taking her hand, he led her closer. "Because I don't think this painting was ever about being good. The men who painted it had to know they didn't have talent. Or perhaps they thought they did. It doesn't matter. This painting is perfect because of its flaws. You see ugly, I see joy. Passion."

The passion was Frederic's. You could feel it radiating off him as he spoke. Like the day in the Place des Vosges, only ten times stronger.

"Of all the paintings I have seen in my life, this is one of my favorites. Because it is pure."

"When you put it that way." Piper's heart was suddenly too big for her chest. She felt so amazingly honored that he would share the piece with her. Wanting to thank him for the gift, but afraid he'd hear the emotion in her voice, she settled for a smile. "To think, all the other tourists will look and see a saint with swollen lips."

"Poor Saint Michael. He does look like he's had one too many collagen treatments, doesn't he?"

"I'm glad you got to see him again."

"I am, too."

They studied the mural in silence. Or rather, Frederic studied the painting while Piper studied him. From the moment this affair began, back in the kitchen in Paris really, she'd been haunted by a sense of surrealism, unable to believe they were together in the first place. Now this. She could feel herself starting to fall. If she hadn't already fallen, that is.

"Can I show you something else?" he asked.

"Here? At the abbey?" Frederic nodded before catching her hand in his again.

"It is outside," he told her.

Behind the monastery, the land spilled into a large grassy field dissected by boulders and a few errant black-eyed Susans. Still holding hands, they picked their way across the uneven ground until they reached the top of a large swell. From there they could look out over the entire abbey grounds. They were high enough that Piper could make out the shape of the old building in the ruined rock.

Frederic sat down, then tugged on her wrist so she would join him. They sat back on their elbows, legs stretched out in front of them.

"When I was studying the mural, I would take my lunch in this spot," he told her.

"It's beautiful." Taking out her phone, she snapped

a picture. She was going to want to remember this day when she returned to Boston in a couple months.

She was going to want to remember a lot of things.

Off to their left, she spotted a roped-off section where the ground appeared dotted with markers. "Wonder what is going on other there?" she said, pointing.

"Archaeological research, no doubt. Before the abbey, this was a pagan ritual site."

"No way."

"It's the reason the abbey was built here in the first place. They would have painted Saint Michael as a way of discouraging rituals and protecting the land from evil."

"He does look scary. Wonder if it worked."

"You'll have to ask the pagans. From what I understand, there are some who come every solstice."

Kicking off her sandals, Piper wiggled her bare toes, enjoying the feel of the sun on her skin. The air was quiet but for the birds and buzzing bugs. Now that she thought about it, there was a kind of mystical feel to the air. Although she was certain it had more to do with her companion.

She turned and snapped a photo of him. His attention on the view, Frederic didn't notice.

When he was studying something very closely, his focus would grow intense, with all his energy directed at his target. It was more than simply trying to see; it was as if he was trying to see into whatever it was he was looking at. Piper had felt that intensity directed at her more than once. Each time, she'd melted under its strength.

This time she saw a sadness to his stare. She brushed the hair from his face to bring him back. "Trying to find a pagan?" she teased. Seeing the enthusiasm fading from his face had made her heart ache. "You're a million miles away."

"Sorry," he said, giving her a half a smile. "I don't know when I will be back here, so I was trying to memorize the view."

Piper was about to tell him that wasn't necessary because she'd taken pictures when she realized what he was really saying.

"I wasn't thinking," she said softly.

"I have read theories that if you stare at something long enough, the image will become ingrained in your memory. I don't know if blind people can see their memories or not, but in case they can…"

"Is that why you are always looking at the Eiffel Tower?" And at her?

"One of the reasons."

The full force of what lay in his future hit her. It was easy to forget with his matter-of-factness, but there would come a day when he couldn't see the sun or the grass. Not even his own hand. She couldn't imagine. A man who loved visual beauty as much as he did. Who saw beauty in ugly art.

"What are you going to do?" she asked him. "I mean, when…" A sob threatened, and she pushed it back along with the rest of her question.

"Carry on, of course. What else can I do?"

"Nothing, I suppose."

She watched as he plucked at the grass between

them. Tugging blade after blade, only to discard each one atop a small pile of clippings. "Tell you what I won't do," he said. "I won't turn myself into a victim, making the whole world bow to my disability."

Like his father? That was what he meant, wasn't it? He did call his father needy last night.

"I asked him once," Frederic said, switching gears, "when I first learned I might have the disease, what it was like to be blind."

"What did he say?"

"He told me it was awful, and that I would find out for myself soon enough."

"That's it?" No reassurance, no advice? Surely the man wouldn't be so self-involved as to leave his son to face the unknown without some kind of support?

But then parents could be selfish. Hadn't her mother been more interested in everything other than Piper?

"Saying more would require him dealing with his own blindness. My father was more interested in wallowing. And in his cocktails," he added, swiping at the grass clippings. "Did you know I could make the perfect *soixante-quinze* when I was eight years old? That is gin and champagne, if you were wondering."

Piper wasn't. The little boy forced to make them was far more interesting. She wished she could tell him she understood what that was like, that she'd been in his shoes. Oddly enough, however, alcohol abuse wasn't one of her mother's many crimes.

"I can still picture him. Proving you can memorize an image," he added with a toneless laugh. "He had this giant easy chair where he would sit and listen to the stereo. All day long. Every day. He only left the house if my mother took him. I was so relieved when they decided to send me to boarding school, because it meant I wouldn't have to see him in that chair anymore."

Relieved, but guilty, too. Piper could hear the regret in his voice. He'd escaped to school, but his mother had stayed behind.

"I'm sorry," she said. "He must have been in a lot of pain."

"What he was, was a selfish bastard who never should have married my mother in the first place. He knew he was going blind. A real man wouldn't have asked her to stay."

No, he would have lived in the present and made no promises for tomorrow. A chill swept through Piper. "How do you know your mother didn't want to stay?" She already knew his answer from last night; Frederic believed his mother stayed out of guilt.

"How would she know that life would stop the moment my father lost his sight. If you're trying to defend him, you're wasting your time. I lived it. I watched day in and day out while she took care of him. Waited on him, walked with him. She cut his meat, for God's sake, while I..."

Stayed out of the way and made cocktails. No wonder his mother sent him away finally. Just imagining what it had been like for him made Piper's heart ache.

Frederic looked up. "Sometimes I wonder why they ever had a child."

Because once upon a time, they were in love and believed in the future. At least his mother had. Piper longed to tell him that it was okay. That it was okay for him to want more than a moment in the present.

You mean to want you. Tears burning the back of her throat, she rolled onto her side. "I'm glad your father was selfish," she told him. "Because if he hadn't been, we never would have met."

"Then he did something good after all."

The back of his hand caressed her cheekbone. Piper grabbed it and kissed his knuckles. It was her time to memorize for the future. "Thank you for showing me your ugly mural," she said.

"It's not my ugly mural. It belongs to Great Britain."

As far as she was concerned, the painting belonged to him, and she would be forever grateful that he chose her to share it with. Frederic would never know how special being here made her feel. She was beginning to understand the joy the monks must have felt when creating their art. Her heart was suddenly so full she feared it would burst.

She wanted to tell him. But how could she explain without sounding like a lovesick idiot that his sharing this part of himself—that these past few moments of vulnerability—meant everything to her?

There were words, three very huge words that summed up everything in her heart, but she wasn't ready to say them out loud. The feelings were too new, too fresh; now wasn't the time to say them. Piper wasn't sure there would ever be a time.

"I don't care who owns this place," she said. "There's still no place in England I would rather be."

Damn his sunglasses for blocking his eyes. She

couldn't tell if he was happy or frightened by her admission. Halfway committed, there was nothing to do but keep going. "Or anyone else I'd rather be with."

"Piper, you know that I can't give you...I won't be selfish like my father."

"I know." But it broke her heart, too. He was telling her that he planned to live out his blindness alone because his father was a self-absorbed drunk, and he couldn't be more wrong. He could—should—have more. Arguing the point, though, would only break the moment. And in the end, he'd still believe the same way.

Better she go along. At least for now. "Hey..." Reaching for his sunglasses, she pulled them away so she could finally look him in the eye. "You're not blind yet. And I'm right here."

She watched as slowly the gray grew black with desire. "Here, and beautiful."

His palms were warm as they brushed the hair from her eyes. "I never want this picture to fade."

His kiss was slow and possessive. It wrapped around her soul, binding them together. Piper gladly gave herself over. Their surroundings disappeared. It was just them, the birds and the grass. When his hands grew bold, she clutched at his back. When they slipped beneath her shirt, she whimpered. And when the moment was over, and he lay heavy, his breath sounding in her ear, she had to bite back the emotions fighting to get out. Her heart belonged to him. Taking one day at a time had just become impossible.

And she was sunk.

* * *

Later that night, Frederic lay in bed staring at the ceiling. In the pitch-black bedroom, he couldn't see beyond shapes, but that did not matter. His mind was at the abbey. He was reliving the afternoon frame by frame so as to not forget a moment. *Thank you for showing me your ugly mural.*

What an amazing five days. To think, all these months there'd been a treasure living under his roof and he'd had no idea. Piper wasn't like other lovers he'd shared a bed with, and not simply because she was American and from a world different from his. The difference had nothing to do with sophistication or worldliness, although her guilelessness was amazingly erotic.

No, what made her different was the way everything felt magnified when he was with her. Bigger, brighter, stronger. *More.*

If only he'd discovered her gifts sooner. So much time wasted.

Well, he would not waste further. Between now and when Piper returned to Boston, he would show her a time she'd never forget.

When Piper returned to Boston... The thought left a chill. He'd miss her. More than he thought possible. Somehow, over the past five days, she'd slipped under his skin to become someone special.

What was he supposed to do, though? Ask her to stay indefinitely? How fair was that?

No, better to give her a magical few weeks and then set her free. She would move on. Find a man who appreciated her, and he would have a wonderful memory to hold on to when the world grew dark.

Beside him, there was the rustle of sheets as Piper curled her body closer. Sliding one arm across his chest, she rested her head on his shoulder. Automatically, he began stroking her skin, seeking the contact that he could never seem to get enough of. "I thought you were asleep."

"Couldn't. Someone is thinking too loudly. Is everything all right?"

The gentle concern in her voice made his heart seize. For a brief moment, he let himself be wrapped up in her compassion. *If only*, he caught himself thinking.

"That wasn't thinking, that was my stomach," he said. "We missed dinner, you know."

"Whose fault is that?"

"Yours. For being irresistible." He kissed the teasing out of her voice, smiling at the tiny moan she made deep in her throat. "But now I am hungry."

"I can fix that," she whispered against his lips.

"Can you now?" In the back of his mind, he wondered if the hunger he felt for her could ever be completely satisfied. Like everything else, it was greater than he thought possible.

He reached for her, but to his disappointment, she slipped from his grasp. There was more rustling. Clothes. She was getting dressed.

"What are you doing?" he asked when she opened the door. Light from the hallway spilled through the crack into the room.

"Told you," she said. "I'm taking care of your hunger. Be right back."

"I know a better way," he called to her. But she'd already closed the door.

Alone, he went back to contemplating the dark ceiling. His eyes were unusually scratchy and tired tonight. Too much time in the sunlight. He had been overdoing things the past few days. Perhaps he should slow down. Or perhaps not. There would be plenty of time to slow down when he was alone.

He must have lost track of time, because before he realized, the door swung open.

"Voilà!" Piper announced. "Food."

Squinting, Frederic tried to see what Piper held in her hands. With the light behind her, however, all he could see was a hazy silhouette. "We have apples, candy bars and a package of something called McVitie's, which I think are cookies."

"How on earth did you find all this?"

"Mrs. Lester keeps a stash of snacks in the front room in case guests get hungry when the kitchen is closed. I found it when she asked me to restock the cabinet this morning."

"She asked you to restock *and* cook?" Even though she couldn't see him, Frederic grinned. "Should I be worried that Mrs. Lester hired you while I wasn't looking?"

A cellophane-wrapped package landed on the pillow near his head. "Shut up—I was doing her a favor. Can you switch on the nightstand lamp? My hands are full."

"Do you mind if we leave the lights off?" he asked her.

"Why? Are your eyes bothering you?"

Again, the concern in her voice gripped him with a warmth that made him want to hold her tight. "No," he said. "My eyes are fine." A small lie, not that it mattered. His eyes weren't the reason. There was an intimacy to the darkness he wasn't ready to give up.

Sliding out from beneath the covers, he crossed to the window and pulled back the wooden shutters. A beam of soft silver lit the floor by his feet.

"A picnic in the moonlight," Piper remarked as she joined him on the bed. "Romantic."

"I blame the company," he teased. "You inspire the romantic in me."

"You'd be the first." Her voice was soft, barely a whisper. Had there been street traffic or some other kind of outside noise, Frederic would have missed the comment altogether. Realizing he heard her, she quickly added a louder, "Sorry."

"Don't be." If it was up to him, she'd have romance every day. He cursed those idiots at school who were too blind to see her gifts. "Anyone who isn't inspired by you is a fool."

"Eat your snacks," she murmured. Frederic could practically hear the blush darkening her cheeks.

A comfortable silence settled over the room, punctuated only by the occasional sound of cellophane crinkling. This was nice, he thought. Comfortable. A man could become very attached to feeling this way if he wasn't careful. So attached he might not want to let go. Longing sprang to his chest, its strength catching him off guard. *You're going to be very hard to give up, aren't you, Piper?*

Piper's voice drifted from across the bed. "Penny for your thoughts?"

"I was thinking we should make the most out of the next couple months," he replied. "Make them unforgettable."

"I'd like that."

"Good. Why don't we start right now?" Rolling to his side, he kissed her into the pillow.

He woke to his face buried in a pillow and an empty bed. Vaguely, he remembered Piper saying something about cooking with Mrs. Lester. The older woman was definitely taking advantage of having another chef in the house. Looked as if he was going to have to go pry Piper away again. Yawning, he lifted his head.

No...

Something was wrong. While he could see, everything he looked at was hazy and faded, as though someone had wrapped the world with a thin gray film.

Frederic held up his hand. His trembling fingers were five muted shapes. Not even squinting could bring back the sharpness.

He willed himself to take a deep breath. No need to panic yet. His eyes could simply be overtired. God knows, he'd pushed himself very hard the last couple days. Give his eyes a little more rest; that is what he should do. Sleep a little longer. He closed his eyes and focused on his breathing.

An hour later, however, nothing had changed. He was still staring into a haze.

Frederic's heart started to race. He wiped a hand over his face. *Do not jump to conclusions*, he reminded himself.

Making his way to the bathroom, he grabbed his shaving kit and dumped the contents on the vanity. He must have packed eye drops in case his eyes got tired. Slowly, he scanned the items on the counter. Which one was the eye drops? In his new blurry world, all the small bottles looked suspiciously alike. For all he knew, he could squirt his eyes with alcohol. Perhaps Piper...

No. He wasn't going to run to Piper, no matter how appealing the thought might be. The situation wasn't anything he hadn't struggled with before. Inhaling deeply, he looked again. The bottles were color-coordinated. Eye drops were in the green bottle. Where was the green bottle?

On the edge of his bathroom sink at home. He had used them right before they departed. Distracted by thoughts of Piper, he forgot to repack them.

No problem. He would simply go into the village and buy more.

Took some stumbling around the room—the room was foreign and he hadn't exactly been thinking of maintaining order when taking Piper to bed last night—but he finally got dressed. Then, with one hand on the wall, he made his way down the stairs.

His foot was barely on the landing when he nearly collided with a warm, familiar body.

"Whoops! You almost ended up wearing your coffee.

Sorry about that." Piper's voice greeted him, warm and sweet. His first thought was to lean into her until the knot in his stomach went away. "I was going to leave the pot on the nightstand for when you woke up. Guess I was down here longer than I thought."

Her fingers touched his cheek. "I don't think I've ever seen you without a shave. I like the look. Very sexy." She stepped back. "Is everything all right?"

No, he wanted to say. *Your features have been blurred by a film.* The words were on his tongue, and he swallowed them. Piper's voice was still rough with the remnants of last night; he couldn't kill the spell by complaining.

Instead, he focused on her face with all his might, hoping that by sheer will, he could bring it into focus. "I'm fine," he said. "I'm still waking up."

"Well, then go into the dining room and I'll get us some coffee. I told Joan—I mean, Mrs. Lester—I'd make more breakfast potatoes, but I'm sure she won't mind if I back out to eat with you. After all, I am a guest."

"No, don't." Frederic wasn't ready to navigate breakfast yet. "That is, I need to get something at the apothecary first."

"Do you want me to come with you?"

Yes. Please. "Why don't you help Mrs. Lester? I will be back as soon as I can, and we'll have breakfast then."

"Okay."

He couldn't help himself. He needed contact, to reassure himself everything would be all right. Cupping her face, he kissed her, tasting her as though it were his last taste. *Which is could very well be.*

"Whoa, cowboy," Piper said with a laugh. "You're going to spill the coffee. Go run your errand. We can finish what you started when you get back."

The sun was already bright when Frederic stepped outside. He'd hoped the light would improve things, but no. If anything, the colors were more muted.

He wished he had thought to count the steps yesterday. He remembered turning right and crossing the street at the corner, but after that...

A car horn blared, forcing him back on the curb.

Frederic, you arrogant idiot. This wasn't Paris, where he knew every street with perfect familiarity. This was a strange village in a foreign country. A town made up of identical stone facades that, thanks to the film, blurred into one giant building. He scanned the storefronts looking for a sign that would tell him his location.

"Pardon," he murmured as he bumped a woman's shoulder. "Excuse me," he said when he bumped into another. He couldn't look where he was heading and read the store signs. If he had Piper come with him she could have...

...helped.

Disgusted with himself, he stopped in his tracks.

"Your butter is browning."

Shoot. Piper snatched the frying pan off the burner, but it was too late. The butter was already dark. "Sorry. I lost track of what I was doing."

"You do seem a little out of sorts," the innkeeper replied. She reached over and took the frying pan from

Piper's grip, before gently pushing her backward away from the stove. "I'll tell you what," she said. "You're not in a cooking mood today, so how about I do the potatoes and you finish your coffee and wake up."

Piper didn't really have much choice but to agree. Mrs. Lester was right; her head wasn't into cooking.

"You know…" the innkeeper was saying, "I don't know how they do things at that fancy cooking school of yours, but here in England, we get a good night's rest if we're cooking in the morning." Her lecture came with a twinkling smile. "You new lovers always think you can burn the candle at both ends, don't you?"

"Since I'm not an employee, I'm technically only burning one end," Piper shot back. She pointedly ignored the lovers comment. Was that what she and Frederic were? Lovers? The word sounded so sex-based, and what they shared last night was so much more. It had been for Piper, anyway. Her feelings had shifted while standing on that hill behind the abbey. Just how much, she was still too afraid to say.

It wasn't her late-night activities that were destroying her concentration, however. It was her morning conversation. She couldn't put her finger on why, but something about Frederic was different. He wasn't the same man who reached for her in the middle of the night. Since he stepped outside, Piper had been racking her brain trying to think whether she'd crossed a line and said too much. Maybe her emotions weren't as hidden as she thought. Maybe she was too obvious, and he was worried she wouldn't be able to handle this no-strings relationship they had going on.

That would certainly explain why his kiss felt strangely like goodbye.

On the other hand, maybe she was being a paranoid loon. Frederic was going to a drugstore, for goodness' sake. He probably had a headache.

Meanwhile, Mrs. Lester had taken over cooking duties, giving Piper a silent lesson in bed-and-breakfast cooking.

"Would you like me to sit in the dining room out of your way?" she asked.

"Goodness, no. I like your company. I don't let just anyone in my kitchen, you know." Picking up a nearby cutting board, the woman scraped a pile of diced onions into a heated fry pan. The vegetables crackled, filling the room with aroma. "What were we talking about, anyway?"

"You were giving me your recipe for Cornish pasties."

"Right. Although I'm surprised that someone studying haute cuisine would be interested in making something like hand pies."

"For your information, I happen to like hand pies," Piper shot back.

"I can cook them a lot better than haute cuisine, that's for sure," she added, speaking to the inside of her cup.

"What did you say?"

"Nothing." Now wasn't the time or place to go into her problems with Chef Despelteau. "I'm in a comfort food phase, is all."

"Can't blame you there. I've been in one my whole

life. The mister took me to eat in London on my birthday last year. A couple medallions of beef drowned in sauce and an itty-bitty dollop of risotto. Seems to me, if you're going to charge fifty pounds for dinner, a person shouldn't need a snack when she gets home."

"I totally agree," Piper said. One of her pet peeves about Chef Despelteau was his emphasis on presentation instead of serving size. "I was telling Frederic the other night that sauces are great, but sometimes a steak should be left a steak." She paused to take a sip of coffee. "Good comfort food isn't all that easy to make, either. Half the time the restaurants try to trendy it up, and end up getting it all wrong."

"Like up at the Hen & Rooster. That's why I prefer the old-fashioned pubs. Give me fish and chips any day."

"Same here," Piper said. "Same here."

"Then why are you in that class?" Mrs. Lester asked.

"I beg your pardon?"

The woman shrugged one of her shoulders. "Seems to me if you don't like fancy foods, you shouldn't be in some fancy French school. So why are you?"

Why did everyone ask her the same question?

She had only herself to blame this time. She had opened the door by talking about comfort food.

"Because I want to become a chef, and where better to learn than in Paris?" Her answer sounded flat even to her this time. She was tired. Frederic kept her up half the night. Plus, she was tired of justifying herself.

Justifying yourself or justifying to yourself?

"Well, I suppose if you want the prestige…"

At Mrs. Lester's comment, she shook off the strange

thought. "Of course English cooking is pretty awesome, too." She didn't mean to hurt the woman's feelings. "That's why I want to make Cornish pasties."

"Mine do get a lot of compliments," Mrs. Lester said, smiling. "But so you know, Cornish pasties are Welsh, not English. You don't want to be messing up the two."

"Yes, ma'am."

Just then, the front doorbell rang, signaling an arrival. "I'll get that," she told Mrs. Lester. "It's probably Frederic back from his walk." At least she hoped so. His odd goodbye continued to plague her. "Would you mind writing down your recipe so I can take it back with me?"

"Of course I can," Mrs. Lester replied. "Soon as I finish breakfast, I'll do it. Oh, and if that is a guest, let them know the rooms don't turn over until after twelve. They can leave their luggage in the tea room."

"Will do." Piper had to laugh. Apparently, over the weekend she'd become an employee, only no one told her.

It was Frederic, all right. He stood at the base of the stairs, staring down at his shoes. As lost and distant as she had ever seen him.

Don't overreact. There could be lots of reasons why he didn't go to the kitchen himself.

"Did you get what you needed from the store?" she asked him.

"No. I didn't go."

He didn't? Where had he been, then? As she stepped closer, Piper saw his hand had the banister in a vise grip. His was squeezing the wood so hard his knuckles were white.

"I've got a headache," he said. "I'm going to lie down."

"I'll go with you." She hurried to catch up with him, her fingers brushing his elbow as she reached the bottom step.

Frederic stiffened at her touch. "No," he told her. "I don't need anyone keeping me company." With one hand on the wall and one hand on the rail, he walked slowly upstairs.

Her stomach felt as if it had been kicked.

Pushing her fear aside, she headed upstairs to find out what happened.

She found Frederic sitting on the edge of the unmade bed, staring into space. His head didn't so much as turn when she closed the door. "I thought you were going to lie down."

"I changed my mind."

"Would you like me to see if Mrs. Lester has any aspirin?"

"No, thank you. I will be fine."

The change in his voice frightened her. Last night's warmth had disappeared in favor of a tone so polite and distant it hurt her ears. She hadn't heard him use that voice since the days when she first started work. Back when they'd been strangers.

Where was the man who was whispering sweet nothings in the dark a few hours ago? She raced through everything they said and did yesterday, wondering what could have happened to make him disappear so abruptly.

Oh, no... Not that. It hadn't even been twenty-four hours...

"It's your eyes, isn't it?"

Frederic stood up, only to stand stock-still, as if he wasn't sure where to go. "Yes."

"Oh, Frederic." It wasn't fair. She hugged him from behind, holding him as tightly as possible. Letting him know best she could that he wasn't alone, and that he could lean on her in any way he needed to. Frederic's body was rigid. Even with their bodies pressed together, it felt as if he were a million miles away. He was in shock. Who could blame him? Even the most prepared man would need time to adjust.

"Everything will be all right," she told him. Ignoring the hairs rising on the back of her neck, she kissed his shoulder blade. "I'm here, and I'll do whatever you need me to do."

For a moment, she felt Frederic's body relax as he leaned against her. Before the moment could take hold, however, he stepped away, leaving her standing alone at the foot of the bed.

"I have to pack," he said. "Can you let Mrs. Lester know we're checking out?"

It couldn't have sounded more like she was being dismissed if he had tried.

CHAPTER NINE

IT WAS LATE when they returned to Paris. Frederic called ahead to his doctor, and the man met them at the hospital. To run tests, he said. Personally Frederic thought it a waste of time. What would a battery of tests show that his eyes couldn't tell him already?

Now that the shock had time to wear off, he was coming to terms with his new reality: his vision had deteriorated again, and while he wasn't completely blind, he was much, much closer. The translucent film draping his view wasn't going away. He would never see sharply again. Only a matter of time before he woke up and his sight was gone forever.

He always knew this day would come—the day he moved another step closer to blindness. His eyes getting worse had always been a matter of when, not if. He only hoped to have more time. With Piper, that is.

Frederic closed his eyes. After the catastrophe in the village, he had managed to rally fairly well. Until Saint Pancras station with its crowds and low lighting. The confusion made his head pound. If not for Piper playing guide dog... *Watch your step. Turn left. Wait here.*

Her voice echoed in his ear, steady and soft. Like the woman herself. A calm in his storm.

It was so easy to hand over control. Terrifyingly so. More terrifying was the security he felt when she linked her arm with his. He followed her lead with complete trust, knowing that if something went wrong, she would be by his side.

Finally, after all these years, he understood how his father had become so needy. Surrendering control—the peace that came from surrendering control, that is—was addictive. Why not let someone else carry the burden, especially when they offered things like goodness and light in return?

He couldn't do that to Piper. Life had dragged her down enough.

At least he would always have yesterday at the abbey.

The sound of sandals flapping caused his pulse to speed up. He already knew the sound of her walk, he thought dejectedly. So much for his goal of a quick, un-encumbered affair.

The curtain drew back. "You've got to love Paris. The hospital cafeteria has better pastries than most American bakeries. I brought you a croissant. Do you want it in front of you or…?"

"Leave it on the side table."

"Are you sure? You haven't eaten all day."

"I think I would know if I was hungry." The words came out far sharper than he meant. She had no idea her kindness made things worse. "I'm sorry," he said. "I didn't mean…"

"You've had a long day."

"So have you."

"I'll live."

"It's late. You should go back to the house."

"Not so late," she said, pulling one of the plastic chairs closer to the bed. The metal legs scraped against the floor with a loud *squeak*. "At some point, Dr. Doucette will release you, and we'll go home together."

The idea of the two of them as a team left Frederic warm all over. Another warning bell. "I'd rather you left now. I'll have Michel drive me home later."

"Don't be silly. I'm sure Dr. Doucette will be here very soon."

"Piper, I want you to go." This time, he didn't mince words.

There was no mistaking Piper's confusion. "You don't want me here?"

Exactly the opposite. Frederic wanted her by his side so badly it hurt. "I think it would be a good idea if you left," he told her.

"I see."

For several minutes, she stared at the floor. Frederic assumed she was angry, and after she'd taken a couple long, clearing breaths, she would leave. Thus, when her hand settled over his, he started. "You're not alone," she said. "You know that, right?"

That was the whole point. He wasn't, but if he was any kind of decent human being, he would be. He should have never pursued her in the first place. But no, he'd been selfish, thinking with his desire, not with his head. Warmth spread up Frederic's arm, mocking his already-aching heart. If he let her stay, he would lean on her. And lean, and lean and lean.

He would never let her go.

"Please go, Piper. You are not obligated to stay here." Painful as it was, he tried to pull his fingers free of her grip. She surprised him by holding on with ferocity, as though she was the person leaning on him.

"Yes, I am," she said. "I know we haven't been to-gether very long, but I…"

"Don't." He didn't want her to say something that couldn't be forgotten. A sentiment that would make the inevitable that much harder.

Forcing his voice to stay as even as possible, he said the words that really needed to be said. "We had a good time together, but we both knew from the start that this was a short-term relationship. No promises."

"No strings. Thanks for reminding me." At last, she yanked her hand free, the loss of contact traveling straight to his chest. "Funny how you decided tonight is the perfect night to cut me loose. Here I thought that after last night… What happened to having an unfor-gettable couple of months?"

Frederic dropped his gaze to the sheet. Ironic that even with his deteriorated vision, he couldn't look her in the eye. He knew that even the gauzy haze couldn't obliterate the hurt he would see there. "Last night we were both carried away. Now that I have had a chance to think clearly, I've come to realize that the longer we continue this affair, the harder goodbye will be. We should make things easy by ending it while we both have happy memories."

"Easy on who? Me or you?"

"Both of us."

She let out a derisive snort. "Right."

The chair legs scraped across the linoleum as she stood up. Her sandals made angry slaps as she paced the floor. "Tell me something, Frederic. Would you have come to this decision if you hadn't woken up this morning with your eye problem?"

Denying the truth would only insult her. "No."

"I didn't think so. Honestly, do you think I care that your eyes got worse?"

"I care." And while she might not now, she would come to resent it, and by extension, him. "I would rather you remember me fondly."

"No problem. Dumping me is the perfect way to do that."

"Better I dump you than drag you down."

"Drag me…? Is that what you think would happen?"

It was what he *knew* would happen. Last night he had promised her romance. "It's not very romantic if your lover can't see."

"Except as you've pointed out many times, you can."

"But at some point I won't. Today was a reminder of that fact. That is why we would be smart to end things now. Before either of us gets too attached." He refused to listen to the voice telling him it was too late.

"What if I don't want to? End it, that is."

Frederic sighed. *Stubborn woman.* He accepted that this was the way it was supposed to be; why couldn't she?

His eyes searched the room until he found her standing near the foot of his bed. Staring straight at her, he spoke with great deliberation, to make sure she understood. "You don't have a choice. This is for the best."

"Says you."

She didn't move. She stood at the foot of the bed, with her eyes bearing down on him. Frederic could feel their wounded glare. "You're wrong, you know. You wouldn't drag me down."

You say that now... "I have no doubt my mother said the same thing to my father." And look how well that turned out. A woman so broken from taking care of the man, she wasn't able to live a life for herself. A son who grew up never respecting the man who fathered him. "I'm not going to be selfish enough to make the same mistake." Not with Piper or anyone else.

"Even though you can see, and I'm scheduled to go back to Boston in a couple months."

They both knew if their affair continued, he wouldn't be able to let her return to Boston. The feelings between them were already deeper than a mere affair. "Even though," he replied.

Through his haze, he saw that Piper was trembling; she was fighting to keep herself from crying. Keeping her pride. Admiration swelled in his chest, along with deeper, unmentionable emotions. Someday she would thank him.

"You deserve nothing but the best, Piper." He meant every blessed word.

"Go to hell."

Frederic listened to the slap of her sandals until he couldn't hear them anymore before giving in to the frustration gnawing at his insides and punching at the bed as hard as he could. As moments went, this was not his finest.

I did the right thing. What would prolonging the affair do other than make the pain of saying goodbye worse? At least this way, her heart wasn't so damaged it wouldn't heal. She would meet someone else, a man who wouldn't grow to need her quite so much.

Dammit! His chest felt as if someone had torn it open. Who knew you could fall so hard so fast?

He should have. He should have realized it the other night in his kitchen when his body was on fire and his head was warning him that Piper wasn't like other women. All he could do was dream of making love to her. This... He punched the bed again, this time hitting the side rail so hard it rattled. This was his punishment for being selfish.

At least he would have a lifetime of solitude to get over his mistake.

"Is everything all right?" A nurse suddenly appeared in the doorway from which Piper just left. "Monsieur, do you need anything?"

Frederic stared blankly at the space across the room. "No," he replied. "I don't need anything."

Better to break things off before either of us becomes too attached, Frederic had said.

Too late. Piper made it as far as the taxi before giving in to her tears. The driver stared at her through his rearview mirror as tears streamed down her face.

"Mademoiselle?" he asked in a soft voice. "Are you all right?"

"Fine," she replied, sniffling.

A moment later, the safety glass slid back and he handed her a tissue through the opening. Seeing it reminded her of how Frederic offered her a paper towel, and she burst into a fresh batch. "Thank you," she managed to choke out between sniffs.

Damn Frederic Lafontaine. Why couldn't he have left her alone and miserable? Why did he have to decide to get involved in her art search and make her fall for him? Now instead of lonely and miserable, she was brokenhearted and miserable.

Here she thought living in Paris couldn't feel worse.

She blew her nose. Frederic was wrong, too. Two days, eight weeks—the length of their affair didn't matter because she had already fallen in deep. What she felt for him went way beyond lust or romantic fantasy. She loved him. With all her soul. Blind, sighted, purple, green, two-headed…none of that mattered. The part she loved was inside. The tender, intelligent man who loved art and history, and who made her feel as though she could do anything.

Stupid her, she thought Frederic felt the same. Really stupid her, she still thought it.

Surely she didn't imagine the feelings between them last night. Frederic said himself that they would still be together had his eyes not gotten worse this morning.

All because of his parents. Why was it that parents always screwed things up for their kids? Her mom's leaving Patience and her to survive on their own. Fred-

eric's parents' making him think his disease was better
suffered alone. If Frederic's parents were alive, she'd kill
them for turning their son into a self-sacrificing idiot.
Why couldn't he see that he wasn't like his father? The
Frederic she knew was far too strong to let blindness
beat him, if and when he finally lost his sight.

So what now? Suck it up and soldier on as she always did? How was she supposed to go back to being
Frederic's housekeeper after the last two days? Simply
being in the same room as him made her pulse race. No
way could she live in the same house.

She'd have to move out, she realized, letting out a
sigh. Move out and find some place cheap to finish
out the term. Great. Twenty-four hours ago she was
wrapped in Frederic's arms, listening to him sleep and
dreaming of the days ahead. Now she was on the brink
of homelessness with nothing to look forward to but
days filled with being lectured by Chef Despelteau.

She wished she'd never come to Paris.

Who was she kidding? If she hadn't come to Paris,
she wouldn't have met Frederic, and lousy as she felt,
she wouldn't have traded the past five days for anything.

Then fight for them. Patience's voice was loud in her
head. *Figure out a way to fix the situation.*

Her sister was right. Wasn't the whole point of coming to Paris so that she could achieve her dreams? Frederic was part of those dreams now.

She wasn't walking away without a fight.

CHAPTER TEN

SHE WAS IN the kitchen waiting on a pan of brownies when Frederic finally returned home. "What are you doing?" he asked.

The day had been hard on him. His face was pale and drawn, with dark circles under his eyes. She moved to take him in her arms, then stopped. Any compassion she offered would only get rejected.

She returned to the sink and the bowl she was washing out. "Making brownies. They'll be ready in a few minutes if you want to wait."

"I wasn't expecting you to be here."

"Where else would I be? This is my job. Unless I'm fired, too," she added, turning the bowl upside down.

From behind her, she heard him let out a long sigh. "Why would you want to stay?"

For you. "Because I've already done homeless once in my life. I don't feel like doing it again."

"I wouldn't let that happen. I'll pay for you to stay at a hotel or find a new apartment."

"Would you find me a new job, too?"

"We would find some kind of arrangement."

"Wonderful. In other words, you'll pay me to stay away." The oven timer rang. "If it's all the same to you, I'll finish out my contract here," she said, reaching for the oven mitt.

"I know what you're doing," he said. "Staying won't make me change my mind."

"Then it shouldn't be a problem for you." Dropping the pan of brownies on the cooling rack, she waited for him to mount a new argument. Dared him to.

"It won't work," he said. "I'm going to bed. Dr. Doucette wants to meet with me before I go to the university."

"What for?" Did something show up in the tests they ran today?

"To fit me for a white cane, I presume. He mentioned something about transition lessons. I won't need breakfast."

The last part meant to remind her she was back to being a housekeeper. Very well, she'd let him have his way tonight. She sighed. "Yes, sir."

As it turned out, Frederic found a reason to not need breakfast or dinner the next two days. For all she saw of him, he might have been the one who took a room at a hotel. Not that he ignored her. No, he talked to her when their paths crossed. Politely worded requests about laundry and other household business. In other words, they'd turned back the clock to when she was simply his housekeeper.

On the third morning, she found him asleep in his chair.

He must have come home very late. She'd waited until well after midnight before going to her rooms.

For a few minutes, Piper contented herself with simply watching him sleep. Kind of on the obsessive side, she knew, but she couldn't help herself. She hadn't had a good look at his face in two days, and she needed to see how he was doing.

In England, she had noticed how Frederic's features would relax while sleeping. His lips would part in a smile as if he was dreaming happy thoughts. There was no smile today. His face was drawn tight. "You foolish man," she whispered. "We could be sleeping together."

A lock of his hair hung over his eye. She brushed it aside, letting her fingers linger on his face. Felt so wonderful to touch him again. It might have been only two days, but it seemed like an eternity.

Frederic stirred. "Mmm, nice," he said in a drowsy voice.

This was the Frederic she knew in England. Stuck between sleep and consciousness, he hadn't raised his defenses yet. Piper's heart ached for his reappearance. "You fell asleep in the chair again."

"I was watching the tower."

With his eyes still closed, he curved into her touch, catching her hand in his and pressing a kiss to the palm. Piper gave a soft sigh. *I missed you.*

His eyes fluttered open. The defenses returned. "Piper…"

She lifted her hand away, but it didn't matter. The moment was there, between them. Frederic could protest all he wanted, but it was clear that the feelings they discovered in England weren't about to go away.

"Nothing's changed," he said, pushing to his feet.

"I can tell," Piper replied.

"That's not what I meant, and you know it." She watched as he stalked his way to his favorite window. He stood with his hands pressed against the molding, the muscles in his shoulders playing beneath his jacket as he attempted to push the wooden frame apart. "This isn't going to work," he said. "You staying here. Let me…"

"Find a hotel? No, thanks."

"For God's sake," he said, spinning around to face her again. "Why are you being so stubborn?"

"Why are you?"

When he didn't answer, Piper stepped closer. "Tell you what." She kept her eyes locked with his, so he would be sure to see the determination on her face. "I will leave if you can honestly tell me you don't care about me as much as I care about you."

Frederic looked away. "You know I can't." Piper's heart skipped a beat.

"But," he said, raising his eyes again, "that doesn't mean we have a future. Not even a short-term one. I can't."

Good Lord, but she was tired of hearing the word *can't*. He most definitely could, if he let himself. "What are you so scared of?"

"I'm not scared of anything."

"Liar. I think you're terrified. You're afraid of the day you wake up and can't see anymore."

"That's where you're wrong. I've been expecting to go blind since I was fifteen years old. I know exactly how my life will play out."

"And how is that?" she challenged.

"Alone."

He said the word with such finality, it ripped her insides in two. Did he really believe that he was meant to be by himself for the rest of his days? How could one man be so incredibly wrong?

"It doesn't have to be that way," she said.

"Yes, it does. I've known that since I was fifteen years old, too. I will never turn the life of the person I... I care about upside down the way my father did ours."

"Even if the person is willing to take the risk?" She touched his wrist, offering.

"It's always easy to be willing at the beginning. It becomes obligation."

"Not necessarily."

"Says the woman who is attending a school she hates because she owes her sister."

Piper stepped back. "That's not true."

"Isn't it?" Frederic asked. "Then tell me when the last time was that you enjoyed cooking?"

When she made him pot roast.

"Do you even like French food?"

"What does that matter?" she countered. "People cook things they don't like all the time." Why were they talking about school all of a sudden, anyway? This wasn't about her.

Narrowing his eyes, Frederic stared down at her with so much intensity it made her insides squirm. "The other night you asked me 'what if' to prove your point, remember? Now it is my turn. What if Patience hadn't been so excited about you going to Paris? What if she hadn't sacrificed so much? Would you still be here?"

"I…" She couldn't say the answer aloud.

"That's what I thought. You're so determined to give back to your sister. Have you ever asked if she cared what you did for a living?"

"She sacrificed for me to be here."

"No, she sacrificed for you to have a *good life*. You were the one who decided that meant being a French chef."

"Not true." France was both their dreams. Hers and Patience's. Frederic was using this as an excuse.

"You can keep telling yourself that all you want, but I will not be another person to whom you feel obligated."

"For crying out loud, Frederic, *I'm not your mother*. Don't treat me like I am." It was the only argument she had left.

Like all her other arguments, it fell on deaf ears. "Finish your school and go home, Piper," he said as he brushed past her.

Piper gnawed the inside of her cheek as she watched him make his way to the staircase. How dare he twist her argument against her? Cooking school was an entirely different situation. For starters, she and Patience dreamed this dream together, meaning it was 50 percent her sister's. Maybe 60 percent. Or 70.

Stupid "what-if" games. Sinking into the chair, she threw her head back to stare at the ceiling. Maybe she was sticking it out because of Patience. If she hadn't, though, she never would have started her affair with Frederic. And wanting to be with him was 100 percent her idea. There wasn't a drop of obligation involved.

Of course, she could see how that might be hard to believe. Why would he think she was sticking with him by choice if her Paris track record said otherwise?

What should she do now? Maybe Patience…

She stopped halfway to her pocket. No. The solution had to be her own. Besides, there was nothing Patience could say that Piper hadn't heard a hundred times before. *Go for your dreams. You can do anything. I just want you to be happy.*

Happy.

That had always been her sister's dream: for Piper to be happy. *So long as you're happy, then it's all worthwhile*, she used to say whenever Piper felt guilty.

She wasn't happy in culinary school. *Face it, Piper, you'd rather be cooking mac and cheese instead of foie gras.*

Was it any wonder her assignments were uninspired? She didn't love making them the way she loved making good old-fashioned comfort food. If she wanted to be brutally honest, she'd been going through the motions the past couple months. Frederic was right; she might have come to Paris on her own, but she'd stayed out of obligation to her sister. Patience would smack her if she knew.

Suddenly Piper was very disgusted with herself.

But it wasn't the same when it came to Frederic. Being with him, being needed by him, could never be an obligation. She didn't fall in love with his ability to see. She fell in love with the man who accepted his blindness and survived anyway.

How could she make him see that they weren't doomed to repeat his parents' mistakes?

The first step would be to get her own life in order.

"Leave?" Chef Despelteau said. "There are only eight weeks left in the program."

"I know," Piper replied. "Trust me, this wasn't an easy decision."

That wasn't true. Actually, the decision had been very easy, once she thought everything through.

The best way to thank Patience wasn't struggling to become something she wasn't simply because she was afraid she would let down Patience. In fact, just the opposite. She was letting Patience down by being so unhappy. If she wanted to truly thank her sister, she should create a life she loved. Cooking would be part of that dream. Just not French cooking.

"I've decided to take my cooking in a different direction," she told Chef Despelteau.

"I am very sorry to hear that. You had the potential to be a great French chef."

Piper smiled. His attempt at sincerity was uninspired.

She left his office feeling a hundred pounds lighter. Now if she could only get through to Frederic, then she would be truly happy.

Frederic was there when she returned home. He was standing by his window as usual. Something about it felt off, though. It didn't take long for her to realize what. Propped against the wall was a white-and-red cane. "Dr. Doucette wants me to use it when I'm walking around the city to avoid accidents," he said when she asked about it. He didn't say anything further.

Leaving the floor open for her announcement. "I quit culinary school."

Frederic turned away from the window to look at her. "You what?"

"You were right," she told him. "The only reason I was staying was because I thought I owed Patience. I realized that was wrong. She would never want me to do something that made me miserable out of obligation. She would want me to choose what made me happy."

"Oh."

That was it? She thought he would show a little more reaction. Maybe not jump up and down, but something more than a flat monosyllable.

"I assume that means you'll be leaving for home soon, then," he said. There was a strange note to his voice that Piper couldn't decide was disappointment or relief.

She certainly knew the emotion deadening her stomach. "No, I'm not leaving," she said. "Don't you understand? I quit because I know the difference between doing something for obligation and choosing something I want to do. *I know the difference.*

"I also know what makes me happy." What she wanted to say next was important. She cupped his face in her hands, so he had no choice but to look her in the eye. "You make me happy, Frederic. For months I was miserable. I hated Paris—I hated school. Then you shoved a paper towel in front of my face and everything changed. I wasn't miserable anymore."

"Piper—"

"Let me finish. Do you know what made me so happy? It wasn't dancing by the river or a whirlwind trip to the English countryside. It wasn't just physical, either. It was sitting next to you on the train and listening to you complain that England had terrible coffee. It was hearing you explain why you loved that God-awful mural. It was being with you. You were all I needed to make Paris worthwhile."

She could see his defenses crumbling. The cracks showed in his eyes. "Everyone feels that way at the start of a new romance," he said. "You'll get over it."

"I don't want to get over it. I don't want to get over you. I'm falling in love with you."

She kissed him, letting her lips do the rest of the talking for her, and for a moment, as he kissed her back, everything slid back into place. *Say you don't love me back, Frederic. I dare you.*

His hands reached up to cover hers and gently pulled them away. "Then walk away," he whispered. "Don't let me drain you dry."

"Damn you!" Damn him *and* his parents. She shoved at his chest, then shoved again. "I am so sick of your dumbass self-sacrificing. For what? Because your parents had a bad marriage? Because your dad was a needy jerk? Did you ever stop to think that maybe it wasn't helping your father that burned your mother out, it was his constantly feeling sorry for himself? News flash Frederic. You're acting as badly as he ever did."

"I am not my father."

"Oh, that's right. You're not going to drag anyone down with you. No, you'll just shove aside anyone who cares about you. To hell with what they want."

Frederic didn't answer. He looked past her, to the tower, his expression more distant than ever. They were back where they began. Two people, separate and alone.

Piper was done. What fight she had left disappeared as soon as she saw his expression. Some situations couldn't be fixed, no matter how hard you tried.

"I'm going to Gloucestershire," she told him. The backup plan she hoped to never use. "Mrs. Lester said I was welcome to come and cook any time I wanted—I'm going to take her up on the offer. I'll be packed and out of here by the end of the day."

Halfway across the room, she paused, unable to help one parting shot.

"There's a difference between needing help and self-pity, you know. Too bad you're too blind to see it. But then, maybe you're too blind to see a lot of things."

Leaving him to his solitude, she went to her room and packed. Frederic never came to say goodbye. She didn't expect him to.

The Eiffel Tower greeted her as she stepped onto the sidewalk. Tall and gray, it would forever be her symbol of Paris. A reminder of both the best and worst of her time in this city. Taking out her cell phone, she took one last picture.

And said goodbye.

* * *

Time, Frederic decided, was playing tricks on him. When he was with Piper, time whipped by. Their few days together were over before he realized. So how was it the forty-eight hours since Piper moved out had stretched endlessly?

Oh, he was busy enough. He had his classes to teach, and classes to take. The life transition classes Dr. Doucette suggested. There were the social and professional obligations that kept him out until late at night. His eyesight might have dropped another notch, but his lifestyle hadn't missed a beat. There was only one problem: he missed Piper.

At night, he would lie in bed and remember the afternoon at the abbey. The way her eyes had looked so blue as he hovered above her. Frederic cherished the memory. It had been his last day of clear sight, and life had blessed him with a wonderful view. Funny, he always thought the visual memory he'd long for most would be some piece of art. Or the tower, perhaps. His trusty friend, whose lights twinkled invitingly, albeit a little hazier now.

No. It was the memory of Piper's eyes that he prayed he'd never forget. He wouldn't trade the memory of her eyes for a thousand Eiffel Towers.

God, he missed her. Breathing hurt without her. The air was too thin, and his shirt collars were always strangling him. He missed her voice. He missed her smell. He missed her touch. And who did he have to blame? No one but himself.

Thanks to him, she was in a completely different

country, charming the locals with her bright smile. He bet she was making plans for her return to America right now, too. All because he was afraid she would bail when things got hard.

You fool. He could have had Piper in his life for as long as she'd have him. Instead, he didn't have her at all.

There's a difference between needing help and self-pity, Piper told him. His father had needed *so* much. He remembered when he was a kid, wanting to go to the tower, but his father had refused because of the crowds. *I can't handle all those people*, he'd said. And so Frederic had gone with the nanny while his mother stayed home, because his father didn't want to be alone. The man couldn't handle being by himself any more than he could handle being with people.

Was there ever a day when his father didn't remind them he couldn't see? How many family events did they miss? How many holidays had to be rearranged? His father wore his blindness like a shield and demanded that it—no, *he*—be acknowledged at every turn.

Had Frederic done the same? Was his insistence on bearing the burden alone a different version of the same self-absorption?

Exhaling long and slow, he closed his eyes. His brain still believed breaking up with Piper was the right thing to do. His heart, on the other hand, needed her. He'd tried listening to his brain, and as a result, he was sitting in a giant house by himself while his heart threatened to break in half.

It didn't have to be this way. He could go to England.

Then what? Beg her to come back, and risk her falling out of love with him?

Better to risk than to live as he had the last forty-eight hours. Piper made the days worthwhile. Without her, they were simply days.

It was time he listened to his heart.

"So I said to myself, why are you playing hardball? There is no reason why you should be hangin' on to that gorgeous painting when Ana Duchenko is in Boston, heartbroken and alone. You can tell her nephew I am more than willing to sell."

Digging into the paper bag he set on the table earlier, John Allen pulled out a blueberry scone. Immediately, Mrs. Lester scoffed. "I'll have you know, there's a perfectly good scone right here."

"I'm sure you make a wonderful scone, but these are gluten-free. I make them with my own flour mix. Try one."

The innkeeper pinched a bite from the pastry on his plate. "Not bad," she said, chewing slowly. "Not as good as mine, but not bad. Do you want to try some, Piper? Piper?"

"Huh?" Piper looked up from her coffee to find John and Mrs. Lester staring at her.

"Sorry," Piper said. "I'm trying to concentrate, but my head doesn't want to cooperate." It was too busy thinking about a stubborn idiot who didn't—no who *couldn't*—love her.

"Still out of sorts, are ya?"

"Afraid so." She was beginning to think she would

be out of sorts forever. "Maybe I should have stayed in Paris."

"And do what?" the older woman asked. "Finish at that snooty cooking school?"

"No. Chef Despelteau and I parted ways for good." Quitting school was the one decision Piper didn't regret. Frederic was right; Patience didn't care whether she stayed enrolled or not. On her way out of Paris, Piper had texted her sister and asked that very question.

All I've ever cared about is you being happy, whatever you decide to do, her sister had texted back. Is everything okay?

Piper gave her one last lie and said everything was fine. This time it wasn't to appease her sister, but to avoid feeling worse. Her sister and Stuart had repaired their relationship and were in a serious honeymoon phase. Piper was afraid hearing the happiness in her sister's voice would cause her to break down.

"I don't think it's the school she's missing," John said.

"I keep thinking if I stayed in Paris, I might have been able to convince Frederic he was being a stubborn idiot." She couldn't believe how much she loved him after such a short time.

"People gotta work out their demons for themselves," Mrs. Lester said. "You stickin' around waiting on him won't make the process go any faster."

"True." In a way, staying where she wasn't wanted would be as bad as staying out of obligation.

Staying with Mrs. Lester might have been a mistake as well. Everywhere she looked she saw some kind of reminder of the weekend she spent with Frederic. Even the damn kitchen wasn't safe. Nights were worse. She lay in bed reliving the ones they had shared.

"Why don't you come stay with me?" John said when Mrs. Lester went to answer the front doorbell. "We could experiment with grain-free recipes."

Piper smiled. "You are a very sweet man, Mr. Allen, but I think I'm better off staying here." Perverse as it was.

"For the last time, call me John, and if you change your mind, the offer will always be there. It's the least I can do for a fellow Ana lover."

Just then, Mrs. Lester called from the front hallway. "Piper? Could you come here a minute, dear? I need you for something."

"Coming, Mrs. Lester."

She found the innkeeper standing at the base of the stairs waiting for her. The older woman had the oddest expression on her face. "Is something wrong?" she asked.

"You tell me," Mrs. Lester replied, nodding her head toward the entryway.

Piper gasped. "Frederic?"

She couldn't believe her eyes. Was he really standing in Mrs. Lester's doorway?

At the sound of her voice, he took off his sunglasses. Piper saw that his hand was trembling. He looked as bad as she felt, with circles turning his eyes dark and gloomy.

"What are you doing here?" she asked.

"You were right," he said. "I *was* blind."

"You were?" She had to ask to make sure she wasn't dreaming. When she walked out of his house, she was certain she would never see Frederic again. Now he was here, and echoing the words she left behind... It was all too unreal.

Frederic stepped closer, stopping just short of her arms. "I thought the only way I could avoid being like my father was to shut myself off. If I didn't need anyone, then I couldn't drive them away. I didn't see that..." He let out a breath. "I thought I was protecting you. Instead I was doing exactly what I swore I would never do. And that was drive the woman I love away."

"Do you mean that?" Out of the corner of her eye, she saw Mrs. Lester disappearing into the kitchen to give them privacy. It was just her, Frederic and the declaration he made.

"That I love you? More than I thought possible. And I was an idiot for pushing you away. You are the best thing that has ever happened to me, Piper. I never should have let you walk out the door. Can you ever forgive me?"

"I..." She wanted to laugh and cry at the same time. Could she forgive him? "You put me through hell," she reminded him.

"I know, love. And I understand if you can't forgive me. I took too long to come to my senses." He lowered his head. "Perhaps if I hadn't been so stubborn..."

"I can't believe you came to England," Piper said. She wasn't quite ready to forgive him, but she also didn't want him to leave.

"I would have gone twice as far. I had to come. I had to let you know that while I don't deserve your forgiveness—not for one second—I...I need you."

That was all she needed to hear. Before he could say another word, Piper was in his arms, lost to the warmth of his embrace.

"I missed you so much," he whispered against her cheek. "My world was dark without you. Please, please tell me you forgive me."

"I forgive you," she whispered back. She had to squeeze her eyes shut to keep the tears back.

Frederic's eyes were as wet as hers. "There's a lot we have to work out. Being with a blind man isn't going to be easy."

"I know."

"There might be days when the frustration gets to me, and I become a selfish boor."

It wasn't funny, but Piper had to laugh. "You mean more so than these past few days?"

"I only want to make you happy."

"Then..." She took his hand. "Then be strong enough to let me help you. Don't push me away."

"Never again," he said. "But you have to promise that if you are ever unhappy..."

"I will let you know, and we'll work on a solution together."

"I love you, Piper Rush, and I want...no, I *need* you by my side." Cradling her face, he kissed her, a kiss so much like the one they shared at the abbey, and Piper gave up battling the tears.

"Please don't cry, love," he said, wiping at the dampness. "This is a happy time. Besides, I don't have a handkerchief."

"Maybe we can steal a paper towel from Mrs. Lester," she said with a laugh. It felt good to feel light again after all these days. She sniffed back as many tears as she could. "And I am happy. More than you can imagine."

Frederic looked wonderful in his tuxedo. He balked at renting one at first, but Piper insisted. *If I'm wearing a gown, then you're wearing a tuxedo*, she told him. After all, the man was born to wear black tie. Especially for his wedding.

It wasn't a real wedding ceremony. Two weeks was way too soon for any kind of official ceremony, especially when neither of them knew what the future held. Frederic had a lot of adjustment ahead of him. Preparing for a sightless future. And Piper needed to figure out what she wanted to do with her life now that she'd parted ways with French cooking. She and Mrs. Lester had talked about maybe opening a small bistro in Paris specializing in classic comfort food. There would be plenty of expatriates looking for a home-cooked meal.

One thing she was certain of, though, was that Frederic owned her heart and that, when the time came, she would be thrilled to make their commitment legal. In the meantime, she was more than happy with being his makeshift bride.

They "married" themselves in the field behind the abbey. Frederic's idea. "I want to watch you walk down the aisle," he said. "In case…" He didn't need to finish his reason why.

Frederic held her hands in his. "I promise to never push you away again," he said. "I will accept your help, and I will never let you lose yourself."

"And I promise to never act out of obligation," Piper replied. "Whatever happens in the future, we will face it together."

She smiled a watery smile at the man she planned on loving forever. Funny how things worked out. She came to Paris with one dream and found another. One that was far better. As for the future…they would simply have to figure it out as they went along. Time was theirs to make what they wanted. So long as she and Frederic stood together, they would be fine. More than fine. She'd be happier than she'd ever imagined.

And to think it all started with Ana's missing portrait.

"Oh, no!" The exclamation burst from her mouth, disrupting the moment and turning Frederic pale.

"What's wrong, love?"

"I never called Patience. With everything going on between the two of us… It's been almost two weeks since I've talked to her." Her sister hadn't called her, either, a point she would make if Patience complained. "She has no idea what's going on." She held out her hand. "Can I borrow your cell phone?"

"Married for two minutes, and already you are pushing me aside for your sister? I have not even kissed the bride."

Piper kissed him long and slow, a promise of what was to come. When they finally broke apart, she rested her forehead against his. "That better?"

"Perfect."

"Good. Give me your phone." She was grinning from ear to ear. "Patience! Did I wake you? I've got good news and I've got more good news. The good news is we found Ana's portrait and the owner's willing to talk to Stuart about selling." Legs bouncing, she waited impatiently for her sister to relay the news. Frederic laughed and kissed her forehead.

Finally, Patience's voice came back on the line. "You said there's more good news. What is it?"

"I got married!" she exclaimed.

And, holding her husband's hand, she filled her sister in on her happy ending.

Christmas Day

Ana knew something was up from all the looks Patience and her nephew exchanged during Christmas dinner. Of course, she assumed they planned to announce their engagement, so when Stuart asked her to close her eyes, she was confused.

"Why do I have to close my eyes?" she asked him. "We've already opened the gifts."

Stuart gave her one of his annoying smirks, the one he reserved for when he had a secret. "Maybe not. Maybe there's a surprise present."

Goodness, how could there be more gifts? You could barely move around the room as it was, what with the tree and all the presents.

A slender arm wrapped around her shoulders. It was Patience, her nephew's partner in crime. "Please, Ana. I promise you won't be disappointed."

"Oh, all right." She couldn't say no to that girl if she tried.

Although she should have pointed out that no matter what the surprise, she couldn't possibly be disappointed. Certainly not after such a wonderful Christmas celebration. In addition to Patience and Stuart, Patience's sister was visiting from France along with her boyfriend. *Boyfriend*, Ana chuckled. Frederic was no boy. Her Nigel would have said *sa grande passion,* the way the two of them lit up whenever the other entered the room. But then, he would use the same phrase for Stuart and Patience as well.

How wonderful it had been to spend the day surrounded by love. To see the people she loved in love. It thrilled her to know that while she had lost her chance, others had not. She ran her hand over the cat nestled in her lap. Sweet Nigel. He'd be thrilled, too. He used to say it was love that gave his art life. For a man who claimed to be a rebel, he was a hopeless romantic.

"Okay, *babushka*. Open your eyes."

No… It couldn't… Ana's heart leaped to her throat. "How…?" Her legs were shaking so hard, she was afraid they wouldn't hold her.

Patience was at her elbow, supporting her. "Piper and Frederic tracked her down in England," she said.

"Turns out a man named Gaspard Theroux held out on Grandpa Theodore," Stuart told her. "He never told him that he owned one of Nigel's works."

"Dear sweet Gaspard. He believed in Nigel's talent before anyone else." She ran her trembling fingers across her younger self, along the brushstrokes she remembered so well. Nigel painted with such vitality, such passion. "He was so proud of this work."

Time turned backward, and she was in Paris, stretched across the velvet settee. "Don't move, *mon amour*. The light on your skin is perfect. I want the whole world to see you the way I do."

She would have lain in place forever if that's what he needed.

A tear ran down her cheek. "Please don't cry," Patience said.

The dear girl didn't understand. These were happy tears. Nigel's work survived. In spite of all Theodore's efforts to erase it, proof of their love lived on.

Leaving the tears to fall, she turned to Piper and Frederic. "Thank you."

"No," Piper said. "Thank you. If not for your painting, Frederic and I would still be…"

"The two loneliest people in Paris," Frederic supplied, pressing a kiss to her forehead. "Your Nigel brought us together."

He would have been so glad to know that. Ana turned back to the portrait. The years hadn't diminished its strength. She could still feel the emotion in every stroke. *I miss you so much, my darling.*

"We'll be together soon enough, mon amour."

In the meantime, she would celebrate. She would bask in the love shared by the young people around her, and give thanks for the happy endings she knew would be theirs.

With Nigel close by. "This moment calls for a celebration," she said. "*Lapushka*, go get some champagne

from the wine cellar. And you, my furry rascal..."
Reaching down, she scooped up the cat she'd unceremoniously dumped when she stood up. "Let us toast to your namesake. And to happy endings."

It was exactly what Nigel would have wanted.

* * * * *

IT HAPPENED
IN PARIS...

ROBIN GIANNA

For my wonderful children, Arianna, James and George. You three are truly the light of my life.

A big thank you to good friend Steven J. Yakubov, M.D. who has been conducting TAVI clinical trials overseas and now in the US for years, and who inspired this story. I so appreciate it, Steve, that you called me to answer all my questions even after you'd had almost no sleep for three nights. Thanks bunches!

CHAPTER ONE

JACK DUNBAR STUDIED the map in his hand, trying to figure out where the heck he was in this city of two million people. He was determined not to waste his first hours in Paris, and never mind that he'd only had a few hours of sleep while folded into an airplane seat, couldn't speak French and had no idea how to get around.

But, hey, a little adventure never hurt anyone. Even getting lost would be a welcome distraction from thinking about the presentation he had to give tonight. The presentation that would begin the new phase of his career he'd worked so hard for. The presentation that would launch the newest medical device, hopefully save lives and change forever the way heart-valve replacement surgery was performed.

Before any sightseeing, though, the first thing on his list was coffee and a little breakfast. Jack stepped into the hotel restaurant and saw that a huge buffet was set up just inside the open doors. Silver chafing dishes, mounds of breads and cheeses, fruits and you-name-it covered an L-shaped table, but the thought of sitting there eating a massive breakfast alone wasn't at all appealing. He approached the maître d'. "Excuse me. Is there just a small breakfast I can grab somewhere?"

"Voilà!" The man smiled and waved his arm at the buffet with a flourish. *"Le petit déjeuner!"*

Jack nearly laughed. If that was the small breakfast, he'd hate to see a big one. "Thank you, but I want just coffee and something quick. What's nearby?"

"Everything you could wish for is right here, *monsieur.*"

"Yes, I see that, but—"

"I know a little place that's just what you're looking for," a feminine voice said from behind him. "When in France, eat like the French do. And that spread in there is most definitely meant for Americans."

He turned, and a small woman with the greenest eyes he'd ever seen stood there, an amused smile on her pretty face. He smiled back, relieved that someone might actually steer him in the right direction, and that she not only spoke English, but sounded like she was American, too. "That's exactly what I want. To immerse myself in French culture for a while. And soon, because I need a cup of coffee more than I need oxygen right now."

Those amazing eyes, framed by thick, dark lashes, sparkled as her smile grew wider. "Caffeine is definitely the number one survival requirement. Come on."

Leaving barely a second for him to thank the unhelpful maître d', she wrapped her hand around his biceps and tugged him toward the door and out into the chilly January streets of Paris. "Just down the street is the perfect café. We can get coffee and a baguette, then we'll be good to go."

We? Jack had to grin at the way she'd taken over. Not that he minded. Being grabbed and herded down the street by a beautiful woman who obviously knew a little about Paris was a pleasure he hadn't expected, but was more than happy about.

"I'm Avery, by the way."

"Jack." He looked at her and realized her unusual name went well with a very unusual woman. A woman who took a perfect stranger down the street to a coffee shop as though she'd known him for days instead of seconds. A red wool hat was pulled onto her head, covering lush dark brown hair that spilled from beneath it. A scarf of orange, red and yellow was wrapped around her neck and tucked inside a short black coat, and tight-fitting black pants hugged her shapely legs. On her feet she wore yellow rain boots with red ducks all over them, and a purple umbrella was tucked under her arm. Dull she most definitely was not.

"Nice to meet you, Jack." Her smile was downright dazzling. The morning looked a whole lot brighter than it had a few moments ago, despite the sky being as gray as pencil lead. "How do you like your coffee? American style? If you really want to be French, you'll have to drink espresso. But I won't judge you either way."

Her green eyes, filled with a teasing look, were so mesmerizing he nearly stumbled off the curb when they crossed the street. "Somehow I think that's a lie. And while I can handle being judged, I like espresso."

"I knew you were a man after my own heart."

He'd be willing to bet a lot of men were after her heart and a whole lot more.

The little coffee shop smelled great, and he followed Avery to the counter. She ordered in French, and the way the words slipped from her tongue, it sounded to him like she spoke the language nearly like a native.

"You ordered, so I'm paying," he said.

"That's what I was hoping for. Why else did you think I brought you along?"

"And here I thought it was my good looks and sophistication."

"I did find that, combined with your little-boy-lost look, irresistible, I must admit."

He chuckled. Damned if she wasn't about the cutest woman he'd been around in a long time. They took their baguettes and tiny cups of espresso to a nearby tall table and stood. Jack nearly downed his cup of hot, strong coffee in one gulp. "This is good. Just what I needed. Except there isn't nearly enough of it."

"I know. And I even ordered us double shots. I always have to get used to the tiny amounts of espresso they serve when I'm in Europe. We Americans are used to our bottomless cups of coffee."

"Are you here as a tourist? With friends?" Jack couldn't imagine she was traveling alone, but hoped she was. Maybe they could spend some time together, since he'd be in Paris for an entire month. With any luck, she was living here.

"I'm in Paris to work, and I'm alone. How about you?"

"Me, too. Working and alone. But I do have a few hours to kill today. Any chance you'll show me around a little in exchange for me buying lunch?"

"We're eating breakfast, and you're already thinking about lunch?" More of that teasing look, and he found himself leaning closer to her. Drawn to her. "I've already proved I plan my friendships around who'll buy. So the answer is yes."

He smiled. Maybe this great start to his trip to Paris was a good omen. "Where to first? I know nothing about Paris except the Eiffel Tower, which I know is close because I saw it from the hotel."

"Paris is a wonderful city for walking. Even though it's cold today and may well rain. Or even snow. Let's walk toward the Seine and go from there. If we hit the tower early, we'll avoid some of the crazy lines."

"There are lines this time of year? I didn't think there would be many tourists."

"There are always tourists. Not as many in January and February as in spring and summer, but still plenty. Lots come to celebrate Valentine's Day in Paris. Romantic, you know?"

He didn't, really. Sure, he'd had women in his life, some briefly and some for a little longer. But, like his father in the past and his brother now, his life was about work. Working to help patients. Working to save people like his grandfather, who'd had so much to live for but whose heart had given out on him far too soon.

Avery finished her last bite of bread and gathered up her purse and umbrella, clearly ready to move on.

"I don't suppose they give little to-go cups of espresso, do they?" he asked.

"You suppose right," she said with a grin. "The French don't believe in multitasking to quite the same degree we do. They'd shake their heads at crazy Americans who eat and drink while walking around the city."

"I'll have to get a triple shot at lunch, then," he said as they stood. He resisted the urge to lick the last drop from his cup, figuring Avery wouldn't be too impressed. Might even come up with an excuse not to take him to the Eiffel Tower, and one drop of coffee wasn't anywhere near worth that risk.

They strolled down cobbled streets and wide walks

toward the tower, Avery's melodic voice giving him a rundown of various sights as they strolled. Not overly chatty, just the perfect combination of information and quiet enjoyment. Jack's chest felt light. Spending this time with her had leeched away all the stress he'd been feeling, all the intense focus on getting this study off the ground, to the exclusion of everything. How had he gotten so lucky as to have her step into his first day in France exactly when he'd needed it?

"That's L'Hôtel des Invalides," she said, pointing at a golden building not too far away. "Napoleon is buried there. I read that they regilded the dome on the anniversary of the French Revolution with something like twenty pounds of gold. And I have to wonder. Wouldn't all that gold have been better used to drape women in jewelry?"

"So you like being draped in gold?" He looked at the silver hoops in her ears and silver bangles on her wrist. Sexy, but not gold, and not over the top in any way.

"Not really. Though if a man feels compelled to do that, who am I to argue?" She grinned and grasped his arm again. "Let's get to the tower before the crowds."

She picked up the pace as they walked the paths crisscrossing a green expanse in front of the tower. Considering how cold it was, a surprising number of people were there snapping pictures and standing in line as they approached. "Are you afraid of heights?"

"Who, me? I'm not afraid of anything."

"Everyone's afraid of something." Her smiling expression faded briefly into seriousness before lightening again. "Obviously, the Eiffel Tower is super tall, and the elevators can be claustrophobic even while you're thinking how scary it is to be going so high. I'll hold your hand, though, if you need me to."

"You know, I just might be afraid after all."

She laughed, and her small hand slid into his. Naturally. Just like it belonged there.

"Truth? I get a little weirded out on the elevator," she said in a conspiratorial tone. "So if I squeeze your hand too tight, I'm sorry."

"I'm tough, don't worry."

"I bet you are." She looked up at him with a grin. "The lines aren't too bad, but let's take the stairs anyway."

He stared at her in disbelief. "The stairs?"

"You look like you're probably fit enough." Her green eyes laughed at whatever the heck his expression was. "But we don't take them all the way to the top. Just to the second level, and we'll grab the elevator there. Trust me, it's the best way to see everything, especially on a day like today, when it gets cloudier the higher you go."

"So long as we don't have to spend the entire day climbing, I'm trusting you, Ms. Tour Guide. Lead the way." The stairs were surprisingly wide and the trek up sent his heart beating faster and his breath shorter. Though maybe that was just from being with Avery. For some inexplicable reason, she affected him in a way he couldn't quite remember feeling when he first met a woman.

They admired the views from both the first and second levels, Avery pointing out various landmarks, before they boarded the glass elevator. People were mashed tightly inside, but Jack didn't mind being forced to stand so close to Avery. To breathe in her appealing scent that was soft and subtle, a mix of fresh air and light perfume and her.

The ride most definitely would challenge anyone with either of the fears Avery had mentioned, the view through the crisscrossed metal of the tower incredible as they soared above Paris. On the viewing platform at the top, the cold wind whipped their hair and slipped inside Jack's coat, and he wrapped his arm around her shoulders to try to keep her warm.

"You want to look through the telescope? Though we won't be able to see too far with all the clouds," she said, turning to him. Her cheeks were pink, her beautiful lips pink, too, and, oh, so kissable. Her hair flew across her face, and Jack lifted his fingers to tuck it beneath her hat, because he couldn't resist feeling the softness of it between his fingers.

"I want to look at you, mostly," he said, because it was true. "But I may never get up here again, so let's give it a try."

Her face turned even more pink at his words before she turned to poke a few coins in the telescope. They took turns peering through it, and her face was so close to his he nearly dipped his head to kiss her. Starting with her cheek, then, if she didn't object, moving on from there to taste her mouth. Their eyes met in front of the telescope, and her tongue flicked out to dampen her lips, as if she might be thinking of exactly the same thing.

He stared in fascination as her pupils dilated, noting flecks, both gold and dark, within the emerald green of her eyes. He slowly lowered his head, lifted his palm to her face and—

"Excuse me. You done with the telescope?" a man asked, and Avery took a few steps back.

"We're all done," she said quickly. The heat he hoped he'd seen in her expression immediately cooled to a friendly smile. "Ready to go, Jack? I think we've seen all there is to see from up here today."

Well, damn. Kissing her in the middle of that crowd wasn't the best idea anyway, but even the briefest touch of her lips on his would have been pretty sweet, he knew. "I'm ready."

They crammed themselves onto the elevator once more, though it wasn't quite as packed as it had been on the way up. He breathed in her scent again as he tucked a few more strands of hair under her hat. "Thanks for bringing me up here. That was amazing." *She* was amazing. "So what now, Ms. Tour Guide? Time for lunch?"

"There you go, thinking about food again." She gave him one of her cute, teasing looks. "But I admit I'm getting a little hungry, too. There's a great place just a little way along the river I like. There will be a few different courses, but don't worry—it won't break your wallet."

He didn't care what it cost. Getting to spend a leisurely lunch with Avery was worth a whole lot of money.

They moved slowly down a tree-lined path by the river, and he felt the most absurd urge to hold her hand again. As though they'd known each other a lot longer than an hour or two. Which reminded him he still hardly knew anything about her at all. "Do you live here? You obviously speak French well," he said.

"My parents both worked in France for a while, and I went to school here in Paris for two years. You tend to learn a language fast that way. I'm just here for a month or so this time."

"What do you do?"

"I— Oh!" As though they'd stepped out from beneath a shelter, heavy sheets of rain mixed with thick, wet snowflakes suddenly poured on their heads, and Avery fumbled with her umbrella to get it open. It was small, barely covering both their heads. Jack had to hunch over since she was so much shorter than him as, laughing, they pressed against one another to try to stay dry.

He maneuvered the two of them under a canopy of trees lining the river and had to grin. The Fates were handing him everything today, including a storm that brought him into very close contact with Avery. Exactly where he wanted to be.

He lifted his finger to slip a melting snowflake from her long lashes. "And here I'd pictured Paris as sunny, with beautiful flowers everywhere. I didn't even know it snowed here."

"You can't have done your homework." Her voice was breathy, her mouth so close to his he got a little breathless, too. "It rains and snows here a lot. Parisians despise winter with a very French passion."

He didn't know about French passion. But hadn't Avery said when in France, do as the French do? He more than liked the idea of sharing some passion with Avery. "I'm not a big fan of winter, either, when snow and ice make it harder getting to and from work."

"Ah, that sounds like you must be a workaholic." She smiled, her words vying for attention with the pounding rain on the nylon above them.

"That accusation would probably be accurate. I spend pretty much all my time at work."

"I must have caught you at a good moment, then, since you're sightseeing right now. Or, at least, we were sightseeing before we got stuck in this."

"You did catch me at a good moment." Maybe the romantic reputation of Paris was doing something to him, because he lifted his hands to cup her cheeks. Let his fingers slip into her hair that cascaded from beneath her hat. After all, what better place to kiss a beautiful woman than under an umbrella by the Seine in the shadow of the Eiffel Tower? "I'm enjoying this very good moment."

Her eyes locked with his. He watched her lips part, took that as the invitation he was looking for and lowered his mouth to hers.

The kiss was everything he'd known it would be. Her sexy lips had tormented him the entire time they'd been together in that elevator and standing close to one another on the observation deck. Hell, they'd tormented him just minutes after they'd met as he'd watched her nibble her baguette and sip her espresso. He could still faintly taste the coffee on her lips and an incredible sweetness that was her alone.

He pulled back an inch, to see how she was feeling about their kiss. If she thought it was as amazing as he did. If she'd be all right with another, longer exploration. Her eyes were wide, her cheeks a deep pink as she stared at him, but thankfully she didn't pull away and he went back for more.

He'd intended to keep it sweet, gentle, but the little gasp that left her mouth and swirled into his own had him delving deeper, all sense of anything around them gone except for the unexpected intimacy of this kiss they were sharing. Her slim hand came up to cradle his neck. It was cold, and soft, and added another layer of delicious sensation to the moment, and he had to taste more of her rain-moistened skin. Wondered if she'd possibly let him taste more than her face and throat. If she'd let him explore every inch of what he knew would be one beautiful body on one very special, beautiful afternoon.

Lost in sensory overload, Avery's eyelids flickered, then drifted shut again as Jack's hot mouth moved from her lips to slide across her chilled cheek. Touched the hollow of her throat, her jaw, the tender spot beneath her ear. She'd never kissed a man she'd just met before, but if it was always this good, she planned to keep doing it. And doing it. And doing it.

His hands cupping her cheeks were warm, and his breath that mingled with her own was warm, too, as he brought his mouth back to hers. Her heart pounded in her ears nearly as hard as the rain on the umbrella. She curled one hand behind his neck, hanging on tight before her wobbly knees completely gave way and she sank to the ground to join the water pooling around their feet.

The sensation of cold rain and snow splattering over her face had her opening her eyes and pulling her mouth from his. Dazed, she realized she'd loosened her grip on the umbrella, letting it sway sideways, no longer protecting them. Jack grasped the handle to right it, holding it above their heads again, his dark brown eyes gleaming. His black hair, now a shiny, wet ebony, clung to his forehead. Water droplets slid down his temple.

"Umbrellas don't work too well hanging upside down. Unless your goal is to collect water instead of repel it," he said, a slow smile curving the sexy lips that had made her lose track of exactly where they were. Lips that had traveled deliciously across several inches of her skin until she nearly forgot her own name.

"I know. Sorry." She cleared her throat, trying to gather her wits. "Except you didn't bring an umbrella at all, so you would have gotten wet anyway."

"True. Not that I mind. I like watching the raindrops track down your cute nose and onto your pretty lips." His finger reached out to trace the parts he'd just mentioned, lingering at her mouth, and she nearly licked the raindrops from his finger until she remembered a few very important things.

Things like the fact that she barely knew him. Like the fact that they were standing in a public place. Like the fact that she wasn't looking for a new relationship to replace the not-good one she'd only recently left.

She stared at the silkiness of his dark brows and the thickness of his black lashes, all damp and spiky from the rain. At the water dripping from his hair, over a prominent cheekbone, down the hollow of his cheek and across his stubborn-looking jaw. The thought crossed her mind that she'd never, ever spent time with a man so crazily good-looking. Even more good-looking than her ex-boyfriend, Kent, and she'd thought at the time he was a god in the flesh. At least for a while, until she'd figured out the kind of overly confident and egotistical guy he really was. Until she'd found out he was actually the one convinced he was godlike.

Getting it on again so soon with another man was not something she planned on doing.

She drew a deep breath. Time to bring some kind of normalcy to a very abnormal day. "Let's go to the café, dry off a little and get some food. You being Mr. Hungry and all."

"I've realized there's only one thing I'm hungry for at the moment." His lips moved close to hers again as his eyes, all smoldering and intense, met hers. "You. All of you."

All of her? Was he saying what she thought he was saying? She tried to think of a quick, light response and opened her mouth to speak, but no words came out. Maybe because she could barely breathe.

He kissed one corner of her mouth, then the other. "What do you say we head to the hotel for a while? A little dessert before lunch. I want a better taste of you."

Her heart leaped into her throat. Never having kissed a man she didn't know also meant never having had a quick fling with one. Never dreamed she ever would. But something about the way he was looking at her, the way his fingers were softly stroking her cheek and throat, something about the way her body quivered from head to toe and heat pooled between her legs had her actually wondering if maybe today was the day to change that.

After all, her last two relationships had ended with loud, hurtful thuds. Didn't she deserve some no-strings fun, just this once? She'd only be in Paris for one month, busy at work most of the time. The perfect setup for exactly what he was suggesting. And what would be the harm of enjoying what she knew would be one exciting, memorable afternoon with an exciting, memorable man?

"I...um..." She stopped talking and licked her lips,

gathering the courage to shove aside her hesitation and just say yes.

"I know. We've just met, and it's not something I usually do, either. Honest." He cupped her cheeks with his cold hands and pressed a soft kiss to her mouth. "But being with you here in Paris just feels right. Doesn't it? It just feels damned right."

She found herself nodding, because it did. For whatever crazy reason, it felt all too right. A no-strings, nothing-serious, no-way-to-get-hurt moment with a super-sexy man to help her forget all about her past disappointments.

Another drop of water slid over her eyelid, distracting her from all those thoughts, and she swiped it away. "Except I'm all wet, you know."

The second the words left her mouth his eyes got all hot and devilish, and she felt herself flush, realizing what she'd said. "That's a plus, not a problem."

A breathless laugh left her lips. Before she could change her mind she decided to give herself a little present to make up for what she'd been through with her past jerky boyfriends.

Silent communication must have zinged between them, because they grasped one another's hands and headed in a near run to the hotel. To her surprise, the closer they got, the more excited she felt. She was entering unknown territory here, and hadn't she always promised herself she'd live life as an adventure? Plunging into bed with Jack for an hour or two seemed sure to be one thrilling adventure.

With her heart thumping so hard she feared he could hear it, Avery followed Jack as he shoved open the door to his hotel room. Once inside, the nervous butterflies she'd expected to flap around earlier finally showed up. She stared at him, hands sweating, as he shut the door behind her, trying to think of what the heck she should say or do now that they were actually here.

"Wouldn't you know that the minute we come inside, it stops raining?" she said lamely. Why was she so suddenly, crazily nervous? A little fling was no big deal, right? People probably did things like sleeping with someone they barely knew all the time. Especially in Paris. She didn't, but surely plenty of women did.

"Maybe if we're lucky, it'll start raining again when we go out. I like kissing it off you." The brown eyes that met hers held amusement and a banked-down hint of the passion that had scorched between them just minutes ago.

He shut the door and flipped the lock, his gaze never leaving hers. The heat and promise and that odd touch of amusement in the dark depths of his gaze all sent her heart into a little backflip before he pulled her into his arms and kissed her.

Unlike their previous kiss, this one didn't start out soft and slow. It was hard and intense, his tongue teasing hers until she forgot all about what she should say or do. Forgot where they were. Forgot to breathe. His fingers cupped the back of her head, tangled in her hair, as the kiss got deeper, wilder, pulling a moan from her chest that might have been embarrassing if she'd been able to think at all.

His mouth left hers, moving hot and moist to the side of her neck to nuzzle there. "You feeling more relaxed now?" he murmured.

How had he known? Though relaxed probably wasn't

quite the right word to describe how she was feeling. "Um, yes. Thank you."

He eased back, his fingers reaching for the buttons of her coat and undoing every one of them before she'd had a chance to blink. "I don't know about you, but I'm feeling a little warm," he said as he slipped it from her shoulders and tossed it on a chair.

"Must be from all that running to the hotel," she said, breathless, but not from their fast trek to his room. "I figured it was a good chance to start training for the spring marathon."

His lips curved. "I thought we were running for a different reason." This time, his hands reached for the buttons of her blouse, the backs of his fingers skimming her skin and making it tingle as he slowly undid them one by one. "The reason being that I can't wait to see what you're wearing under this."

Her lacy white blouse dipped low over her breasts, and pure, feminine pleasure swept through her at the way his eyes darkened as he stared down at them. At the way a deep whoosh of breath left his lungs. His fingertips slipped down her collarbone and inside her bra to cup her breast at the same time that his mouth covered hers.

Oh. My. The man was certainly one amazing kisser. World class, really, and her bones nearly melted at the sensations swirling around her. His cool hand on her breast, her nipples tightening into his palm. His hot mouth tracking along her skin, her bra now slipping completely off her to the floor. Her pants somehow magically loose enough to allow his other wide palm to slide inside to grasp her rear before it moved to the front and touched her moist folds, making her gasp.

The loud patter of rain again on the window had him pausing his intimate exploration, and he lifted his head, his dark eyes gleaming. "Guess it's a good thing we came in here out of the rain."

"Good thing," she managed before he resumed kissing and touching her until she was trembling with the intense pleasure of it all.

"Avery." The way he said her name in a rough whisper, the way he expertly moved his fingers while kissing her mouth and face and throat, had her nearly moaning. It all felt so wonderful, every bit of nervousness evaporated, replaced by want and need.

How she ended up on the bed she couldn't say, but when his mouth left hers she looked at him, foggily realizing that she was somehow flat on her back completely naked, while he stood there, staring at her.

"You are every bit as beautiful as I'd fantasized you'd be," he said. "Looking at you takes my breath away."

If that was true, then neither of them had much of an ability to breathe at the moment.

"My turn to look at you. Strip, please."

Those bold words coming out of her mouth shocked her, but he just laughed. "Your wish is my command." His gaze stayed on her as he quickly yanked off his shirt, and her breath caught at his lean but muscular torso. As he shoved off his pants, his erection became fully, impressively but all too briefly visible before his body covered hers, hot and deliciously heavy.

"You didn't give me much time to look at you," she managed to say.

"Sorry. Couldn't wait to feel all your gorgeous, soft skin against all of mine."

Well, if he put it that way. She had to admit it did feel amazingly, wonderfully, delectably good.

Was she really doing this? Lying naked with a man she barely knew? The feel of his body on hers, his mouth pressing sweet kisses to everything within reach of it, his smooth, warm skin beneath her hands told her the answer was yes, but to her surprise she didn't feel tense or strange or regretful. All she felt was toe-curlingly excited and turned on.

His hands and mouth roamed everywhere until she found herself making little sounds and moving against him in a way that would have been embarrassing if she hadn't been so totally absorbed in the sensations and how he made her feel. Nearing orgasm more times than she could count before he backed off and slowed things down, she was close to begging him when he finally rolled on a condom, grasped her hips with his hands and pulled her to him.

Instinctively, she wrapped her legs around his waist, inviting him in, and the way they moved together made her think, in the tiny recess of her brain that could still function, that it seemed impossible they'd met only that morning. That this dance they danced hadn't been etched in both their bodies and minds many a time before.

And when she cried out, it was his name on her lips and hers on his as they fell together.

CHAPTER TWO

"JUST SO YOU KNOW...it's really true that I don't usually do this." Her pulse and breathing finally slowing to near normal, Avery managed to drag the sheet up to cover her breasts. She glanced over at Jack, whose head lay on the pillow next to hers, eyes closed, looking as sated and satisfied as she felt. She wasn't sure why the words had tumbled out, but once they had, she wasn't sorry. She didn't want Jack to think she routinely picked up men, showed them around, then dove into bed with them.

"Do what?"

The expression on his face was one of bland innocence, completely at odds with the amused glint in the eyes that slowly opened to look at her. She couldn't help but make an impatient sound. "You know very well what. Sleep with men I've just met. Heck, I've never even kissed a man I just met."

He rolled to his side, his warm body pressing against hers. "I believe it was I who kissed you. Figured it was a Parisian tradition. The city of romance and everything. And what's more romantic than a rainstorm in the shadow of the Eiffel Tower?"

"Well. There is that." Though she was pretty confident that if it had been any other man she'd invited to breakfast that morning, there wouldn't have been any kissing on their trek around town or any rolling around in the sheets, complete with a lovely afterglow. And, to her surprise, no feelings of regret at all. Maybe because she knew it would happen just this once.

The moment she'd stepped off the hotel elevator that morning, her attention had gone straight to him like a magnet. Tall, lean and obviously American, with an adorably befuddled expression on his handsome face as he'd spoken to the maître d', she'd moved toward him without thinking, inviting a stranger for coffee and breakfast as though she did it every day. Which he doubtless assumed she did.

"I hope you're not regretting it. Our kiss, and now this." He propped himself up on his elbow and slowly stroked his finger down her cheek. "I know I don't. Being so close to you under that umbrella, there was no way I could stop myself. And once I'd kissed you, all I could think of was kissing you more."

No way she could have resisted his kiss, either. Or the bliss that had come afterward. Not that she'd tried at all. "Well," she said again, as though the word might somehow finalize the whole crazy afternoon, "we've shared *le petit déjeuner*, walked a bit of the city and gone up the tower. Kissed under an umbrella and made love while it rained outside. I guess it's a good time to find out a little about each other. I hope you're not married?"

She said it jokingly, but a small part of her suddenly wondered if he possibly could be. If he was the type of man who philandered when working out of town. Her stomach clenched at the thought. After all, she knew that type way more intimately than she wished she did. Would Jack admit it if he was?

"Not married. Never have been. Remember, I told you, all I do is work. Which probably makes me pretty boring."

Whew. She looked at him carefully and managed to relax. Surely no one could lie about a wife so convincingly. "Don't worry, you're not completely boring." His twinkling dark eyes and devilish smile proved he knew he was darned exciting to be around. "Tell me something else about you. What's your favorite food? Besides espresso, that is."

"Sorry, coffee definitely is number one on my list of life's sustenance. Though I'm sure anything licked from your lips would qualify, too."

She laughed and shook her head. "I don't have to ask you about talents, because I already know a few of them. Blarney being one."

"And my other talents?" His eyes gleamed as his wide hand splayed on her back, pressing her close against him, and the heat of his skin on hers made her short of breath all over again.

"I'm not stroking your ego any bigger than it already is."

"How about stroking something else, then?"

"Already did that. And I see I'll have to watch what I say around you."

He chuckled as he kissed her shoulder, and she found herself thinking about his mouth and those talents of his and wasn't sure if it was that or his body heat making her feel so overly warm. Again. "So what are your hobbies?" he asked.

"I don't know if I'd call it a hobby, but I like to run.

Helps clear my mind when it gets too busy. And I like marshmallows. A lot."

"Marshmallows?" He laughed out loud at that. "You're kidding."

"Unfortunately, no. I pop the little ones when I'm working on the computer. Which is why I have to run. Don't want to *become* a marshmallow."

"You're about as far from a marshmallow as anyone could be." His hand stroked feather-light up her arm and across her chest to slide down the other, making her quiver. "I'd like to run more than just on a treadmill, but my work just doesn't leave me that kind of time."

"So what is this work you spend all your time doing?"

"I'm a cardiologist."

Every muscle froze, and her breath stopped as she stared at him. A cardiologist? *Cardiologist?* Could this really be happening?

He was probably used to women swooning when he announced that, but not her. She'd worked with more cardiologists than she cared to think about, and being arrogant and egotistical seemed to be a requirement for becoming that kind of specialist. Something she'd allowed herself to forget for too long with her last two boyfriends.

Along with her shock came another, even more chilling thought, which now seemed all too likely since they were staying at the same hotel. Her heart thumped hard in her chest, her body now icy cold as she tugged the sheet up tighter around it. "What's your last name, Jack?"

"Dunbar." He smiled, obviously not sensing the neon "oh, crap" vibes she had to be sending off. "I'm working for the next month at the Saint Malo Hospital, testing a new heart-valve replacement device. I've worked damned hard to get the design finished and to get the arrangements for the trial finalized. Can't believe it's finally about to happen."

Oh. My. Lord. She couldn't quite believe it, either. Not the trial starting. This unbelievable coincidence.

How was it possible that the man she'd just slept with was Dr. Jack Dunbar? The Jack Dunbar she'd be working with and observing at the hospital? The Jack Dunbar who was testing the procedure many, including her, hoped would someday always be used, instead of open-heart surgery, to replace faulty heart valves? The Jack Dunbar who had helped develop the next generation of valve replacement catheter based on her original design?

A next generation she feared wasn't any better, or safer, than her own had been.

And if it became necessary to voice her opinion that the trial should be halted, he wouldn't feel like kissing her or making love with her again, that was for sure. Not that she planned on more kisses and lovemaking, anyway.

A cardiologist was the absolute last kind of man she wanted in her life. Again.

"How about you?" He lay back, reaching to grasp her hand, his thumb brushing against her skin. Just as it had earlier when they'd been walking in such a lovely, companionable way. This time the feeling it gave her wasn't electrifying and sweet. The sensation felt more like discomfort and dismay. "So, what kind of last name goes with Avery? And what kind of work brings you to Paris?"

She swallowed hard. "Funny you should ask. My work has a lot to do with your own, Dr. Dunbar."

"Your work is similar to mine?" Jack asked, obvious surprise etched on his face. "In what way? Are you a doctor?"

"No. I have a doctorate in biomedical engineering." She left it at that, which was absurd, since it was all going to come out sooner or later, and it might as well be now. Lying naked in bed with him.

That realization had her shaking off her stunned paralysis to leap out of bed and grab up her clothes.

"That's…impressive." He propped himself up on his elbow, obviously enjoying the view as she scrambled to get dressed. His dark eyebrows were raised even higher, an expression she was used to seeing when she told people what she did for a living. She was young to be where she was careerwise and being petite made her seem younger still.

"Not really. I just worked hard, like you. Then again, in my experience cardiologists are pretty impressed… with themselves." And was that an understatement, or what?

"I should be insulted, except it might be true." He grinned at her. "So what brings you to Paris?"

"Well, as I said, my work has to do with yours." And could there be a much worse situation? The very first time she had a one-time thing with a man, he turned out to be someone she'd be working with closely.

She still couldn't quite wrap her brain around this mess. With a nervous laugh threatening, she pulled on her shirt, relieved to be finally clothed. After all, being naked when they made their formal introductions would be all kinds of ridiculous, wouldn't it?

She smoothed down her clothes and took a deep breath as she turned to him.

"As you know, your company hired the designer of the first valve replacement catheter to come study and observe the trial of your new one. That designer would be me."

His mouth actually fell open as he stared at her. It seemed he shook his head slightly, and that jittery laugh finally burst out of her throat. Clearly, he was as shocked by this crazy coincidence as she was. Though maybe it wasn't so crazy or much of a coincidence— after all, the Crilex Corporation was putting them both up at the same hotel where they'd met.

"You can't be...Dr. Girard," he said, still wearing an expression of disbelief.

"I am. And I'm equally shocked that you're Dr. Dunbar." Awkwardly, she stuck out her hand. "Avery Marie Girard. Nice to meet you."

That slow, sexy smile she'd found all too attractive throughout the day slipped onto his face again before he laughed. He reached to shake her hand, holding onto it. "It's an honor, Dr. Girard. Obviously, I've read about all you've accomplished. Your designs for various medical devices. Studied them for more hours than I care to think about as I worked with engineers to design the one we'll be testing. I...can't believe that you're...her."

"Because I'm young?" Or more likely because he'd already seen her naked, but maybe she could pretend it hadn't happened. As though *that* was possible.

"Because you're beautiful. And fun. And spontaneous. With silky hair you don't wear in a bun and crazy, colorful clothes instead of drab gray. Rain boots with ducks instead of orthopedic shoes." His eyes crinkled at the corners. "I'm obviously guilty of thinking of a very stereotypical brainiac scientist, and those stereotypes don't include any of the things you are."

"Jack Dunbar!" She shook her head mockingly, having heard it all before. "You shouldn't admit any of that. The Society of Women Scientists will publicly flay you if you say that aloud. Maybe mount your head on an energy stick and parade the streets with it, denouncing stereotypes of all kinds."

"And I'd deserve it." The eyes that met hers were warm and admiring. That admiration would doubtless change into something else if he knew about her true role in his project. A slightly sick feeling seeped through her. Why, oh, why, hadn't she learned who he was before she'd slept with him?

"Glad you admit it. Scientists come in all ages, sizes, genders and personalities."

"You're right, and I'm sorry." He got out of the bed as well, and she averted her gaze from his glorious nakedness. "Sounds like you buy into some stereotyping, too, though. That cardiologists are all egotistical and impressed with themselves."

Guilty. But she had good reason to believe that, and it wasn't based on a stereotype. It was based on personal experience. And then, today, she'd dived into bed with another one. How stupid could she be? "Let's agree to set those preconceived ideas aside, shall we?"

"Agreed." He shook his head as he pulled on his own clothes. "Wow. I'm just blown away by this. I'd been interested in meeting the famous Dr. Girard and pleased to have her participate in the trial with me. Little did I know she'd be an incredible tour guide, have the greenest eyes I've ever seen and..." he paused to look at her, speaking in the low, deep rumble that did funny things to her insides "...the sweetest lips on either side of the Atlantic Ocean."

Oh, my. And his were beyond sweet, as well. "Except you realize this was a bad idea. Now that we know we'll be working together."

In fact, he didn't have any idea exactly how bad an idea it had been.

Robert Timkin, the Crilex CEO, had spun to Jack and everyone else involved that Avery would be there just to observe the trial for her own education. But the company knew she had concerns about the new device and had really hired her to evaluate the data, giving her the power to stop the rollout of the next trials if she thought it necessary.

Jack had worked on designing the new device and organizing the trial for over a year, and he'd doubtless flip out if the data forced her to shut it down.

"Working together." His warm smile faded and his brows lowered in a frown. "I guess you're right. That is a problem."

"It is." She drew a calming breath. "Listen. This afternoon was wonderful. A lovely day in a wonderful city between two strangers. But now we're not strangers. And I have to be an objective observer as I gather data on the trial. From now on, we're just working colleagues, nothing more."

He stared at her silently for a moment, his expression serious, before he nodded. "You're right. Business and pleasure never mix well."

"No. They don't." Not to mention that she'd sworn off cardiologists for good.

He stepped forward and pulled her close, pressing

his lips to hers in a soft, sweet kiss. Despite her words and thoughts and conviction, she found herself melting into him.

"That was from Jack to Avery. Thank you for an unforgettable day," he whispered against her lips before he stepped back. "Dr. Dunbar will be meeting Dr. Girard tomorrow in the cath lab as we both concentrate on why we came to Paris. Okay?"

"Okay."

He dropped one more lingering kiss on her mouth before he picked up her coat and draped it over her arm. She stepped out to the hall and the door clicked quietly behind her. She lifted her fingers to her lips, knowing with certainty this had been the only one-time fling she'd ever have. That she'd savor the memory, and pray that over the next thirty days it didn't come back to sting her in more ways than one.

CHAPTER THREE

Avery stood behind a wall of glass to one side of the operating table in the hospital's cath lab, watching the procedure on the X-ray fluoroscopy viewing monitor. She'd gowned and masked like everyone else in the room, but unlike anyone else, she held a tablet in her hand to record the notes she'd be taking.

"The prosthetic valve is made from cow tissue," Jack said to the nurses and doctors assisting or observing the procedure, as he and Jessica Bowman, the nurse he'd brought with him from the States, readied the patient. "This version doesn't require a balloon to open it as the previous one did."

He continued to explain, as he had last night during his presentation, how a transcatheter aortic valve implantation, TAVI, worked. The details of how the catheter was designed, and why the stent and valve were in an umbrella shape, designed to push the diseased valve aside before the umbrella opened, seating the new valve in its place. With the procedure not yet started, Avery had a moment to watch him instead.

Today, he was all business, his dark eyes serious above his mask, his voice professional and to the point. In stark contrast to yesterday's amusing and witty companion. As they'd laughed and walked through Paris, his eyes had been perpetually filled with interest and humor, his mouth curved in a smile, his attention on her as much as it had been on the landmarks she'd shown him.

A very dangerous combination, this Dr. Jack Dunbar. So dangerous she'd thrown caution off the top of the Eiffel Tower. Thank heavens they'd agreed that no more hot, knee-melting kisses or spontaneous sex could be allowed.

Though just thinking about those kisses and their all-too-delicious lovemaking made her mouth water for more.

She gave herself a little mental smack. Date a cardiologist? Been there, done that. Twice. Fool me once, shame on me, fool me twice, shame on me again. Fool me three times? Well, her genius status would clearly be in question.

Then there was the other sticky issue. Obviously, the best-case scenario would be for the device to work fabulously, for the trial to be a success and for it to be further rolled out to other countries and hospitals. After all, in the U.S. alone over one hundred thousand people each year were diagnosed with aortic stenosis, and a solid third of them were high risk who might not do well with traditional open-heart surgery or weren't candidates at all.

But, from studying this stent and catheter, she worried that it didn't fully address the significant problem of postoperative valve leakage and subsequent pulmonary edema, which her own design had not solved and was something she was trying to fix in her new prototypes.

"I'm going to establish a central venous line through the right internal jugular," Jack said as he made an incision in the patient's neck. "Then insert a temporary balloon-tip pacemaker. Both groin areas of the patient have been prepped, and I'll next insert an introducer sheath into the femoral artery."

Avery watched as his steady hands worked. After completing the first steps, he made another incision in the patient's groin, moving the guide wire inside the artery. "Contrast dye, please, and monitor the heparin drip," he said as he watched his maneuvering of the wires on the overhead screen. "You'll see that it's important to puncture the artery with a high degree of angulation to minimize the distance from the artery to the skin."

The man was an incredibly skilled interventional cardiologist, that was obvious. She quickly focused on the careful notes she was taking to squash thoughts of the man's many skills he'd thoroughly demonstrated to her yesterday. Why, oh, why, would she have to be around him every day when the whole reason she'd given in to temptation had been because she'd thought she'd never see him again?

Finally, he finished stitching the access sites and the patient had been moved to Recovery. Jack shook hands with all those in the room congratulating him.

"Thank you, but I'm just one cog in this wheel that will hopefully change valve transplantation forever," Jack said. "One important cog is right here with us. The designer of the first catheter-inserted replacement valve, Dr. Avery Girard."

Taken off guard, she felt herself blush as Jack turned, gesturing to her with his hand, then actually began to clap, a big smile on his face, as the others in the room joined him. She'd been keeping a low profile, and most of the hospital had just assumed she was a Crilex representative. Most cardiologists she knew—most definitely both of her old boyfriends—loved to play the big shot and preen at any and all accolades. Neither one of them would have shared the glory unless they had to.

"I appreciate your nice words, Dr. Dunbar," she said, feeling a silly little glow in her chest, despite herself. "I have every hope that the new design you've helped develop will be the one that works. Congratulations on your first procedure going smoothly."

"Thank you." His warm eyes met hers, reminding her of the way he'd looked at her yesterday, until the doctors observing converged on him to ask questions and he turned his attention to them.

Avery took off her gown, mask and hat, and caught herself watching Jack speak to everyone. Listening to his deep voice and the earnest enthusiasm there. She wanted to stay, to listen longer, but forced herself to move quietly from the room to go through her notes. Limiting her interactions with him to the bare minimum had to be the goal, and since there was just one surgery scheduled today, there was no reason to hang around.

Satisfied that her notes were all readable, in order and entered correctly into her database, Avery walked toward the hotel, feeling oddly restless. She'd planned to work in her room, but a peculiar sense of aloneness came over her. Since when had that ever happened?

Still, the feeling nagged at her, and she stopped to work for a bit at a little café, which seemed like a more appealing choice. After a few hours she headed to her room and settled into a comfy chair with her laptop.

Projects on her computer included ideas on how to fix her previous TAVI design if the one Jack had in trial had significant issues.

That unsettled feeling grew, sinking deep into the pit of her stomach, and she realized why.

If she had to recommend the trial be discontinued, would Jack think it was because she wanted Crilex to develop one of her designs instead? That her concerns would be from self-interest instead of concern for the patients?

She'd been doing freelance work ever since abruptly leaving the company that had funded her first TAVI design. They'd insisted on continuing the trials long after the data had been clear that the leakage problems had to be fixed first, which was why she'd been glad to observe this trial before that happened again.

If only she could talk to Jack about it, so he'd never think any of this was underhanded on her part. But her contract with Crilex stated she was to keep that information completely confidential.

She pressed her lips together and tried to concentrate on work. Worrying about the odd situation didn't solve anything and, after all, Jack knew she'd designed the original. Wouldn't he assume she was likely working on improvements to it and observing his with that in mind?

She couldn't tell Jack the power she had over the trial. But maybe she should tell him she had concerns with the design. To give him that heads-up, at least, and maybe nudge him to look for the same issues she would be as the trial continued.

Avery caught herself staring across the room for long minutes. With a sigh she shut the lid of her laptop and gave up. Clearly, she needed something to clear her head. Fresh air and maybe a visit to somewhere she hadn't been for a while. A place popped into her head, and she decided it was a sign that it might be just what she needed to get back on track.

A half hour later, jostling with others passengers as she stepped off the metro, she saw the sun was perilously low in the sky. She hadn't torn out the door in record time to miss seeing the Sacré Coeur at sunset and headed in that direction in a near jog, only to bump into the back of some guy who stepped right in front of her.

"Oh, sorry!" she said, steadying herself.

"No, my fault. I'm trying to figure out how to get to the Sacré Coeur to see it at sunset, and I…"

She froze and looked up as the man turned, knowing that, incredible and ridiculous as it was, the man speaking was none other than Jack Dunbar. Saw his eyes widen with the same surprise and disbelief until he laughed and shook his head. "Why is it that whenever I need a tour guide, the best one in Paris shows up to help me?"

Fate. It was clearly fate, and why did it keep throwing her and Jack together? Should she even admit that was exactly where she'd been going? "I wish I had the answers to the universe. But somehow I don't think you'll be surprised to learn that's where I'm headed, too."

He looked at her a long, serious moment before he gave her a slow smile, his eyes crinkling at the corners, and the warmth in them put a little flutter in her chest. "You know, somehow I'm not surprised. And who am I to argue with the universe? Guess this means we're going together."

A buoyant feeling replaced the odd, unsettled feeling she'd had for hours. Bad idea? Yes. Something she could walk away from? Apparently not.

"Then we've got to hurry." She grabbed his hand, knowing she was throwing caution away again. But how could she say no to the happy excitement bubbling up inside her? And after all, it was just a visit to the Sacré Coeur, right? "The sun's setting soon, and we don't want to miss it."

"Lead on, Ms. Tour Guide. For tonight I'm all yours."

CHAPTER FOUR

JACK LOOKED AT the adorable woman dragging him through the streets and wondered, not for the first time, how he could have gotten so lucky to have met her before they'd started working together. A personal connection before a professional one got in the way of it.

The professional part was unfortunate, since he'd vowed he'd never again get involved with a woman at work. For just one more night, though, he'd let himself enjoy being with Avery. After all, here they were, together. And, smart or not smart, he just couldn't resist.

"A lot of people think it's really old, but did you know the Sacré Coeur was consecrated after World War I in 1919?"

"I didn't know. Are you proving again to me that female scientists are well versed in many subjects?"

"I don't have to prove anything about women in science," she said in a dignified tone, "seeing as I'm not wearing orthopedic shoes."

He laughed. "True. And they're even bright green, which I've never seen in leather ankle boots."

"Clearly, you live a sheltered life. Maybe you should get yourself some brightly colored shoes."

"Somehow, I think my patients would worry about

my skills if I dressed that way." His eyes met her twinkling ones, an even more vivid green than her boots, and just looking at her made him smile. "You get to hide in your lab and behind your computer. I don't."

"You could wear them while your patients are under anesthesia." She had that teasing look in her eyes that he'd found irresistible yesterday when they'd gone up the Eiffel Tower, then spent that magical time in his hotel room. That he'd found irresistible since the moment she'd grabbed his hand and led him to breakfast. That he had to somehow learn to resist, starting again tomorrow.

"Except most of my patients are awake during procedures, so I'll stick with black or brown."

"Where's your sense of adventure?"

"Here with you tonight."

She looked up at him, an oddly arrested expression on her face. "Mine, too." She stepped up their pace. "We're almost there, and since January's off season, hopefully there won't be big crowds. Good thing the sun's peeking through. I think it just might be a beautiful night."

"It already is."

A blush filled her cheeks as she realized what he was saying. And maybe it sounded hokey, but he meant it. His intense focus on work usually didn't allow him to notice things like a beautiful sunset or, though he probably shouldn't admit it, even a beautiful woman sometimes. But she'd grabbed his attention from the second he'd met her, and he didn't know what to do about that.

She led him around a corner then suddenly stopped, turning her full attention in front of them. "*Voilà!* We made it! And, oh, my gosh, I think it's about the most spectacular I've ever seen!"

His gaze followed hers, and the sight was beyond anything he'd expected. At the end of the street behind a beautiful old building with large columns, the Sacré Coeur rose high above everything else. Its numerous cupolas and spires were bathed in pink and gold from the sunset, emerging from the pale sky and looking for all the world like a stunning mural in the mist.

"That's...incredible."

"It is, isn't it?" She took her hand from his, moving it to clutch his arm, holding him closer. He looked down to see her eyes lit with the same wonder he was feeling and that strange sense of connection with her, too, that had prompted yesterday's memorable interlude. "I haven't seen the basilica for a long time."

He moved his arm from her grasp and wrapped it around her shoulders, wanting to feel her next to him. They stood there together a long while, staring as the pastels changed hue and darkened. Eventually, the sun dipped low, taking the color and light with it, and Jack turned to her, pulling her fully into his arms without thinking. "Somehow, I don't think it would have seemed quite as beautiful if you hadn't been here with me."

She smiled and lowered her head to rest her cheek against his chest as she gazed down the street at the now shadowed church, and he couldn't believe how natural it felt to hold her like this. Like they'd been together a long time instead of one day. Like there weren't good reasons not to.

He stroked his hand up her back, sliding it beneath her thick hair to cup her neck. "How about we take the funicular up to see the city below?"

She lifted her head and leaned back to look up at him. "How do you know about the funicular?"

"What, you think you have all the dibs on tour guiding?" He tucked her hair under her cute hat, a yellow one this time, letting his fingers linger on the softness of her locks before stroking briefly down her cheeks. "I read a Paris tour guide book because I didn't know I'd have a personal one tonight."

"And yet here I am."

"Yeah. Here you are."

For a moment her green eyes stared into his until, to his surprise, worry and utter pleasure, she lifted herself up on tiptoe, slipped her arms up his chest and around his neck and pressed her lips to his. The touch was instantly electric, surging through every cell in Jack's body as he tightened his arms around her. Until he forgot they worked together. Until he forgot they were standing near any number of other sightseers who were snapping photos and admiring the church. On the side of a busy street where cars and motorcycles and scooters veered all too perilously close.

Just as had happened yesterday under that umbrella, Avery managed to make him forget everything but the drugging taste of her mouth as it moved softly on his.

The roar of a scooter zooming by had him breaking the kiss. He leaned his forehead against hers, their little panting breaths creating a mist of steam in the cold air between them. "Wow. That was nice."

"What, you think you have all the dibs on initiating a kiss?"

He chuckled at her words, mimicking his. "Believe me, I'm more than happy to share the dibs. But as much as I'd like to keep kissing you, I don't want either of us sent to the hospital by one of the crazy drivers around here." Or get into a sticky situation because of their jobs. "Let's go on up to see the view."

She pulled away and something, maybe embarrassment, flickered in her eyes. He reached for her chin and turned her face to his. "Hey, what's that look for?"

"I don't know why I kissed you. Why I keep kissing you, even when we agreed not to." She shook her head, a little frown between her brows. "It's like something comes over me and I lose all common sense."

"If you have to lose your common sense to kiss me, I hope you don't find it," he teased, earning a small smile. He took a few steps backward, bringing her with him, until he came up against the wall of a building. Even as he knew he shouldn't, he lifted his hand to cup her cheek, gently stroking her beautiful lips with his thumb. "You taste damned good to me."

"Except we need to work together. So kissing or… anything else…isn't a good idea."

"I know. It's a hell of a bad idea." He kissed her again, and the sigh that slipped from her lips, the way her body relaxed into his nearly had him going deeper, and to hell with the risk of being struck by a car. But he forced himself to let her go, reaching for her hand. "Come on. Your funicular awaits, princess."

They rode to the top and enjoyed the incredible views of the city as he held her close to shelter her from the colder air and wind. They meandered along the cobbled streets of Montmartre as Avery filled him in on some of the history of the village that had long been a haven for artists, including Picasso, Monet and Van Gogh. Today it attracted young artists who peddled their work on the streets.

"I don't know about you, but I haven't eaten," Jack said as they passed a restaurant with an appealing exterior. He looked at the posted menu and laughed when he realized it was, of course, in French. "I don't know what this place serves, but you want to grab something to eat?"

"My parents and I lived right here in Montmartre the two years we were in Paris, but I've never eaten here," she said, looking at the menu. "It's pretty expensive."

"We deserve something besides hospital food, which we'll be eating a lot of. Come on."

The food turned out to be good, and they enjoyed a lively conversation and occasional debate about medical devices like stents and implants until they both laughed about it.

Jack grabbed the bill when he saw her reaching for it, handing his credit card to the waiter. "My treat. I like a woman who eats all her food and talks about something besides shopping," he said to tease her.

"You treated me yesterday, so it should be my turn. And it sounds like you've been dating the wrong kind of women."

"No doubt about that." In fact, she didn't know how right she was, and it was a good reminder why he couldn't date Avery, no matter how attractive she was. No matter how much he wanted to.

"I don't always practically lick the plate, though," she said with a grin. "Thank you. The food was amazing, but you spent way too much."

"You forget I'm a rich, egotistical cardiologist. When I'm not working like crazy, I like to throw money around to impress beautiful women."

"You're right. Somehow I'd forgotten."

Her smile disappeared. He had no clue why and tried for a joke. "It's my pleasure to shower money on gorgeous scientists who wear colorful shoes."

Still no smile. In fact, an odd combination of unhappiness and irritation had replaced every bit of the pleasure that had been on her face.

Well, damn. But it was probably just as well, considering everything. "Time to head back to the hotel," he said, shoving back his chair to stand. "We have two surgeries tomorrow I need to get ready for."

She nodded and they headed toward the metro. It felt strange not reaching out to hold her hand, and a pang of regret filled him. But wishing their circumstance could be different didn't change a thing.

"Oh! I think that's Le Mur des Je T'aime! I've never seen it."

"What's Le Mur…whatever you said?"

He followed her as she moved closer to look at a wall of tiles with words scrawled all over it and splashes of red here and there in between. "It's the Wall of I Love You. An artist named Baron conceived of the wall, with 'I love you' written in something like three hundred languages. As a place for lovers to meet."

A place for lovers to meet? That bordered on overly sentimental as far as Jack was concerned. "Sounds like something from a chick flick, with a gooey happily-ever-after."

After he'd said it he thought maybe he should have kept his opinion to himself, and was relieved when she laughed. "Typical man. Not that I know much about lasting relationships and happily-ever-after."

"That makes two of us."

"Nobody you'd meet here at the wall? Old flame or old pain?"

"I've been too busy." The only woman who qualified as an "old pain" was the medical device sales rep he'd dated who, it had turned out, had used him big-time to advance her own career. He hadn't come close to being in love with her, but it had been damned embarrassing. Which was why he never dated anyone remotely connected to his work. And he needed to remember that.

She began walking toward the metro again, and they were mostly quiet on the way back to the hotel. Another sudden shower burst from the night sky that had them wet in an instant and nearly running the last blocks, intimately tucked beneath Avery's little umbrella.

Finally sheltered under the overhang in front of the hotel doors, she shook the rain from it. "Clearly, I'm going to need to get a bigger umbrella," she said, her voice a little breathless. "This one isn't nearly big enough for both of us."

Except, after tonight, they wouldn't be touring Paris together anymore. "I could invest in a big, yellow rain poncho and leave the umbrella to you. That would be pretty masculine and sexy, don't you think?"

"I don't know. People might mistake you for a giant lemon."

He loved her laugh and the way her eyes twinkled. Fortunately, other people loaded onto the elevator with them or he just might have found himself kissing that beautiful, smiling mouth of hers again. He grasped her elbow when they arrived on her floor and moved into the hall.

"What are you doing?" she asked. "You're staying on the eighteenth floor."

"I always walk a lady to her door."

"I don't think hotels count."

"Why not? There are so many doors in this huge place, you might get lost." He thought she'd smile at his teasing tone, but she didn't, and he sighed. "If that look on your face means you think I'm planning to jump your bones again, I'm not. Much as I'd like to, I get that it's different now. And agree it needs to be. Okay?"

"Okay."

She smiled, and it was her real, sunny smile. So real he had to kiss her one last time. She tasted the same as she had before, an intoxicatingly sensual mix of chilled, damp skin and warm mouth. The smell of rain and a slight, perfumed scent from her hair filled his nostrils, and the feel of her body through her coat filled his hands. He wanted to strip it off of her so that barrier wouldn't be between them.

A little sound came from her throat, and the sound inflamed him, his own low groan forming in response as he deepened the kiss. Damned if this woman didn't knock his socks off in every way a woman could.

She pulled back, her gloved hands a softly fuzzy caress on the sides of his neck. Her eyes were wide, her mouth wet from his kiss, her breathing choppy. "What is it about you?"

"Funny, I was just thinking the same thing. About you. Except I know the answer. You're amazing, and we have chemistry about equal to a nuclear explosion. Which makes it nearly impossible not to kiss you, even when I know I shouldn't." He pressed his lips to hers for another long moment before looking into the deep green of her eyes again.

She stared at him a moment longer before her beautiful mouth curved in an answering smile. "I guess we need to think of this as one last time Avery and Jack meet one another."

"I like that. A kiss dictated by the universe."

"By the universe." She rose up and kissed him again. Just as he was trying, in the midst of the thick fog in his brain, to mentally calculate how many hours it was until he had to be at work and alert, and how much longer he could enjoy the taste and feel of her, she drew back.

Her eyes were lit with the same desire he felt, and he was glad one of them had enough presence of mind to stop while they still could.

"There's something I want to be honest with you about," she said, clasping her hands together in an oddly nervous gesture. "And when you hear it, it'll probably help us keep our distance from one another."

"That sounds ominous. Is it that you're actually the one who's married?"

She smiled and shook her head. "No. It's about your TAVI device. I'm worried it doesn't address the flaw mine had. Leakage resulting in pulmonary edema."

He stared at her in surprise. "Why? We've barely begun the trial."

"I know. But I'm just not sure the corrections you've made will be enough, and feel it should have been tested longer on animals before a human trial."

What the hell? "The bioengineers and I worked hard to improve it. It's more than ready."

"I just wanted you to know I believe we should both pay extra attention to that aspect of the data."

Maybe this was how people felt when someone said their baby was ugly, and it wasn't a good feeling. "Duly noted. Good night, Dr. Girard."

He headed to his room, still reeling a little from her announcement. He was damned proud of the new device and would never have guessed she had any bias whatsoever about it. Surely she would remain scientifically impartial as she collected the data. Her announcement, though, did seem to make it easier to step away and keep his distance, which he tried to see as a positive development.

But as he attempted to sleep, he was surprised and none too happy to find himself thinking about Avery nearly as much as he was thinking of the work waiting for him early in the morning.

CHAPTER FIVE

JACK SAT AT the small desk the hospital had given him to use and finished his notes on the procedures they'd just completed. Now that surgery was over for the day, he let himself think about Avery and this uncomfortable situation.

For the first time in his entire career he'd had trouble getting one hundred percent of his focus on the patient and surgery in front of him before the procedure had begun. To not notice Avery standing behind the glass, ready to watch the TAVI procedure on the monitor, taking her notes. He'd finally managed, but somehow, some way, he had to keep Avery Girard and her premature concerns about the device from invading his thoughts.

He shoved himself from the chair to concentrate on what he'd come here to accomplish. He pulled up the patient records and headed toward the room of the second patient they'd done the procedure on.

Simon Bellamy was eighty-six years old and had been referred to them because of his severely diseased aortic valve. Although reasonably healthy otherwise, his age put him at high risk for open-heart surgery. He'd been doing well the past two days, and Jack expected he could be released tomorrow.

The satisfaction he was feeling as he looked at the patient's chart disappeared the instant he walked into the man's room.

Short, rasping gasps were coming from his open mouth, and he sat bolt upright in his bed, eyes wide. Jack grabbed his stethoscope from his scrubs pocket as he strode to the bedside. "What's wrong, Mr. Bellamy? Are you having trouble breathing?"

The patient just nodded in response, his chest heaving. Jack listened to the man's lungs, and the obvious crackling sounds were the last thing he wanted to hear. "Ah, hell." He pushed the button for the nurse, then got the blood-pressure cuff on the man. He stared at the reading, his chest tightening at the numbers. While it had been normal earlier today, it had soared to two hundred and twenty over one hundred.

The nurse hurried into the room. Jack kept his attention on his patient as he spoke, checking oxygen saturation levels, and was damned glad almost everyone in the hospital spoke English. "We need to reduce his heart's workload by getting his blood pressure down immediately. Also administer furosemide and get a Foley catheter placed, stat."

The man's oxygen level proved to be very low, which was no surprise. It was disturbingly obvious what was happening here. "I need to get a chest X-ray. Can you...?" He glanced at the nurse, who was busy getting the Foley placed. "Never mind. I'll call down to have the portable brought up."

And damned if the minute he finished the call to X-Ray, Avery walked in with her tablet in hand, stopping abruptly.

"What's wrong, Dr. Dunbar?"

For a split second he didn't want to tell her, after her revelation to him last night. Which would be childish and unprofessional, not to mention pointless, since she'd figure it out anyway. "Acute onset aortic insufficiency. Getting a chest film to confirm."

Just his luck that she was witnessing exactly what they'd just talked about. A significant complication from the valve leaking. He knew her being there or not didn't change the reality and told himself he was mature enough and confident enough to handle it. For a small number of patients it wasn't an unusual complication, anyway, and Jack discussed with everyone all the risks and potential side effects.

Avery gave a single nod and stepped out of the way as the tech rolled the X-ray machine into the room and got the patient prepared to get the picture of his lungs. To her credit, there was no sign of I-told-you-so smugness on her face, just concern.

"Have you given him a diuretic and blood-pressure meds?"

Had she really asked that? He nearly let loose on her, until he saw the deep frown over her green eyes and the genuine worry there. He managed to bite back the words he wanted to say, which was that he knew what he was doing, for God's sake, and to butt out. Did she really think he was a lousy doctor? "Having a Foley catheter placed and gave him furosemide and BP meds. With any luck, he'll be more comfortable shortly."

She nodded again, moving farther away to one side of the room as she opened her tablet. Her head tilted down and her silky hair swung to the sides of her cheeks as she began to tap away at the screen.

Frustration surged into his chest and he stuffed it

down, a little shocked at the intensity of it. His years of practicing medicine had taught him how to remain calm even in critical situations, and he was fairly legendary for being cool under fire.

He inhaled a deep, calming breath and turned away from her to check on Mr. Bellamy. Already the man was breathing a little easier and able to lean back against the raised bed. The X-ray tech ambled off with the films, and Jack hoped they'd be done fast, though he didn't expect them to show anything he didn't already know. There was no doubt in his mind this was pulmonary edema, the patient's lungs full of fluid from the valve leakage.

"Feeling slightly better now, Mr. Bellamy?"

The man nodded, still mouth-breathing but not nearly so labored as before. Jack reached for his hand and gave it a squeeze. "I know that's a scary thing, when you can't get a breath. You've been given a water pill to get your lungs clear, and we're going to keep the Foley catheter in to catch the fluid. It will have to stay there until we get the volume of fluid we want to see and make sure it's nice and clear. Okay?"

The man nodded again, giving his hand a return squeeze before Jack headed out of the room to check the X-ray.

"Dr. Dunbar."

Avery's voice stopped him in the hall and he turned. He folded his arms across his chest, wondering if this was the moment for an *I told you so*. Which he absolutely would react calmly and professionally to, damn it, if it killed him.

"Yes?"

She stepped close to him and, to his surprise, placed

her cool palm on his forearm. He couldn't figure out exactly what her expression was, but it didn't seem to be self-satisfaction. More like...remorse?

"I owe you an apology."

He raised his eyebrows. That was about the last thing he'd expected to come out of her mouth, and he waited to hear what she was apologizing for.

"It was completely inappropriate of me to ask if you'd administered blood-pressure meds and furosemide. You're the doctor in charge and far more knowledgeable about patient care than I am."

"Yes, I am."

A little laugh left her lips. "There's that egotistical cardiologist finally coming out. I knew he was in there somewhere." She dropped her hand from his arm and gave him a rueful smile. "During the clinical trial on my original device, I was often required to give instructions to nurses post-op when the doctors weren't around. I guess it's an old habit that's hard to break. Sorry."

She bit her lip, and damned if the thought of how incredible it had been kissing her came to mind.

How could he be thinking about that now? He looked into the green of her eyes, filled with an obvious sincerity, and felt his frustration fade. "Just don't let it happen again, or everyone in the hospital might start to wonder if you know something they don't. Like that I bought my MD online."

"It would take more than me blurting something dumb to tarnish your awesome reputation, Dr. Dunbar. Everyone here thinks you walk on water." Those pretty lips of hers curved. "But, believe me, I'll do my best to keep my trap shut. You know that old saying about how if looks could kill? Seeing the expression in your eyes at that moment, if that was true, I'd be lying on the floor lifeless."

In spite of everything, he felt himself smile, and how she managed that, he didn't know. "Cardiologists do have superpowers, you know. Better not test me to see if that's one of mine."

Her smile widened, touched her eyes and sent his own smile even wider. They stood looking at one another, standing there in the hallway, until Jack managed to shake off the trance she seemed to send him into with all too little effort.

He couldn't allow himself to fall any further for her obvious charms. Her work was too tangled up with his, and he'd promised himself never again.

He brought a cool, professional tone back to his voice. "I'm going to check on Mr. Bellamy's X-ray. I'll put the notes in his chart for your database."

He turned and strode down the hall, fighting a stupid urge to look over his shoulder to see if she was still standing there. When he stopped at the elevator he glanced back up the hall, despite his best intentions not to, and his heart kicked annoyingly when he saw her backside as she moved in the opposite direction. Riveted, he stared at the view. Her thick, shiny hair cascading down her back. That sexy sway of her hips, her gorgeous legs with their slender ankles, her delicate profile as she turned into a patient's room.

And found himself powerless against the potent memories of how she'd felt held close in his arms, the taste of her mouth on his, the feel of his body in hers.

Damn.

He focused on the gray elevator doors. This just might prove to be the longest month of his life.

CHAPTER SIX

"So, LADIES AND GENTLEMEN," Bob Timkin said, smiling at the group attending the late dinner meeting at the hotel, "we are encouraged at the success so far after a full week of the clinical trial. Patients and their families are pleased with the results, and I have great optimism as we look forward to the rest of the month."

The forty or so attendees clapped, a number of them turning their attention, smiles and applause toward Jack. He shifted slightly in his seat, wondering why it felt a little awkward. Not long ago he'd felt pleased with the media attention he'd gotten for his role in the development of the prototype device and the work involved in getting it finished and the trial set up. Happy that his mother, father and brother—all doctors—were proud of him and what he was trying to accomplish in memory of his granddad.

A large group effort had made it happen. The biomedical engineers had taken his suggestions to heart when they'd created the device. Crilex had funded it. French officials had seen the value of conducting the first trials here. He'd always been sure to include every one of them in his presentations and mention them in interviews.

But when it came down to it, the focus of others had been primarily on his work and his skills.

Avery's gaze met his across the room, and damned if he didn't have to admit she was probably why he felt this sudden discomfort. Her original design was the whole reason he had a new TAVI device at all. And while a slight valve leakage in a small percentage of patients was normal, he didn't like it that now three of the patients in this trial so far had experienced that complication. Statistically, that was far higher than the expected six percent, and that knowledge, along with Avery's announcement of her concerns, added to his unease.

He and Avery had managed to be simply cordial and professional to one another for the remainder of this first week. She also hadn't said anything to him about the latest patient with the valve leakage, which he'd been surprised but glad about. She must have finally seen it was still way too early to become truly concerned.

Jack nodded in acknowledgement of the recognition being sent his direction, but as his gaze again met Avery's he knew he couldn't stand her believing he was egotistical enough to think he alone merited the applause. Why what she thought of him mattered so much, though, wasn't something he wanted to analyze.

About to get to his feet and give a little speech about all the people deserving credit for the trial, Jack saw Bob moving from the lectern. Discomfort still nagged at him, but he figured it would be ineffective and even weird to start talking as the crowd began to stand and disperse.

Next thing he knew, he was looking at Avery again, and, disgusted with himself, quickly turned away. He would not allow himself to wonder what she was doing the rest of the evening. Would. Not.

He should go to his room and look over the history of the patient he'd be doing surgery on tomorrow. But an odd restlessness left him thinking he needed to do something else first, so he could concentrate later. Maybe a little downtime, listening to music in the lounge, would help him relax.

He moved toward the table where Jessica was sitting with some other nurses, yakking away like they'd become best friends. "Hey, Jess. How about a drink at the bar? We only have a single surgery tomorrow afternoon, so I think we can stay up one night past ten p.m."

"You don't have to ask me twice." She smiled at the women she was with. "Anybody want to join us?"

One by one they shook their heads. "I need to get home to get my little ones ready for bed," a young woman said. "Their papa will let them have crazy fun all night if I'm not there, then they will be tired and crying in the morning before school."

Another nodded in agreement, rolling her eyes. "*Oui.* My Raoul thinks that, if Maman's not home, dinner can be a chocolate croissant."

Jack smiled as everyone at the table laughed in agreement. It sounded just like his sister-in-law's gripes on the rare occasions his brother took over with the kids. If he was ever a dad, he'd try to remember this conversation and be more responsible.

That the random notion came to mind at all took him aback. Since when had he even thought about having a family? The answer was never. Work consumed his life.

For the first time, he wondered if that was all he wanted. If work could always be everything.

He shook his head, trying to shake off any and all peculiar and unwelcome notions. Paris was clearly doing strange things to him and had been since day one. He'd be glad when the month was over and the clinical trials continued elsewhere. Maybe he should consider talking to the Russian government about a winter trial in Siberia—if that didn't freeze some sense into him, nothing would.

He moved into the hotel lounge with Jessica, passing the dance floor as the heavy beat of music pulsed around them. "I can't believe I've worked with you for three years, but don't know your tipple," he said to Jess as they settled into a round, corner banquette.

"Like that's a surprise?" she said with a grin. "I don't think we've ever been out for a drink before. Ever. You're always still at work when I leave."

"We haven't?" He thought back and realized with surprise that was the case. "It bothers me to realize you're right. Though I'm pretty sure a big part of that was you falling for Brandon. And the two of you getting married thing was kind of a big deal."

"Okay, maybe that's true," Jess said, chuckling. "A cosmopolitan makes me pretty happy. Sounds extra-good after the constant demands you've put on me this week."

"Cosmo it is."

He ordered from the waitress and was just about to ask Jess a few of the questions he realized he'd never bothered to ask her before when, out of the corner of his eye, he saw Avery walk into the lounge. Not alone.

Every ounce of the relaxation and good humor he'd managed to feel for the past five minutes died when he saw the guy who accompanied her.

Jack recognized him as a doctor from the hospital, though he didn't know him. A urologist, maybe. French. Well dressed, like most Parisians, and good looking to women, too, he supposed.

Jack watched the guy laugh at something she'd said. As she gifted him with her amazing smile in return, he pressed his palm to Avery's lower back and led her to the dance floor.

The way she moved, the way she smiled, the way she rested her hand on the man's shoulder made it hard for Jack to breathe, reminding him of the moment they'd first met. Every muscle in his body tightened at the way the guy was looking at her as they moved to the beat of the music. Like she was first on his list of desserts.

"Earth to Jack. Should I call the bomb squad before it goes off?"

Jessica's words managed to penetrate his intense focus on Avery and the guy, and he slowly turned to her. "What?"

"You look like you're about to explode. Which I don't think I've ever seen from you. Jealous a little?"

"Jealous? That's ridiculous."

"It may be ridiculous, but I hate to break it to you. It's all over your face."

Somehow he managed to control his accelerated breathing. To school his expression into something he hoped was neutral. "I don't date women I work with. You know that."

"Uh-huh. Except this one's making you rethink that, isn't she?" Jack hadn't even realized the waitress had brought their drinks until Jessica took a sip of hers, studying him over the rim of her glass. "Listen. I get it. She's smart and pretty and, other than me, you're alone here in France. But acting on your attraction to her? That's just trouble calling your name."

Trouble with a capital *T*. Unfortunately, he'd felt that trouble calling his name ever since he'd arrived in Paris. Trouble in the form of a small woman with soft skin, smiling eyes and a mouth that tasted like bright sunshine on a gray day.

Had she joked with the guy that she chose dance partners based on who would buy her a drink? The thought squeezed his chest so tight he had to force out his response to Jess.

"Since when are you my guardian angel? Believe me, I know all of that, and you don't have to worry. I'm keeping my distance." At least, he'd managed to for the past week or so.

"Guess you'd better run, then, because she's heading toward our table."

He stiffened and turned. Then couldn't help the relief he stupidly felt when Dr. Frenchman wasn't with her. And hoped like hell he wasn't looking at Avery the same way that guy still was, watching her from a corner table.

"Dr. Dunbar, may I speak with you for just a moment?" Avery asked when she stopped in front of them, her gaze flicking from him to Jessica and back.

He sat back, trying to pretend she didn't affect him in any way, which stretched his acting skills to the limit. "What's on your mind?"

She stood silently for a moment. Jack took in how perfectly the yellow shift dress she wore fit her slim body. How she folded one hand over the other in a nervous gesture before she stilled them against her sides. How her silky eyebrows twitched the way he'd noticed before when she pondered what to say.

"I wanted to suggest that, when you have a day off soon, you let me show you—"

As though pulled by a string from some invisible puppeteer, he reached out to grasp her wrist, tugging her down onto the bench seat. Her hip bumped into his as her eyes widened in surprise. Jessica's presence had nearly helped him resist the urge but, God help him, the hot jealousy that had grabbed him by the throat took control. Wanting to send a message to the guy still sitting across the room. Prompting Jack to say what he couldn't stop thinking about, and before he knew it the words were coming out of his mouth.

"Show me the correct way to use an umbrella?" Of its own accord, his voice went lower as he dipped his head, his lips nearly touching hers. "Or explain the mysteries of chemistry and spontaneous combustion? In which case, we can find a more private place to talk."

She stared at him, and even through the darkness of the bar he could see the surprise and confusion on her face. "Um, no. I wanted to talk to you about the trial."

"What about it?"

"With three patients already experiencing valve leakage, I'm sure you see why I'm concerned."

He watched her lips move, thinking about how good it was to kiss her. Let his gaze travel to the V of skin below her throat, which he knew was soft and warm. "The trial's barely started. We haven't had nearly enough patients to come to any kind of conclusions yet."

"I know. But as I said before, sometimes there are red flags right away." Deeply serious, her green eyes locked with his. "I want to introduce you to a patient who underwent one of the first TAVI procedures with my original device. I'd like you to see what he's living with."

He laughed, disgusted with himself. While he couldn't stop thinking about the taste of her mouth and the softness of her skin, she didn't seem to be having any trouble focusing on work.

He realized he was still holding onto her wrist, and dropped it. "I know what people with postoperative complications live with, Avery. I treat them every day."

"Just think about my offer." As she lifted her hand to his shoulder, a part of him liked having it there, while the saner part reminded him she'd just had that same hand on Dr. Frenchman's shoulder. "You might find it enlightening to meet this man and his family."

She slid from the seat and walked away. To Jack's surprise, she didn't sit with Dr. Frenchman. Instead, she exited the bar entirely, and he was glad he didn't have to watch her cozy up to the man, at the same time annoyed as hell that he felt that way.

What was it about this woman? First he'd grabbed her and pulled her down next to him like he had a right to. And in spite of it being a beyond-bad idea, every time he looked at her, all he could think of was how much he'd enjoyed being with her and kissing her and having sex with her. How much he wanted more of all of it.

"Boy, you've got it bad." Jessica shook her head. "I hope you can keep from getting so tangled up with her that you lose perspective on what we came here to do."

As he watched Avery's bright yellow, curvy behind disappear into the hotel foyer, he could only hope for the same thing.

CHAPTER SEVEN

AVERY STEPPED OFF the hotel elevator to head to the front doors, then stood frozen when she saw Jack standing right where she wanted to go. An absurdly handsome Jack, wearing a pale blue dress shirt, necktie and sport coat.

She and Jack had been friendly but professional over the past two days of surgeries and patient follow-ups, and she hoped it could stay that way. Without the uncomfortable attraction that remained in a low hum between them. The attraction that had clearly prompted Jack to do the caveman thing and pull her down next to him after she'd danced with the French doc she'd met. Jessica was walking toward him, and Jack's mouth tipped into a smile when he spotted her. Normally wearing scrubs all day, Jessica had dressed up tonight, looking very attractive in a black dress with a coat slung over her arm. Obviously, the two were going to dinner somewhere, and when Jessica reached Jack she said something that made him laugh.

Could there be something going on between them, now that she and Jack had agreed to keep their professional distance?

The thought twisted her stomach in a strange little

knot, which was ridiculous. Must be just a residual re-action to the shock of her ex cheating on her.

Still, the thought of walking past Jack and Jessica to leave the hotel made her feel uncomfortable, though that wasn't very mature. Hoping they'd move on to wherever they were going, she saw Jack pull his phone from his pocket. In just seconds his expression went from relaxed to a deep frown, and the sudden tension in his posture was clear even from all the way across the room.

Jack shoved his phone back into his pocket, spoke briefly to Jessica, and pushed open the doors to head out into the night. Was there a problem with a patient? Without thinking, Avery hurried to talk to Jessica, to see if there was anything she could help with.

"Jessica?"

The woman turned, and when she saw Avery the concern on her face morphed into a neutral expression. "Yes?"

"I couldn't help but notice that Jack ran out of here quickly. Is something wrong?"

Jessica seemed to study her before she answered. "One of the patients we performed surgery on today is experiencing slurred speech and weakness in one arm."

Obviously, a possible stroke. "Which patient?"

"Henri Arnoult."

"All right. Thanks." Avery took a step toward the doors to head over there, but Jessica's hand on her arm stopped her.

"There's nothing you can do, Dr. Girard. He'll either make it or he won't, and you know as well as I do that stroke is one of the major risks of any kind of surgery involving stents."

"I do know. But it's my job to record every bit of data

on every patient, whether it's a normal complication or not, and whether it's a good outcome or a bad one."

"Jack told me you have some concerns about this TAVI device. I hope your personal bias wouldn't interfere with—or influence—that data."

"I don't have any personal bias. Concerns, yes. Bias, no." Jessica regarded her with clear skepticism, and Avery sighed. "Listen. I appreciate that you support Jack, and I assure you that any and all data I record and analyze will be done carefully and scientifically. I'd love for this trial to be a success as much as you do."

"Good. Jack is the best surgeon I've ever worked with, and this groundbreaking work is extremely important to him. Important to heart patients, too."

"I know."

"Okay," Jessica said, nodding. "Please ask Jack to let me know how things go. Even if it's in the middle of the night."

"I will." As soon as Avery pushed open the door, cold wind whipped down her neck and up her dress. She closed her coat as tightly as she could and hurried the two blocks to the hospital.

She found Jack in the patient's room in the ICU, talking to the house doctor who had likely been the one to call him in. Avery hung back, not wanting to intrude inappropriately. It seemed like forever before the house doctor finally left the room. Avery inhaled a fortifying breath before she entered. Jack stood there, his back to the door, his hands in his pockets, looking down at the patient lying in the bed. She moved to stand beside him, her heart sinking when she saw that Mr. Arnoult was unconscious and connected to a breathing machine.

Without thinking, she tucked her hand through the

crook of Jack's arm and his elbow, pressing it close against his side. "These are the tough days, I know, Jack," she said softly. "Do you know what's wrong?"

"He seemed fine when I saw him this afternoon. But I'm told his blood pressure soared and his speech became slurred, so they quickly got a CAT scan. Which confirmed he's had a large hemorrhagic stroke."

"It's not impossible that his condition could improve."

"No. Not impossible. We've given him meds to try to control the brain swelling, among other things, but I don't know. It's a big bleed."

"Have you…checked to see how the TAVI looks? Is it still in place?"

"Not yet. I just ordered an echocardiogram. I hope to God it hasn't moved, because there's no way he could survive open-heart surgery on top of this. Hell, he wouldn't have survived that kind of surgery before this." A deep sigh lifted his chest. "I suppose this is more confirmation to you that the trial might be premature."

He turned to look at her as he spoke, his eyes somber with concern. Her heart filled with the certain knowledge that it was for this ill man and not concern for himself or for the future of the trial.

"Will it shock you when I say no?" She pulled her hand from his arm to rest it against his cheek. "Risk of stroke is an unfortunate complication of any procedure like this. Give an elderly patient with serious underlying health problems the blood thinners necessary for this kind of surgery, and sometimes it doesn't go the way everyone hopes it will. It's no one's fault. It's not your fault or the device's fault. It just is."

He stared down at her for a suspended moment before, to her surprise, he gathered her in his arms. Another deep sigh feathered across her forehead as he rested his head on top of hers. She pushed aside his necktie before pressing her cheek against his chest, and she wrapped her arms around him, too, since he clearly needed that connection right now. He smelled wonderful, just as he had on their first day together, holding her close beneath that umbrella, and she found herself closing her eyes at the pleasure of it as she breathed him in.

"I'd hoped we wouldn't have any catastrophic events," he said as his hand stroked slowly up and down her back. "But you're right. It is a reality that this happens sometimes. And I appreciate you not making it even worse by stomping up and down and yelling about it."

"Wow. Sounds like you think I'm a troll or something."

"A troll?" She could hear the smile in his voice. "That, I've gotta say, never occurred to me."

It took great force of will for Avery to lean back and break the close contact between them. She glanced at Mr. Arnoult and the steadily beeping monitors and figured they should continue their conversation elsewhere.

"I could use some coffee. You?"

At his nod, she took his hand and they walked to the nearly empty coffee shop on the first floor. Sitting at a round table so tiny their knees kept bumping, Avery sipped her espresso before asking the question she needed to know the answer to. "Jessica seemed to think I might skew the data based on what she called my bias about the device. Do you, too?"

"Honestly?" He quirked a dark eyebrow. "I'd be lying if I said it hadn't crossed my mind."

Her chest ached a little at his words. Obviously, there'd be no friendship between them if that was how he felt. And she realized, without a doubt, that she very much wanted that friendship. More than friendship, but under the circumstances friendship was all they could have.

And even friendship was probably a bad idea, considering Jack didn't know all that Crilex had hired her to do.

"I find, though, that for some damned reason," he continued as he leaned closer, his mouth only inches from hers, "the uncertainty seems to turn me on."

A startled laugh left her lips. "And my wondering if you're different or the same as most other cardiologists apparently has kept me interested, as well."

He leaned closer still, so close his nose nearly touched hers. "Or maybe it's that we just have this undeniable chemistry that refuses to be snuffed out by little things like that."

The timbre of his voice, the expression in his dark eyes made her a little breathless. "Well, I did get straight As in chemistry. It's something I'm good at."

"Now, that I already knew." He closed the tiny gap between them and gave her the softest of kisses. "I'm going to go check on Mr. Arnoult again and see if the echocardiogram's been done. You might as well go on back to the hotel, or wherever you were going to go tonight, and collect his data tomorrow. Unless your plan was to go out with Dr. Frenchman. He's a total player, and even more egotistical than I am."

"You mean the man I danced with?" Was it wrong

of her to be pleased at the tinge of jealousy in his voice, to know that he'd noticed and had obviously been bothered by it? Was it also wrong of her that she'd secretly hoped he would, even though she'd been disgusted with herself when the thought had occurred to her? "I didn't realize you knew him."

"I don't. I just know his kind."

"Uh-huh. Aren't you the man who told me I shouldn't judge you negatively just because of what you do for a living?"

"That's totally different. Trust me, I know how guys think and saw the way he was looking at you."

"What way?"

"Like I do." She'd never known something like a hot twinkle existed, but there it was in his eyes as he stood. "I'm going to spend the night here so I can keep tabs on Mr. Arnoult."

A sudden desire to stay right here with him, supporting him, came over her, but she knew it didn't make a lot of sense. She wasn't Mr. Arnoult's family, she wasn't a medical doctor, and she and Jack needed to keep a professional distance. Though, at that moment, as her gaze stayed connected with his, she knew with certainty that was getting more difficult every day.

Concern for Mr. Arnoult and thoughts of Jack staying up much of the night, working, left Avery unable to sleep well, either. Up early and in the hospital just after 7:00 a.m., she stopped in the hospital coffee shop to get double shots of espresso for both her and Jack, knowing she'd find him there somewhere.

She checked Mr. Arnoult's room first, relieved to see Jack was there, able to drink his coffee while it was still somewhat hot. Her heart squeezed the second she saw him standing next to the patient's bed, his dark head tipped toward the nurse and another doctor as he spoke to them.

Mr. Arnoult was still connected to the ventilator, and from her distance by the door it appeared he was still unconscious or heavily sedated. The squeeze in her chest tightened when she saw his head was thickly bandaged, which most likely meant they'd decided to try draining the hemorrhaging blood from around his brain.

Jack glanced up as she entered the room, and his gaze held hers for a moment before he finished his conversation and walked to meet her in the doorway.

"I could smell that coffee all the way across the room," he said. His hair was uncharacteristically messy, dark stubble covered his cheeks, and the lines at the corners of his eyes were more pronounced. "Nothing better than a woman who understands a caffeine addiction."

"I nearly got you a triple, but thought maybe I could get you to go to the coffee shop I took you to that first day. It would be good for you to get out of the hospital for a breath of air."

He shook his head. "Not yet. Maybe later."

"How is he?"

He grasped her elbow and led her down the hall to the little office he'd been working from, pulling the single chair from behind the desk for her to sit on.

"No, you sit," she said, perching on the side of the desk. "You're the one who's been up most of the night."

"If I sit, I might fall asleep." He set down his coffee, giving her a shadow of a smile as he took hold of both her shoulders and gently lowered her into the chair. "A woman who brings coffee deserves not only the chair but being draped in gold, like you said women should be."

"Well, coffee is worth its weight in gold." She sipped her espresso and resisted the urge to ask again about Mr. Arnoult. Forced herself to be patient and wait for him to speak when he was ready.

With his body propped against the side of the desk and long legs stretched out, he drank his coffee and stared out the door. Just when she thought she couldn't keep silent another second, he put his cup down and turned to her. "Things aren't good. We couldn't control his brain swelling, so the neurosurgeon drained the blood from his brain about two this morning. I had hoped that releasing the pressure would work, but the swelling continued. Tests show there's now severe, irreversible brain damage—his pupils are fixed and dilated. No movement of his extremities, no gag reflex. Just received CAT scan images that confirm it. Which I'm going to have to share with the family when they get here."

"I'm so sorry, Jack." She stood and moved in front of him to hold both his hands in hers. "I know this is never the outcome anyone wants. But as I said yesterday, we both know this risk exists in a patient like him. He was extremely ill before the procedure. You'd hoped to give him a new lease on life, which he had no chance of having without replacing his valve, and he wouldn't have made it through open-heart surgery for that. You tried your best."

He released her hands, his tired eyes meeting hers. "Thanks for all that. I do appreciate it. I know it, but it still feels crappy."

Without thinking, she slipped her hands around his neck and kissed him. Just like she had in front of the Sacré Coeur. This time, it was to comfort him, soothe him. But the moment her lips touched his, the moment his arms wrapped around her and held her close, the moment his warm, soft mouth moved against hers she nearly forgot the goal was comfort and not something entirely different.

But they were in an office attached to a busy corridor, which both of them seemed to remember at the same time. Their lips separated, and she rested her head on his shoulder as she hugged him, working on the comfort part again, stuffing down the other feelings that wanted to erupt.

It felt good to hold him. Felt good to try to offer him comfort. But as the moment grew longer, warmer, she reminded herself that she was there for another reason, too. She should ask him about the prosthetic valve and if he'd checked it or not, but she didn't want to break the closeness they were sharing. Not quite yet, anyway. The valve wasn't the reason the man had had the original stroke, and she'd find out soon enough if it had moved or leaked after the brain had begun to bleed.

Apparently, though, this connection between her and Jack seemed to include mind reading. "I already know you well enough to guess you're dying to know about the valve," he said, loosening his hold on her to lean back. "We've done two separate Doppler echocardiograms, neither of which showed any fluid flow around it. It's fitting tight as a drum, which makes me all the sadder that he stroked before he could enjoy his life a little more."

She nodded. "That's encouraging for other patients

but, yes, it's very sad for Mr. Arnoult. Would you like for me to join you when you talk to the family?"

"No. This is a part of what I do. The hardest part, but the buck has to stop with me."

She nodded again, and instantly pictured the caring and sympathy that Jack would show the man's family when he shared the bad news, because it was obvious that was simply a part of who he was.

"Then I'll leave you. How about letting me give you a little TLC later? I'm good at that." As soon as the words came out of her mouth and a touch of humor lit his eyes, she knew how he'd interpreted it. And found her heart fluttering, even though that wasn't how she'd meant it.

"I bet you are. And despite us agreeing we shouldn't mix business with pleasure, I can't seem to keep all that in the forefront of my mind when you're around." He tipped up her chin. "Something else seems to take over instead. Like serious anticipation of some TLC from you."

He gave her a glimmer of a smile, his dark eyes connecting with hers for a long, arrested moment. Then he kissed her in the sweetest of touches. The rasp of his beard gently abraded her skin, and he tasted of coffee and of deliciousness, and she could have kept on kissing him for a long, long time. But his lips left hers to track, feather-light, up her cheek and linger on her forehead before he drew back. "Thanks for being here. I'll find you later, okay? Maybe dinner?"

She'd barely had time to respond before he left the room, his posture proud and erect despite the exhaustion he had to be feeling. And at that moment she knew with certainty that Jack was nothing like her old boyfriends. He had an integrity and warmth and depth they couldn't even begin to match.

Avery concentrated on seeing all the patients who were still in the hospital after their procedures, carefully recording their vitals, test results, state of mind and comfort levels. But throughout those hours she often found herself thinking of Jack having to continue on and do his job. How he'd still operated on the patient scheduled for early that morning, his focus never wavering throughout the procedure as she'd watched, despite the obvious fatigue in his eyes.

She'd bumped into him once, rounding on patients, spending a long time talking with each of them, recording his own notes. She wondered if he'd spoken with Mr. Arnoult's family yet, and her chest tightened at how tough that was going to be on all of them.

As she moved down the hall to see a different patient, she heard the rumble of his voice in Mr. Arnoult's room and the sound of quiet weeping. Her stomach clenched, and when she glanced in she saw two middle-aged men standing, flanking an elderly woman who sat in a chair, dabbing her face with a crumpled tissue. Jack was crouched in front of her, one hand patting her shoulder, the other giving her another tissue he'd pulled from the box on a chair next to her.

Avery found herself pressing her hands to her tight chest at the sweet and gentle way Jack was talking with the woman, the deeply caring expression on his face. A part of her wanted to go into the room and stand next to him for support, but she knew he wouldn't want or need that. It wasn't her place to spy or eavesdrop, either, and she quickly moved on to the last patient she needed to see.

At that moment, she knew she wanted to somehow help him feel better about it all. While she knew this was far from the first time in his career he'd had to deliver bad news to a family, and certainly wouldn't be the last, giving him a reason to smile suddenly became her priority for the day.

How, though? They'd already been up the Eiffel Tower and seen the Sacré Coeur at sunset. Her mind spun through her favorite places in Paris, but many of them were more fun to go to in the summertime, when you were lucky enough to enjoy some sunshine and the gardens were glorious. Still, there was something to be said for just walking the city on a cold night, cuddling to stay warm on a bench in one of the gardens or by the Seine.

Cuddling? Her plan for the evening was about cheering Jack up, not kissing him or having sex or anything like that.

Except she'd be lying to herself if she pretended that she hadn't thought about throwing aside the very good reasons they shouldn't be together for one more memorable night. A night to help him forget a very long and difficult day. Knowing it would be more than memorable for her, too, would be the icing on the cake.

CHAPTER EIGHT

AVERY'S HEART, WHICH only moments ago had felt all bubbly at the thought of spending the evening with Jack and finding ways to make him happy, stuttered, then ground to a halt.

Standing stock still now just outside the doorway to Jack's office, she stared at what seemed like a reenactment of her warm and intimate time in that room with him earlier. A woman had her arms wrapped around his waist, and he held her close with his cheek resting on her head.

But unless Avery was watching some holographic image of that moment in time, Jack was not holding her. He was holding a different woman.

Jessica.

Barely able to breathe, Avery backed up a few steps, then turned to hightail it out of there.

She'd become completely, utterly convinced he wasn't at all like the last two doctors she'd been involved with, which proved how incredibly bad she must be at judging character. Clearly, every one of them charmed, lied and cheated as easily as they breathed, and she thrashed herself for forgetting. For thinking Jack was different.

She stalked down the hall, her throat tight with embarrassment as she thought of the really good fantasies she'd been dreaming up about their night together. Gullible idiot. Fool. IQ genius with no brains.

"Avery." Jack's voice and footsteps followed her, and she walked faster. "Avery, stop, damn it!"

His fingers curled around her arm, turning her toward him. She yanked her arm from his hold. "What is it, Dr. Dunbar? It's been a long day, and I have a date." A date with herself and her computer and her work, which she'd just remembered she'd promised herself would be her only focus until she'd let a certain man change her mind about that.

"Your date is with me. And if you're running off in a huff because I was hugging Jessica, you know damned well that she's married."

"Like that matters to some people."

"It matters to me. And to her. We've worked together for three years. She's my coworker and my friend. And as my friend, she felt bad about Henri Arnoult. Just like you did. That's all." He grasped both her arms this time, tugging her closer. "It's been a hell of a bad day. Mr. Arnoult's family had to make the hard decision to take him off the ventilator. We had to let him go. And, yeah, that's one damned difficult part of being a doctor, and I'm tired inside and out. The last thing I want is for you to be upset and thinking things that are all wrong."

She stared into his dark eyes, which were filled with frustration and exhaustion and worry. Could she have been wrong? Jumped to conclusions too fast? And hadn't she wanted to comfort him, not add to his stress, if she was wrong?

She definitely didn't want to make his day any worse

than it already had been. But her heart didn't feel up to being exposed to more punishment, either. "Listen. I think it's a good idea for you and Jessica to be together tonight. She knows you better than I do, and you'll have a nice time, I'm sure."

"Except that, even though I shouldn't, I want to know you better." He glanced down the hall, which was fairly quiet this late in the day, before turning back again, lifting his hands to cup her cheeks. "After the great time we've spent together, how could you even think I might have something going on with Jess?"

She stared up into his eyes and could see he really wanted to know. But she didn't feel like sharing her past. Her embarrassment that she hadn't seen her exes for who they were.

"I didn't. Not really. I was just being weird."

His eyes crinkled at the corners in a smile. "The only way you're remotely weird is the odd color combinations you sometimes favor." His thumb stroked along her cheekbone before he bent his head and kissed her. Maybe it was stupid, but the soft warmth of his lips managed to sap every ounce of the worry and self-deprecation she'd felt just moments ago. The feel of his mouth slowly moving on hers sent all of that to the outer reaches of her brain and her thoughts back to the fantasies she'd been having before she'd seen him with Jessica and freaked.

He broke the kiss, and the eyes that met hers were so sincere she knew she couldn't let what had happened with her stupid exes mess with her mind anymore. No way did she want to live her life suspicious of people and their possible agendas, backing away from potential pain instead of exploring all the wonderful things the world had to offer.

That Jack just might have to offer, if their potentially disastrous professional relationship didn't ruin everything before they had a chance to spend more time together.

"It would sure be nice to kiss you without knowing there are hundreds of people who might be spying on us at any moment. Which is pretty much the only times we've kissed so far. Let's get out of here."

She wanted that, too, but felt she had to ask about Jessica's plans. After all, the woman probably had nothing to do, and maybe she shouldn't hog Jack all to herself. Even though that was all she wanted, darn it. "Shouldn't we ask Jessica to join us for dinner?"

"One of the reasons she was happy to come and assist me in the trial here is because she has a cousin with three little kids living in Paris. She's enjoying spending time with them. And even if she wasn't," he added, his eyes gleaming, "I wouldn't ask her along. Three's a crowd, and you're the one who said you're good at TLC and offered to comfort me, right?"

"I did make that offer, though you probably don't need it. You're pretty tough, I know."

"Tough or not, a guy always appreciates some TLC from a beautiful woman. Looking forward to being with you tonight is the only thing that made today bearable." He placed his mouth close to her ear, and his words, the rumble in his voice, made her shiver. "I know you don't back out on your promises. And I can't wait to be on the receiving end of some tender, loving care from the talented Dr. Girard."

* * *

Chilly wind nipped what little skin they had exposed, and Jack watched Avery tug her blue and purple scarf more tightly around her neck. Figured it was the perfect excuse to hold her even closer to his side as they walked through the Palais-Royal gardens. Though gardens would be an overstatement at the moment, since everything was dormant from winter, and the only things remotely green were the carefully trimmed evergreen shrubs.

"I love this park in the summertime, when all the roses are in bloom and you can sit and enjoy the quiet and seclusion from the busyness of the city," Avery said, smiling at him, her cute nose very pink from the cold. "And the trees are trimmed in an arching canopy that's fun to walk beneath on the way to the fountain. I'm sorry it's not all that pretty right now."

"You're sorry because you could do something about it being the end of January? Are you a magician as well as a scientist?"

"Wouldn't that be nice?" She laughed. "Sadly, no. I just wish I could show you the Paris I love all year round, but we'll have to settle for now."

Her words struck him with a surprising thought, which was that he wished for that, too. For more than just these brief weeks with her. But that wasn't meant to be. He had his work and his TAVI trials, which would take him to various parts of the world, and finally, assuming all went well, to trials back in the States. He didn't have time in his life for any kind of real relationship and felt a pang of regret about that reality.

"I'm enjoying the now with you," he said. "What's the next part of now, Ms. Tour Guide?"

"Let's pop into a few of these boutiques. Anything in particular you like to look at? Or want to buy?"

"Yes. The one thing I particularly like to look at is you." Which had been true from the moment he'd met her. He tugged her close enough that her steamy breath mingled in the cold air with his own. "And I'd like to buy a thin gold chain to slip around your neck, except you'd accuse me of being an egotistical player again. When the only reason would be to please you. Okay, and touch your skin, too. I'm definitely looking for ways to make that happen."

She blushed cutely, and he loved the humor that shone in her green eyes. "You don't have to buy me gifts to make that happen."

Maybe she saw exactly where his thoughts had immediately gone, because she stepped out of his hold to walk through the doorway of a little shop.

"In truth, I'm into this kind of thing more than gold," she said as she picked up a delicate, inlaid wooden box.

"Music boxes? Any special kind?"

"I love old ones. But any kind makes me smile. Like lots of little girls, I had one with a dancing ballerina and fell in love with them after that." She opened the lid and a tune began to play. An adorable smile lit her face and eyes, making him smile, too. "Isn't it beautiful?"

"Beautiful." He damned near took it from her hand to buy it for her, but was sure she'd protest. It would probably make her feel uncomfortable to receive a gift from him at that point in their relationship—or whatever you'd call the powerful force that kept drawing him to her.

They stared at one another, and the hum in the air between them was so strong it nearly drowned out the soft tune tinkling between them. She put the box down and, to his surprise, grabbed his hand and trotted quickly out of the store, the sexy blue ankle boots she wore clicking on the pavement.

"Where to now?" he asked.

"I just thought of something that would be fun to do with you."

He hoped that "something" was her hauling him off to the hotel to get naked for the TLC she'd promised, but had a feeling that was wishful thinking. "And that would be?"

"This." They ran until they got to a carousel, the music filling the air around it not all that different from the music box, except a lot louder. She jumped onto its platform, turning to him with the bright eyes and brilliant smile he'd come to see in his dreams. "Come on! Which horse do you want?"

"Whichever you're on."

She laughed and walked between the rows of wooden animals, finally straddling a white horse with a bright green saddle and carved mane that looked to be flying in the wind. Jack swung himself up behind her. As her rear pressed against his groin, as he wrapped one arm around her waist and one hand on top of hers on the pole, as he breathed in the scent of her hair and her skin, he knew he'd never see another carousel without remembering this moment with her.

"I never knew I loved merry-go-rounds until this moment," he murmured in her ear.

"Doesn't everybody?"

"Everybody lucky enough to have a gorgeous woman sharing their horse."

The music grew louder, and as the carousel began

to turn, their horse rose and fell, pushing his body into hers, rubbing them together. And damned if even through their clothes and jackets it wasn't just about the most erotic thing he'd ever experienced outside a bedroom.

He tried to scoot back, away from her a little, so she wouldn't feel exactly how aroused he was, but had a feeling she already knew. He dipped his head and let his lips wander over what skin he could reach, which wasn't nearly enough. Her cheek and jaw, her nose, her eyebrow. Her soft hair tickled his face as he nibbled her earlobe, tracing the shell of her ear with his tongue until her sexy gasp, the shiver of her skin he could feel against his lips, took every molecule of air from his lungs and sent him on a quest for her mouth.

The arm he had wrapped around her tightened as he lifted his hand from the pole to grasp her chin in his fingers, turning her face so he could taste her lips. Her eyes met his, a dark moss green now, full of the same desire he knew she could see in his.

Her head tipped back against his collarbone, and he covered her mouth with his and kissed her. Kissed her until he wasn't sure if the spinning sensation he felt was from the earth turning, the carousel revolving, the horse rising and falling or his brain reeling from Avery overload.

The sound of people laughing and talking seeped into his lust-fogged brain, and apparently Avery's, too, as they both slowly broke the kiss, staring at one another, the panting breaths between them now so steamy he could barely see her moist, still-parted lips. He brushed his thumb against her lush lower lip, and it was all he could do not to kiss her again.

"Didn't I say I'd like to kiss you, just once, without people standing around, watching?" he said when he was able to talk. "I don't think this accomplishes that."

She gave him a breathy laugh. "No. So let's accomplish it now."

As the carousel slowed to a stop, he slid from the horse, then helped her down. "Any ideas on how?"

"Oh, yeah." Her lips curved, and the only word to describe her expression would be *sensual*, which kicked his pulse into an even faster rhythm than it was already galloping in. "They don't call me the 'idea gal' for nothing."

CHAPTER NINE

JUST LIKE THE first time—the one she'd been sure would be the only time—Jack had her coat and blouse off before she'd barely drawn a breath. Time to get with the program and get his coat off, too. Her fingers weren't quite as swift as his talented surgeon ones, and she wrestled to get it unbuttoned.

He shrugged it off and tossed it on top of hers before reaching to touch his thumb to the top of her bra as he had before, slowly tracing the curve of it, and her breath backed up in her lungs at the expression in his eyes, at the low, rough sound of his voice. "Bright blue lace this time. Hard to decide if I like this or your pretty white one better."

"I have matching panties on. Does that help?"

His eyes gleamed in response. "Don't care if they match. I can't wait to see you in them." He lowered his mouth to hers, softly, sweetly, before moving it across her jaw, down to her collar bone, slipping farther until his tongue traced the lacy top of her bra. Sliding down to gently suck her nipple through the silky fabric until her knees wobbled. Avery clutched the front of his shirt, hanging on tight, wondering if she just might faint from lack of oxygen and the excruciating pleasure of it all.

She wanted to see his skin, too. Wanted to touch him and lick him, as well. "No fair that you're ahead of me," she managed to say, reaching for the buttons of his shirt. "No more distractions until I get your shirt off."

He lifted his head, ending his damp exploration of her bra, and his dark eyes gleamed into hers as she attempted to wrangle his buttons. "Happy to assist, if you'd like."

Oh, yes. She'd like. Mesmerized, she stared as he flicked open one button at a time, slowly exposing the fine, dark hair on his smooth skin, before finally pulling the shirt off entirely. About to reach for him, she lifted her gaze to his. Saw that his focus was on her breasts, and the hunger in his eyes sent her heart pounding even harder.

"You have one beautiful body, Dr. Girard."

"Funny, I was just thinking the same about you, Dr. Dunbar."

With a smile, he closed the gap between them, reached behind her, and in one quick motion had her bra unhooked, off her arms and onto the floor. His hand cupped her breast and his thumb moved slowly back and forth across her nipple until her knees nearly buckled.

"As I said before, those are some quick fingers you have, Dr. Dunbar. Should have known you were a surgeon or guitarist or something." She pressed her palms to his hard chest, sliding them through the dark, soft hair covering it. On up to wrap her arms behind his neck, holding him close, loving the feel of his body against hers as she moved backward, bringing him with her.

"You haven't seen anything yet," he said in a gruff voice so full of promise she found herself mindlessly touching her tongue to his jaw to taste him as she pressed her body to his. His mouth moved to capture hers as they continued their slow meander to the bed. She didn't even realize he'd unbuttoned her pants, too, until she felt his hands moving on her bottom, inside her silky underwear and on down her thighs until every scrap of clothing was pooled at her feet.

She gasped in surprise, which sent the kiss deeper. Until the backs of her legs hit the bed, and the impact jolted her mouth from his. He stared at her a moment before he slowly kneeled, pulling her undies and pants off her ankles as he nipped and licked her knees, making her jerk and laugh.

"Stop that," she said. "My knees are ticklish."

He grasped her calves as his tongue slipped across the inside of one knee, then the other, interspersed with tiny nibbles. "How ticklish?"

"Very." She gasped and wriggled, the sensation of his teeth and tongue on her bones and skin both sensitive and exciting. "And if you don't stop, it's not my fault if my reflexes send one up to crack you in the jaw."

"Risk noted." His hands slipped up to widen her legs as his tongue moved on in a shivery path to her inner thighs. "But I think we already agreed that life is full of risk. If it's potentially dangerous to taste you all over, then, believe me, that's a risk I'm more than happy to take."

Her breath coming in embarrassing little pants now as he moved northward, she knew it was time to change direction. While part of her wanted, more than anything, for his mouth to keep going to the part of her currently quivering in anticipation, it seemed that mutual pleasure was more in order.

"Come up here and kiss me." She placed her hands on his smooth shoulders, trying to tug him back up.

"I am kissing you." And, boy, he sure was. His lips were pressing inch by torturous inch against her shivering flesh.

"My mouth. Kiss my mouth." She tugged harder at his shoulders. If she didn't get him away from where he was headed, she knew she just might combust. "I'm the one who's supposed to be administering TLC here, remember?"

He lifted his gaze to hers. His eyes were heavy-lidded with desire, but touched with amusement, too, and the smile he gave her was full of pure, masculine satisfaction. "For some reason, I forgot. Probably because I'm already feeling much less stressed. But if it will make you happy, who am I to argue?"

With one last kiss so high on her inner thigh she nearly groaned, he got to his feet. Which reminded her he still had his pants on, while she was sitting there utterly naked. His gaze traveled across every inch of her skin, hot enough to scorch, and she was a little surprised that his perusal was exciting instead of embarrassing.

She reached for his pants and undid them, happy that he took charge and quickly finished off the job. Then stared at the now very visible confirmation that he was every bit as aroused as she was.

"So now what, Dr. Girard?" He placed his hands on the bed, flanking her hips, and leaned close. "The TLC ball is in your court."

She gulped. All the things she'd fantasized about seemed to have vacated her mind, along with every rational thought. Except how much she wanted to grab him and pull him on top of her and feel him deep inside.

"I...I can't remember exactly what I had in mind to soothe you and make you feel better. Give me a minute."

"That's okay," he said between pressing soft kisses to her mouth. "As I said, I already feel a whole lot better. Expecting to feel even better real soon."

His strong hands wrapped around her waist and he lifted her up to him, nudging her legs around his waist as he kissed her again. She was vaguely aware of the sound of the covers being yanked back and the cool sheets touching her skin at the same time Jack's hot body covered hers.

"I've realized the one thing that will soothe me the most," he whispered against her lips.

"What?"

"Making you feel good." He kissed her again. His body was deliciously heavy on hers as his hands stroked her everywhere, exciting and tantalizing. Their kiss grew deeper, wilder as his talented fingers finally delved into her moist core until she feared he might bring her to climax with just his touch.

Then the sudden, harsh ring of her hotel phone startled them both, sending their teeth clacking together. "Holy hell!" Jack frowned. "Are you okay?"

With her breath still short, she slid her fingers across his moist lips. "No blood, I don't think. You?"

"Fine. More than fine." His eyes gleamed into hers. "Except for the damned interruption just when things were getting very...soothing."

She chuckled breathily as they both turned their heads to the still-ringing phone.

"Do you need to get that?" he asked.

Was he kidding? Even if it was the French president, she wasn't about to talk on the phone at that moment.

"Whoever it is will leave a message. Or call back. Now, where were we?" She reached for him, squeezed, and the moan he gave in response sent her heart pumping faster and her legs around his waist in silent invitation.

He quickly ripped open a condom. "About to get to the next step in making us both feel good," he said, grasping her hips as they joined. Slowly, wonderfully, but as the tension grew she had to urge him to move faster, deeper. The room seemed to spin dizzily like the carousel had, but this time there were no barriers between them. She held on tight, loving the taste of him and the feel of him, until she cried out in release, wrenching a deep groan from his chest as he followed.

Jack buried his face in her neck, their gasping breaths seeming loud in the quiet of the room. Until another sound disturbed her bone-melting, utter relaxation and tranquility—the muffled ringing of a cell phone.

Jack lifted his head and looked down at the floor with a frown. "Who the hell keeps bothering us? I hope nothing's happened at the hospital."

He dropped a kiss on her mouth, lingering there, before he got up and dug his phone from the pocket of his discarded pants. Avery enjoyed the very sexy view of him, standing there comfortably naked, his skin covered with a sheen of sweat.

"Dr. Dunbar."

She watched his frown deepen and sat up, beginning to get alarmed. Hopefully this wasn't a crisis with a patient.

"And you can't give me some idea what this is about now?" he asked. "Fine. I'll be there."

"What is it?"

"I don't know." His warm body lay next to hers

again, propped on his elbow. "Bob Timkin wants to meet with me—with both of us—tomorrow morning at eight. Says he has to talk to me right away about something to do with the trial."

"What? Why?"

"He wouldn't say. You don't happen to know, do you?"

The pleasure of the evening began to fade at the expression on his face. Beyond serious. Maybe even a touch suspicious? She couldn't even imagine how he'd react if he knew Crilex had given her the power to shut down the trial if she deemed it necessary, and the thought chilled her formerly very toasty body. "No. I don't. If I did, I'd tell you."

"Did you tell him you were concerned about the number of patients who've had the valve leak? You know I feel strongly that we haven't treated nearly enough patients to make any kind of judgment on that yet."

"Of course I didn't speak with him about Mr. Arnoult. For one thing, I haven't had a chance to finish compiling the data on his...situation. And I also told you I know the valve design was not why he died."

A long sigh left him before his mouth touched hers with a sweet, tender connection at odds with the tense tone of his voice. His finger tracked down her cheek before he slipped from the bed and got dressed, his expression impassive when he turned to her.

"I wish mixing...this...with work didn't create a hell of a complication for both of us. But there's no getting around it that it does." He stepped to the bed and took her chin in his hand, tilting her face up for another soft kiss. "Thank you for the TLC tonight. Sweet dreams."

And then he was gone, the door closing behind him

with a sharp click. A whirl of emotions filled her chest, and she didn't know which one took center stage in her heart. Frustration that he still clearly didn't completely trust her to report the data scientifically and not emotionally? Disappointment, even sadness, that this obvious "thing" they had between them was a huge problem because of their jobs? Anxiety, knowing he would definitely not like having been kept in the dark about her authority to decide if the trial was rolled out further or not?

She flopped back onto the bed, her body still feeling the remnants of their lovemaking, and remembered how wonderful every second of it had felt.

Now, instead of stealing a kiss or two with him tomorrow, she knew the smart thing to do was go back to a strictly professional friendship. And she also had to wonder what in the world Bob Timkin had planned.

CHAPTER TEN

JACK SWALLOWED THE last of his morning coffee, wishing it didn't make him think of Avery and how her mouth always tasted after they'd shared espresso. Made him think of that first morning they'd spent together, that entire, magical day, and how beautiful and adorable she'd been. Realizing, from that moment on, he'd been fascinated by her in every way. Her looks, her brains, her personality.

He couldn't shake that fascination and attraction. An attraction that had grown even deeper after their time together last night, making love again to her beautiful body. Except his heart rate had barely slowed when the phone call had come, bringing a lot of questions with it. A harsh reminder of what he kept forgetting whenever he was with her. Which was that mixing business with pleasure was always one hell of a bad idea, no matter how incredible that pleasure was.

He thought he'd learned that painful lesson all too well. A lesson that had come in the form of doubt cast on his professional character and integrity, resulting in some very personal questions from a hospital ethics board. A lesson in why he should never get involved with a woman connected in any way with his work.

Except he knew Avery was nothing like Vanessa. She wasn't the kind of woman who would advance her own career at the expense of someone else's.

He took the elevator to the hospital's administrative offices on the top floor, where Bob had a nice, cushy office that someone had clearly given up for him. About to knock on the doorjamb, he was surprised to hear Avery's voice speaking through the partially open door, then the rumble of Bob's voice in answer.

He knocked on the door and didn't wait to be asked in before pushing it all the way open to step inside. Timkin looked up, then stood, a broad smile on his face. "Jack. Thanks for coming. Have a seat."

"I'm good standing, thanks."

"Dr. Girard was just updating me on the patient data from the trial so far."

"Seems impossible to have any kind of real report, considering we've operated on all of twelve patients so far."

"Well, yes. But all of them came through it nicely, I see."

"Actually, that's not entirely true," Avery said. "Several of the patients have had significant paravalvular regurgitation, as Dr. Dunbar and I have discussed."

"And in that discussion I noted that a certain percentage of patients are expected to have that complication and can live fine with it." His chest began to burn a little. Was she about to tell Timkin she thought there might be a flaw in the design? He was confident that Bob was completely behind this trial and the next phase of the rollout to other hospitals.

"We do know that is a normal, and expected, complication, Dr. Girard," Timkin said. "While I'm aware the numbers of patients experiencing that are currently slightly higher than we would have wished, the procedure hasn't been done on nearly enough patients for those numbers to be meaningful."

Jack relaxed a little, and he waited to hear why Timkin had called the meeting. Avery's brows were lowered in a frown, and he could practically see the wheels spinning in that brain of hers, probably coming up with various data she wanted to spout.

"Which is why I asked you both to come here this morning," Timkin said. "We've decided to significantly increase the number of patients in this clinical trial, which I'm sure will please you, Jack."

"What do you mean, you want to increase the number of patients in the trial?" Avery asked, her eyes wide.

"It seems logical to me that we get as many patients in the trial as we can for these last two and a half weeks," Timkin said. "We need as much data as possible before we decide how many hospitals to roll this out to next. I have a few of my people looking for good patient candidates and screening them as we speak, and of course I'd like your nurse to work on finding some, as well."

"Frankly, I don't think that's a good idea," Avery said. Her gaze flicked to Jack, then away, before she continued. "With the comparatively high percentage of the prosthetic valves experiencing leakage, I think the trial should be conducted on a smaller number of patients so we can keep our eye on that until we know more."

"I respect your opinion, Dr. Girard. But increasing the numbers can't be anything but good, giving us the conclusive data we all want."

Jack smiled at this great news. "I appreciate the vote of confidence, Bob. Dr. Girard is, of course, the leading expert on this device but isn't as familiar with patient care. Those in the trial experiencing the valve leakage are all doing well as we manage their situation."

As he turned to leave, his gaze paused on Avery, and he was surprised to see the look on her face was completely different from that of a moment ago. Instead of concern, her green eyes held deep disappointment. He'd even call it hurt. Was it because of what he'd said when he'd reassured Bob he had the leakages under control?

This trial was beyond important to him, the patients it was helping and the future of interventional cardiology. Avery knew that as well as anybody. Why she was so overly concerned about the valve leakage, he didn't understand and refused to worry about yet.

But as he headed to the cath lab, the image of the hurt in her eyes went along with him.

Jack headed for the hotel fitness room, needing a physical release from another long day at the hospital, his muscles tense from hours of standing on his feet doing surgeries. He had to give Crilex credit—they'd gotten additional patients lined up incredibly fast, and he and Jessica had been working flat out. Which he welcomed for the clinical trial and welcomed for himself.

The busy pace had left him with little time to think about Avery. During the brief moments he'd had free, though, she'd been on his mind. Thinking about all the great things he'd learned about her over the past weeks. Knowing she wasn't the kind of self-interested person who would skew data to benefit her career, and feeling bad that had even crossed his mind. They might not always agree, but the woman had absolute integrity.

That it seemed he'd accidentally hurt her made him feel like crap. Made him want to head to her room and apologize, then grab her to explore more of Paris and laugh together. Kiss and make love together. That desire was so strong he could only hope that running hard on the treadmill would somehow blank it all from his mind.

At 9:00 p.m. there were only two other people in the exercise room, and he was glad he wouldn't have to wait around for any of the machines or weights to become available. He slung a towel around his neck and started out jogging on the treadmill, increasing the pace until he was running, breathing hard, sweating. To his disgust, even that didn't stop his thoughts from drifting to Avery. To the softness of her skin and the taste of it on his tongue. To her laugh and the amazing green of her eyes.

Which made him one damned confused man. He adjusted the treadmill settings and picked up the pace, noticing out of the corner of his eye that the middle-aged man who had been lifting crazily heavy weights was now sitting strangely sideways on the bench, leaning on one hand.

Jack looked more carefully at him, realizing the guy didn't look like he felt very well. He slowed to a stop, quickly wiped the sweat from his face and walked over to the man, concerned at the ashen color of his face.

"You okay?"

The man shook his head and laboriously said a few words in French. Jack hoped like hell he could at least understand a little English, even if he couldn't speak it. "I'm a doctor. I'm going to check your pulse."

Thankfully, he nodded, and Jack pressed his fingers to the man's wrist to see if his heart was in a normal sinus rhythm. It was fast, very fast, and he'd begun to sweat buckets, too, neither of which were signs of anything good. Just as Jack was about to ask the man if he thought he might be having a heart attack he slumped sideways and started sliding clear off the bench.

"Whoa!" Jack was able to grab him midway, managing to keep him from cracking his head on the hard floor.

"What is wrong, monsieur?" The other person in the room had come to stand next to him, staring.

"Get the hotel to call the medical squad."

The guy ran off just as the man opened his eyes again, thank the Lord. His brows lowered as he blinked at Jack, saying something Jack wished he could understand. Pressing his fingers to the man's wrist again, he grimly noted his pulse was thready, which meant his blood pressure was high, which again meant nothing good.

"Good God, Jack, what's wrong?" To his surprise, Avery crouched next to him, deep concern on her face as she looked from the ill man to him.

"I think he's having the big one. Going in and out of V-fib, and his pulse is really tachy." He looked up at her, relieved she might be able to communicate with the man. "Ask him how he's feeling, where it hurts."

She quickly spoke to the man in French and he managed to answer her back. "He says he's nauseated and his chest feels strange."

"Damn. The chances of this not being a heart attack are slim to none." He scanned the room and didn't see what he'd hoped for. "I wish this place had a defibrillator. His arrhythmia is bad, and if he crashes, I don't think CPR's going to do it."

"They do. Over here." She ran around the other side of the L-shaped room and returned with exactly what he needed if the man went into true V-fib.

"How did you know that was there? I've been in this gym ten times and never noticed."

"It's by the plié bar, which I'm guessing you don't use."

She gave him a quick grin, and he grinned back before turning to place his fingers against the man's carotid artery. "You'd guess right. I—"

With a sudden, strangled sound the man, who'd been lying on his side, flopped onto his back, obviously unconscious again. Jack shook him, then rubbed his knuckles against the man's sternum. "Hey, buddy! Wake up. Can you hear me? Wake up!"

But the guy just lay there like he was dead, and Jack cursed. "We've got to get his shirt off so I can check his heart rate with the defib."

They wrestled the T-shirt off the man as quickly as they could, then Jack grabbed the defibrillator. Both moved fast to get the paddle wires untwined as he pressed them to the man's chest. Then stared at the EKG monitor on the paddle in disbelief.

"He's code blue. I'm going to have to bust him." He looked up at her tense face. "Can you set it at three hundred joules while I get it placed? Then get the hell out of the way."

She nodded and her fingers got it adjusted impressively fast.

"Okay. Ready? Clear!"

She jumped up and backpedaled as Jack sent the electricity to the man's heart.

Nothing.

"Clear again." His own heart pounding like he'd just jumped off the treadmill, he busted the man once more. When the man's chest heaved and his eyelids flickered, then opened, Jack exhaled a deep breath he hadn't even realized he'd been holding in his lungs.

"Thank God," he heard Avery say devoutly as she came back and kneeled next to them, reaching to hold the man's hand.

"Yeah." Jack pressed his fingers to the man's throat. "Pulse is down to ninety. And his color's even a little better. I think we did it, Dr. Girard."

Their eyes met briefly across the poor, supine guy, and a wordless communication went between them. Relief that they'd been able to help and joy that he was hopefully out of the woods.

The man weakly said something in French, and Avery smiled and answered before turning to Jack. "He asked what happened. I told him his heart stopped, and you saved his life."

"We saved his life. You were awesome."

Her smile widened before she turned back to speak to the man again, and Jack could see her squeezing his hand. Now that he could take a minute to breathe, he had to marvel at how calm she'd been through the whole thing, and how comforting him obviously came as second nature to her. Doctors and nurses were trained how to react to this kind of crisis, but he doubted there was a lot of that kind of education in biomedical PhD school.

The door to the fitness room clattered open as several emergency medical techs wheeled in a gurney. The guy who'd run from the room to get help followed, along with several people Jack recognized as hotel management. He stood and updated the med techs on what had happened and where the man's heart rate was now.

The hotel guys talked with Avery. She handed them the defibrillator, and he heard her saying what a hero Jack was. Part of him absolutely hated that, since he was no hero. He was a doctor who'd been in the right place when he'd been needed.

But another part of him couldn't be unhappy about Avery praising him that way. The hotel staff pumped his hand and thanked him, and he repeated that it was just lucky he'd been in the right place and gave them credit for having the defibrillator there for him to use. If they hadn't, he was certain the outcome would not have been good for the man.

It seemed the room went from full of people to empty in a matter of minutes, and he noticed what he'd missed before in all the excitement. Avery wearing tiny, sexy exercise shorts that showed off her toned legs and a tank top that revealed a whole lot more of her skin than he'd ever been able to see before, since she was always dressed for the cold or the hospital.

Well, except for their two blissful moments together, when he'd been privileged to see every inch of her body.

His heart went into a little atrial fibrillation of its own at the memories and the current vision standing right in front of him.

"That was one lucky man," Avery said. "How many people have a cardiologist around when they're having a heart attack? Were you in here working out when it happened?"

"I was running on the treadmill. Trying to loosen my

muscles." *Trying to forget about you.* "He was lucky all right. Lucky that you came in when you did and that you knew where the machine was. I've got to tell you, I'm pretty impressed at how calm and cool you were, helping with what needed to happen without freaking out."

"Believe me, I was freaking out on the inside." She grinned. "But that's a sweet thing for you to say. Much better than the stinging barbs you've thrown lately."

"Listen." He rubbed his hand across the back of his neck to loosen the knots there. Hoped she'd accept his apology. "I'm sorry I said you didn't know much about patient care. I'm sure you do. I just wanted Bob to know the leakages so far are minor, but I shouldn't have implied you're clueless about postoperative treatment."

"No, you shouldn't have. I may not be a medical doctor or nurse, but gathering the data teaches me plenty, believe me."

"I'm sure it does." He cupped her chin in his hand because he wanted that connection. Wanted to show her he truly cared how she felt. "Did it hurt you when I said that?"

"Honestly? To my core." Her words pricked his heart, but the sweet smile she gave him soothed the wound. "Though I just might have not very nicely accused you of certain things, as well. Like maybe you were sleeping with a married woman the same week you were kissing me."

"You know, you're right. That wasn't nice of you at all." He caught her elbows in his hands, tugging her against him. "So we're even."

"Even."

As he looked into the green of her eyes he tried hard to conjure all the reasons he had to keep a professional distance from her. But he couldn't. All he could think about was how much he enjoyed kissing her and making love with her, and how he wanted more of all of it.

"What is it about you that makes it impossible for me to keep a professional distance? Even when I try?" he asked, genuinely baffled.

"Maybe because we share a love of espresso?"

"Maybe," he said, dipping his head down to speak against her lips. "Or maybe it's just you."

"No." She shook her head, her lips slipping back and forth across his mouth as she did, and that simple touch nearly made him groan. "It's us. That mysterious and unexplainable chemistry, whether we like it or not."

"Sometimes not," he said. "But I find I can't help that, way more often, I like it very much."

Knowing he damned well shouldn't, he kissed her, loving the way she instantly melted against him, her arms sliding around his back to hold him tight. Their mouths and tongues moved in a slow dance that already felt seductively familiar. A tiny little sound came from her throat as the kiss deepened, a sound so full of desire it sent his blood pumping and nearly had him slipping his hands into those tiny shorts she was wearing, not caring at all about the consequences.

Somehow, though, he managed to summon every ounce of inner strength he had to break the kiss, dragging in a few desperate breaths to clear his head. Not only were they in a public place, which seemed to always be a problem whenever he kissed her, but nothing had really changed.

The chemistry—hell, more like a nuclear reaction—was most definitely there. But so was the inescapable

conflict in their jobs. And that situation was one harsh
reality.

"Right now, there's nothing I'd like more in the world
than for us to head upstairs and take up where we left
off a few nights ago," he said, and the truth of that statement nearly had him grabbing her hand, hightailing it
to his room and acting on exactly what he wanted. "But
that would just make our jobs more difficult. The work
I'm doing here is damned important to me. And I know
your work is important to you."

"It is. Which is why I'm going to stretch on the bar,
then get running. Good night, Jack." She rose on her
toes to give him a quick peck on the cheek and turned
to walk to the plié bar.

The sight of her sexy rear in those shorts and the
thought of how she might contort herself around that
bar practically made him groan. A mini war raged in
his chest, with the part of him that wanted her yesterday, today and tomorrow fighting with the cool, rational part of his brain that seemed to short-circuit every
time he was around her.

He thought about pretending to continue his work-
out while really watching whatever she was about to do,
but he managed to move to the elevator instead. Giving
work one hundred percent of his focus was something
he'd been good at for a long time. Time to get with
that program and somehow forget the vision of Avery's
shapely butt cheeks peeking from beneath those shorts.

Yeah. Like that was going to happen. Which made
him wonder. How cold, exactly, could he get the shower
in his room?

CHAPTER ELEVEN

JACK STARED IN frustration at the Doppler echocardiogram. The paravalvular regurgitation from the prosthetic valve was more than obvious. The valve looked like it was fitting tightly, but there was no denying the image of the fluid seeping slightly from around it. Why had the past two patients experienced this problem when it hadn't been an issue with the last ten?

"What do you think, Jack?" Jessica asked, peering over his shoulder at the echocardiogram.

"I don't know what to think. I'm trying to figure out if I somehow did something different with these two patients. Maybe I'm not being careful enough as I insert the cath to remove the diseased valve. Or when I place the new one."

Jessica shook her head. "I'm watching almost every second you're working, and if I'd noticed you doing anything different at all, I'd say so."

His mind spun back to past procedures, wondering if the increased patient load had made him hurry in any way. He didn't think so, but he would be extra careful from now on to be sure to take his time and triple-check the monitor as he was putting the prosthetic valve in place.

Jessica glanced around, then leaned close, speaking in a near whisper. "Do you think it's a design flaw, like Dr. Girard has been worried about all along?"

His chest tightened. He'd have to be as stubborn as a mule to not have wondered exactly that. "I don't know. It's possible. The percentage of patients with medically manageable leakage is more than we expected, but not dramatically more. We're just going to have to wait and see the numbers as the trial unfolds."

Jessica nodded. "This patient's pulmonary edema is improving nicely, and the liquid from her Foley is crystal-clear now. She's going to be fine, I think."

"Good. I'll check on her again this afternoon."

"Dr. Dunbar!"

He and Jessica both turned to the nurse who'd run in. "Yes?"

"Madame Belisle is having trouble breathing. I fear it may be another aortic insufficiency."

He stiffened. Another one? Damn it to hell. "We'll be right there."

Jack grimly strode to Mrs. Belisle's room, with Jessica right behind. When he saw that Avery was in there, standing by the patient's bed, his heart knocked hard in his chest. He wasn't sure if it was from seeing her, or if it was because he knew she was taking notes on the third patient with this problem in a matter of days.

He took the woman's pulse, checked her blood pressure and went through the process to confirm the diagnosis, but it was pretty clear. Same song, different verse, and he hated that they had no idea why this kept happening at this rate.

As he gave orders to Jessica and the other nurse, he was painfully aware of Avery observing all of it, tapping away at her tablet. Watching as the patient received the medications needed to reduce her blood pressure, the diuretic to clear her lungs and the Foley catheter to catch the fluids. Continued tapping away as the portable echocardiogram was brought to the room to get images of Mrs. Belisle's heart activity.

He resolutely ignored her presence, concentrating on the situation. A half hour later, relieved that the patient was breathing a little easier, Jack let himself glance up at Avery, surprised to see her green eyes staring straight into his. This time there wasn't a hint of the humor he loved to see there. They were beyond serious.

"I'm going to look at the echocardiogram," he said to no one in particular. He knew his voice was gruff, but he couldn't help the slightly sick feeling in his gut that maybe this clinical trial was heading downhill fast.

"I'd like to look at it with you, Dr. Dunbar," Avery's voice said from behind him as he moved down the hall.

Of course she would.

His gut tightened a little more. No matter how disturbing all this was, though, he knew he couldn't blame her or feel ticked at her. She was doing her job and, ultimately, if it turned out she'd been right all along, he had to accept that. Should welcome it, really, because if the device was truly flawed, he wouldn't want to put patients at risk any more than she did. If he had to spend another year working with Crilex's biomedical engineers to improve it before testing it on humans again, then that's what would have to happen.

Way premature to be thinking like that, Jack fiercely reminded himself. This clinical trial was only half over, and it was very possible they'd just had a run of bad luck and the next twenty patients would all do fine.

"What are you thinking, Jack?" Avery asked quietly as they studied the Doppler echocardiogram of Mrs. Belisle and the obvious, slight leakage from around the valve.

He looked at her, measuring his response. He trusted her. He did. But loose lips sank ships, as the old saying went, and there was too much riding on this trial to jeopardize it by being too forthcoming with the woman who'd been concerned about this risk all along.

"I'm thinking that I will carefully examine how I'm inserting the catheter and device. As I do that, we'll continue to compile the data. We're also going to perform the procedure on all the very sick patients who've lined up to receive it. Even those with this complication will be better off than they were before the surgery, you know."

"So you're not worried that this is clear evidence the device design just isn't yet where it needs to be?"

The expression on her face showed loud and clear that's what she thought, with maybe a little contempt thrown in. Or was it disappointment? Either way, he didn't want to see it and turned his attention back to the monitor. "Too soon to say. There's not enough evidence, and worrying about it when we don't have the data from a full study is pointless."

She was silent for so long, with such an odd, thoughtful expression as she studied him, it made him jittery. When he couldn't stand it any longer, he abruptly turned. "I have some other patients to see."

"Jack."

He paused and looked back at her, bracing himself for a lecture, willing himself to not let his frustration over all this send his temper flaring. "Yes?"

"I have a great idea," she said, her voice suddenly, surprisingly, light and playful. The same voice she'd used that first, very memorable day they'd spent together.

"Sounds scary."

"Not scary. I think you'll like the proposal I have in mind."

That mischievous smile that usually made him smile back was in her eyes once more. Right now, though, it made him wonder why her demeanor had changed so abruptly. He folded his arms and waited.

"You've been working long and hard and don't have any patients scheduled this weekend. You're looking pretty haggard, which is going to worry your little old lady patients who think you're the most handsome thing in the world."

"You think?" He actually did smile at that, and how she managed to change the entire atmosphere of the room in one minute, he didn't know. "Is that what's called a backhanded compliment?"

"Maybe. So here's my proposal." She moved closer to him and pressed her hands to his chest. He felt some of his stress seep away at their warmth through his scrubs, at how good they felt there.

It made him realize how much he'd missed her touch. Missed touching her.

He let himself cup her waist with his hands because he wanted to, and she was the one who'd started the touching after all. "Does it have anything to do with espresso? If it does, a triple sounds pretty good right now."

"It might." Her smile could only be described as flirtatious, which ratcheted up Jack's interest tenfold. At the same time, he felt even more perplexed. "I promise some serious espresso consumption if you agree. Wine consumption, too."

"Wine consumption? You sure know how to intrigue a guy. What other guilty pleasures might be included in this proposal?"

"You'll find out, if you just say, 'Yes, Avery.'" Her coy words were accompanied by the sparkle in her eyes he'd fallen for the first day they'd met, oddly mingling with a tinge of seriousness.

"I never say yes until I know what I'm agreeing to. What's the catch, and is it going to hurt much?"

"It might hurt, but you're tough enough to handle it," she said, the sparkle fading a bit. "I'd like you to come to Alsace with me, to a little village northeast of Paris. Not too far and easy to get to by train. It's beyond beautiful, so I'll get to show you more of France, and you'll get to shake the dust of this place from your feet and be all refreshed when you come back to work."

He tipped his head to study her, trying to figure out where she was going with this. "Despite the wine consumption promise, I suspect you're not inviting me there for a weekend of sightseeing and wild sex." Though just thinking about spending two days alone with her sent a hot zing through every nerve ending, which he quickly tamped down. Hadn't he sworn off sex or anything else with her?

Yeah, right. If that was her proposal, he'd be saying yes in half of one second and to hell with the consequences.

"Maybe it is about wild sex," she said, giving him the adorable teasing look he'd missed almost as much as her touch, and his heart pumped harder. "Along with meeting the patient I mentioned before, who was one of the first to receive my original TAVI device. I'd like you to hear his story."

"Uh-huh." Here was the damned big letdown he'd known was coming. "How about we go for the wild sex and forget the rest?"

"It's a package deal. We'll be out of Paris and away from the hospital to relax."

"You want me to meet this guy so much you'll risk more of us mixing business with pleasure?" The part of him that wanted his hands and mouth on her again was already yelling yes, but going there with her would be one bad idea. "I know the problems patients with leaky valves live with, Avery. And much as I'd like nothing better than to go on a weekend away with you, it'd just complicate an already complicated situation."

To his shock, she reached up to wrap her arms around his neck and kissed him. Kissed him until his knees nearly buckled and his heart raced. Kissed him until he couldn't breathe and his stress had completely evaporated. Kissed him until he'd say yes to pretty much anything she asked.

When she finally stopped, he could see in her eyes the same delirious desire he felt pumping through every cell in his body. Even though she was obviously using her all-too-irresistible feminine wiles to get him to see that guy, it was also clear she was every bit as turned on as he was.

"How about it, Jack?" she whispered against his lips. "I know you need a break. And meeting this man will just add to your data, so there's nothing to lose. Except, maybe, your virtue."

"Pretty sure I lost my virtue that first day we met."

He had to chuckle, but he shook his head, not quite believing her tactics. "You drive a very hard bargain, Dr. Girard."

She pressed closer against him, and when his erection pressed into her stomach she gave him the wickedest smile. "Very hard, Dr. Dunbar. Which I hope means your answer is yes."

In a sign that this trip just might go as well as Avery hoped, the gray clouds parted and the sun cast its golden fingers across the vineyards and snowy mountains that surrounded Riquewihr. Jack parked the little rental car outside the town's ancient walls and turned to her with a smile.

"This place is amazing," he said. "I can't believe that one minute we're driving through endless vineyards, then all of a sudden here's this beautiful old medieval town parked right in the middle of it all."

"You should see it in the summertime, when everything's green and flowers are everywhere," she said, glad he already seemed to like this place. "Wait till we get inside the walls. The town itself is every bit as amazing and lovely."

She smiled, pleased that he again looked like the upbeat man she'd met in the hotel that very first day, and not the cardiologist whose tense and tired expression the past week had made her want to gather him up and hold him and give him more of that TLC she'd promised him before. It wasn't good for his patients or for Jack if he worked endless hours under stress, and in a sudden decision not too different from the moment she'd first met him in the hotel, she'd wanted to do something about it.

For days, a disturbing feeling had nagged at her. As the number of patients in the trial had more than doubled, the problems had increased, too. She knew Jack was as concerned about it as she was. But she also knew him well enough to guess that his fatigue and worry would turn into defensiveness if she suggested again that he ratchet the trial back to its original numbers, or even fewer.

Inspiration had struck on how she could accomplish two things at once. Get him to come here to Riquewihr for a much-needed break—and to meet Benjamin Larue. A lovely man with a lovely family, whose life had been damaged irreversibly during the first TAVI trials.

Jack's loose stride already seemed much more relaxed than the fast pace he kept in the hospital, moving from surgeries to patients to various test results and back. They headed toward the old clock tower, walking through the gate beneath it in the ancient wall.

"How many times have you been here?" he asked. "Just in the summertime?"

"I've been here twice. Once in winter and once in summer. Totally different things to do, of course. I love to hike the mountains, but the snow cover at the moment requires a different approach. So I figured maybe we'd cross-country ski or snowshoe. Have you ever tried it? I made a reservation for us just a half hour from now, so we'll have to hurry to get there. Unless you'd rather do something else."

"I haven't tried either one." He leaned closer, the devilish smile that had knocked her socks off—among other things—back in full force and electrifying the air. "But I'm all for any kind of exercise you might think up to get our blood pumping."

Her blood was already pumping just from looking at him and thinking about the kind of physical exercise he obviously had on his mind.

The curve of his lips, the light in his eyes as he looked at her and the various landmarks they passed reminded her so much of the Jack she'd shown around Paris that first day. The Jack she'd tumbled into bed with, before she'd thought long enough about it. Before she'd found out exactly how ill-advised that decision had turned out to be.

But pretending that hadn't happened, and deciding not to let it happen again, had come to seem pretty pointless. When the trial was over and she'd studied the data, her recommendation to Crilex would be the same no matter whether they were sleeping together or not. She knew Jack wanted what was best for the patients, and she had to believe, either way it went, that he'd come to the same conclusion she did.

She smirked at herself. Like before, she seemed to have a much easier time talking herself into being with him than the other way around. Probably because he looked sexier in scrubs than about anybody she'd ever seen, and asking her to not think about stripping them off him to see that lean, muscular body of his was like asking her to give up coffee.

She glanced at him out of the corner of her eye, smiling at the memory of his shocked expression as she'd coerced him to come on this trip. She'd never tried seducing someone to get them on board with a different agenda. Now she knew it was pretty exciting to know how well her sex appeal apparently worked on the man.

They walked down a cobbled street flanked by beautiful medieval buildings, with Jack commenting on all of it in amazement, before they checked into their small hotel. From the moment she'd first seen the place she'd been awed and delighted by the beautiful pastel blues, yellows and mauves of the buildings, like something from a fairy tale.

"Some cities in France had to rebuild after World War II, so a lot of the buildings are really replicas rather than the original medieval structures," she said. "I'm told that only two bombs dropped here, though, so it's nearly all original. Isn't the whole place incredible?"

"It is. I've never seen anything like it."

Pleasure fluttered inside her at the fact that he liked it as much as she did. As they made their way down the narrow, stone-lined hallway, Jack smiled at her. "Gotta tell you, the whole town reminds me of a Hollywood movie set."

"I know what you mean." The first time she had come here, she had thought the Renaissance-style stone and half-timber homes were almost too enchanting to believe. "I've always wondered if the animators who did *Beauty and the Beast* came here for inspiration."

"I confess I haven't watched that movie and also confess I hope that's not part of your agenda for the weekend." He shoved open their room door and looked down at her with the teasing humor she'd enjoyed that first day they met. Humor that had been in short supply the past week. "Or watching *The Sound of Music*. Have to wonder if that's the plan, though, considering the dirndl that you're wearing."

"Dirndl?" She set her suitcase on the floor and fisted her hands on her hips, giving him a mock glare. "My dress is not a dirndl, Dr. Dunbar. It's a blouse beneath a corduroy jumper."

"If you say so." He reached to unbutton her coat, pulling it apart to look at her dress. "No need to get defensive, though. I like it. A lot."

He ran his finger along the lacy top of her blouse that dipped low to just above her breasts. Avery looked down, watching the track of his finger, her breath growing short. Vaguely, she pondered that maybe the skirt did look a little like a dirndl. Her main thoughts, though, were that his touch felt wonderful, that she'd missed it, and that, unlike the first two times they'd briefly shared a hotel room, she didn't feel at all nervous. All she felt was a delicious anticipation of the day and night they'd be spending together.

She looked back up at him, and a warm flush crept through her body at the way he was looking at her. The small smile was still on his face, but his eyes were filled with something entirely different that told her he, too, was feeling that same breathless anticipation.

"Bonjour, monsieur...mademoiselle."

They both turned to the open door and saw an older gentleman with a wide, curled mustache smiling at them. "I wanted to suggest that you join us this evening at five o'clock for a wine tasting from our local vineyards. There will be complimentary hors d'oeuvres as well, in our wine cellar."

"Thank you," Jack said. "We haven't made any plans yet, but that sounds great."

He shoved the door closed behind the man and turned to her again. "Are you sure Riquewihr isn't just some elaborate Hollywood hoax? I mean, how often do you see a guy with a mustache like that outside the movies?"

Her laugh morphed into more of a little hiccup when his fingers tugged apart the lapels of her coat again.

"So," he asked in a low voice, "are we staying in or going out?"

"I…um…" She struggled to decide, wanting to show him the amazing and wonderful things about Riquewihr during the daylight hours of this single Saturday that they had. Wanted to enjoy the same delight she'd felt, that she was sure they'd both felt, seeing the Eiffel Tower and the Sacré Coeur. Have those kinds of lovely moments before they stopped at the Larue family winery to meet Benjamin.

But she also wanted that heady give and take they'd had before. The overwhelming sensations when they let go of all the external problems, shared their bodies and simply let the chemistry between them ignite into a searing, physical passion like none other she'd ever experienced.

She drew a breath to try to finish her sentence, but it was a shaky one at best. Because it was clear he could read exactly what she'd been thinking, and she nearly caught fire just from the look in his eyes before he lowered his head.

His lips covered hers, teasing, tasting, as his hands moved to her waist. Slid up to cup her breasts, his fingers again brushing the filmy top of her blouse as he deepened the kiss, the sweep of his tongue so delicious she had to bite back a moan.

When he broke the kiss, his eyes were so heavy-lidded she could barely see the gleam in the darkness of his eyes. "Didn't you say we have a time schedule to hit the mountain for a little skiing or snowshoeing?"

She nodded, knowing any verbal answer she gave at that moment would just come out as a whisper until she caught her breath. "Yes," she finally managed. "I thought you'd enjoy the fresh air and how gorgeous it is up there. But we don't have to. We have the day off to do whatever makes us happy."

"Just being with you makes me happy," he said, and she was surprised the words didn't hold a sensual tone. They sounded beyond sincere, and her heart tripped in her chest. "And since we have only so many hours of daylight, I think we should do what you'd already planned for us. Because I sure haven't been disappointed in any of our activities in France so far, Ms. Tour Guide."

She stared at Jack and realized he was being utterly genuine. He truly enjoyed just being with her, here or in Paris or wherever they happened to be, and hadn't come here with her just for the "wild sex" she'd teased him with. As she thought back to her two previous relationships, she realized that the physical part of them had been the primary element.

Which wasn't at all what she had with Jack. What they had between them went deeper than the sexual chemistry they'd talked about, which was thrilling and scary at the same time. Because she knew his job was not just his priority, it was his life. She was a brief interlude in that life—an interlude he'd made clear he felt uncomfortable participating in.

And if it became necessary to halt the trial, she could only hope and pray he understood why.

Her heart giving an odd little twist, she gave him a soft kiss before grasping his hand and smiling into his beautiful eyes. "Then let's head to the Vosges mountains. I think you'll love it, and afterward we'll both be more than ready for a little après-ski."

"Lead on, Dr. Girard. I'm all yours."

CHAPTER TWELVE

"Even without the potential for wine and wild sex, I'm glad I agreed to this trip," Jack said, looking handsome as all get-out with his cheeks flushed and his dark hair poking from beneath his knit hat. "Growing up, a few of my friends went skiing in the winter with their families. Both downhill and cross-country. We never went places like that, but now I wish I'd tried this kind of thing at home."

"I knew you'd like it." The crisp mountain air was filled with the rhythmic crunch of their snowshoes and Avery's heavy breathing from tromping practically straight up for the past fifteen minutes. "Also knew the only thing that would convince you to take your mind off work by coming here was the potential for sexual favors."

"Already, the woman knows me well." He sent her his most devilish smile, and she was pretty sure it was his expression and not the cold air that made her insides quiver.

"So, where did your family go on vacation?" The tracks of the cross-country ski course had been grooved into the snow next to them, and they followed that line to be sure to not get lost. A straight uphill line, and Avery's lungs and legs sure hoped for a downhill slope soon.

"We didn't, much." He shrugged. "Both my parents are workaholic doctors, with my dad being the worst. We mostly took the occasional short trip to New York or the beach. Just for a few days, so they wouldn't be gone long."

"Ah. So you took after them?"

He flashed her a grin. "Probably. My brother, too. But I'm beginning to see the value of a little vacation time."

The path curved in a C shape to finally slope slightly downhill, thank heavens, but it was one long way down. Avery had thought she was in pretty good shape, but the burning in her thighs and lungs after the uphill climb told her maybe not so much. "Let's cut through here. Catch the path on the other side."

"I may not be a skier, but I've heard you shouldn't go off the trail. What if we fall into a crevasse?"

"You're such a rule follower. Come on."

She grabbed his hand and veered to the right near a line of trees that went all the way down the mountain.

He slid her a look that said she was crazy, but his lips were tipped into an amused smile. "There are times to follow the rules and times when it makes sense to break them. Wandering around on a mountain doesn't seem like the best time to me, but you're the tour guide. Lead on."

Even though the snow was deeper there, going downhill made it easier to breathe. And she was glad she wouldn't be panting when she asked the question she'd been wondering about. "Was there some bad situation in your life that made you not want to spend time with me after we found out who each other was? When I said it wasn't good to be involved with someone you had to work with, you were very quick to agree, and I thought there must be a reason."

"First, there was never a moment I didn't want to spend time with you. I just knew it was a bad idea." She relaxed at his teasing expression, glad he wasn't going to get all stiff again now she'd brought up the unsettling back and forth between them. "But your observation is very astute. And here I'd always heard genius types were book smart but not people smart."

She rolled her eyes. "Again, the stereotype. I thought we were done with that."

"Sorry." He took a sideways step, his shoulder bumping into hers as his eyes got that wicked glint in them. "Learning that female scientists wear lacy, colorful underwear has changed my perspective forever. Don't think I'll ever be able to see techs with their test tubes and not wonder what they have on under their lab coats."

It was utterly stupid, but his words pricked at her heart. It wasn't like they were a real couple. One that would be together after the trial was complete in just over a week. He was a career-driven man who liked women in small doses, and fantasizing about lingerie and wild sex was part of that package.

"Hey." He must have seen something in her expression because he stopped walking and tipped her chin up. "I was teasing. There's only one woman whose underwear I wonder about."

She forced a laugh. "And I just might have to keep you wondering. But you haven't answered my question."

They continued their trek as several cross-country skiers slid by in the tracks above them, and the sound of his deep sigh mingled with the swish of the skis. "When I first found out who you were I was amazed. Well, I was amazed a whole lot of ways that day." He aimed that glint at her again.

Warmth crept into her cold cheeks at his words, remembering exactly how she'd behaved and how she'd never done such a thing in her life before. "I'd prefer you didn't remind me I slept with a man I'd just met. I'm embarrassed by that, and you know it."

"You shouldn't be." He wrapped his arm around her and tugged her close to his side. "The romance of Paris and our chemistry together made it inevitable. If it hadn't happened that day, it would have happened another day. From the second I turned to see the knockout woman talking to me in the hotel, I knew it was meant to be."

His words, his low voice and the expression in his eyes caught her breath. "Maybe it was," she replied softly. "And you're still doing a darned good job of avoiding answering me."

"You just want to gloat when you hear I made a stupid mistake. Because you know I never do, and admitting I made one once isn't something I like to do."

"I know, Dr. Dunbar, that you think you're perfect."

"Hey, my mom calls me Prince Perfect. What do you expect?" That quick grin flashed again, almost as dazzling as the sunshine on the snow, and Avery had to admit he just might be as close to perfection as a man could be.

A minute went by, silent except for the crunch, crunch of their shoes, and she'd begun to think he'd never tell her when he finally spoke. "My crown slipped a few years back, though. I dated a medical supplies rep who sold, among other things, stents for angioplasty. I switched to the stent she repped because I honestly thought it might be superior to the ones I'd been using. You can imagine how many stents we use a month, and because it was more expensive, the hospital bean counters questioned it. When it came out that she and I had a personal relationship, all hell broke loose. Hospital bigwigs accused me of behaving unethically, and as it all unfolded, a whole lot of dirty laundry spilled out."

She couldn't imagine Jack having a whole lot of dirty laundry. "Like what?"

"Turned out the beguiling Vanessa was sleeping with numerous docs, in multiple hospitals, who used high-end surgical and biomedical products. She was trying to get a big promotion at her company and used me, and the other saps, to get the sales record and promotion."

He shook his head, his lips twisted into a grimace. "What a fool I was. My relationship with Vanessa was pretty much strictly physical, but knowing the truth, that she'd used me, made me feel sick. I hated answering to the ethics board, having them question my professionalism. I was cleared of any wrongdoing, but vowed I'd never so much as look at a woman involved in any way with my job."

"Wow." His story might even be worse than her former boyfriend mistakes. And explained why the wall between them had been wider even than she'd thought their situation warranted.

"Wow?" He raised his eyebrows at her. "Maybe I shouldn't have confessed. You think I'm an idiot now?"

"No, of course not. But I've gotta tell you. While I feel bad you went through that, you've made me feel a little better about my own poor judgment."

"Which would be what?"

Part of her didn't want to share something so embarrassing, but he'd shared with her, so it was only fair. "I dated a couple of cardiologists for a while. The first one traveled a lot, teaching his specialized procedures. Turned out he had a woman in every port. Or every hospital, to be more accurate."

He stopped walking to stare at her. "I can't believe there's a human alive who could be stupid enough to not hang onto you with both hands when he had the chance."

He looked genuinely astonished, and what woman wouldn't feel pretty good about his words? "The second one started talking down to me, saying disparaging things."

"What kind of disparaging things?"

"Oh, like when people asked me questions about angioplasty and stents, which happened sometimes because that's what he did, he'd say I was the 'equipment' girl and wasn't qualified to talk about medical procedures."

"You've got to be kidding me." The astonishment was still there on his face, along with anger. "No wonder you wrote off cardiologists as being total jerks. But he was probably jealous of your amazing smarts. That kind of guy isn't worth having, and you know it."

"I do know. But I guess that whole experience has made me hypersensitive. Which is why I was suspicious of you and Jessica. Sorry. But there are some real winners out there."

"Yeah. There are." His eyes and voice warmed and he stopped, turning to wrap both his arms around her and draw her close. Her own arms slipped around his back, and the sizzle between them could be felt all the way through their coats and hats, warming her from the inside out. "The kind of winner that makes a man do something he swore he wouldn't do. So maybe I'm still a fool. But I can't seem to keep you out of my head."

His cold lips touched hers, and in an instant both their mouths were toasty warm as they shared a slow, sweet kiss. Just as Avery angled her head, inviting him to delve deeper, the swishing sound of skis on snow came from above them. They pulled apart and looked up the hill to the trail they'd abandoned to see nearly a dozen skiers following one another in single file on the trail.

"Are you kidding?" Jack said. "Even out here in the middle of a mountain we have an audience?"

She wasn't about to let a few strangers ruin the heavenly moment. Of all the places she'd kissed Jack, holding him close on this wild, beautiful mountainside, his cold nose touching hers and his mouth so hot and delicious—this place was her very favorite. "Who cares? We're in France."

She tried to go up on tiptoe to kiss him again, but found it pretty difficult with snowshoes on her feet. Luckily, the superheated gleam in his eyes showed he knew exactly what she wanted and he kissed her again, sending her heart pounding even harder. Her legs wobbled, whether from the kiss or the hiking or both she wasn't sure. She hung onto Jack's coat as his mouth moved across her cold cheek and beneath her earlobe in a shivery path that made it very hard to breathe.

Frigid wind swept the cheek not currently covered by Jack's warm one and at the same time clumps of snowflakes dropped onto her face. She opened her eyes to see Jack lifting his head, a slow, sexy smile curving his lips as his finger swept the snow from her eyelashes.

"Guess we should have thought to bring your umbrella up here on the mountain with us." His hat and shoulders were covered with snowflakes, too, and she looked behind him to see the wind catch more of the snow loaded on the evergreen trees and swirl it onto them, like Mother Nature was playing a joke and tossing it with her hand.

"Who knew?"

Their steamy, breathless laughter flitted between them as they separated, her gloved hand in his, to trudge on down the mountain in a companionable silence. She pulled in a deep, satisfied breath, realizing she felt as comfortable and relaxed as she'd felt in a long, long time, and hoped Jack was feeling the same.

Except he probably wouldn't be much longer.

"So here's the other thing we have scheduled today," she said, hoping her announcement wouldn't ruin the beautiful, quiet mood between them.

"Dare I hope it's the wild sex or the wine consumption? Or both combined?"

"Not yet. That might come later, if you're good."

"Oh, I'm good. You know I'm good."

She hated to squash the teasing heat in his eyes and sucked in another breath, this one no longer relaxed. "After we turn in our snowshoes, we're going to take the car out to the Larue family vineyards."

Something in her expression obviously told him this wasn't just another pleasure excursion. "Your TAVI patient?"

"Clearly, I'm not the only astute one." Suddenly she felt nervous. Would meeting Benjamin make Jack go all defensive again? Snuff out the smile on his face, the relaxed posture, the teasing looks? Make it difficult for them to enjoy the hours together in this beautiful place?

Maybe it would. But with the complications that patients were experiencing increasing, her gut told her Jack needed to step back from how deeply he was wrapped up in the trial and think about it objectively. If meeting Benjamin didn't do that, probably nothing would. "Are you...okay with that?"

"I told you this morning, Dr. Girard," he said, his gaze steady on hers, "I'm all yours."

The house looked to be hundreds of years old, though at the same time it was still in pristine condition. Proof that most people had been shorter long ago, Jack had to duck beneath the ancient beam above the thick, wooden front door when he followed Avery, who was being kissed on both cheeks and warmly greeted by a woman who was probably in her early forties. Both were yammering on in French, and since he couldn't understand a word, he took time to look around the cozy room. A welcoming fire burned inside a huge stone fireplace, and a wooden table was covered with so many plates of finger foods you'd have thought every guest at the hotel was stopping by.

He blew out a breath. He'd known all along this was the catch to an otherwise great weekend with Avery, but now that he was here, dread began to seep into his gut. What did Avery really want from him? And what could this man have experienced that he hadn't seen before, anyway?

It wasn't as if he didn't know all too well about the challenges people with bad hearts faced every day. He stood by his statement that a less-than-perfect outcome was still better than what most had lived with before the procedure. This TAVI trial was doing important work, critical work, work that might have helped someone like his own grandfather, who had died with so much left to live for. Help a lot of people who couldn't get a new heart valve any other way.

Benjamin Larue must not have had luck on his side. Sometimes bad things happened to good people, and every doctor experienced days when it felt like a shower of bricks came down on everyone's head. When it did, it hurt like hell and left bruises that lasted a long time.

"Jack, this is Vivienne Larue. Vivienne, Dr. Jack Dunbar."

"Welcome, welcome! Please sit and make yourself comfortable while I get Benjamin. He is very happy you've come to visit."

Jack wasn't sure *visit* was the right term—why did he suddenly feel a little like he was standing in front of a firing squad? The feeling persisted, even though he sat in a comfortable chair by the flickering fire. Maybe it was the way Avery's green eyes were focused on him—*expectantly* would be the word—and that fueled his discomfort.

"So were you telling secrets about me in French?" Maybe making a joke would lighten up the awkward mood that hung like a cloud in the room.

"I don't know many of your secrets, though that one you shared on the mountain was a doozy. Can't wait to hear more and spread them all over the hospital."

Damned if the woman couldn't make him smile in the midst of an avalanche. "I might have to make up some juicy ones, just to surprise you."

"You've been surprising me since the minute we met." A sweet, sincere smile accompanied her words, and he felt himself relax a little.

"Likewise, Dr. Girard."

"Vivienne makes the best cheesy puff pastries," Avery said as she put a few things on her plate. "You should try one."

Before he could answer, he heard a sound behind him and turned to see Vivienne pushing a man in a wheelchair into the room.

It wasn't an ordinary wheelchair. It was semi-reclining, the kind someone who couldn't breathe well would use, and the man sitting in it had a prosthetic leg. His head was raised to look at his guests as introductions were made, and a friendly smile didn't mask his pallor or the thin, drawn look to his face.

So much for feeling less tense. His gut tightened all over again when he saw how young the man was to have this kind of disability. Probably only in his early forties, like his wife. It was damned unfair that sometimes a guy drew the short straw, and medical science just wasn't advanced enough to replace it with a longer one.

And wasn't that exactly why the work he was doing was so important? Advancing medical science to help patients was the critical goal.

"*Bon après-midi*, Dr. Dunbar. I'm honored to have you visit," Benjamin said in a hoarse, rasping voice as he extended his hand. "Avery tells me you have developed a new prosthetic valve device. I wish you well with it."

Jack stood and leaned over to shake his hand. "Thank you. Avery thought that speaking with you might help me do the best I can for other patients as we move forward."

Benjamin's smile broadened. "And I hope that you will taste our latest wine vintages to help me with those, as well. We make the finest wines in France right here, you know. Pinot Gris, Pinot Noir and Rieslings are our specialties."

"I didn't know. I don't pretend to be a wine expert, but I'm more than happy to lend my palate to you."

"Excellent." Benjamin beamed, then turned to talk to Avery. As Jack watched them banter, the room seemed to lose its claustrophobic feeling and he relaxed, taking a bite of the cheese Vivienne offered. Which made him realize he'd been prepared for criticism or attack or who knew what from all of them.

"So, Dr. Dunbar. Avery is determined that I tell you my story. Why she continues to take responsibility for God's hand in my life, I do not know. It is what it is. So I will recite it quickly, then we can enjoy more important things." Benjamin looked at her with an expression similar to that of a fond uncle, and her emotions were right there on her face, visible to anyone who wanted to look.

Warm friendship. Caring. Heartache and guilt.

She'd been through tough times with this man, he saw, surprised at that revelation, though he shouldn't have been. She had obviously had her own days where bricks had fallen all too hard on her head. She might not be a medical doctor, but she cared about the patients using the devices she'd designed as much as any of them. Cared about them deeply enough to forge this bond that obviously both hurt and soothed.

"I'd like to hear your story, Benjamin," he said. "More than anything, I want to help people like my late grandfather, and like you, with challenging heart valve problems."

He thought he was focused on Benjamin, but realized he was glancing at Avery, too. At her smile, and the softness in her eyes that told him she liked his response. He'd always thought he didn't care what others thought, that he worked for his patients and for the goals he'd set for himself, and that was all that mattered. But at that moment her approval brought a smile to his own face and made his chest swell a little, even though he knew that was absurd.

"At the age of nine I was diagnosed with diabetes," Benjamin said, staring at the swirl of red wine in a glass his wife had poured. "As the years went on, I was one of the less fortunate. Many complications, and eventually I lost my leg."

"Juvenile-onset diabetes can be a difficult disease to manage." Jack saw all too many patients with terrible complications from diabetes and hoped like hell researchers would eventually find a cure.

"It is." Benjamin nodded. "Then, when our boys were only seven and nine, my kidneys began to fail. We fit weekly dialysis into our schedules somehow. Along with caring for the vines and harvest and crush and all the other things that must happen for a winery to survive. For me to survive." His hand reached to Vivienne and she clasped it tight. "My beautiful wife has stood by me through all of this, and why that is I do not know. I only know that I am blessed."

"It is your stubbornness, Benjamin Larue. Your irresistible stubbornness."

Jack saw tears fill Vivienne's eyes, and he glanced at Avery to see hers had filled, as well. In her line of work she probably didn't often work with sick people. He dealt with it every day, but that didn't make it any easier. "When did you begin to have heart problems?"

"Not long after my dialysis began. When I worked with the grapes or played with my sons, I tired quickly, becoming very short of breath." His eyes met Jack's. "Do you have children, monsieur?"

"No."

"Then you do not know the joys and frustrations of their abundant energy. Energy I wanted to keep up with."

Jack might not know about wanting to play with his own children, with any children, but could easily imagine how that inability could cut away at your soul. "So you and your doctors decided a valve transplant would help. Except you weren't a candidate for open-heart surgery because of your other health issues."

"*Oui.* I was pleased to think a new procedure might help me breathe easier, work longer and play ball with my boys for more than five minutes." He grinned. "You may look at me and wonder, but I got pretty good at kicking with my pretend leg, which amused my children."

"Amused everyone," Avery said, smiling, too. "When his doctor and I came here to talk about the risks and benefits of the TAVI trial, I couldn't believe how Benjamin could practically do spin moves. His boys joked that he was Iron Man and had an unfair advantage. Tiring quickly was his primary problem, which we'd hoped to fix."

"But the surgery didn't go well." Jack wanted to get to the crux of the matter, though he already knew.

"*Non.*" Benjamin's smile faded. "Afterward, I was

much worse, not better. Now if I lie flat, my lungs fill. I cannot kick the ball with my boys at all anymore or work in the vineyard. My kidney problems make it impossible for me to take a diuretic to lessen the fluid buildup, and my body is not strong enough to handle open-heart surgery." He gestured at himself. "So this is it for me. I accept it, but hurt for my family that they must do all the things in the vineyard and at home that I no longer can."

"Bottom line, Jack? It was an utter failure," Avery said, her eyes intent on his. "We wanted to make Benjamin's life better, but we made it much worse instead. I know you see patients with bad outcomes. But you've been convinced that those with leakage from the prosthetic valve are medically manageable and still better off than before. Benjamin's situation proves that's not always the case. The percentage having this problem must be very small to justify the risk."

What was he supposed to say to that? All procedures carried risks. Every single one of them, from the simplest to the most complex. But he understood the frustration and deep disappointment. Benjamin may not have had the exercise capacity he'd wanted before the procedure, but now he had none at all and couldn't even sleep in a bed with his wife.

"Papa! Papa!" Two boys careened into the room, nearly skidding to a halt next to the wheelchair, speaking fast in French until he held up his hand.

"English, please. Our guest does not speak French, and it is good for you to practice."

Both boys took a breath, and Jack was impressed at how polite they were during a brief introduction, before launching into their story again.

"*Les chevreuils* got through the fence that has a hole and into the berry bushes. They were eating up the brambles before we chased them off! Why do deer eat thorny things like that, Papa?"

"The same reason you like your mother's macaroons, I suppose."

"Are you saying that eating my macaroons is like swallowing thorns, Benjamin Larue?" Vivienne said in faux outrage, her hands fisted on her hips.

"*Non, non*, my dearest, I am saying the brambles are like a delectable delicacy to *les chevreuils*, as all your wonderful dishes are to me." His chest filled with a deep chuckle that morphed into a horrible coughing fit that immediately swept all amusement from everyone's face.

Jack tensed, wishing there was something he could do to help Benjamin breathe more easily, but there wasn't. The fluids had to work loose on their own, and he was sure everyone was as relieved as he was when the poor man's coughing finally subsided. Benjamin took a moment to catch his breath, then spoke to his sons, telling them where to get materials to repair the fence. Pride lit his eyes as they kissed both his cheeks, said their goodbyes and ran off as fast as they'd run in.

Jack thought of his own brother and how the two of them had always looked up to their dad. The man hadn't done much around the house, always busy working at the hospital. On the occasions they'd tackled a project together, though, he still remembered how he'd admired his father's smarts and physical strength. Not having that physical strength had to hurt Benjamin like hell, but thank God he still could guide and mentor his boys in other ways.

"You have a fine family, Benjamin," Jack said. "Think they'll continue the family tradition of wine making?"

"If they do not, we will disinherit them." His eyes twinkled. "Now it is time for that wine tasting, *oui*? I cannot walk down the stairs to the cellar, so we will have to enjoy it here. Vivienne, will you uncork them, *s'il vous plaît*?"

Jack saw the closeness between husband and wife just from the way they smiled at one another, and he found himself looking at Avery. Thinking about sharing that kind of lifelong bond with a woman had never been on his list of things to accomplish in his life. Wasn't sure it ever would be. But he had to admit there just might be something good about having that kind of steady love and support in good times and bad.

The Larues had managed to keep that through plenty of bad times.

Jack didn't have to know them well to hurt for them. He got why Avery wanted him to see what Benjamin lived with, but at the same time he felt she was being naive. If he counted the number of patients living less than optimal lives, he'd spend all day doing it. Life wasn't fair, that was for sure.

The clinical trial he was working so hard on was all about trying to level the playing field just a little. Trials existed for a reason, and that reason was to test new procedures and devices. If everyone threw in the towel halfway through because potential questions arose, nothing good would ever get accomplished from most of them.

Did Avery think meeting this great family that had to live with adversity and challenges would change his goals, or make him question what he wanted to accomplish? He damned well had plenty of his own patients who had to endure a life with far less than optimal physical ability. Surely she knew that.

Improving the lives of patients was all he wanted to accomplish. If she didn't understand or believe that, their time alone together this weekend wouldn't turn out the way he hoped it would.

CHAPTER THIRTEEN

SEEING THE LARUE family always left Avery with a tumble of emotions. Pleased about spending time enjoying the closeness of their family. Grateful for her own health. Sad for what they had to deal with every day. Guilt that she hadn't done a better job designing the TAVI device before it had gone to human trials.

At that exact moment she wasn't sure which emotion was winning.

Jack's arm wrapped around her waist, holding her close, might not be helping much with the guilt and sadness, but it did feel good there. Warm and comforting. Despite their height difference, their bodies seemed to fit perfectly together as they strolled through the village in search of a *biscuiterie* and the coconut macaroons Riquewihr was famous for. The shop she usually went to was closed for the winter, and she peered hopefully at dimly lit signs, trying to find another one that was open.

"There's one," Avery said, pointing down a crooked little street. "I don't remember it, but I'm sure every one of the *biscuiteries* are good."

"So you claim these cookies are the best things in the whole world?"

"The best. I guarantee you'll love them."

They went into the tiny shop and selected a few macaroons and espresso before sitting at a small table. Avery felt pretty much sapped of small talk and nibbled her cookie, hoping its deliciousness would cheer her up and make her a better companion, which she knew she couldn't claim to be at that moment.

"I have a confession to make," Jack said, looking extremely serious.

She paused with her macaroon halfway to her mouth. "A confession?"

"Yes. I'm not a big fan of coconut. In fact, I usually avoid it like flesh-eating bacteria. But if sharing coconut macaroons with you banishes the melancholy in your beautiful eyes for even a split second, I'll gladly choke one down."

As he said it, she could swear he actually shuddered, and she managed a laugh. "You believe it would cheer me up to watch you eat something you liken to flesh-eating bacteria? What does that say about the kind of person you think I am?"

"That you are caring. And that you obviously feel all beat up right now."

"There's that astute thing again."

"Don't have to be astute to see it, Avery. How you're feeling is written all over your face."

"Good to know." She closed her eyes and swallowed at the sudden lump in her throat. "I do feel beat up whenever I see them. Who wouldn't? I designed the prosthetic valve, and that valve is why his life is awful now. It's hard for me to see that wonderful family dealing with what they deal with. See Benjamin barely able to walk, when I saw him running with the boys before my TAVI device destroyed that."

"For all you know, his heart might have gotten worse anyway. The man's been dealt a bad hand of cards, and I feel for him, too." He reached for her hand, and its warmth had her holding it tight. "But if I blamed myself for every patient who didn't do well, or who died, like Henri Arnoult, I'd never be able to function and do my job. Medicine is both rewarding and damned difficult. The only way to help people is to forge on and do the best you can. Would it help people if you just stopped designing biomedical devices? Never came up with an improved stent or something no one's invented yet?"

"No. But I should have insisted it be tested further on animals first." Not that the manufacturer and sponsor would have listened anyway. "I'd hoped you'd come to see you should consider that, too, for yours."

"I am listening to you, Avery. Hearing you loud and clear, and paying attention to the reason for your worries. I want you to know that." Seeing how deeply serious and sincere he looked brought her hope that he truly meant it. "While it's impossible to know how Benjamin's health would be right now without the TAVI, I understand your point about possibly making it worse for some patients than others. This trial is already under way with patients who have no other options. I still believe we're doing far more good than harm. But since we have more than double the number of patients now giving us additional data, I will keep him in mind as we look at how things are going."

The weight in her chest lifted at the same time it squeezed even tighter. Not only did Jack respect her opinion, it sounded like this trek had accomplished her goal. How could she have thought he might be too narrow focused, too hell-bent on success, to at least listen? She'd already seen what a committed and caring doctor he was.

"Okay, for that you don't have to eat the macaroon," she said, managing a smile. "I can't believe you were going to, if you don't like coconut. Though I admit I'm incredulous that's even possible."

"Maybe I'd like it after it's touched your lips." His finger gently swiped her bottom lip and she could see bits of cookie on his finger just before he licked it off.

Had she really been yakking away with crumbs all over her mouth? Her embarrassment at that realization got shoved aside by serious body tingling at the oh-so-sensual look he was giving her.

"You know what?" He sounded genuinely surprised. "It is better. Definitely. Sweet and delectable, in fact."

"Not like flesh-eating bacteria?" She found herself staring at his mouth, and to keep herself from diving in there and tasting for herself the crumbs and espresso on his tongue, she tried for a joke. "I'm not a big fan of escargots, which I saw you gobbling up at the hotel hors d'oeuvre party. Maybe you could hold one between your lips and I'll nibble it from there. Just to see."

His laughter made her grin and realize he'd managed to squash much of the sadness she'd been feeling. Had also managed to blast away every negative thought her former relationships had stuck in her brain nearly from the first day she'd met him. Had managed to prove himself the complete package of what a sexy man should be. At that moment she knew the attraction and lust she'd felt when she'd first met him had evolved into very much more.

The thought both scared and thrilled her, and she

wasn't at all sure what to do with the realization that had just slammed her between the eyes.

"Somehow, nibbling snails from my lips doesn't sound nearly as appealing as licking cookie crumbs from yours. I think we need further research on this, Dr. Girard."

"I think we need further research on why talking about flesh-eating bacteria and nibbling snails hasn't at all dulled my desire to kiss you, Dr. Dunbar." Further research on that, and on the tender emotions swirling around her heart as she seriously considered pressing her mouth to his right then and there.

"Then I definitely want to find out what will happen if I suggest you nibble *chocolat* from my lips. Which you can bet I'm pulling from the minibar in our room the minute we get there." His voice had gone so low, his expression so wicked that her belly quivered in anticipation of any and all nibbling action.

He tossed back the last of his espresso and stood, grasping her hand and leaning down to speak close to her ear. "Bring your cookies back to the hotel so I can see how they taste licked from your lips. After I lick off the chocolate. In fact, I like the idea of keeping a database of how all kinds of things taste from your lips and other beautiful parts of your body."

Whew, boy. She felt so hot she nearly didn't bother putting on her coat before they moved out into the chilly night. Jack walked fast, and because he was holding her hand she had to nearly run to keep up.

"Slow down a little. My legs aren't as long as yours."

"Having a hard time slowing down, thinking about our future data collection." His eyes glittered in the darkness. "And I figured the pace would keep you warmer."

No need to worry about her being warm. At all. About to skirt the ornate fountain in the center of a square, she found herself, ridiculously, wanting to make a wish like she always did when she was here. She tugged his arm so he'd stop. "Let's make a wish in the fountain. I always hope it's like the Trevi Fountain in Rome."

He pulled a couple of coins from his pocket and handed one to her. "What are you going to wish for?"

"It won't come true if you tell." She looked skyward to make her wish, surprised to see how remarkably clear it was for a winter night in France, which made her think about how wonderful it would be to make love to Jack outdoors deep in the vineyards when it was warmer, which briefly sidetracked her from her mission.

She yanked her thoughts back to ponder her wish as the stars seemed to twinkle down on them. She closed her eyes and tossed the coin into the fountain with a satisfying plunk.

"Your turn."

He tossed his coin. It landed just a millimeter from hers, and she wondered if that meant something. Which was beyond silly—it was just water in a fountain, and what would she want it to mean anyway?

"Maybe you'll get lucky and your wish will come true," she said.

His expression as his eyes met hers was odd, almost serious. It was too bad it wasn't really a magic fountain, because she'd love to ask it what his wish was.

"I'm already feeling lucky. Though I very much hope I'll get even luckier."

Her insides went all quivery again, as there was no mistaking the superheated gleam that returned to his eyes as he spoke. If the two of them making love again was what he'd wished for, he'd wasted his wish. Her breath caught just looking at his handsome face and sexy smile, and she fully intended to enjoy these hours with him before the stress of work faced them once again. Before he moved on to his next trial and she went wherever her job took her.

This time, it was Avery setting the pace, giving a quick greeting to the hotel manager before running up the two flights of stairs to their floor and into the room.

"For some reason, I'm feeling a little déjà vu," Jack said as he shoved the door closed behind them. "If it was summertime, I'd be sneaking into one of the vineyards and feeding you grapes while making love to you under the stars."

Did the man have mind-reading powers, too, or was it just part of this electric connection they seemed to have? "Funny, I was just thinking the same thing. We could add grapes to the database." Breathlessly, she wrangled off her coat and tossed it on the chair. "It does seem like we've done the same dash into a hotel room several times since we met, wearing an awful lot of heavy clothes."

"Not exactly the same dash. For one thing, it seemed like you weren't too sure you wanted to unbutton your coat before. This time you're ahead of me." He reached for her and pulled her close. "Not to mention that, each time, it's gotten even sweeter. I'm betting tonight will be also, not even counting the macaroons you brought."

"Know what? You do taste sweeter than any cookie." She stood on tiptoe and slid her hands behind his head before she kissed him. Deeply, deliciously, pouring herself into it, wanting to show him how much she'd come to care for him. To tell him without words how impressed she was that he'd shared his honest view about Benjamin and medicine, while still listening to her, respecting her, caring what she thought. To enjoy the connection they shared that was of both mind and body.

He kissed her back. And kissed her. Until her breath was choppy and her knees nearly stopped holding her up. Figuring she'd like to be sitting or something before that happened, she backed them both toward the bed, but he stopped the movement and broke the kiss. He stood there just staring at her with eyes that were peculiarly serious behind the obvious desire shining there.

"What?" she whispered.

"When I came to Paris I was keyed up and couldn't think about anything but how all my work was about to pay off. Being with you that first day seemed like a great way to take the edge off before the trial started." He slowly shook his head. "But it didn't quite work out that way. Instead, you've added another edge."

"What do you mean?"

"I hate not having complete control over how I feel about you." He pressed her body so close to his it was hard to breathe. "I've spent my adulthood being in control of my life and my career. Not having that makes me damned uncomfortable."

Her heart constricted into a cold little ball at the fact that she was the one who had control over this current phase of his career that was so important to him. And he'd be very angry and upset that she hadn't shared that reality with him, if he ended up finding out. Or if she had to wield that control and power.

And yet somehow her heart swelled, too, at his words and the way he looked at her. Like she'd come to mean as much to him as he had to her. "Is being in control all the time important? Because right now I wouldn't mind you losing control a little."

"Yeah?" She thought he was about to resume their motion toward the bed, but he veered sideways toward the bathroom. At the same time he somehow managed to slip her blouse over her head, unzip the back of her skirt, yank off his own shirt and pants, and throw a condom onto the floor until they were standing naked just outside the tiny shower.

"I've heard the verse 'Jack, be nimble, Jack, be quick,'" she said, amazed and more than excited as she stared at his all-too-sexy physique. "Was that written about you?"

"You make me want to be quick. For some things, not everything." His lips curved. "Not jumping over any candlesticks, though. Wouldn't stay lit for what I'm planning next."

"And what are you planning next?" Avery quivered at the superheated gleam in his eyes, knowing whatever it was would be a whole lot better than any snail nibbling.

Jack turned the faucet on, then tugged Avery's breathtakingly naked body into the cubicle and closed the door.

"My plan is to lick water from every inch of your skin," he said. The closeness of the space sent her pink nipples nudging against his chest and his erection into the softness of her belly, making him groan. Still-cold water rained onto his back as he shielded her from it until it warmed, but it didn't do a thing to cool the heat pumping through every one of his pores.

"It's small in here, I know. But I don't care. I liked kissing the rainwater from your face and mouth so much I've been fantasizing about getting you in the shower ever since."

"Should I get my umbrella? I kind of liked kissing you under that before we got all wet."

"Maybe next time." God, she was adorable. "I'm already all wet, and soon you will be, too."

He kissed her, letting one hand palm her breast while the other stroked down her soft skin and between her legs to make his last statement come true. The little gasping breaths and sexy sounds coming from her mouth into his nearly had him diving into her right then and there, but tonight was about slow and easy. Being together just this once without work and patients and the trial hanging around with them.

The water pounding on his back had finally warmed, and he pulled her under it to join him. He shoved her wet hair back so he could see her beautiful face and started with her forehead, sipping the water from her skin as it tracked down her cheek, her throat, her breasts.

Her fingers dug into his back as he tasted as much of her as her could reach, and the feel of her tongue licking across his shoulder, too, up his neck and around his ear, made him shiver and burn at the same time.

"You taste so delicious," he murmured against her damp sternum as her other slick wetness soaked his fingers and the scent of her touched his nose, making him want to taste her there, too. Probably not possible in the tiny shower, but later? Oh, yeah. "The best dessert any man could ask for."

"This water doesn't taste as good as the rain, though." Her chest rose and fell against his mouth. "Maybe we should try bottled water, since I don't think they drink tap water here."

"Too late for that." He chuckled and looked up at her, then paused in mid-lick. Arrested by the look on her face. It was filled with the kind of intimate connection between them he'd only felt with her—a humor and euphoria and something he couldn't quite define. He wanted to see more of it, wanted to look into her eyes as he kissed her mouth. Every bit of her tasted beyond wonderful, but that delectable mouth of hers was his absolute favorite of all.

Grasping her rear in his hands, he wrapped her legs around his waist, then realized he had to get the condom from the floor. He crouched down, juggling her on his knees as he reached for it, but she slid sideways. Mashing her close against him so she wouldn't crack her head on the tile wall, he fell back on his tailbone, his erection nearly finding home base as she slid forward on top of him.

"Well, hell. Note to self. Even the best idea can be ruined by poor planning." He steadied them both, resisting the urge to massage his sore butt, and saw she was stifling a laugh.

"NOT RUINED. ALTERED." She grabbed the trouble-making condom and tore the wrapper, and he thought he might come unglued as she opened it and rolled it on, then slowly eased herself onto him.

"Is this a good alteration to the plan?" she asked in a sultry voice as she moved on him, her eyes all smoky green, her beautiful lips parted, and he had to try twice before he could manage a short answer.

"Yes. Good." The back of his head was against the hard tile wall, his neck all kinked, and he was practically folded into a pretzel as the water still flowed and pooled on the shower floor, but none of that mattered.

All he could feel was her heat wrapped around him. All he could see was the vision that was her—her breasts, her hips, her face, the total goddess that was Avery Girard. He reached up to touch all of it, all of her, pulling her to him for the deepest kiss of his life as she increased the pace. As he felt her orgasm around him and followed her there.

Warm and bonelessly relaxed, Jack held Avery close beneath the sheets and down blanket. Round two in bed with the promised *chocolat* from the minibar had been every bit as good as the shower, which he'd never have believed until he'd experienced it.

"You were right, you know," he murmured against her silky hair.

"I usually am." He could feel her lips curve against his arm, and he smiled, as well. "What was I right about this time?"

"I did need a break. I needed to relax so I have a clear mind when I get back to work tomorrow. So thank you for that."

"Thank you for coming to meet Benjamin and listening to my worries with an open mind. That's all I wanted."

"All you wanted? Not me licking water and chocolate from you?"

"Okay, I wanted that, too."

He loved that little gleam in her eye and got distracted for a few minutes from something he'd been wanting to ask, having to kiss her again. When he finally came up for air he slipped her hair from her eyes and refocused his attention from the libido that kept leaping onto center stage around her.

"I've been wondering why you haven't come up with a next-generation TAVI device," he said. "You had to have heard through the biomedical grapevine I was working with Crilex on one. Is it because of Benjamin?"

"No. I can't quit trying to come up with a design to help people like him. I have a couple I'm working on. But I want the most promising device to be tested on animals until we're as sure as we can be of a positive outcome for patients. If I let a trial get started too soon, it's out of my hands after that."

"You didn't have much say during your first one?"

"No. Even after the percentage of patients with aortic insufficiency was too high and then Benjamin had his catastrophic problem, the sponsor insisted on finishing the trial."

Finally, he got why she wasn't working for that company anymore, doing freelance work instead. "So you quit."

"I quit. I know trials carry risks, and patients know those risks. But for the cardiologist and corporation to ignore them when things have obviously gone wrong? That's unacceptable."

"And you think that's what I'm doing?"

"No." Her lips pressed softly against his arm, and he pulled her closer against him, glad that was her answer. "I don't think this trial is there yet. But it might get there, and if it does, I hope you'll do the right thing and shut it down."

"I want to finish the trial and study the data for the rollout, because I think we have to do that to come to any real conclusion." He hoped she understood his perspective. "If there was an extreme and obvious high risk, though, I wouldn't put patients' lives in harm's way to accomplish that."

"I know that now." Her teeth gleamed white in the low light. "That's why I'm lying here in bed with you, sticky with chocolate."

"Happy to lick you more to clean it off, if you like."

"Need to record the current data first. Macaroons, wine, espresso, chocolate." She pushed up onto her elbow. Her soft hand stroked across his chest, and he captured it in his, kissing her fingers and sucking the chocolate still clinging to one until she laughed and yanked it free. "So, you know my dirty little secret about the failure of my device and the failure of the people in charge to abort the mission. Tell me how you became so passionate about a second TAVI device."

He sighed. The subject of his grandfather still had the power to bring an ache to his chest. So much knowledge and grace had died with the man.

"My dad, my brother and I all decided to become cardiologists because of my granddad. I wish you could have met him—he was just a great guy and a great doc. Always seemed ironic that he had a heart attack when he was only in his fifties and suffered for years from a faulty valve afterward. He eventually had open-heart surgery, but he was one of the small percentage who didn't make it through."

"I'm sorry, Jack."

Her hand slipped up his chest to cup his cheek, and he liked the feel of it there. He turned his face to kiss her palm. "The more I worked with various stents in interventional cardiology, the more convinced I got that we could solve that problem. Help patients without other options and someday have the TAVI procedure completely eliminate the need to perform open-heart surgery for valve replacement. I want that to happen. And I want to be a part of it."

"You already are. No matter how things end up, this step you've taken is a huge one. Mine was, as well. Unsuccessful, yes, but each time, no matter what, we learn something that will help us do it better next time."

"Is that the biomedical engineering creed?" While he admired the hell out of her attitude, and agreed with it, he couldn't help teasing her a little, wanting to bring a smile back to her now somber face.

"My creed. Yours, too, I bet."

"Yeah. Mine, too." He wasn't even close to giving up on this device. He was still convinced, even if Avery wasn't, that rolling it out to other hospitals remained the ultimate way to study it.

CHAPTER FOURTEEN

"Ah, Dr. Dunbar, you will promise I can tend my garden after you fix me, *oui*?"

"No promises, Mrs. Halbert. But I'll do the best I can. What do you like to grow in your garden?"

The smile Jack was giving the woman, the way his eyes crinkled at the corners and how he seemed genuinely interested in her garden all made Avery's heart feel squishy. It wasn't the first time that organ had felt that way around him. In fact, he'd made it squish a little their very first day together, and it had gotten to the point where it became pretty much a melted mess whenever he was around.

That she'd ever believed the success of this trial was important to him for his personal fame and fortune—more important than the success of the patients' health—made her cringe now. It was so obvious he was doing this to help people with no other surgical option. To someday change valve replacement surgery altogether, as she had wanted to do. To honor the memory of his beloved grandfather.

"I know I cannot dig my leeks from the ground. But grow chard and cucumbers, *oui*? My grandchildren love it when I fix them. And to prune my roses. *Est-ce que je serai capable de la faire?*"

He glanced at Avery, and she quickly translated. "She wants to know if she'll be able to do that after the surgery."

Jack placed his hand on the woman's gnarled one. "I hope so, Mrs. Halbert. Maybe I'll be here when you come for checkups this summer. I'd like it if you would bring me one of the roses you've pruned, to see and smell what you love to grow."

"Oui, oui." The woman beamed and patted his hand resting on hers. *"Quelle couleur? Rose? Blanche? Rouge?"*

Avery was about to translate again, but he was obviously able to figure it out as he smiled first at the woman, then at her in a slow perusal from head to toe. "I'm fond of every color, Mrs. Halbert. Preferably enjoyed all at once."

As his eyes met hers, that squishy feeling rolled all around in her belly. When he turned back to the patient she glanced down at herself and the yellow blouse and red shoes she wore. She decided she just might have to buy a new scarf in multiple hues to go with them for the next time she and Jack went out together.

The thought surprised her. Since when had she ever dressed for anyone but herself? Apparently the answer was, *not until she'd met Jack.*

Nurses came in to prep Mrs. Halbert for surgery, and as Jack spoke with them Avery quietly left the room. She pulled up the data from the past three days of surgery after she and Jack had returned from their weekend together. The weekend that had left her with the unsettling yet exhilarating knowledge that, for good or bad, her heart was in Jack's hands.

She hadn't planned on falling for him. For anybody. And she was pretty sure Jack was in the same boat. But since it was too late to keep it from happening, she fully intended to see just where these new feelings she hoped he shared might take them.

Yet there was that one potentially huge, very worrying issue with that, and she felt a little queasy just thinking about it. More than a little queasy, as she studied the information she'd gathered onto her tablet.

The dramatically increased patient load in the trial and the resulting data had waving red caution flags written all over it. If it continued like this, she would have to try to convince Jack to halt the trial. If that couldn't be accomplished, she'd have no choice at that time but to recommend to Bob it be halted and that future trials be discontinued.

Her stomach churned more, even as she hoped against hope that things would improve with the surgeries scheduled over the next couple of days. But if they didn't, if that's what had to happen, would Jack understand and agree?

She didn't know. But one thing she did know. No matter how much she'd come to care for him, those feelings would not get in the way of her professional integrity.

"Breathing better now, Mrs. Halbert?" Jack asked. It felt like he'd said those words a dozen times in just the past eight days, and it took a major effort to keep his voice calm and steady when he wanted to slam his fist into the wall and kick something.

"*Oui.* Better."

This déjà vu wasn't the great kind he'd shared with Avery, running to hotel rooms together. This was a recurring nightmare for both his patients and himself.

After taking the weekend off with Avery, Jack had returned to work feeling ready to take on the world. That feeling of energy and optimism had been quickly replaced by stress and anxiety as no fewer than three patients from last week and two from this one were already suffering with leakage from their new valves.

He studied Mrs. Halbert, very glad to see that her hands had loosened their grip on her chest and each inhalation seemed more even and less labored. He checked her vitals, asked the nurse to look at the fluid in her Foley and listened to her lungs, which were definitely clearer. Blood pressure improved, oxygen improved. Crisis hopefully over, and she'd be okay.

"Sorry you got that scare." He reached for her hand. "I know it feels bad when you can't catch your breath. But I believe you're going to feel pretty good by the time you go home to prune those roses."

"*Merci beaucoup.*" She gently patted his hand as she'd done every time he'd talked with her. If the woman had been in an advertisement playing a dear, lovely grandma, people would have bought whatever she was selling, and his chest felt a little heavy as he wondered if the sweet woman would be thanking him in a few months.

Think positively. He checked her pulse again and reminded himself she'd likely do just fine with meds to control the leakage, which was thankfully minor. But as he looked at the smile on her wrinkled face he saw someone younger. Benjamin Larue, who couldn't even sit upright without drowning in the fluid that collected in his lungs.

"I'll be back to check on you later, Mrs. Halbert." He shoved to his feet, spoke again to the nurse and said his goodbyes. Then saw Avery standing in the doorway.

Her expression bore no resemblance at all to the flirtatious, fun Avery he'd spent the weekend with. The woman looking at him rivaled a grimly stern principal about to haul a student off to her office, and Jack braced himself for the lecture she'd given before that he absolutely did not want to hear again at that moment.

He walked past her into the hallway, and she followed. He closed his eyes for a moment, trying to find his calm, before he turned to her and held up his hand. Needing to stop whatever she was about to say before it started, because it had been a damn long day and week and he knew his nerves were worn thin enough that he just might say something he regretted. He liked her—hell, more than liked her—and respected her, and getting into an argument with her was the last thing he wanted to do.

"I know the percentage of patients with problems is higher than we expected," he said. "I know you're worried that some won't be medically manageable, and I know you think we should perform the procedure on fewer patients as we finish the trial. I know, Avery."

"So what are you going to do about it?"

What *was* he going to do about it? Very good question, and one he didn't have a clue how to answer. He scrubbed a hand over his face, and when he looked at her again, saw her beautiful green eyes were somehow both soft and hard as they met his.

"Last week I was worried, but still watching. This

week, in just ten surgeries, you've had two major leakages, and now Mrs. Halbert, which makes it thirty percent. Sweet Mrs. Halbert, who just wants to be able
to prune her roses." She shook her head. "I think you
know what you should do. The real question is whether
or not you will."

"First, Mrs. Halbert's original valve was so diseased
she could barely walk twenty steps. Second, thirty percent of patients in three days isn't thirty percent over
the entire trial, which you may not be aware is how data
must be collected."

Her mouth dropped open. "That's a nice insult. Reminds me of another cardiologist I used to be involved
with."

Damn it. "I'm sorry, that was just frustration talking.
You know I admire and respect you and your expertise."
The disappointment he saw in her eyes made him want
to punch himself the way he'd wanted to punch the wall.
Saying something he shouldn't was exactly why he'd
wanted to avoid the whole conversation. "But you think
it's black and white. It isn't. If we reduce the number of
patients, there might be fewer with problems, but there
will also be fewer who get the help they need. Some
who might die soon because their aortic valve barely
works. Have you taken the time to talk to any of them
or their families? Because I have."

He knew his voice was rising, and he sucked in a
breath to control it, walking farther down the hall away
from the rooms. He turned to her again, and she had
that damned tablet clutched to her breast like a shield.
"I've told them exactly how the trial is going, good and
bad, and asked if they still wanted to participate. And
you know what? They do. For almost all of them this

is their last shot at a decent life. Or life at all. We won't have the conclusive data we need until trials are conducted over the next year at various hospitals."

"The data is screaming at you, Jack, but you're not listening."

"I am listening. I'm hearing the patients talk and the data talk. After it's rolled out everywhere it's scheduled to be, we'll listen to the entire conversation and go from there." He dropped a quick kiss on her forehead, knowing even that connection would ease his frustration with her and the situation. "I've got to get to my next surgery."

He scrubbed, then headed to the cath lab, working hard to bring his focus where it needed to be. Jessica was already there, arranging the last items needed for surgery, and she handed him his lead apron.

"Can I talk to you privately for a minute before surgery gets started?" she asked, glancing around at the doctors and nurses starting to filter in behind the glass wall in the cath lab to observe. Then she focused a laser look at Jack that was odd enough to grab his attention. He nearly asked why before just giving her a nod and moving to a quiet corner where he didn't think anyone would be able to hear them.

"What's up?"

"I found out something this morning that you're not going to like." Jessica's lips were pressed into a tight line and a deep frown had formed between her brows. In the three years they'd worked together she hadn't been a woman prone to drama. Big drama was written on her face now, though, and he felt a little fissure of concern slide down his spine.

"This sounds ominous. We're getting started soon, so make it fast, please."

She glanced behind them again before speaking, keeping her voice low. "I was in the back room finishing up some things after your last surgery yesterday evening. Bob Timkin was there, talking to a hospital administrator type from a different French hospital who had just arrived in Paris to observe the trial. Timkin was showing him the TAVI device and talking it up. But when the guy asked him about conducting a trial at his hospital in Nice, I was surprised when Timkin put him off. Said we had to finish this trial first and see what the results were before they considered any rollout."

Jack frowned. "That can't be what he said. The whole reason French interventional cardiologists have been here observing how the procedure is done is so they can conduct their own trials. The trials at other French hospitals are about ready to begin."

"How long have we worked together, Jack?" Jess fisted her hands on her hips. "I heard him say it with my own ears. Are you implying I'm confused?"

"I believe you heard something. But it just doesn't make sense, so I have to think you missed some important part of the conversation." He trusted that Jessica must have heard a conversation that had been out of the ordinary. But it didn't add up. "Crilex has poured money into the development of the device and this trial for that exact reason—to conduct additional trials elsewhere for the next year. We've just begun to collect the data."

"I know. But, believe me, I didn't misunderstand. So, when he left to take the guy to dinner, I was glad he left his Crilex binders behind. He must have gotten them later, though, because this morning they were gone."

"You were planning to snoop through them?" Jack nearly smiled despite concerns about this conversation they were having. Jessica was the queen of snooping into things around the hospital she ordinarily wouldn't be privy to. "Must have ruined your morning that they were gone."

"A little." A small, return smile flitted across her face before that deeply serious expression came back. "But I did get a chance to snoop through them some. Quite a bit, actually, until a couple of people came in. Enough to surprise and worry me. I didn't call you about it then, because I'd hoped to look more this morning, to make sure I wasn't reading it wrong. So here's the other part you're not going to like."

Her expression was so dark and downright grim his chest tightened and the alarm bells rang louder in his brain. "Spill it, Jess. We don't have all day."

"Genius biomedical engineer Dr. Girard isn't here to just observe and possibly use ideas from this device on a new one she might design in the future. Crilex hired her to give her evaluation of your device regarding its safety and effectiveness. At the end of the thirty days, if she gives them the green light, they'll roll out the trials elsewhere. If she doesn't, Crilex won't fund any more clinical trials with it."

Jack stared at her in utter disbelief. "There's no way you can be right about that. No one can make any kind of final judgment call on a device's success or failure after just one month of clinical trials. That's ridiculous."

"It may be ridiculous, but I'm telling you it's true. And there's more." She stepped even closer, speaking in a conspiratorial whisper. "I wanted to make sure you knew before the procedures today, so you could watch your back and be careful what you say and do. Here at the hospital and before you get in any deeper with her."

The numb shock he was feeling started to take over his whole body. "Make sure I knew what?"

"The whole reason Dr. Girard is here is because she approached Crilex after seeing, in all the medical journals, details on the new design for the upcoming trials. And articles about you, working together with bioengineers to develop it. She told them, just like she told you, that she believes your design hasn't fixed the valve leakage problem hers had. Crilex decided they should listen. They don't want to pour millions more into something if it has an obvious defect. They'd rather put that money into a new design, then conduct trials with that one. I don't know about you, but I'm thinking she'd rather design her own for them, which is why she's 'concerned' about yours."

The numbness faded, morphing into a hot, burning anger. Could any of this possibly be true? That, all along, Avery had withheld from him the fact that she had full control of the future of this trial? That she'd told the product developer and sponsor of these trials she thought the device he'd worked on for over a year was bad?

He sucked in a calming breath. Jessica hadn't had time to read through all the binders. Maybe she was wrong. Maybe there was a mistake.

One thing was certain, though. After this procedure, he was damned well going to find out.

Avery stood in Bob Timkin's office, waiting for him and Jack. After the last surgery, Jack had asked her to meet them here in such a tense voice she wondered if he might be coming around to her suggestion to halt the trial.

Except when he walked into the room her stomach clenched when she saw the hard look on his face. It didn't seem to be a "you might be right" expression, but who knew?

He folded his arms across his chest and stared at her. "I've been trying to figure out how to ease into this, but I'm just going to ask. Did you go to Crilex with your concerns that I thought you'd only shared with me about the new TAVI device? And did they then hire you to evaluate the device and give your opinion on its safety and effectiveness? To decide if more trials should be conducted or not?"

Avery felt like she'd swallowed the big bomb he'd just dropped. How had he found out? And what should she say? She was contractually bound to secrecy on the subject.

"I've been here to observe the new device and the clinical trial. You know that." Which was true. Just not all of it.

"Cut the crap, Avery." Anger flared in his eyes. "I may have only known you a few weeks, but I can tell when you're lying. So tell me the damned truth. I think you owe me that."

"I like you a lot, Jack, and I respect you and the work you do. But I don't owe you anything." She breathed deeply before forging on. "The people I owe are the patients who went through the trial with my first device. People like Benjamin Larue. The people I owe are the patients going through this trial now."

"So it is true," he said in a rough, disbelieving voice. He shoved his hand through his hair. Stared at her like he was seeing her for the first time. "So you get to decide if it works or if it doesn't? If it's worth putting money into the next trials? That while you've feigned interest in how I think it's all going, you haven't really given a damn because you're calling the shots?"

Her hands felt icy cold and she rubbed them together. Wrung them, really, before she realized what she was doing and flattened them against her stomach. "Yes." She braced herself for whatever reaction he was going to have to what she had to say. "After I voiced my concerns Crilex management decided that if patients have significant problems during this trial, it might make more financial sense to put their money into a next-generation device. They don't want to spend millions on multiple and extended clinical trials only to have to redesign the device and start all over again."

"You know damned well that this trial, even with the increased patient load, won't provide close to enough data to make any kind of final judgment." The anger rolling from him now was nearly palpable. "Who do you think you are? Just because you designed the first device, it doesn't make you qualified to make that kind of call on a procedure like this. You're not the cardiologist doing detailed study of the patients' history. You're not the doctor performing surgery on the patients, taking their vital signs and carefully monitoring them postop. Taking notes from the charts the *doctor* has written isn't even close to the same thing as medically caring for them."

Her own anger welled in her chest. Here it was. The same kind of insult her old boyfriend had liked to give her—that she'd been so sure Jack would never throw at her. "I may not be a cardiologist or a medical doctor but, believe me, I am more than qualified to know whether the device is safe or not and effective or not."

His eyes narrowed at her. "This whole thing smacks of unethical self-interest to me. You collect data on the trial, tell them the device is flawed and the roll-out should be stopped, and suddenly Crilex hires you to design the new one. No more messing around doing freelance work. You'll have a nice steady job and pay-check for a long while."

"That's beyond insulting." How had she thought he might be different from other egotistical, jerky cardi-ologists? "I have no expectation of being hired by Cri-lex. They have a great team of bioengineers, which you know very well since you worked with them to get this catheter designed. I resent you questioning my ethics and integrity."

"And I resent that you kissed up to me. Now I know why you approached me in the hotel and invited me out for the day, ending up in bed. You knew who I was and hoped I'd let slip some concerns of my own about the device or trial that you could use against me." He pointed his finger at her. "Stay out of my cath lab, Avery."

"For the record, I had no idea who you were. But it doesn't matter. You may be the brains and brawn behind this trial, Jack, but Crilex is the sponsor, which means they're running this show, not you. And they have given me authority to decide the next act."

Jack's heart was pounding so hard he thought it might burst from his chest. He'd thought the déjà vu with Mrs. Halbert had been unpleasant? This reenactment of the way Vanessa had used him to advance her career stunned him. Avery had pretended to like him when, in reality, she'd used him and the situation to snatch the reins of the trial from him, design a new catheter and run with it in her deceiving little hands.

"Doctors." Timkin came into the room to stand between them, frowning. "What's the disagreement here?"

"I've just discovered you gave her the authority to evaluate this TAVI device. Behind my back, keeping me in the dark. I've worked almost two years on this damned project, but you leave its future to someone else?"

"Jack. We simply wanted her expertise to contribute to the data collection. While it's true we asked her to give her opinion at the end of the trial, we have always fully expected there to be a full rollout when it's complete."

"Why didn't you tell me?" He wouldn't have let himself get so wrapped up in her if he'd known. He found himself looking at her beautiful, lying face, and wanted to kick himself. Wrapped up in her? Damn it, he felt so entwined with Avery he knew the pain of all this would twist him in knots for years to come.

"It seemed best to not have you distracted by any concerns about the future trials. You had enough on your plate getting everything set up for this one."

"I think you deemed it best for *you* not to have me go off on you. I don't appreciate my sponsor not being up-front with me, hiring someone to collect data behind my back and report to you."

"You knew I was collecting data for the study, which I've encouraged you to look at, so don't accuse me of doing it behind your back," Avery said, her eyes flashing green sparks. "Except you haven't wanted to really look at it."

"Tell me this." He turned to Timkin. "If Dr. Girard claims the device is unsafe, will Crilex hire her to design the next-generation one?"

"I already told you," Avery said hotly, "that Crilex's own biomedical engineers—"

"Yes," Timkin interrupted. "We would offer that position to Dr. Girard, should that be the case."

Jack could hardly breathe. He'd known it and had to believe she'd known it, too. "Funny, these self-interested concerns of yours, that you said you wanted to be 'honest' with me about. What a joke."

"My concern now is that thirty percent of patients have had serious to mild valve leakage just this week," she said. "Fourteen percent overall so far, which is more than double the expected number. The trial should be stopped and the data analyzed before any more procedures are performed."

"How do you feel about that, Jack?" Timkin asked.

How did he feel about her deception and the way she'd used him and her wanting to stop the trial right now so she could get started in her new, cushy job? Shocked and furious barely covered it. "It's a normal risk. All patients are being medically managed, and we've barely begun to have any kind of big picture here. You've already invested a lot in this device, and we need the year's worth of data," he said to Timkin. "Are you going to listen to her or to me?"

"Both. We'll decide on the rollout after everyone in this trial has received the TAVI. I need sufficient data to give shareholders as we decide to fund either this device or the next one."

"Now, there's some impressive corporate talk. Numbers instead of lives." Avery stared at them both, slowly shaking her head. "You told me, Jack, that you wouldn't put patients in harm's way if the risk became obvious."

"I said extreme risk. Fourteen percent isn't extreme."

She didn't rebut his statement, simply looking at him like he'd disappointed her ten times as much as her past boyfriends combined.

He told himself he didn't care. She'd used him and lied to him. He'd screwed up big time, believing in her, but that was over with. "Is this meeting done? I have work to do."

Slowly and carefully, she held the tablet out to him. "Good luck and goodbye. I can't be a part of something I no longer believe in."

She was quitting? Jack couldn't analyze the burning sensation in his gut, but he wasn't sure it was relief.

He watched the sway of her hips as she walked away, hating that he still wanted to. Watched as she moved all the way to the end of the hall and out the door, because he knew it was the last time he'd get to enjoy the view he never should have enjoyed to begin with.

He squared his shoulders. Work was what he did and who he was—always had been. It was past time to remember that.

CHAPTER FIFTEEN

AVERY WANDERED THROUGH Montmartre on her way to the apartment she'd been lucky enough to find available to rent for a few months.

She'd always loved this neighborhood. Loved walking the cobbled streets, window shopping in all the art stores and seeing the Sacré Coeur, which was beautiful any time of day.

Today, though, her soul wasn't filled with the pleasure of it all, bringing a smile to her face. Instead, it felt hollow and empty, because all she could think about was Jack. How angry and shocked he'd been, as she'd known he would be. How obviously beyond disappointed in her that she'd kept the secret she'd been asked to keep. Maybe she should have handled it differently somehow, but it was too late now.

There was plenty of disappointment to go around. She just didn't understand him. How could he be so blind to the fact that there were simply too many patients having problems to go on with business as usual?

She knew he was an excellent, caring doctor. An incredible man. But it seemed he cared more for his career and the future of the trial than he did for his patients.

Or maybe his determination and narrow focus was keeping him unrealistically optimistic when it was clearly time to look at everything more objectively.

Out of the corner of her eye she saw a couple kissing and realized she was standing at the Wall of I Love You. It was the day before Valentine's Day, which hadn't been her favorite holiday anyway, but now was a day she wished would forever disappear from the calendar.

Her heart ached, thinking of being here in Montmartre with Jack. Thinking of their time together all over Paris, and in Riquewihr, and how much she'd come to care for him.

How she'd come to fall in love with him.

Her throat clogged, and she sniffed and swallowed hard, quickly moving away from the wall. There'd be no reunion with Jack, here or anywhere. The universe had gotten it wrong somehow, and it just wasn't meant to be between them the way she'd come to think maybe it was.

Time to get back to her computer and back to work on a new TAVI device that maybe some company would want to fund. And tomorrow, on Valentine's Day?

Tomorrow she'd load up on tissues and romantic movies and marshmallows and coconut macaroons, giving herself a whole day to cry.

Jack stared at the X-ray fluoroscopy as he seated the prosthetic valve into the patient's heart, surprised and none too happy that in the midst of it a thought of Avery flashed through his mind. The thought that he wished she was watching. That she could see she'd been wrong to quit. Wrong to want to shut down the trial since, so far, not a single one of the last eight patients had had any problems with their new valves.

He told himself it didn't matter whether she was there or not. That he should be glad. But he couldn't deny that, without her behind that glass wall, the cath lab felt empty. The air flat and dull. The woman brought an effervescence and energy everywhere she went, and even though he hated that he did, he missed it.

"Valve looks like it's fully in place and seating nicely, so I'm withdrawing the catheter and guide wires," he said to those watching. There were some new docs there today from outside France, interested in bringing a trial to their own hospitals, and he was damned glad things were finally going more smoothly.

Except, suddenly, they weren't. The wire wouldn't release from the valve the way it was supposed to. With a frown, he gently pushed, pulled, and twisted it, but it was stuck like a damn fish hook in rocks on a riverbank.

"Get the patient's feet up in the air to see if a change in position helps the wire release."

Jessica did what he asked, and he worked at it a few more minutes, but nothing. "Try helping him roll onto his right side. If that doesn't work, roll him to the other side." More minutes, more tugging and jiggling, more nothing.

Damn it to hell. "Jess, grab my cellphone and get Toby Franklin on the line. The bioengineer from Crilex who helped design the device. Quick."

Jess hurried to make the call, explained the problem, then held the phone to Jack's ear.

"Toby. I've been trying for ten minutes to get the guide wires loose. Any ideas?"

"Put the patient in the left lateral decubitus position," Toby said. "See if having him take a deep breath to increase the pressure in his chest cavity helps. Then give it a good twist to the left, pull, and pray like hell."

Sweating now, Jack did what Toby had suggested and nearly shouted *Hallelujah!* when the wires finally released from the valve and he was able to slowly withdraw them. "Okay. We're almost done. Get ready to clamp the artery so I can close the access site."

He dragged in a deep, relieved breath as Jessica and the other nurse put a weight on the artery in the man's leg, then clamped it. Able to take a brief break, the thought of Avery flashed into his brain again. This time he realized he was glad she hadn't been there to see the problem, though he shouldn't feel that way. He couldn't take every damned thing that went wrong as a personal failure. But the fact that it had happened at all would suggest a design flaw different than any they'd seen so far. He didn't want to talk about it with her, but definitely planned to discuss it with Toby.

"Dr. Dunbar, patient's pressure is dropping."

He looked up from closing the access site in the man's leg to see Jessica frowning at the monitors. "What is it?"

"Was one twenty. Now it's one hundred—no, ninety—and his pulse is dropping." Her eyes were wide with concern as she looked at him over her mask. "Oxygen saturation is falling, too."

What the hell? "Give him a liter of fluid and get an echo."

Jessica quickly rolled over the echo machine and got a picture. Jack stared at the image of the man's heart. The valve looked snugged in right where it belonged.

He peered closer and his own heart practically stopped when he saw the one thing he dreaded to see.

"Oh, no," Jessica whispered. Obviously, she'd seen it, too, and they stared together for a split second before Jack snapped himself back into action.

"We have a large, pericardial infusion," he announced to the room, his throat tight. "Jess, page Anton Maran. He's the thoracic surgeon on call. Somebody get in touch with Anesthesia. Everybody move to get the patient to the OR fast. We don't have a single second to spare."

The room became a flurry of activity as they got the patient ready, running down the hall with Jack as he pushed the gurney, because saving the man's life would require fast work and a lot of luck.

Breathing hard, his mind spun back to the whole procedure. How could he possibly have perforated the man's ventricle? There was just one, obvious answer. Somehow, when he'd had to twist and pull the wires to get them to release from the valve, the catheter had torn it.

"Is he going to make it?" Jessica asked as she ran along beside him.

"Stitching the cut will be easy for Anton. Getting him to the OR on time will be the hard part. The other part of the whole equation is whether or not he can recover from the open-heart surgery we were trying to avoid."

Jack said a prayer of thanks that Anton Maran and the anesthesiologist were already scrubbed up and in the OR when they wheeled the patient in. He briefed Anton, but they'd already spent time going over each patient just in case there was an emergency like this one, so he was able to get to work fast.

Jack watched throughout the whole procedure. The shock of the man's ventricle getting perforated had worn off, leaving a stabbing ache behind. An ache of disappointment that the trial had ultimately not been the success he'd so wanted and expected it to be. An ache for the patient having to recover from this intense surgery, if he did recover.

An ache for Avery, who was long gone to who knew where. And all because he'd refused to listen to her.

Avery not being there, standing next to him through this thing, felt all wrong. How had that happened in a few short weeks? He had no idea, but somehow her absence felt like a huge, gaping hole in his life. In his heart.

All he'd wanted or needed in his life had been his work. Something he loved and was damned good at. Until Avery had shown up. Avery, in her colorful clothes with her beautiful green eyes, a teasing smile on her face and every bit as strong a work ethic as he had.

He'd wanted just a day or two of fun with her. To his surprise, she'd given him that and so much more. And what had he given her? Not a damn thing. Not even the respect he'd slammed her old boyfriend for not giving, either.

He shook his head at himself. What a damn fool.

Hours later, the surgery was over and a success, and Jack could only hope that the man remained in a stable condition. Feeling wiped out, he changed out of his scrubs and went to his hotel room. The thought of going out to eat without Avery sounded miserable, and he didn't feel like hashing out the day's events with Jessica, either. As he pondered room service, a knock at the door sent his heart slamming against his ribs.

Had Avery heard what had happened? He moved toward the door, wishing it would be her standing there, ready to give him another lecture that, for once, he'd be happy to listen to.

But it wasn't. "Jessica."

"Wow, my ego's gotten even bigger at how excited you sound to see me," she mocked. "Can I come in for a minute?"

"I'm always glad to see you. I'm just tired."

"Of course you're tired. I don't think you've rested for more than a few hours all week, and today was rough."

She sat on the side of the bed while Jack perched in the wooden chair by a small table and looked at her. "I've decided to stop the trial. I'm telling Timkin tomorrow morning."

He hadn't even realized he'd made that final decision, but now that the words had come out of his mouth, he knew without a doubt it was the right one.

Jessica nodded. "I figured you would. But that's not what I want to talk to you about."

He raised his eyebrows at her, hoping she didn't have some marital problem with Brandon. He wasn't up for that kind of conversation.

"Are you interested in where Avery Girard is?"

Hell, yes. He sat up straight. "I might be."

"Might be. Right." She snorted. "You've been glum and cranky ever since she quit the trial, even before today's scary event. Which I guess proved maybe she was right, which means maybe you should find her and apologize and kiss her and then we can all be happy again."

If only it were that easy. "I don't think she has much interest in my apologies." Or in his kisses, and the thought made his chest ache all over again.

"I bet she does. But there's only one way for you to find out." She dug into her purse and pulled out a piece of paper, leaning over to wave it in his face. "Her address in Montmartre. She's rented an apartment for the month."

"How did you find that out?"

"Nurses at any hospital know everything." She stood and patted him on the head like he was a little kid. "Now, go. I'm heading to dinner with my cousin and expect a full report tomorrow."

He stared at the door closing behind her as adrenaline surged through his blood.

He knew he'd disappointed Avery, but he could fix that. Tomorrow was Valentine's Day, and he had to admit he didn't know much about romance. But the woman who'd held his clinical trial in her hands held his heart now instead, and she'd given him a few ideas about what just might work on her.

Avery frowned at the knock on her door, wondering who the heck could be bothering her at 9:00 p.m. in an apartment few knew she'd moved into. While she was eating marshmallows and macaroons and crying over movies. Cautiously, she peeked through the peephole and the shock of who was standing there stole her breath.

How had Jack found out where she was? And why? She knew it couldn't have anything to do with it being

Valentine's Day. The man probably wasn't even aware of the holiday.

She took a moment to wipe her nose and eyes, smooth down her skirt and conjure the frustration and deep disappointment she'd felt the last time she'd seen him. Except the sight of his handsome, tired face made her want to wrap her arms around him and hold him close instead.

Disgusted with herself, she opened the door. "Lost in Paris?"

A small smile touched his mouth, but didn't make it to his eyes. "I am lost. Looking for a tour guide. You available?"

"No, I'm not."

"Can you give me just ten minutes? Please?"

She willed herself to resist the entreaty in his beautiful brown eyes, but felt that darned melting sensation inside her chest that seemed to happen whenever he was near. She sighed and figured she may as well spend ten minutes with him. Who knew? Maybe it would help heal the huge hole he'd left in her heart.

"Ten minutes."

She grabbed her coat from the rack by the door, and the feel of his fingers touching the back of her neck as he gently tugged her hair from inside made her eyes sting again. Lord, if she'd known what a heartbreaker the man was, she'd have avoided him that first day in the hotel like flesh-eating bacteria.

A little half laugh, half sob formed in her throat as she thought about their ridiculous conversation about that and snails and about the magical time they'd spent in Riquewihr. Which hadn't accomplished a thing, except to make her fall even harder for the man.

She was a little surprised he didn't touch her the way he always did as they walked to wherever it was they were going. Clearly, this must be a business visit and nothing more. Which, of course, she'd known anyway. Tears again blurred her eyes, and she forcefully blinked them back, getting really annoyed with herself now. Why would it even cross her mind to think it might be anything else?

When her vision cleared, she glanced at her watch, noting the time and fully planning on only ten darned minutes of torture with the man. Then realized they were standing by the Wall of I Love You. As she looked at him in surprise, the memory of kissing him there clogged up her breath.

"Someone told me this was a special place created just for lovers to meet. And this day, of all days of the year, seems like a good one for that to happen." He reached for her hands. "At the time, I thought that was a little hokey. I didn't realize how important such a place could be until my lover left me."

His lover. She closed her eyes at how wonderful that had been. But it wasn't meant to be. "We were supposed to be lovers just that one day. We should have left it that way."

"If that was all it was supposed to be, it would have been. But it was more than that. A whole lot more, at least for me. You brought a joy into my life I didn't even know was missing."

His words, the intense way he was staring at her squeezed her heart. But what was she supposed to say to that? He had his work and she had hers, and trying to combine that with being lovers had created nothing but conflict and pain.

"I love you, Avery." His hands tightened on hers. "I thought my work could be everything. But now I know. Even if I never see you again, it will never be enough. There would always be an empty place where you belong."

He loved her? Stunned, she stared at him as he drew her close, wrapped his arms around her and kissed her. So sure she'd never feel his lips on hers again, the pleasure of it had her melting into his chest and sighing into his mouth.

He pulled back slightly to look at her. "Remember when we made a wish at the fountain? I got my wish."

"I know. I figured you wished for sex, except I was going to give you that anyway."

"No, though I wasn't counting on that. Just hoping." A small smile touched his lips before he got serious again. "I wished for the wisdom to know when to keep at something and when to quit. It didn't kick in any too soon, but thank God it finally did."

"You're stopping the trial?"

"Yes. I'm sorry I didn't listen to you, because I should have. But that's not what I got the wisdom for. My wish kicked in when I knew I had to find you and tell you how much I love you and ask you to forgive me for all the things I've done wrong."

"You…you're not still mad about me not telling you the truth?"

"I wish you'd been honest with me, but who knows? Maybe we would have really kept our distance from one another, and we wouldn't be standing here tonight, kissing, on Valentine's Day."

"Maybe you're right. Who knew you were such a romantic?" Swallowing back tears, she reached to cup his face in her hand, barely believing this was really happening.

His lips curved in his first real smile of the night, and he gave her a long, delicious kiss that wobbled her knees before he let her go and reached into his pocket. To her shock, he pulled out the music box she'd looked at with him. The little tune tinkled when he opened it, and she started to shake all over when she saw what was inside it.

"Jack. What—"

"You said you wanted to be draped in gold." His fingers grasped the ring tucked into the red velvet folds of the box and held it up. A diamond flanked by sapphires, rubies and emeralds. "I thought a plain diamond was too dull for you, and I'm not sure this qualifies as draping, except around your finger. But I hope it's good enough for now. Will you marry me and be my forever Valentine, Avery?"

"You're asking me to marry you?" She stared into the intense brown of his eyes, barely breathing.

"I'm asking you to marry me. Begging. And since I'm about to have a heart attack because you haven't said you love me, too, please tell me. One way or the other."

"The answer is yes. *Oui, oui, oui.* And I do love you. Crazily love you. Wildly love you."

"Insanely love *you.*" He pulled her close and pressed his face to her hair. "I don't deserve you, but I'm keeping you anyway." He held her for a long time before sliding the ring onto her shaking finger. She sniffed at the tears stupidly popping into her eyes again and wished she could see it better.

He held her hand tight as he pressed soft kisses down her cheek. "What do you say we team up to create a new TAVI device, Dr. Girard?" he whispered against her skin. "Sound like a good idea?"

"Une très bonne idée." She tunneled her hands into his hair and tipped his face so she could look into his beautiful eyes. Eyes that looked at her with the same kind of love she felt all but bursting from her chest. "I think we'll make a very good team, Dr. Dunbar. One very good team."

* * * * *

HOLIDAY WITH THE BEST MAN

KATE HARDY

To Gay, the best stepmum in the world.

PROLOGUE

ROLAND'S FACE ACTUALLY ached from smiling, but he knew he had to keep it up. Apart from the fact that it was his best friend's wedding day—and of course Roland was delighted that Hugh had found the love of his life—he also knew that half the guests were remembering that Roland's wife had been killed in a car accident nearly two years ago, and were worrying that he was finding it hard to cope with today.

As he'd said to Hugh at the altar, today had brought back good memories of his own wedding day. Roland just hoped that Hugh and Bella would have a lot more years of happiness together than he and Lynette had had—and none of the misery that they'd both kept secret, even from their family and their closest friends.

He knew he ought to make the effort to go and dance with the chief bridesmaid. Even though his friend Hugh had opted to have two best men, and Tarquin—the other best man—was dancing with Bella's sister right now, Roland knew that he couldn't use that as an excuse. If he didn't dance with Grace, everyone would assume that it was because he was thinking of Lynette, and the last thing he wanted right now was another dose of pity. He'd had more than enough of that after the crash.

One dance. He could do that. All he had to do was ignore the fact that the ballroom in the Elizabethan manor house was full of fairy lights, creating the most romantic mood. And to ignore his misgivings about the chief bridesmaid, because it wasn't his place to judge her—even though the little he knew about her pressed all the wrong buttons. Grace had been so drunk the first time she'd met Hugh, that she'd thrown up over him in the taxi; plus she'd cancelled her wedding at the last minute. Sure, everyone had an off day or made mistakes, but to Roland it sounded as if Grace was a spoiled princess who liked alcohol too much.

And a spoiled, princessy drunk driver had shattered Roland's life with her selfishness, nearly two years ago. Having to be nice to a woman like that for even a few minutes really stuck in his craw. But he'd do it for his best friend's sake. His best friend who, even now, was dancing with his bride—and Roland was pretty sure that the glow around Hugh and Bella was due to more than just the fairy lights. This was real happiness.

Which left him to man up and do his duty. Right now Grace looked perfectly demure in her dark red bridesmaid's dress with its ballerina skirt and sweetheart neckline, and she was even wearing flat shoes rather than spindly heels so she didn't tower over the bride. Though her dark hair was in a sophisticated up-do with wisps of hair curled into ringlets that framed her face—a seriously high-maintenance style—and her eyelashes had most definitely been enhanced. So maybe Roland was right about the princessy tendencies. And even Tarquin—who saw the good in everyone—had admitted that Grace was nothing like sweet, bubbly little Bella.

One dance, he reminded himself. Do your duty and don't let your best friend down.

At the end of the song, he walked over to Grace and Tarquin. 'As the other best man, I believe the next dance is meant to be mine,' he said, forcing himself to keep smiling.

'It is indeed,' Tarquin said, and clapped him on the shoulder. 'See you later, Grace.'

'See you later, Tarquin,' she echoed, then turned to Roland. 'I don't think we've been properly introduced yet. I'm Bella's sister, Grace. You're Roland, aren't you?'

'Yes.'

'Nice to meet you.' She held out her hand to shake his.

Thinking, oh, please, just hurry up and let us get this over with, Roland took her hand and shook it. And he was truly shocked to find a prickle of awareness running down his spine.

Close up, Grace Faraday had the most incredible eyes: a deep cornflower blue. Her mouth was a perfect cupid's bow. Her complexion was fresh, almost dewy. And there was something that drew him to her. Something that made him feel protective.

And that really threw him.

Based on what he'd heard from the two people whose opinion he trusted most in the world, Roland had expected to dislike the woman. Instead, he found himself attracted to her. Attracted to someone he'd been sure was the last woman he'd ever want to date. And he really didn't know what to do about it.

'It was a lovely wedding, wasn't it?' Grace said. 'And that song Hugh wrote for Bella—that was amazing.'

'Mmm,' Roland said, too confused to string a coherent sentence together, and gave her his best attempt at a smile.

* * *

Grace was shocked by how different Hugh's two best friends were. Tarquin had been sweet and funny, and she'd felt really comfortable with him; Roland was taciturn to the point of making Grace feel awkward and shy, the way she usually was with strangers.

It didn't help that she'd felt a weird prickle of awareness when he'd shaken her hand. By any standards, Roland was good-looking, and the tailcoat, dark trousers, dark red waistcoat and matching cravat he wore emphasised it even more. His dark hair was brushed back from his forehead, and his slightly olive skin was clean-shaven. He could've been a model for a wedding suit company, and Grace wasn't sure if she found that more attractive or intimidating.

Maybe if she treated this as work—if she was professional and sensible with him, the way she'd be with a client—they could get through this dance without it being a total disaster.

Not having a clue what to say to him, she went through the motions of dancing with him and really hoped that pinning a smile to her face would be enough to get her through the next song. Just as well she'd talked Bella into letting her wear flat shoes; if she'd worn heels, she would probably have tripped over Roland's feet and made a complete and utter fool of herself.

Though it felt odd to be dancing with someone who was six inches taller than she was. Howard, her ex-fiancé, had been five foot eight, so she'd always worn flat shoes to make him feel less self-conscious about the fact that she was the same height as he was. Roland was broad-shouldered, where Howard had been slight. Being in his arms made Grace feel petite and feminine—something she wasn't used to. She was sensible, no-nonsense, and way too tall to be treated as if she was fragile.

She noticed that Roland's dark eyes were watchful. Why did he look so wary? Grace wondered.

Then she realised with a sinking heart just why she was feeling so awkward with him: because Roland was looking at her in exactly the same way that Howard's mother always had. Rather than smiling back at her, his lips were thinned. It was pretty clear that he'd judged her and decided that she wasn't quite good enough.

No wonder he wasn't chatting to her, the way Tarquin had. The guy clearly disliked her—even though he'd never met her before.

Well, that was his problem. She'd be polite and dance with him to this song, fulfilling their duty as the chief bridesmaid and the best man. Then she'd make sure she stayed out of his way for the rest of the evening, spending her time with her parents and Hugh's family.

And as for that weird prickle of awareness just now—well, that was just how weddings made everyone feel. Especially a glitzy wedding like this one, held in the grounds and ballroom of a manor house that had been in Hugh's family for generations. Yet behind the glamour was a warm-hearted, loving family who adored Grace's bubbly, slightly unconventional baby sister for who she was. And Grace had seen Roland hugging Bella earlier—with a proper smile on his face—so clearly he liked Grace's sister.

But this taciturn, slightly forbidding man clearly wasn't going to extend that warmth to Grace. And she absolutely refused to let it get to her. Why should his opinion of her matter? She didn't know anything about him, other than that he was Hugh's other best friend from school and was a sleeping partner in Hugh's record label. But, even if Roland was single, he was the last man Grace would even consider dating. She wasn't going to repeat her mistake with Howard. The next man she dated would be one who made her heart skip a beat and who'd sweep her off her feet. Someone who'd make her feel good about herself.

Which meant absolutely not Roland whatever-his-name-was.

Even if he was one of the most good-looking men she'd ever met.

CHAPTER ONE

Two days later

YET AGAIN GRACE missed Bella. Her little sister was the person she most wanted to call and talk to about her job interview today. But Bella was in San Francisco right now with Hugh and, even without having to take into account the eight-hour time difference, Grace had no intention of interrupting her baby sister's honeymoon. She'd wait for Bella's daily 'postcard' text, and casually mention in her reply that she thought the interview had gone OK. And hopefully later in the week she'd be able to report good news.

Please let her have got the job.

Temping was fine, but Grace knew that she functioned at her best with a solid structure in her life, and when she was able to plan more than just a couple of days ahead. The last couple of months, since she'd called off her own wedding, had changed her entire life. Not only had her relationship ended, she'd lost her job and her home because of it, too.

Bella was the bubbly one who coped just fine with change and seizing the day, always living life to the full; whereas Grace was more cautious, weighing things up and doing the sensible thing every single time. Even though calling off the wedding had been the right thing to do, it had caused her a huge amount of heartache and guilt. Bella had stood by her, as had their parents. But Grace hated the ensuing chaos.

At least she had a flat of her own again now. She'd been let down at the last minute with the flat she'd managed to find, but Bella as usual had been a bit scatty and forgotten to give her landlord her notice on time. And it had all worked out perfectly for both of them, because the landlord had agreed to let Grace take over the lease; she was just awaiting the paperwork. So that was another little bit of her life rebuilt.

Trying to push away the thought that she wasn't adjusting terribly well to her new life so far, Grace opened the front door of the house that had been converted into three flats—and saw with horror that the hallway was an inch deep in water. *Water that was coming from underneath her front door.*

OK. Forget the panic and work with your common sense, the way you always do, she told herself. Turn off the water supply at the mains to stop any more water gushing out from wherever the leak is, turn off the electricity to avoid any problems there, run the taps to make sure the system drains fully, and *then* find out where the leak is coming from and call the landlord to organise a plumber.

Fortified now she had a plan to work to, Grace opened the flat's front door to find water everywhere. The carpet was soaked through and she could see from the change in the colour of the material that the water was soaking its way up into the sofa, too. What a *mess*. She took a deep breath, took off her shoes, and put them on the kitchen

table along with her handbag and briefcase so they'd be
out of the way of the water.

Stopcock. Where would the stopcock be? The house
had been converted into flats, so there was only a fifty-
fifty chance that the stopcock would be inside her flat.
But, to her relief, when she opened the cupboard under
the sink in the hope that it was the most likely place to
find the stopcock, the little wheel on the water pipe was
clearly visible. She turned it off. Another switch dealt
with the electricity supply, and when she went into the
bathroom to turn on the taps to drain the system she
could see the problem immediately: water was gushing
through a burst pipe underneath the sink.

She grabbed the washing up bowl from the kitchen
sink and put it there to catch the water that was still gushing from the burst pipe, then turned on the taps in the
bath so the system would start to drain.

Those were the most important things. Now to call
the landlord—and she really hoped that he'd be able to
send an emergency plumber out to fix the pipe tonight.
Though, even when the pipe was fixed and the water supply was back on, Grace knew that she was still going to
have to find somewhere else to sleep tonight, because
the flat was too badly flooded to be habitable. She'd also
have to find somewhere to store all her stuff.

Although part of her wanted to burst into tears of sheer
frustration and anger and misery, she knew that crying
wasn't going to solve anything. She needed to stick with
the practical stuff. Once she'd sorted that out, she could
start weeping. But absolutely not until then.

There was a note in Bella's handwriting underneath
a magnet on the door of the fridge, with a telephone
number and the words, *Call if any problems.* Obviously

this was the landlord's number; Grace was truly grateful that for once her little sister had been organised, despite spending the last three weeks knee-deep in plans for her whirlwind wedding to Hugh. Grace grabbed her mobile phone from her bag and called the number on the note.

Roland didn't recognise the number on his phone's screen, so he let the call go through to voicemail. A cold caller would give up as soon as Roland's recorded message started playing, and anyone who really wanted to talk to him could leave a message and he'd return the call when he had time.

There was an audible sigh on the answering machine. 'Hello. This is Grace Faraday.'

Bella's sister? Roland frowned. Why on earth would she be calling him?

'Please call me back urgently.' She said her telephone number slowly and clearly. 'If I haven't heard from you within thirty minutes, I'll call an emergency plumber and assume that you'll pick up the bill.'

Why did she need an emergency plumber? And why on earth did she think that *he'd* pay for the cost?

Intending to suggest that she called her landlord or her insurance company instead, he picked up the phone. 'Roland Devereux speaking.'

There was a stunned silence for a moment. 'Roland? As in Hugh's other best man Roland?' she asked.

'Yes.'

'Um, right—if you didn't catch the message I was in the middle of leaving, it's Bella's sister Grace. There's a flood at the flat and I need an emergency plumber.' Her voice took on a slightly haughty tone. 'I assume that you, as the landlord, have a list of tradesmen you use.'

So *that* was why she thought he'd pay the bill for an emergency plumber. 'I'm not the landlord.'

'Ah. Sorry.' The haughtiness disappeared, and there was the slightest wobble in her voice. 'I don't suppose you know the landlord's contact details?'

Why on earth would he know something like that? 'No.'

'OK. Never mind.'

And there it was.

The tiniest sob. Muffled quickly, but he heard it.

It brought back all the memories of Lynette. Her heart-wrenching sobs every single month they'd failed to make a baby. The guilt about how badly he'd let her down and how he'd failed her at the last.

Plus Grace was his best friend's sister-in-law. If Roland's sister had called Hugh for help, Hugh would've come straight to Philly's rescue. So Roland knew he had to do the right thing.

'I'm sorry to have bother—' she began.

'Grace. How bad is the flood?' he cut in.

'You've just told me you're not the landlord, so don't worry about it.'

He winced, but he knew that he deserved the slightly acidic tone in her voice. But there was one thing that was bothering him. 'Where did you get my number?'

'Bella left me a note on the fridge—a phone number for emergencies.' She sighed. 'Again, I apologise. I assumed it was the landlord's number. Obviously I was wrong.'

That didn't matter right now. He was focused on the flood. 'Have you turned off the water?'

'Yes. I'm not an airhead,' she said drily. 'I also turned off the electricity supply to prevent any problems there, and I'm currently draining the system to try and stop any more water coming through. I need a plumber to fix the burst pipe, and I also need to tell the people in the flats upstairs, in case the problem in my flat has affected their water supply, too.'

He was surprised that Grace sounded so capable and so organised. It didn't fit with what he'd been told about her. But she'd said there was a burst pipe, and clearly she didn't have a number to call for help—apart from his, which Bella had left her in case of emergencies. He could hardly just hang up and leave her to it. 'What's the address?' he asked abruptly.

'Why?'

'Because you just called me for help,' he said.

'Mistakenly,' she said crisply. 'For which I apologise. Yet again.'

'Bella obviously left you my number in case of emergencies—and a burst pipe counts as an emergency.' Although Bella had forgotten to tell him she'd given Grace his number, that wasn't Grace's fault. 'Where are you?'

'Bella's flat.'

'I don't actually know the address,' Roland explained.

'Oh. Right.' Sounding slightly reluctant, she told him the address.

'OK. I'm on my way.'

'Are you a plumber or something?'

'No, but I know a good one. I'll call him on the way and have him on standby in case you can't get hold of the landlord.'

'Thank you,' Grace said. 'I appreciate this.'

Roland called his plumber from the car, warning him that it was possibly a storm in a teacup but asking him to stay on standby. But, when he turned up at the flat, he discovered that Grace had been underplaying the situation, if anything. The water had clearly been gushing for a while and the carpets were soaked through; they'd need to be taken up and probably replaced. The sofa also needed to be moved, because water was seeping into it. And he felt another twinge of guilt as he noticed that Grace looked as if she'd been crying. Although she was clearly trying to be brave, this had obviously upset her.

'Did you manage to get in touch with the landlord?' he asked.

She shook her head. 'His details are probably somewhere in Bella's shoebox—but I'm not blaming her, because I should've checked everything properly myself before she and Hugh left. I live here now, so it's my responsibility.'

'Shoebox?' he asked, mystified.

'Bella's not really one for filing,' Grace explained. 'She has a shoebox system. Business receipts go in one shoebox, household stuff in another, and you just rummage through the shoeboxes when you want something.'

'That sounds a bit chaotic.' And it was definitely not the way Roland would do things. It wasted way too much time.

Grace shrugged. 'At least she has the shoeboxes now. It took a bit of nagging to get her that far.'

What? This didn't fit, at all. Wasn't Grace the drunken, princessy one? And yet right now she was wearing a sober grey suit and white shirt; plus that looked like a proper briefcase on the kitchen table, along with a pair of sensible black shoes and an equally sensible-looking handbag. Her nails weren't professionally manicured, her dark hair was cut simply in a long bob rather than being in a fussy high-maintenance style like the one she'd had at the wedding, and her make-up was minimal.

Maybe he'd got her totally wrong. More guilt flooded through him.

'The neighbours aren't home yet, so I've left a note on their doors to tell them what's happened,' she said. 'And I really need to find the landlord's details and check the insurance.'

Again, there was that tiny wobble in her voice.

'Are you OK?' he asked, hoping that she wasn't going to start crying.

'I've had better days.' She lifted her chin. 'And worse, for that matter. I'll live. Sorry. I would offer you a cup of tea but, as I don't have water or electricity right now...' She shrugged. 'I'm afraid I can't.'

'It's not a problem,' Roland said. 'My plumber's on standby, so I'll call him again to get him up to speed with the situation—and we need to shift that sofa in a minute before it soaks up any more water, to try and minimise the damage.'

'And the bookcase. And the bed. And...' She blew out a breath. 'It's just as well my car's a hatchback. I'm going to have to move everything I can out of here until this place dries out. And find somewhere for storage— though, as all my friends have flats just as tiny as this and none of them have a garage I can borrow, even temporarily. It's probably going to have to be one of those lock-up storage places.'

'Give me a moment.' Roland went outside and made a swift call to his plumber and then to one of the restoration specialist firms he'd used in the past. He also remembered seeing a café on the corner as he'd driven here; he made an executive decision to grab two takeaway black coffees, packets of sugar and two chocolate brownies. It would give them both enough energy to get through to the next stage. And if she didn't drink coffee—well, now would be a good time to start.

Grace had talked about finding a lock-up place to store the stuff from the flat. At this time of the evening, she'd be lucky to find somewhere to sort it out. And he had more than enough space to store her stuff. Even though part of him didn't really want to get involved, part of him knew that if something like this had happened to his sister, he'd want someone looking out for her. Grace was his best friend's sister-in-law. So that kind of made him responsible, didn't it?

On the way back to her flat, he called one of his team and asked him to bring a van.

She was already loading things into the back of her car when he got there.

'Coffee,' he said, and handed her one of the paper cups. 'I didn't know if you took milk or sugar, so I got it black and there are packets of sugar.'

'Thank you. How much do I owe you?' she asked.

He shook his head. 'It's fine. And I have a van on the way. Do you have some bags, boxes or suitcases I can start filling?'

'A van?' she asked, looking puzzled.

'The flat's small, but we're not going to be able to fit its entire contents into your car and mine,' he pointed out.

'So you hired a van?' Her eyes widened. 'Actually, that makes a lot of sense. I should've thought of that. Thank you. Obviously I'll reimburse you for whatever you've paid out.'

'There's no need—it's my van,' he said.

She frowned. 'But this isn't your mess, so why...?'

'Because you're Hugh's sister-in-law,' he said. 'If this had happened to my sister when I was out of the country, Hugh and Tarq would've looked out for her. So I'm doing the same, by extension.'

'Considering that you and I didn't exactly hit it off at the wedding,' she said, 'this is really nice of you. And I appreciate it. Thank you.'

Roland was beginning to think that he'd seriously misjudged Grace. If she'd been the spoiled, princessy drunk he'd thought she was, she would've been wailing and expecting everyone else to sort out the mess for her—most probably while she swigged a glass of wine and wandered about doing nothing. Instead, while he'd been away, she'd been quietly and efficiently getting on with moving stuff out of the flat. Not liking the guilt that was beginning to seep through him, he handed her a brownie. 'Chocolate. My sister says it makes everything better.'

Then she smiled—the first real smile he'd seen from her—and he was shocked to discover that it made the street feel as if it had just lit up.

'Your sister sounds like a wise woman.'

'She is.'

Roland Devereux was the last person Grace had expected to come to her rescue, but she really appreciated the fact that he had. And today he was very different from the way he'd been at the wedding. This time, he didn't make her feel the way that Howard's mother always made her feel. He treated her like a human being instead of something nasty stuck to the bottom of his shoe.

Fortified by the coffee and the brownies, between them they had most of Grace's things outside in boxes and bags by the time Roland's van arrived. And in the meantime, Grace's neighbours had returned, offering sympathy when they saw the mess and thankfully finding the landlord's number for her.

She called the landlord, but there was no answer, so she left a message explaining what had happened and giving him her mobile number, and continued moving stuff out of the flat.

Roland's plumber arrived and took a look at the burst pipe.

'It's very old piping around here,' he said. 'The system probably got blocked somewhere along the line, and this pipe had a weaker joint that couldn't cope with the extra pressure.'

'So it wasn't anything I did wrong?' Grace asked.

'No, love—it was just one of those things. I can do a temporary repair now, and then sort it out properly tomorrow.'

She nodded. 'Thank you. Let me have an invoice and I'll pay you straight away.'

'No need—the boss is covering it.'

'The boss?' she asked, mystified.

'Roland,' the plumber explained.

What? But it shouldn't be Roland's bill. OK. Right now she didn't have time for a discussion. She'd sort it out with him later.

She'd just left the plumber when a restoration specialist turned up and introduced himself. He took photographs of everything, and asked her to hold a metal ruler against the wall to show the depth of the water. 'For the insurance,' he explained. And then he brought a machine from his van to start sucking up the water.

'I really appreciate everything you've done to help me,' Grace said to Roland. 'Just one more thing—do you happen to know the number of a good lock-up place as well?'

He shrugged. 'There's no need. You can store your things at my place.'

She blinked. 'But you don't know me. You only met me once before today. For all you know, I could be a thief or a fraudster.'

He shrugged again. 'You're my best friend's sister-in-law—that's good enough for me.' He paused. 'You really can't stay at the flat until it's dried out properly.'

'I know.' She grimaced. 'Hopefully I can persuade one of my friends to let me crash on their floor tonight, then I'll find a hotel or something to put me up until the flat's usable again.'

It was a sensible enough plan, and if Roland agreed with her he wouldn't have to get involved.

But something in her expression made him say, 'I have a spare room.'

She shook her head. 'Thank you, but I've already imposed on you far too much.'

'It's getting late,' he said, 'plus your stuff's all in the back of your car, my car, and the van. You can't do anything else here until the landlord calls you back and the insurance assessors turn up—which won't be until at least tomorrow. And you said yourself that none of your friends have the room to put you up, let alone store your stuff as well. So come and stay with me.'

'That's—that's really kind of you.'

He could see her blinking back the tears and lifted his hands in a 'stop' gesture. 'Don't cry. Please.' He didn't cope well with tears. He never had. Which had been half the problem in that last year with Lynette. He'd backed away when he shouldn't have done. And she'd paid the ultimate price.

Grace swallowed back the threatening tears and scrubbed at her eyes with the back of her hand. 'OK. No more tears, I promise. But thank you. I owe you.'

CHAPTER TWO

ONCE THE RESTORATION man had finished getting rid of the worst of the water and Grace had locked the flat, she programmed Roland's address into her satnav in case she got stuck in traffic and lost both him and the van on the way, then followed him back to his house—which turned out to be in a swish part of Docklands. Once she'd parked behind his car, outside what looked like a development of an old maltings, Roland and the van driver helped her transfer her things from their cars and the van to his garage.

'Everything will be safe here for tonight,' he said when they'd finished.

'And dry,' Grace added. 'Thank you.'

There was a row of shops on the ground floor of the building, and Grace assumed that Roland had a flat on one of the upper floors; to her surprise, she discovered that his house was at one end of the building. And when he showed her into the townhouse itself, she saw that the entire back of the house was a glass box extension. It was incredibly modern, but at the same time it didn't feel out of place—and the views over the river were utterly amazing.

'This place is incredible,' she said.

He looked pleased. 'I like it.'

'But—' she gestured to the floor-to-ceiling windows '—no curtains? Don't you worry about people peering in?'

'I have a little bit of trickery instead. It's much cleaner, design-wise. And I loathe frills and flounces—my idea of hell is those swags of fussy fabrics.'

And those were just the kind of thing Grace had in mind for her own dream home—a pretty little Victorian terraced house, with sprigged flowery wallpaper and curtains to match, and lots of cushions in cosy armchairs.

He flicked a switch and the glass became opaque, giving them complete privacy.

'Very clever,' she said. And although she would've preferred the kind of curtains he hated, she could understand what he liked about it. 'Did you have an architect design this for you?'

'That,' Roland said, 'would be me.'

Grace stared at him in surprise. 'You're an architect?'

He nodded. 'I designed Hugh and Tarquin's offices,' he said, 'and I had a hand in remodelling Hugh's place so it's soundproof—for the sake of his neighbours, if he gets up in the middle of the night and starts composing on the piano.'

'This is amazing.' She shook her head. 'What an idiot I am. I thought you were some sort of builder, given that you had a plumber and a van.'

He smiled. 'You weren't that far off. I'm in the building trade, and I was pretty hands-on with this place. I guess this was my prototype.'

'How do you mean, prototype?' she asked, not understanding.

'My company makes eco-prefab buildings—either extensions or even the whole house. They're all made off site, and they can be put up in a matter of days.'

'You mean, like the ones you see on TV documentaries about people building their own houses or restoring old industrial buildings and turning them into homes?' she asked.

'They've been featured on that sort of programme, yes,' he said.

'That's seriously impressive.'

He inclined his head in acknowledgement of the compliment. 'I enjoy it. Let me show you to the guest room.'

Like the rest of the rooms she'd seen so far, the bedroom was very modern, simply furnished and with little on the walls. But, with one wall being pure glass, she supposed you wouldn't need anything else to look at: not when you had a whole panorama of London life to look at. Water and people and lights and the sky.

There was a king-sized bed with the headboard set in the middle of the back wall, a soft duvet and fluffy pillows. The bed linen was all white—very high maintenance, she thought. The en-suite bathroom was gorgeous, and was about six times the size of the bathroom in Bella's flat; Grace still wasn't quite used to thinking of Bella's old place as her own flat.

She took the bare minimum from her case—it seemed pointless to unpack everything just for one night, when tomorrow she'd be moving to a hotel or whatever alternative accommodation the insurance company offered—and hung her office clothes for the next day in the wardrobe so they wouldn't be creased overnight. Just as she was about to go back downstairs in search of Roland, her phone rang; thankfully, it was the landlord, who'd spoken to the insurance company and could fill her in on what was happening next.

Roland was sitting at the kitchen table, checking his emails on his phone, when Grace walked into the kitchen, looking slightly shy.

'Can I get you a drink?' he asked.

'No, thanks. I'm fine,' she said. 'The landlord just called me. He's talked to the insurance company and they're getting a loss assessor out to see the flat—and me—tomorrow morning at eleven.'

She sounded a little unsure, he thought. 'Is getting the time off work going to be a problem for you?'

She wrinkled her nose. 'I'm temping at the moment—but if I explain the situation and make the hours up, I'm sure they'll be fine about it.'

He was surprised. 'Temping? So you're what, a PA?'

'An accountant,' she corrected.

Which made it even more surprising that she didn't have a permanent job. 'How come you're temping?'

'It's a long and boring story. It's also why I've moved into Bella's flat.' She flapped a hand dismissively. 'But it's not because I'm a criminal or anything, so you don't need to worry about that. I just made some decisions that made life a bit up in the air for me.'

He wondered what those decisions had been. But she was being cagey about it, so he decided not to push it. It was none of his business, in any case. 'You can keep your stuff here as long as you need to, so that isn't a problem.' He glanced at his watch. 'You must be hungry. I certainly am, so I was thinking of ordering us a takeaway.'

'Which I'll pay for,' she said immediately.

'Hardly. You're my guest.'

'You weren't expecting me,' she pointed out. 'And I'd feel a lot happier if you let me pay. It's the least I can do, considering how much you've done for me this evening.'

He could see that she wasn't going to budge on the issue. In her shoes, he'd feel the same way, so he decided to give in gracefully. 'OK. Thank you.'

'And I'm doing the washing up,' she added.

'There's no need. I have a housekeeping service.'

She scoffed. 'I'm still not leaving a pile of dirty dishes next to the sink.'

A princess would've taken a housekeeper for granted. Grace didn't, and she clearly wasn't playing a part. How on earth had he got her so wrong? 'We'll share the washing up,' he said, feeling guilty about the way he'd misjudged her. 'What do you like? Chinese? Pizza?'

'Anything,' she said.

So she wasn't fussy about food, either.

And, given the way she was dressed…it was almost as if she was trying to blend in to her surroundings. Minimum fuss, minimum attention.

Why would someone want to hide like that?

Not that it was any of his business. He ordered a selection of dishes from his local Chinese takeaway. 'It'll be here in twenty minutes,' he said when he put the phone down.

It felt very odd to be domesticated, Roland thought as he laid two places at the kitchen table. For nearly two years he'd eaten most of his evening meals alone, except if he'd been on business or when Hugh, Tarquin or his sister Philly had insisted on him joining them. Being here alone with Grace was strange. But he just about managed to make small talk with her until the food arrived.

His hand brushed against hers a couple of times when

they heaped their plates from the takeaway cartons, and that weird prickle of awareness he'd felt at the wedding made itself known again.

Did she feel it, too? he wondered. Because she wasn't meeting his eyes, and had bowed her head slightly so her hair covered her face. Did he fluster her, the way she flustered him?

And, if so, what were they going to do about it?

Not that he was really in a position to do anything about it. He'd told Hugh and Tarquin that he was ready to date again, but he knew he wasn't. How could he trust himself not to let a new partner down, given the way he'd let his wife down? Until he could start to forgive himself, he couldn't move on.

'Don't feel you have to entertain me,' she said when they'd finished eating and had sorted out the washing up. 'I've already taken up more than enough of your time this evening, and I don't want to be a demanding house guest. If you don't mind, I'm going to sort out Bella's shoeboxes for her so all her papers are in some sort of order.'

So Grace was the sort who liked organisation and structure. That made it even stranger that she'd call off her wedding only three weeks before the big day. There was a lot more to that story than met the eye, Roland was sure; but he didn't want to intrude on her privacy by asking.

'I'll be in my office next door if you need me. Feel free to make yourself a drink whenever you like. There are tea, coffee and hot chocolate capsules in the cupboard above the coffee machine.' He gestured to the machine sitting on the work surface.

'Thanks.' For the first time, she gave him a teasing smile. 'Now I've seen your house, I'm not surprised you have a machine like that.'

'Are you accusing me of being a gadget fiend?' he asked.

'Are you one?' she fenced back.

He grinned. 'Just a tiny bit—what about you?' The question was out before he could stop it, and he was shocked at himself. Was he actually flirting with her? He couldn't even remember the last time he'd flirted with anyone.

'I use an old-fashioned cafetière and a teapot,' she said. 'Though I might admit to having a milk-frother, because I like cappuccinos.'

Tension suddenly crackled between them. And Roland was even more shocked to find himself wondering what would happen if he closed the gap between them and brushed his mouth very lightly over Grace's.

What on earth was he doing? Apart from the fact that his head was still in an emotional mess, Grace was the last person he should think about kissing. He'd just rescued her from a burst pipe situation. She was as vulnerable as Lyn had been. He needed to back off. Now. 'See you later,' he said, affecting a cool he most definitely didn't feel, and sauntered into his office.

Though even at the safety of his desk he found it hard to concentrate on his work. Instead of opening the file for his current project, he found himself thinking of a quiet, dark-haired woman with the most amazing cornflower-blue eyes—and he was cross with himself because he didn't want to think about her in that way. Right now he couldn't offer a relationship to anyone. Who knew when he'd be ready to date again—if ever.

Grace sorted through the contents of Bella's shoeboxes at Roland's kitchen table, putting everything in neat piles so she could file them away properly in a binder. She tried to focus on what she was doing, but the mundane task wasn't occupying anywhere near enough of her head for her liking. It left way too much space for her to think about the man who'd unexpectedly come to her rescue.

And now she was seeing Roland Devereux in a whole new light. He'd been cold and taciturn when she'd first met him. She would never have believed that he was a man with vision. A man who could create such a stunning modern design, which somehow didn't feel out of place in its very traditional setting; he'd merged the old and the new perfectly to get the best of both worlds.

She couldn't resist taking a swift break and looking him up on the Internet. And she liked what she saw on his company website, especially the way they paid attention to detail. Although the houses they built were prefabricated, the designs didn't feel as if they were identikit; from the gallery of pictures of the finished houses, Grace could see that Roland's company had added touches to each one to make it personal to the families who'd wanted to build them. And not only was he great at design, he'd worked with conservation officers on several projects. One in particular involved an eco extension that had enhanced the old building it was part of, rather than marring it, and he'd won an award for it.

There was much more to Roland Devereux than met the eye.

And she had to push away the memory of that moment when he'd flirted with her in the kitchen. Right now, her life was too chaotic for her to consider adding any kind of relationship to the mix. And, although Roland seemed to live alone, for all she knew he could already be committed elsewhere.

So she'd just put this evening down to the kindness of a stranger, and consider herself lucky that her brother-in-law had such a good friend.

Roland had already left for the day when Grace got up the next morning, even though she'd planned to be at her desk by eight. He'd left her his spare door key along with a note on the table asking her to set the house alarm, giving her the code. He'd added, *Call me if any problems*.

She texted him to say that she'd set the alarm and thanked him for the loan of his key, then headed for the office. At work, she explained the situation to her boss, who was kind enough to let her reorganise her work schedule so she could meet the loss assessor at the flat.

But the news from the loss assessor wasn't good. It would take a couple of weeks to dry out the flat, even with dehumidifiers, and there was a chance they might need to take all the plaster off the walls to stop mould developing, and then re-plaster the walls. Which in turn would take time to dry. And the landlord would probably have to look into replacing the plumbing completely in the very near future. And that meant even more disruption.

How could a burst pipe cause so much chaos?

And she could hardly invite herself to stay with Roland for an unforeseeable amount of time. Her parents lived too far out of London for her to be able to commute from their place, and she knew her friends didn't have the room to put her up, so she'd just have to find a room in a budget hotel. Hopefully Roland wouldn't mind her leaving her stuff in his garage for another day or so until she could organise storage.

She called in to a specialist wine shop to buy a thank-you gift for him on her way back to the office, then worked through her lunch hour and left late that evening to make up the time she'd had to take out to meet the assessor. When she returned to the house in Docklands, Roland was in the kitchen, making himself a coffee.

'Hi. Coffee?' he asked, gesturing to the machine.

'Thanks, but I'm fine. Oh, and I got this for you.'

She handed him the bottle bag, and he blinked in surprise. 'What's this?'

'To say thank you,' she said. 'I have no idea if you prefer red or white wine, so I played it safe and bought white.'

'That's very kind of you,' he said.

But she noticed that he hadn't even opened the bag to look at the wine. 'Sorry. Obviously I should've gone for red.'

'Actually, I don't drink,' he said.

Grace wished the ground would open up and swallow her. 'I'm so sorry.' And she wasn't going to ask him why. It was none of her business.

'You weren't to know.' He opened the bag and looked at the label. 'Montrachet is lovely. I know a certain woman who will love you to bits for bringing this.'

His girlfriend? Grace squashed the seeping disappointment. So not appropriate. And it raised another issue. 'I hope your girlfriend doesn't mind me staying.'

'No girlfriend. I was talking about my little sister,' Roland said. 'Just because I don't drink, it doesn't mean that I make everyone else stick to water.'

And the little rush of pleasure at discovering he was single was even more inappropriate. 'Uh-huh,' she said, knowing she sounded awkward, and wishing yet again that she could be as open and spontaneous as her sister.

'So how did it go with the loss assessor?' he asked.

'Not great.' She told him what the loss assessor had said. 'So if you don't mind me staying here again tonight, I'll sort out a hotel room for tomorrow night onwards. I'll find a storage place, and it shouldn't take me too many trips to ferry all my stuff there.'

'Why go to all that trouble when I've already said you can stay in my spare room and store your stuff here?' he asked.

'Because I can't impose on you for an open-ended amount of time,' she explained. 'I know you're my brother-in-law's best friend, but this is way beyond the call of duty, and I'd rather stand on my own two feet.'

'Noted,' he said, 'but you said yesterday that you'd made some choices that made life a bit up in the air for you. I think we all have times like that, when we could maybe use a friend.'

'You're offering to be my friend?'

He looked at her, his dark eyes full of questions, and suddenly there didn't seem to be enough air in the room.

Was he offering her friendship...or something else? She didn't trust her judgement to read the situation properly.

And then Roland said, 'Yes, I think I'm offering to be your friend.'

'But we don't know each other,' she pointed out.

'I know, and I admit I took you the wrong way when I first met you.'

She frowned. 'Meaning?'

He winced. 'Meaning that I've been a bit judgemental and I can see for myself that you're not what I thought you were.'

'You're digging yourself a hole here.'

'Tell me about it,' he said wryly. 'And I'm sorry.'

'So what did you think I was?' she asked.

'Are you sure you want to hear this?'

No, but she'd gone far enough to have to keep up the bravado. 'I wouldn't have asked otherwise.'

'OK. I thought of you as the Runaway Bride,' he said.

He'd thought *what*? Obviously he knew that she'd cancelled her wedding quite late in the day—but he'd assumed that she was some kind of spoiled brat? She narrowed her eyes at him. 'You're right, that's judgemental and that's not who I am—and, for your information, I didn't leave my fiancé at the aisle or even close to it. In fact, I hadn't even bought a wedding dress.'

It was his turn to frown. 'But Hugh said you cancelled the wedding three weeks beforehand. And I've seen by the way you've dealt with the flood that you're organised. This doesn't add up. Why didn't you have a wedding dress that close to the big day?'

'It's a long and very boring story,' she said.

'I don't have anything better to do—do you?' he asked.

She blew out a breath. 'Maybe, maybe not. And I guess if I'm going to stay with you, you probably need to know why my life's a bit chaotic.'

'Let's talk over pizza,' he said, 'and maybe a glass of wine. We could open this bottle now.'

'You just told me you didn't drink.'

'I also told me I don't make everyone else around me stick to water.'

'I don't actually drink that much,' she admitted.

He looked at her. 'But the first time you met Hugh...'

Oh, no. Well, he was Hugh's best friend. Of course he'd know about what happened. 'I threw up over Hugh because I'd drunk three glasses of champagne on an empty stomach. Which is more than I would usually drink in a month.' Shame flooded through her at the memory. 'Does *everyone* know about that?'

'Tarq and I do.'

'Tarquin never mentioned it when he met me.'

He gave her a wry smile. 'Probably because Tarq's nicer than I am.'

'I'm reserving the right to stay silent.' Because Roland had come to her rescue, and he was offering her a place to stay. But she was still annoyed that he'd thought so badly of her without even waiting to hear her side of the story. Maybe she'd been right in her first impression of him, too, and he was firmly in the same box as Cynthia Sutton: cold, judgemental and obsessed by appearances.

He raised his eyebrows. 'Isn't the rest of that speech along the lines that if you want to rely on something later in court, you have to speak now?'

'Am I on trial?' she asked.

'Of course not.' He shook his head. 'Pizza it is, then. And mineral water.'

'Provided I pay for the pizza. I don't want you thinking I'm a freeloader as well as being the Runaway Bride and a lush to boot.'

The slight colour staining his cheeks told her that was exactly what he'd thought of her. Which was totally unfair—he'd jumped to conclusions without even knowing her. If it wasn't for the fact that he'd come to her rescue last night and been kind, right at that moment she would've disliked him even more than she had at the wedding.

'I know now that you're none of those things. And you insisted on paying last night, so this is on me,' he said.

'If you buy the pizza,' she said, still cross that he

thought she was one of life's takers, 'then I want an invoice for the use of your van yesterday.'

'How about,' he suggested, 'we go halves on the pizza?'

She folded her arms. 'I'd prefer to pay.'

He met her glare head-on. 'Halves or starve. That's the choice.'

And how tempted she was to choose the latter. On principle. Except she was really, really hungry and it was pointless spiting herself. 'OK. Halves. But I do the washing up. And, tomorrow, I cook for us.'

'You can cook?' He looked taken aback.

She could guess why. 'I love my little sister to bits,' she said, 'but Bella's a bit of a disaster in the kitchen. If she's cooked for you, then I understand why you're surprised—but her culinary skills don't run in the family.'

'She hasn't cooked for me. But Hugh told me how bad her stir-fry is,' he admitted.

'In her defence, she does make great pancakes and cupcakes.'

He smiled. 'But you can't live on pancakes and cupcakes alone.'

'Exactly. Is there anything you don't eat, or do you have any food intolerances or allergies?'

'No—and you can use anything you like in the kitchen.'

'I'm glad you said that, because your kitchen is gorgeous and it'll be a pleasure to cook here.' She gestured round. 'So do I take it that you're a cook, too, or is this just for show?'

Roland thought back to the times when he and Lynette had cooked together. Never in this kitchen—he'd still been renovating the place when the drunk driver had smashed into his wife's car. And he hadn't had the heart to cook since. Most of the time he lived on sandwiches, takeaways or microwaved supermarket meals; apart from when his family and his best friends insisted on seeing him, he filled the time with work, work and more work, so he didn't have the space to think. 'I don't cook much nowadays,' he said.

'Fair enough.' To his relief, she didn't pry.

'But if you can text me and let me know what time you want to eat tomorrow,' she added, 'that would be helpful.'

'I'll do that,' he said. Though it felt weirdly domestic, and it made him antsy enough not to press Grace about the reason why she'd moved to Bella's flat—just in case she expected him to share about his past, too. The last thing he wanted was for her to start pitying him—the poor widower who'd lost his wife tragically young. Especially because he didn't deserve the pity. He hadn't taken enough care of Lyn, and he'd never forgive himself for that.

Grace's phone pinged. 'I'm expecting something. Can I be rude and check my phone?' she asked.

'Be my guest.'

She glanced at the screen and smiled. 'Oh, I like this. Today's Bellagram is the Golden Gate Bridge,' she said, showing him the photograph of Bella and Hugh posing with the iconic bridge behind them.

'Bellagram?' Roland asked, not quite understanding.

'Postcard. Telegram—the modern version,' Grace explained. 'Bella likes puns.'

'She texts you every day?'

Grace nodded. 'We always text each other if we're away, sending a photo of what we've been doing. Bella forgot about the time difference for the first one, so it woke me at three in the morning.' She laughed. 'But that's Bella for you. It's great to know they're having a good time.'

'Have you told her about…?'

'The flood? No. I don't want her worrying. I just text her back to say I'm glad she's having fun and I love her,' Grace said.

Which was pretty much what his own family had done when he and Lyn had sent a couple of brief texts from the rainforest on their honeymoon, purely to stop everyone at home worrying that they'd got lost or been eaten by piranhas. Another surge of guilt flooded through him. He'd taken care of Lyn then. Where had it all gone so wrong?

He was glad when Grace was tactful enough to switch the subject to something neutral and kept the conversation easy.

Though later that evening Roland still couldn't get her out of his head. He lay awake, watching the sky through the glass ceiling of his bedroom—a ceiling that wasn't overlooked by anyone or anything—and thinking of her.

What was it about Grace Faraday?

He'd misjudged her completely. Far from being a spoiled, princessy drunk, Grace was a capable and quietly organised woman with good manners. She was a little bit shy, very independent, and *nice*. Easy to be with.

Which was why he probably ought to find somewhere else for her to stay. Grace Faraday was dangerous to his peace of mind. She was the first woman in a long time to intrigue him. Or attract him. And for someone like her to call off a wedding only three weeks before the ceremony… Something had to have been very wrong indeed. Even though it was none of his business, he couldn't help wondering. Had she discovered some really serious character flaw in her husband-to-be?

She'd been going to tell him about it, and then they'd been sidetracked. Maybe she'd tell him tomorrow.

And maybe that would be the thing to keep his common sense in place and stop him doing something stupid.

Like acting on the strong pull he felt towards her and actually kissing her.

CHAPTER THREE

THE FOLLOWING EVENING, Roland opened his front door and stopped dead. It was strange to smell dinner cooking; he could definitely smell lemons, and possibly fish.

Then he realised he could also hear music; clearly Grace had connected her MP3 player to his speakers in the kitchen. Odd; he'd half expected her to like very formal classical music, but right now she was playing vintage feel-good pop songs. And she was singing along. He smiled as she launched into 'Build Me Up, Buttercup', ever so slightly out of key.

But were the song lyrics a warning to him that she didn't want her heart broken? Not that he should be thinking about a relationship with her anyway. His smile faded as he went into the kitchen. 'Good evening, Grace.'

'Oh! Roland. Hello.' She looked up from whatever she was doing and smiled at him, and to his shock his heart felt as if it had done a somersault.

When had he last reacted to someone like this?

Then her face went bright red as she clearly thought about what she'd been doing when he'd opened his front door. 'Um—I apologise for the singing. I'm afraid I can't hold a tune.'

'That's not a problem,' he reassured her. 'You can

sing in the kitchen if you like—though actually I had you pegged for a classical music fiend.'

'The boring accountant who likes boring stuff?' she asked with a wry smile.

'Not all classical music is boring. Have you ever heard Hugh play Bach on the piano? It's amazing stuff.'

'No—and, actually, I do like classical music. Not the super-heavy operatic stuff, though,' she said. 'I've always wanted to go to one of those evenings where they play popular classical music to a background of fireworks.' She paused. 'Not that you want to be bored by my bucket list. Dinner will be about another ten minutes.'

Why did Grace think she was boring? Though Roland wasn't sure how to ask her, because she seemed to have gone back into her shell. Clearly she was used to being the shy, quiet older sister, while Bella was the bubbly one. He fell back on a polite, 'Something smells nice.'

'Thank you. I wasn't sure if you'd prefer to eat in the dining room or the kitchen, so I guessed that here would be OK—though I can move it if you like.' She gestured to the kitchen table by the glass wall, which she'd set for two.

It was definitely less intimate than his dining room would be, he thought with relief. He wasn't sure if he could handle being in intimate surroundings with her, at least not until he'd got these weird, wayward feelings under control. 'The kitchen's fine,' he said. 'Is there anything I can do to help?'

'Everything's pretty much done,' she said. 'Can I get you a coffee or something?'

'It's fine. I'll make it,' he said. 'Do you want one?'

'That'd be nice.' She smiled at him and went back

to scooping the flesh and seeds out of passion fruit. 'Thank you.'

This felt dangerously domesticated, working in the kitchen alongside her. Roland made the coffee in near silence, partly because he didn't have a clue what to say to Grace. His social skills outside work had really atrophied. Right now, he felt as gauche as a schoolboy.

'How was your day?' she asked.

'Fine. How was yours?'

'As exciting as any temporary accountancy job can be,' she said with a smile.

'Are you looking for something permanent?'

She went still. 'Roland, if you're just about to offer me a job out of pity, please don't. I'm perfectly capable of finding myself a job.'

'Actually, I don't have anything right now that would match your skill set,' he said. 'But if I did and I offered you an interview, then I'd expect you to be better than any of the other candidates before I offered you the job.'

'Good,' she said. 'And I guess it was a bit previous of me to jump to the conclusion that you were going to offer me a job—but you've already rescued me this week and...' Her voice trailed off and she looked awkward. 'Sorry.'

'And sometimes rescuers don't know when to stop and let someone stand on their own two feet. I get it,' he said. 'And no offence taken.'

'Thank you. Actually, I did have a job interview the other day. And I think it went well.' She wrinkled her nose. 'But then I came home to find myself flooded out, so I haven't really thought about it since then.' She shrugged. 'I probably haven't got the job, or I would've heard by now.'

'That depends on how many they're interviewing,' Roland said.

'I guess.' She brought a jug of what looked like sparkling elderflower cordial over to the table, and then two plates. 'I thought we could have fig, mozzarella and prosciutto skewers to start.'

'Impressive,' he said.

She laughed. 'There's nothing impressive about threading things onto skewers.'

'It's nicely presented, anyway.' He took a taste. 'And it's a good combination.'

She inclined her head in acknowledgement of the compliment. 'Thank you.'

The citrus-glazed baked salmon with sweet potato wedges, caramelised lemons, spinach and baby carrots was even nicer. 'Now this you did have to cook. Don't tell me this isn't impressive.'

'Again, it's much simpler than it looks. I was kind of guinea-pigging you,' she confessed.

'Guinea-pigging?'

'I'm going to teach Bel to cook,' she said. 'So the food needs to look pretty—but it also has to take minimum effort and not involve planning the cooking time for more than two things at once.'

He smiled at her. 'You're obviously a foodie—so why are you an accountant rather than, say, running your own restaurant?'

Because numbers were safe.

Though Grace didn't quite want to admit that. 'I was good at maths when I was at school, and accountancy has good employment prospects,' she said. 'Plus that way I could study for my qualifications in the evenings while I earned money, rather than ending up with a pile of student debt. It made sense to choose accountancy as my career.' And that was who she was. The sensible, quiet older sister who was good at sorting things out.

'Do you enjoy your job?'

She smiled. 'Bella always groans and says she doesn't get why, but actually I do—I like the patterns in numbers, and the way everything works out neatly.' She paused. 'What about you? Why did you become an architect?'

'Because I love buildings,' he said simply. 'Everything from the simplest rural cottage through to grand Rococo palaces.'

She looked at him. 'I can imagine you living in a grand Rococo palace.'

He smiled. 'They're not all they're cracked up to be. They're very cold in winter.'

She blinked. 'So you've stayed in one?'

'The French side of the family owns a chateau or two,' he admitted.

She felt her eyes widen. 'Your family owns *castles*?' Roland had a posh accent, but she hadn't realised just how posh he was. Way, way outside her own social circle.

'Chateaux tend to go hand in hand with vineyards, and our French family produces wine,' he said. 'Christmas in France when I was young was always magical, because there was always the most enormous Christmas tree with a silver star on the top, and there were roaring open fires where you could roast chestnuts and toast crumpets.'

Now she knew he was teasing her. 'Since when do they eat crumpets in France?'

He spread his hands. 'What can I say? We tend to mix the traditions a bit in my family, so we get the best of both worlds. But, seriously, that was probably where the architecture stuff started. Apart from the fact that I liked the lines and the shapes of the buildings and I was always drawing them as a boy, waking up in a freezing cold bedroom with ice on the inside of the windows made me think about how it could be made better. How we could have all the modern conveniences we were used to in London, but without damaging the heritage side of the building.'

'And that's how come you're so good at mixing the old and the new,' she said. 'The front of your house is an old maltings, but the back half is as modern as it gets.'

'All the new stuff is eco,' he said, 'and all the old building is maintained properly.' He shrugged. 'Perhaps I'm greedy, but I like having the best of both worlds. All the comfort and convenience of the modern stuff, and the sheer beauty of the old.'

She smiled and brought over dessert—passion fruit cream with almond *cantuccini*.

'This is seriously nice,' he said.

'Thank you.'

When they'd finished eating, he made them some more coffee.

'You were going to tell me yesterday,' he said, 'why your life got turned upside down. It's a bit unexpected for someone who likes order and structure to make a decision that makes everything messy.'

This time, he didn't sound judgemental, and Grace felt comfortable enough with him to tell him. 'I don't like myself very much for what I did. I know I hurt Howard and I feel bad about that.' She grimaced. 'But if I'd married him it would've been so much worse.'

'For what it's worth,' he said, 'I've already worked out that you're not a spoiled princess. Not even close. So that must've been a serious case of cold feet.'

She nodded. 'If I'm honest, I'd been feeling that way for quite a while, but I thought I could still go through with it.'

'So what happened to change your mind?'

She took a deep breath. 'The Fifty Shades of Beige party.'

Roland almost choked on his coffee. Had he just heard right? 'The *what*?'

'Howard—my ex—it was his parents' golden wedding anniversary,' Grace explained. 'I wasn't looking forward to the party, and Bella drew me this cartoon to make me laugh. She called it "Fifty Shades of Beige".'

He smiled. 'From what Tarq says about her, I can just see Bella doing that.'

'Except the awful thing was that she was right,' Grace said. 'I was the only woman there not wearing beige.'

'And it was a problem?' he asked.

'Not for me. For... Well.' She grimaced. 'Don't get me wrong—I did love Howard. But that's when I finally realised that I wasn't in love with him.'

'And there's a difference?'

'A very big difference,' she said. 'It wasn't fair to marry him, knowing that I didn't love him enough—I didn't love him the way he deserved to be loved. I think we were each other's safe option. We were settling for each other instead of looking for what we really wanted.'

'Why did you need a safe option?' He only realised he'd spoken the question aloud when he saw her wince. 'Sorry. That was intrusive and you don't have to answer,' he said hastily.

'No, it's fine. Just don't tell Bella any of this, OK?'

He frowned. From the way Grace talked, she was clearly very close to her sister. 'Why doesn't Bella know?'

'Because,' Grace said, 'she's my little sister and I love her, and I don't want to burden her with it. Basically, my dad's really unreliable and I didn't want to be like my mum. I wanted my partner to be someone I could trust.'

Roland frowned. 'But I met Ed at the wedding—he seemed really nice and not at all unreliable.'

'Ed is utterly lovely. He's Bella's biological dad, but he's my stepdad and he adopted me after he married Mum,' Grace explained. 'I think of him as my real dad, and he's been a better father to me than my biological dad could ever have been. But the first time round my mum married a charming man who let her down over and over again. He was terrible with money and he never kept his promises. He hardly ever turned up when he'd promised to be there to see me. We've pretty much lost touch over the years. I just wanted to avoid making my mum's mistake.'

'And in the process you made your own mistake,' he said. 'Picking someone who was reliable but not right for you.'

She nodded. 'Howard's a nice man. He's kind and gentle.'

'But?'

'But he made me feel like part of the furniture, and I probably did the same to him,' she admitted. 'I never once felt swept off my feet. And I think we both secretly had doubts—after all, we were engaged for four years.'

In the twenty-first century, that was an unusually long engagement, Roland thought. 'Were you saving up for a house?'

'Avoiding it, I think, if I'm honest,' Grace said. 'We didn't even live together. And if we'd really loved each other, the wedding and everything else wouldn't have mattered—we would've been together regardless. But we weren't.' She dragged in a breath. 'The truth is, if I'd married Howard, his mother would've run our lives—right down to the tiniest detail.'

'Ah, the old cliché—the interfering mother-in-law.'

'Sadly,' Grace said drily, 'in this case Cynthia more than lived up to the cliché. She wanted us to get married on her fiftieth wedding anniversary, and she wasn't very pleased when I said that I thought she ought to be the centre of attention on her special day rather than having to share it with her son's wedding.'

So Grace was tactful and kind, too, Roland thought. Rather than throw a hissy fit at the idea of sharing her wedding day, she'd tried to make the older woman feel important.

'And,' Grace added, 'I wanted my sister to be my bridesmaid.'

Roland blinked in surprise. 'She didn't want Bella to be a bridesmaid?'

'Cynthia didn't like Bella. She said Bel was too head-strong and too quirky.'

'Bella's a free spirit, yes—and she's great,' Roland said. 'I'm beginning to dislike your almost-mother-in-law.'

'Bella didn't like Cynthia, either. She called her "Mrs Concrete Hair".'

'Because it was never out of place?' Roland had to stifle a grin.

Grace nodded. 'Cynthia prided herself on always being turned out immaculately. And she wore a lot of beige.'

'Did you like her?' he asked.

Grace wrinkled her nose. 'Do I have to answer that?'

'Yes.'

She smiled wryly. 'I think Cynthia and I didn't meet each other's expectations. I wanted a mother-in-law who's like my own mum—someone who's warm and supportive, who'd be there if I needed help, but who would always encourage me to stand on my own two feet. Someone I could be friends with and who'd make me feel part of the family.'

Roland thought of his own parents. That summed up their relationship with Lynette—and his own with Lynette's parents. He'd assumed that was completely normal, but maybe they'd both been lucky.

'And what did Cynthia want?' he asked.

Grace looked away. 'Someone who'd keep up appearances at all times and do whatever she told them to.'

'Which doesn't sound like much fun.'

'It wasn't,' Grace said, her voice so quiet that he could barely hear her. 'I hated being judged all the time, and always falling short.'

Which was what he'd done to her. No wonder she'd been so prickly with him, at first.

And now he was beginning to understand her. Grace was the quiet, sensible sister. The one who'd thought she'd wanted her partner to be completely the opposite of her unreliable father. And yet what she'd really wanted was to be swept off her feet…

An idea was forming in his head.

A really crazy idea.

But maybe it could work. Could he ask her?

Should he ask her?

'Obviously cancelling the wedding shook up your life a bit,' he said, 'but why did it mean that you became a temp and you taking over the lease of Bella's flat?'

'Because I worked for Howard's family's accountancy practice,' she said. 'I could hardly keep working there when I'd just cancelled my wedding to the boss's son. I couldn't ask them for a reference, in the circumstances, so temping was my only real option. Plus I'd already given notice to my landlord, and he'd leased my flat to someone else.'

So cancelling the wedding had cost Grace her job and her home, too. Now he understood what she meant about a decision turning her life upside down. And it was a decision she clearly hadn't made lightly.

'So what are you looking for, Grace?' he asked carefully. 'Marriage?'

'Maybe, maybe not. I've just come out of a long relationship, and I guess right now I need to find out who I am and think about what I really want.' She wrinkled her nose. 'I just wanted to be swept off my feet once in a while. Which I know isn't going to happen, because I'm very ordinary—I'm not free-spirited and brave like Bella is.'

The crazy idea suddenly seemed that little bit less crazy. Maybe Grace—quiet, sensible Grace—could help him move on, haul him out of the limbo where he'd spent two long years. 'What if you had the chance to be swept off your feet? Would you take it?' he asked.

'That's *really* not going to happen,' Grace said. 'I have friends who've joined online dating sites or gone speed-dating, and they've all ended up disappointed.'

'What if,' he asked carefully, 'the date was with someone you know?'

'Such as?'

'Me.'

'You?' She stared at him, looking shocked. 'But you don't even like me.'

'I was obnoxious to you at the wedding because I'd jumped to some very wrong conclusions about you,' Roland said. 'I've got to know you better over the last couple of days and I've realised how wrong I was. And I apologise for that.'

'Thank you. I think.' She frowned. 'You're actually suggesting that we should date?'

'That we should help each other out,' he corrected. 'You want to be swept off your feet, and I need to practise my dating skills.'

She frowned. 'Why do you need to practise your dating skills?'

Grace had been brave enough to tell him about her life. Roland guessed he owed it to her to be brave back. 'I assume Bella didn't tell you?'

'Tell me what?'

'That my wife was killed in a car accident nearly two years ago—a year before I moved in here.'

She reached across the table and took his hand briefly, squeezing it gently for just long enough to convey sympathy, then letting his hand go before the contact dissolved into pity. 'I didn't know her, and it's a horrible cliché, but I'm really sorry you had to go through losing someone you loved like that.'

'It was hard,' he said. 'And I miss Lynette. A lot.' Mostly. Apart from the one sticking point in their marriage—the thing that had made him jump at the chance to get away for a few days and be rid of all the pressure. And he still felt guilty about it, even though he knew that the accident hadn't been his fault. But part of him still felt that if he'd been here instead of a couple of thousand miles away, maybe Lynette wouldn't have gone out in the car, and she wouldn't have been hit by the drunk driver. Or, even if the accident had still happened, at least he would've been by her side when she'd died, later that night.

He pushed the thought away. 'But missing her won't bring her back—and there isn't such a thing as a time machine, so I can't go back and change the past. Though, if I could, I'd stop the other driver from guzzling her way through a bottle of wine and several cocktails and then getting behind the wheel of her car.'

Now Grace understood why Roland didn't drink—and why his house was immaculate but didn't feel quite like a home. Because he'd lost the love of his life to the selfish actions of a drunk driver. 'That's so sad,' she said.

He said nothing, but gave a small nod of acknowledgement.

'But I still don't get why you're asking *me* to help you practise your dating skills.'

He reached across the table and took her hand, then drew it up to his mouth and pressed a kiss into her palm.

And Grace tingled all over. Nobody had ever kissed her hand like that before.

'My friends,' he said, 'and my family have tried to find me someone suitable to heal my broken heart.'

'Too soon?'

'Partly,' he agreed. 'But I know Lyn wouldn't have wanted me to spend the rest of my life on my own, mourning her. She would've wanted me to share my life with someone who loves me as much as she did.'

For a moment, a shadow crossed his expression. It was gone before she could be sure it was there. Maybe she'd imagined it, because hadn't he just pretty much told her that Lynette was the love of his life? Or maybe that shadow had been grief that he was still trying to be brave about.

'So,' he said, 'I'm going to start dating again. Put my life back together. But I'm finding it hard.'

'Because you're not ready to move on?'

He dragged in a breath. 'And I'm out of practice. I need to date someone who won't mind if I make mistakes and will help me get better at dating. And you want to be swept off your feet, just for a little while. So that's why perhaps we can help each other out. For two weeks.'

'Until Bella and Hugh are back from honeymoon. And no strings?' she checked.

'No strings. We could just clear our diaries outside work for those two and a bit weeks and spend time together.'

'Like a holiday?'

'I guess,' he said.

A holiday with the best man. Part of Grace wanted to say yes; but part of her wondered just how sensible this was. Roland Devereux wasn't the surly, barely civil man she'd met at Bella's wedding. He was kind and sensitive—and this side of him was seriously attractive. But he still had a broken heart; and, even though he thought he wanted to try looking for love again, that made him vulnerable.

She knew that she was vulnerable, too. Her life was still all up in the air. She wanted to stand on her own two feet and work out what she wanted from life. And did she really want to take the risk of dating someone who wasn't going to be available and maybe falling in love with him? Or would this be the thing that changed her life and made everything right again? 'Can I have some time to think about it?' she asked.

'Of course. Maybe you could tell me your answer tomorrow?'

'All right.' Sitting here at the kitchen table with him didn't feel casual and easy any more; Grace felt hot and bothered, remembering the touch of his mouth against her skin. For the last four years—and for longer than that, if she was honest—she hadn't felt anything like this. Like a teenager about to go on her first date, with her heart pattering away and butterflies dancing a tango in her stomach. 'I'd better do the washing up,' she said, taking the coward's way out of facing him.

'I'll help.'

Which would put them at even closer range. She couldn't risk that. 'There's no need,' she said brightly.

'There's every need,' he corrected. 'It's my kitchen— and I'm not the kind to make other people do my share of the chores.'

She had no answer to that.

But, as they worked by the sink, they ended up brushing against each other. Grace tingled all over—which was ridiculous, because they were both fully clothed and, technically speaking, his shirtsleeve had touched her dress, which was nothing like his bare arm against her bare torso.

And then she really wished she hadn't thought of that, because now she was imagining what it would be like if Roland was skin to skin with her. She went very still, and looked at him. He was exactly the same: still and watchful. So had he felt that strange connection between them? Was he tingling all over, too?

Grace couldn't help glancing at Roland's mouth. His

lips were slightly parted, revealing even, white teeth; how had she not noticed before how sensual the curve of his mouth was? When she looked up again, she realised that he was looking at her mouth, too.

And then he leaned forward and kissed her. It was the lightest, gentlest, most unthreatening brush of his mouth against hers, and it sent shards of desire all through her. She couldn't ever remember a kiss making her feel as hot and shivery as this before.

'Tell me tomorrow,' he whispered.

She shook her head. 'I can give you the answer right now.' Even though part of her knew this was crazy and she ought to be measured and sensible about this, the way she always was, a stronger part of her couldn't resist the challenge. And maybe taking a leaf out of Bella's book—living life to the full, instead of being sensible all the time and holding back—would be good for her.

Two weeks. No strings.

Time to take the leap.

'Yes.'

CHAPTER FOUR

THE MIDDLE OF the next morning, Roland texted Grace.

Do you have a posh cocktail dress?

She thought about it. Was he planning to take her to a cocktail bar or something? Given that Roland was six-foot-two, she could actually wear her one pair of high heels without being taller than he was and making him feel embarrassed. She could team them with a little black dress, and maybe put her hair up.

Yes. Why?

Taking you out for dinner tonight. Need you to be ready for seven. Does that fit in OK for work?

Which meant she had absolutely no idea where they were going; all she knew was that the dress code meant posh. It could be anything from a private dinner party in a castle somewhere—given that Roland's family owned chateaux in France and he mixed in very different circles from her own—to dinner at Claridge's. Was this what it felt like to be swept off your feet, not having a clue about what was happening? Grace was used to being organised and in charge, and right now she felt a bit out of her depth. But she brazened it out.

Sure, can be ready.

Good. Any allergies or things you can't bear to eat?

No to both.

Excellent. See you at seven.

Where are we going? she texted, though she had a feeling that he wouldn't tell her.

Out, was the reply that she'd half expected, leaving her none the wiser.

Roland wasn't at the house when Grace went back to Docklands after work. But he'd asked her to be ready for seven, so she showered, changed and did her hair to make sure she'd be ready. As she started applying her make-up, a wave of nervousness swept through her. This was their 'date'—and it had put her in a complete spin. She knew this wasn't a real relationship, but Roland had promised to sweep her off her feet, and she'd promised to let him practise his dating skills.

Did that mean he was going to kiss her again? And those feelings she'd had last night—would they get to the point of overwhelming her common sense? Would she end up making a fool of herself?

She tried to put the thought from her mind and concentrated on getting ready. By the time she'd finished, it was ten to seven and Roland still hadn't come back from work. Given that he'd asked her to be ready for seven, if he turned up in the next few seconds it wouldn't leave him much time to get ready to go out. But surely if he'd been held up at work or in traffic he would've called her?

Had she just made a huge mistake and agreed to a ridiculous deal with someone who would turn out to be as unreliable as her father? Someone charming who would let her down? That would mean she'd gone from one extreme to the other: from thinking of marrying a sensible man who didn't make her heart beat faster, to dating one who'd break it without a second thought. That wasn't what she wanted. At all.

Maybe she should call the whole thing off and find herself somewhere else to stay until Bella's flat had dried out.

She was about to start looking up hotels when the doorbell rang. Even though it wasn't strictly her place to answer the door, maybe it was a delivery or neighbour who needed something and she really ought to answer. When she opened the door, she saw Roland standing on the doorstep. He smiled and handed her a single red rose. 'Hi.'

'Thank you,' she said. Then she noticed the way he was dressed. He was wearing a formal dinner jacket, with a bow tie—and she was pretty sure that wasn't what he'd normally wear to the office. 'But—but...'

'But what?' he asked, his dark eyes glittering; clearly he was enjoying the fact that she was completely wrong-footed.

She gestured to his suit. 'You didn't come back here to get changed.'

'I can hardly sweep you off your feet if you see all the domestic stuff first,' he pointed out with a grin. 'I came home at lunchtime to pick up my clothes and I got changed in the office.'

'Oh.' Feeling stupid and vaguely pathetic, Grace stared at the floor. Why hadn't she thought of that? And that was why he was here at precisely seven o'clock—the time when he'd asked her to be ready. Of course he wasn't unreliable. She'd jumped to conclusions and been as unfair to him as he'd been to her.

Roland reached out, gently put the backs of his fingers under her chin and tilted her chin until she met his gaze. 'Hey. This was meant to make you feel special, not awkward,' he said. 'But I did warn you my dating skills are rusty. I'm sorry I got it wrong.'

If this was Roland in rusty mode, heaven help her when he was polished. 'It's not you, it's me being stupid,' she mumbled. 'I'd better put this rose in water—and it's lovely. Thank you.' And now she was babbling like a fool. He must be really regretting making that deal with her.

As if he could read her mind, he said quietly, 'Grace, just *relax*. This is about having fun.' Then he leaned forward and brushed his lips very lightly against hers, which sent her into even more of a tizzy. Every nerve end in her lips tingled and her knees felt as if they'd turned to soup.

'You have two minutes,' he said.

She just about managed to get her head together enough to ask, 'Where do you keep your vases?'

'Um—I don't have any, which is a bit pathetic given that my sister Philly is a florist.' He flapped a hand dismissively. 'Just use a glass for now and we'll sort it out later.'

The momentary confusion on his face made her feel a bit better. She put the rose in a glass of water in the kitchen, then joined him again at the front door.

'Your transport awaits, madam.'

She had no idea what she'd been expecting—but it certainly wasn't the gleaming silver Rolls-Royce that waited for them by the kerb, with a chauffeur at the wheel wearing a peaked cap.

'A Rolls-Royce?' she asked.

'In design terms, I prefer this to a stretch limo,' he said with a grin, and helped her into the car.

'Are you quite sure your dating skills need polishing, Roland?' she asked when he joined her in the back of the car. 'Because I think you've already swept me off my feet tonight more than I've ever been swept in my entire life so far.'

He inclined his head in acknowledgement. 'Good. That's the plan.'

They stopped outside a restaurant in Mayfair. The chauffeur opened the passenger door for her, and then Roland was by her side, tucking her arm into his elbow and leading her to the restaurant.

Grace recognised the name of the place as one of the best restaurants in London. It had two Michelin stars and the food was legendary—and it was so far out of her budget that she'd never even dreamed of booking a table here for a special birthday. Yet she noticed that the *maître d'* greeted Roland as if he was very well known here, then ushered them over to an intimate table for two.

She drank in her surroundings. This was definitely a once in a lifetime opportunity. The room was very light and airy, and was decorated in Regency style. There were Venetian glass chandeliers suspended from the ceiling, with beautiful art in gilded frames and a huge antique mirror hanging on the duck-egg-blue walls. The carpet was in a slightly darker shade than the walls, and her feet actually sank into it as she walked. The dark wood chairs had blue-and-cream-striped seats; the tables were covered with plain white damask cloths and were set with silver cutlery, with a simple arrangement of roses and a candelabrum in the centre.

'This is amazing,' she whispered when the *maître d'* had seated her and left them to look at the wine menu, 'but don't you have to book a table here months in advance?'

'Usually,' Roland agreed with a smile.

Which meant there was a reason why Roland had been able to book a table at the last minute. 'So did you go to school with the owner or something?' she asked.

He shrugged. 'I just did a little bit of renovation work for them, about four years ago.'

'They have one of your glass boxes here?'

'Sadly not. Though I do like the idea of a glass wall between the restaurant and the kitchen so the customers can see their food being cooked,' he said. 'Possibly not for here, though, because it wouldn't work with the architecture. I've booked the tasting menu for us, by the way. I hope that's OK?'

'More than OK, thank you. I've always wanted to do something like this,' she said shyly.

'And don't feel that you have to stick to water just because I don't drink,' he added. 'I'm perfectly happy for you to have the paired wines with each course if you'd like them.'

'I don't drink a lot,' she said, 'so it'd probably be a waste for me to do that. Maybe I could have one glass of wine, if they can recommend something?'

He spoke to the sommelier, who returned with a single glass of champagne and a bottle of water.

'Thank you,' she said quietly. 'That's really lovely.'

'What I like about this place is the attention to detail,' Roland said. 'Maybe it's the architect in me, but I like the fact they've kept the Regency styling right down to the glassware.'

She looked at the glass; the stem was sturdy and the bowl was conical, with an engraving of wine leaves just below the rim. 'This is an antique glass?'

'Reproduction—but a good one,' he said.

The waiter brought out the *amuse bouche*—a sunflower seed crisp with a braised artichoke and a bay leaf cream. Grace had never seen anything so beautifully presented; it looked more like a work of art than a dish.

But the first mouthful was even more amazing; the combination of the tastes, the textures and the scent stunned her.

'I've never had food this good before,' she said in almost hushed tones. 'The way the whole thing is put together and presented—it's incredible.'

Roland looked pleased. 'I hoped you'd enjoy this, seeing as you're a foodie.'

'Hey, I'm strictly amateur,' she said ruefully. 'But I like this very much indeed. Thank you so much for bringing me here.'

He smiled. 'That's what tonight's about, doing something we both like. It's nice to come here with someone I know will get this as much as I do.'

Grace wondered, had Lynette not liked this sort of thing? But she didn't ask; it was too intrusive and might spoil Roland's enjoyment of the evening. And Grace was determined to enjoy being swept off her feet, because she knew she'd never eat at a place like this again. Roland's world was in a completely different league from her own.

Course after course followed, all cooked to perfection and plated beautifully. The staff were friendly and attentive without being over the top, and Grace started to lose her shyness and relax with Roland.

'I hope you've got stamina,' he said with a grin. 'There are eight courses.'

'Eight? That's *so* greedy.' But she grinned back. 'Bring it on. I love everything about this. And, as you say, it's nice to do something like this with someone who gets it.'

'So what else do you like doing?' he asked.

She thought about it. 'Curling up on the sofa with a good book, walking in the park, going to the cinema with friends, and dance aerobics class with Bella. You?'

He considered it. 'I probably spend too much time at work. But I like wandering round museums. Especially ones in gorgeous buildings.'

'Where you look at the architecture and think what you'd do if you were given a free hand?'

'Busted,' he said with a grin.

Grace found herself relaxing with Roland, chatting easily about the food. 'A pre-dessert dessert? What a fabulous idea,' she said when the waiter brought a terrine with lemon verbena cream layered with orange curd, and served with the lightest and crispest almond *tuile*. Even better was the dark chocolate *pavé* with fresh blueberries and shards of dark chocolate. And then there was the cheeseboard, with a selection of cheese, tiny crackers, walnuts and black grapes, all served on a long slate board.

'That was utter perfection,' she said with a sigh. 'And right now I feel like a princess. A very greedy, full-to-bursting one, but definitely a princess.'

'Good.' Roland smiled at her. 'I'm glad you're enjoying this.'

While they had coffee and *petits fours*, the chef came out to see them.

'Ro. It's been too long,' he said, clapping Roland on the shoulder. 'And this is…?'

'Grace Faraday, my friend,' Roland said. 'Grace, this is Max Kleinman.'

'Delighted.' Max shook her hand warmly.

Max Kleinman was the equivalent of a rock star in the culinary world, and Grace felt incredibly shy. She knew Bella would've been in her element here and chatted away to him, and not for the first time she wished she had her sister's people skills. But she was the one who was quiet and sensible and good with numbers. All she could think of to say was, 'Your food is amazing.'

To her relief, Max looked pleased rather than embarrassed. 'I'm glad you liked it. I hope this means you'll come back.'

In my dreams, Grace thought, but she smiled. 'I hope so, too.'

Finally, the Rolls-Royce took them back to Roland's house. Grace was shocked to realise that it was almost midnight; they'd spent nearly four hours at the restaurant. She'd never lingered that long over a meal before.

Roland gestured to his coffee machine. 'Decaf cappuccino?'

'I think I'm too full to eat for another week, let alone drink coffee now,' Grace said. 'Thank you, but I'm fine.'

'So was it OK?' Roland asked.

'More than OK. I've never eaten such amazing food in my life,' she said. 'Thank you so much for spoiling me.'

'My pleasure,' he said, sounding utterly sincere rather than being polite.

'Though I have to be honest,' she said. 'I do feel as if

I'm cheating you. The deal is that I'm supposed to help you brush up your dating skills while you're sweeping me off my feet, but as far as I can see you don't need any help with your dating skills at all.'

'I think that's because of you,' he said. 'You made me feel comfortable enough to be myself with you. You're easy to talk to. Maybe—I don't know—maybe next time you can be a bit awkward with me so I have to work harder at it?'

She flushed at the compliment, pleased by the idea that she'd made this complex man feel relaxed with her. 'I'll try. And I'm organising tomorrow night. Though I'm afraid my budget won't stretch to anything as fabulous as tonight was. That is, if you want to do something?' Given that he didn't really need to practise his dating skills, it was a bit forward of her to suggest it.

He frowned. 'You don't have to organise anything. The idea is for me to sweep you off your feet.'

'Yes, I do,' she corrected, 'because I'm not a freeloader and I'm going to feel horrible if you pay for everything and sort everything out. And if I feel horrible, then you're not sweeping me off my feet. Quite the opposite.'

'You're stubborn.' To her surprise, he reached out and stroked her face. 'OK. We'll play it your way and you can organise tomorrow night. We agreed to clear our diaries so I won't be working late. I can make any time after seven.'

His touch made her feel all shivery. His eyes went dark and for a moment she thought he was going to dip his head and kiss her. But then he took a step back. 'It's late and we both have work tomorrow. I'd better let you go to bed.'

Grace was relieved and disappointed at the same time.

And she couldn't get to sleep for ages, tossing and turning and thinking about the situation. She was horribly aware how easy it would be to fall for Roland Devereux. But this wasn't real, and besides she'd only just come out of a long relationship. She needed to stand on her own two feet for a bit, not just fall for the first man to smile at her.

This was a temporary arrangement. She should just enjoy it for what it was and not be stupid enough to want more.

The next morning, Grace spent her entire journey to work looking up something unusual to do with Roland. Finally she found the perfect thing. She texted him swiftly.

Meet you at seven at Docklands. We're going by Tube. Dress code casual. Do you mind maybe eating a bit late?

It took him a while to reply.

Is fine. What are we doing?

She felt brave enough to text back, Wait and see.
Intrigued, he texted back. Bring it on.
She met him back at the house, but managed to keep him guessing about what they were doing until they were standing in the queue for the pop-up rooftop cinema.

'We're seeing *Back to the Future*?' He smiled. 'Considering what Hugh told me about Bella's first meeting with his family, I should consider myself lucky this isn't *The Sound of Music*.'

'I love that film, but no.' She smiled at him. 'Though you very nearly got *Jaws*.'

He laughed. 'I wouldn't have minded. Actually, I really like the idea of a rooftop cinema.' He eyed the sky. 'Though I hope those are threatening clouds rather than actual rainclouds.'

'They give out ponchos if it's wet,' she said. 'I checked the website.'

He brushed his mouth lightly against hers. 'That doesn't surprise me. You're good at organising things and you pay attention to detail.'

The compliment warmed her all through; and the kiss made her shivery at the knees. She was going to have to be so careful and keep reminding herself that she and Roland weren't really dating. This was simply a practice run for him.

There was a bar selling film-themed cocktails—including a James Bond martini, the White Russian from *The Big Lebowski*, and a Cosmopolitan from *Sex and the City.*

'It's my bill, tonight,' she said firmly. 'Have whatever you like.'

Roland glanced down the list of non-alcoholic cocktails. 'A Shirley Temple for me, please,' he said.

She joined him; they had a brief argument over whether sweet or salted popcorn was better, and ended up sharing a tub of each.

The film was as feel-good and fun as she remembered it. And when Michael J. Fox hitched a ride on his skateboard, she nudged Roland and whispered, 'I can't ever imagine you on a skateboard.'

'No, but I can play the guitar badly enough to make Hugh and Tarq cry—does that count?' he whispered back.

She smiled. 'Just.'

And then the butterflies in her stomach started stampeding as Roland took her hand and laced his fingers through hers. Was this still a practice run? Or did he mean it? He held her hand through the whole film, and she still hadn't worked it out when the first raindrops spattered down.

The ushers swiftly handed out ponchos to the audience, who passed them along the rows of chairs. Grace couldn't help laughing when the ponchos that reached them were pink.

'Hey. I'm comfortable enough with my masculinity to wear pink,' Roland said, and helped her with her poncho before putting on his own.

'Uh-huh.' She was still smiling.

He looked at her. 'What?'

'You, looking all pretty in pink. I should so grab a picture of that for Hugh and Tarquin,' she said with a grin.

In response he kissed her until she was breathless.

And her concentration was totally shot to pieces.

After the film, they went for a burger. 'I'm afraid this isn't going to be anywhere near up to the standard of last night's food,' Grace said ruefully.

'You're comparing apples and pears,' Roland pointed out, 'and I'm as happy with a burger as I am with gourmet food.'

She scoffed. 'You don't seriously expect me to believe that.'

'I eat out sometimes for work,' he said, 'or when Hugh and Tarq drag me out for our regular catch-up and suggest we go for a curry or a burger. But most of the time for me it's a ready meal at home or a takeaway because I don't really have the time or the inclination to cook.' He looked at her. 'But that meal you cooked me—it was very obvious that you cook on a regular basis.'

'I like cooking,' she said simply. 'It relaxes me.'

'You're really good at it. Did you ever think about going into catering rather than accountancy?'

'You asked me that before.' She shook her head. 'I'm happy with my job—or I will be, if I get offered the one I had the interview for the other day.'

'I'll keep my fingers crossed.' He paused. 'And if you don't get it?'

'Then I'll keep applying until I get a permanent job. But in the meantime the temping tides me over,' she said. 'Anyway, I don't really want to talk about work tonight. Though I guess work is a good topic for a first date when you're trying to get to know someone.'

'As we're sorting out my rusty dating skills, what other topics of conversation would you suggest for a first date?' he asked.

'Things you like and don't like. Say, what kind of films do you normally watch?' She looked at him. 'I'm guessing action movies?'

'Actually, no. I like the old ones that rely on good direction and acting rather than special effects.'

'Like Hitchcock's films?' she asked. '*Vertigo* and *Rear Window* are two of my favourites.'

'Mine, too,' he said. 'So does this mean you're a film snob at heart?'

She raised an eyebrow. 'Would a film snob go to singalong musical showings?'

He groaned. 'No. Please. Tell me you don't.'

'Oh, I do—that's one thing where Bella and I definitely see things the same way,' she said with a grin. 'You can't beat singing along to *Grease*, *Mamma Mia* or *The Sound of Music* with a cinema full of people.'

'So I really did get off lightly, tonight.'

'You don't like musicals?' she asked.

He grimaced. 'Lyn used to make me watch these terrible rom-coms. I put up with them for her sake, but…' He grimaced again. 'I'm sorry if you think rom-coms are wonderful, too, but they're really not my thing. Musicals aren't quite my thing, either.'

'I'll remember not to drag you along to a rom-com or a musical,' she said. 'Though you're missing out. Doris Day, Gene Kelly—that kind of film is the best thing ever for cheering you up when you've had a bad day.'

'No. That would be going to a gig performed by one of Hugh's pop punk bands,' he corrected. 'Standing right in the middle of the front row, yelling the songs along with them and letting the sound drive everything else out of your head.'

'Pop punk? I'm sure you look great wearing guy-liner,' she teased.

'Oh, please. At thirty, I'm way too old for that.' But he was laughing, and he held her hand all the way to the Tube station—and all the way back to Docklands.

They walked hand in hand along the river frontage in easy silence, watching the play of lights on the water. Grace thought wistfully, if only this was real. But that wasn't the deal, and she needed some space to stand on her own two feet again. So for now she'd just enjoy the moment. Two weeks of being swept off her feet. Wanting more was just greedy.

'I had a really good time tonight,' Roland said.

'Even though it's not the glamorous kind of stuff someone like you is used to?' she asked.

'It was fun,' he said. 'You put a lot of thought into it and came up with something original and different that I really enjoyed. Anyway, it doesn't have to be super-glamorous or cost a lot of money for it to be a good time—like now. There's nothing better than walking by the river at night watching the lights on the water, and that doesn't cost anything.'

'True,' she said. 'I can see why you live here.'

'Is this the sort of area where you'd live, if you had the chance?' he asked.

'Are we talking about my dream home? That would be a pretty little Victorian terraced house, filled with the kind of curtains and cushions you hate most,' she said. 'If I won the lottery, I'd want a place that overlooked somewhere like Hampstead Heath, or have one of those gorgeous houses in Notting Hill that have access to a pretty garden.'

He stopped and turned to face her. 'Like the one in the film where the movie star kisses the ordinary guy?'

'I guess,' she said, and she couldn't help staring at his mouth. Except he wasn't an ordinary guy and she wasn't a film star.

She only realised she'd spoken aloud when he said, 'I'm ordinary enough,' and leaned forward to kiss her.

Time seemed to stop. And she was super-aware of his nearness—his clean male scent, the warmth of his skin, the way the touch of his lips made her skin tingle.

A cat-call from a passing teenager broke the mood, and he took a step back. 'Sorry.'

'It's fine to kiss your date in public,' she said, striving for cool. 'Except maybe not as, um…' How could she tell him that he'd made her feel feverish, without giving herself away? 'A little cooler might be more appropriate,' she said.

'Noted.' But his pupils were huge. Was that because of the darkness around them, or had kissing her affected him the same way it had affected her? She was way too chicken to ask.

And she was even more relieved when her phone pinged. 'This might be my daily Bellagram,' she said. 'Oh, look—they took a cable car ride today.' She showed him the photograph. 'Trust Bella to hang off the running boards like Doris Day.'

'Wouldn't you do that, too?' he asked.

She gave him a rueful smile. 'I'm the sensible one. I'd be thinking of health and safety.' And missing out on the fun.

'Nothing wrong with being sensible. Do you have plans for tomorrow?' he asked as they headed back to his place.

'No.' Even if they hadn't already agreed to clear their diaries for these next few weeks, she didn't have anything planned.

'You do now—and, no, I'm not telling you what. Dress code is whatever you like. Something comfortable. But bring something warm in case it turns chilly, and I'll bring a golfing umbrella in case it rains.'

They'd be doing something outdoors, then, she guessed. 'What, no pink poncho?' she teased, trying to keep the mood light and not let him guess about how much his kiss had affected her.

'A golfing umbrella is much more appropriate,' he said, unlocking the front door.

'We're playing golf?'

'No—and stop asking questions. It's meant to be spontaneous.'

Spontaneous wasn't how she usually did things. Roland was definitely pushing her out of her comfort zone.

'See you in the morning,' he said. 'And thank you for tonight. I really enjoyed myself.'

'Me, too,' she said.

And although part of her was disappointed that he didn't want to sit with her in his kitchen, drinking coffee and talking about everything under the sun, part of her knew this was the sensible option. She'd nearly lost her head as it was when he'd kissed her. If he kissed her again...

Two weeks, she told herself. She might like the way Roland made her feel, but she was his practice date. This wasn't permanent. Wasn't real. And she'd better remember that.

CHAPTER FIVE

THE NEXT MORNING, Roland was horrified to discover that there was only one firework display set to music in a fifty-mile radius of London—and, worse still, all the tickets to it were already sold.

Oh, for pity's sake.

This was the sort of summer evening event that was often held in the park of a stately home, or possibly in a municipal park or seaside resort as part of a week's carnival event. He couldn't believe that there was only one event available that evening. Surely there had to be others?

He widened the radius for his search, and discovered that the nearest music and fireworks event with a few tickets remaining was being held a hundred miles away. A two-hour drive each end wouldn't be much fun for either of them. So much for sweeping Grace off her feet with something that he actually knew was on her bucket list and she'd really love to do.

Even though he didn't usually use the 'get me a ticket at the last minute' type websites, it looked as if that was going to be his only option. To his relief, he managed to get two tickets for the venue he'd wanted in the first place. That was the hardest bit done, he thought, and headed out to the local deli for part two of his plan. A few minutes later, everything was sorted to his satisfaction.

Roland was sure that this would be the perfect way to sweep Grace off her feet. Even if the weather wasn't on his side and it poured with rain, it wouldn't matter. The fireworks and the music would still go on. And he could set the scene for it, starting right now.

He checked the breakfast tray. Coffee, croissants, freshly squeezed orange juice, granola, Greek yoghurt and a bowl of perfect English strawberries. Philly would forgive him for not buying the sweet peas from her; he'd seen them in a shop window on the way back from the deli and they'd just reminded him of Grace, all sweet and shy. And he hoped that Grace wouldn't mind the fact that the flowers were propped in water in a juice glass rather than in a proper vase.

It was almost nine o'clock. He didn't think that Grace was the sort who'd stay in bed all day; but at the same time she would still have had the chance to relax and sleep in a bit longer than she could on a weekday. Hopefully she wouldn't mind him waking her now. He tucked the newspaper under his arm and carried the tray to her room; he balanced the tray between himself and the wall and knocked on the door. 'Grace?'

'Yes?' Her voice sounded sleepy and he felt a twinge of guilt. Maybe he should've left waking her for another half an hour.

'Can I come in? I've brought you some breakfast.'

'I…sure.'

He walked in to the room. She was sitting in the middle of the king-sized bed, nestled into the duvet, with her hair all mussed and her eyes all sleepy, and his mouth went dry. Oh, help. This wasn't in the plan. He wasn't supposed to react to her like this. He was meant to be sweeping her off her feet, not the other way round. And he definitely needed to keep his eyes off her pretty camisole pyjama top. He absolutely couldn't walk over there, slide the straps from her shoulders and kiss her bare skin. Even though his body was urging him to do exactly that.

'I, um, didn't know what you like for breakfast, but I hoped this would be OK. And I brought you the Saturday paper.'

'Thank you. That's really kind of you. And flowers. That's so lovely.'

Her smile was sweet and shy and genuine, and it made him feel warm inside. 'Pleasure.' He handed her the tray. 'I, um...' How come he was suddenly so flustered and inarticulate? He was known for being as good with words as he was with building, and he could talk anyone through even the most complex project so they understood the plan and loved the concept as much as he did. But, in Grace's presence, all his words seemed to have turned into so much hot air. 'I know we said we'd clear our diaries, but I need to nip into the office and do a few things this morning,' he improvised. 'Would you mind amusing yourself?'

'Roland, you really don't have to entertain me all the time,' she said. 'You're already being kind enough to put me up while the flat's drying out. I don't expect you to run around after me as well.'

'OK.' He couldn't take his eyes off her hair; he wanted to twine the ends round his fingers and see if it was as soft and silky as it looked. So he'd better leave before he did something stupid. 'See you later, then.'

She smiled at him. 'Have a good morning. And thank

you for breakfast. This is such a treat. I can't remember the last time someone brought me breakfast in bed.'

Hadn't Howard done that for her? Then again, she'd said they hadn't lived together.

Did that mean they hadn't slept together, either?

That was a question Roland knew he couldn't ask. Not without going into very dangerous territory indeed. Sleeping with Grace… He really had to get that idea out of his head. Fast. Because that wasn't part of the deal he'd made with her. This was about helping her to feel swept off her feet, and helping him to move past the guilt and misery so he could truly live again.

He changed the subject to something safer. 'We need to leave here at about four, if that's OK with you,' he said.

'I'll make sure I'm ready.'

And he knew she'd do exactly that; she prized reliability in others, and that meant in turn that she was always reliable too.

But even when he drove to the office, he found it difficult to concentrate on work instead of thinking about Grace. His foreman, Charlie, who'd come in to the office to debrief him on a project, teased him about being on another planet.

Possibly Planet Crazy, Roland thought, because he just couldn't get Grace Faraday out of his head.

When Roland drove back to London later that afternoon, he had just enough time to drop into the deli to pick up his order and then change into a fresh shirt and a pair of chinos. Grace was ready on time, as he'd expected; her idea of 'smart casual' turned out to be smart black trousers and a pretty strappy top. One which made him remember that pretty camisole top she'd worn in bed that morning, and heat spread through him. 'You look lovely,' he said, meaning it. And somehow he'd have to find that tricky balance between sweeping her off her feet and losing his head completely.

'Thank you,' she said, smiling in acknowledgement of the compliment.

Then he noticed just how sensual the curve of her mouth was. He itched to kiss her, but he managed to hold himself back. Just. 'Ready to go?' he asked, hoping that his voice didn't sound as croaky to her as it did to him.

'Sure.'

He kept the conversation light as he drove Grace to the stately home on the edge of London. Then she saw the banners on the wrought iron fence. 'A classical music and fireworks spectacular? We're actually going to this, right now?'

'You did tell me this sort of thing was on your bucket list,' he pointed out, enjoying the fact that her excitement had sounded in her voice.

'I know, and this is utterly wonderful—but telling you the sort of thing I'd love to do really doesn't mean that I expect you to actually take me to all my dream places,' she said, her face a mixture of delight and guilt.

'But isn't that what you're supposed to do when you sweep someone off their feet? Take them to their dream places?' he asked.

'Maybe.' She bit her lip. 'And that banner says it's sold out.'

'Uh-huh.'

'Don't tell me.' Her voice was dry. 'You called in a favour because you did some work for the people who live here?'

He laughed. 'No. Actually I got our tickets from one of those "get me in at the last minute" sites.'

'What? But they always put a massive mark-up on ticket prices!' She sounded horrified. 'Roland, I need to reimburse you for my ticket.'

He groaned as he followed the car park attendants' direction to a space on the grass. 'Grace, I know you like to be independent, and I appreciate the offer, but you're supposed to be being swept off your feet. Right now, it seems to me that you have both feet very firmly on the ground, so I'm failing miserably.'

She flushed. 'In other words, I'm being an ungrateful brat.'

'No—just a bit difficult,' he said.

'You did tell me that you wanted me to be awkward with you, so you could practise your dating skills on being smooth,' she reminded him.

'Are you telling me you're being difficult on purpose?' His eyes narrowed. 'So how do I know when you're acting and when you're not?'

She spread her hands. 'You tell me.'

He resisted the urge to kiss her until she was breathless—mainly because he knew he'd end up in a similar state, with his head in a spin. Instead, he said, 'Let's go and get set up.' And then maybe the fresh air would help bring him back to his senses. This was meant to be practice dating, not the real thing. She'd made it clear that she didn't want to be let down—and he couldn't trust himself not to repeat his mistakes and let her down.

Roland took a picnic blanket, umbrella, two small collapsible chairs and the wicker picnic hamper from the back of the car.

'What can I carry?' Grace asked.

'Nothing. It's fine.'

'It isn't fine at all. You're totally laden—and there's a big difference between being swept off your feet and being a poor, helpless female who can't carry anything in case she breaks a fingernail.'

He laughed and she narrowed her eyes at him. 'What's so funny?'

'A week ago, I would've said you were exactly that type.'

'Helpless and pathetic? Well, thank you very much.' She scowled at him.

He winced. 'Grace, I've already told you that I know how much I misjudged you. Though this is particularly bad timing.'

'How do you mean?' she asked.

'Because you're right,' he said. 'I'm fully laden. I'll have to put something down before I can kiss you to say I'm sorry for getting you so wrong.'

'You want to kiss me?'

He moistened his lower lip. 'Firstly to say sorry. And then because…'

Her heart skipped a beat. 'Because what?'

He waited until she met his gaze. 'To say I like you.'

And even though they were outdoors, standing in lush parkland, it felt as if there wasn't enough room to breathe.

'I like you, too,' she whispered. Even though she hadn't expected to. And even though she really didn't want to feel this way about him. She wanted to be independent. She couldn't possibly fall for someone this quickly. Especially someone who'd made a deal with her that he'd sweep her off her feet in exchange for her brushing up his dating skills—because she knew that everything he was saying to her was dating practice, not for real.

'I'm glad you like me,' he said, his voice slightly husky.

Grace knew she ought to leave it there, make him give her a couple of things to carry, and keep it light. But Roland was staring at her mouth, and it was a little too much to resist. She closed the gap between them, stood on tiptoe, and reached up to brush her mouth against his.

When she stepped back, she could see a slash of vivid colour across his cheeks and his eyes had gone all dark.

'If we weren't in a public place...' His voice cracked.

'But we are,' she said. 'And you need to let me carry something.'

In the end, he let her carry the umbrella and the picnic blanket. They found a nice spot on the lawns with a good view of the stage and the lake—where the fireworks were going to be set off—and between them they spread out the blanket, set up the chairs and opened the picnic basket.

When Grace had gone on picnics as a child, the food had consisted of home-made sandwiches stored in a plastic box, a packet of crisps, an apple and maybe a cupcake or some sausage rolls; there might have been cans of lemonade or cola for her and Bella to drink. Everything had been stored in a cool box, and they'd eaten without plates or cutlery.

This was a whole new level of picnic. Roland's wicker basket had storage compartments for plates, glasses, cutlery, napkins and mugs as well as for the food. And when she helped Roland unpack the food, she discovered that it was on a whole new level from the picnics of her childhood, too. There was artisan seeded bread and butter curls; cold poached chicken with potato salad, watercress and heritage tomatoes; cocktail blinis with cream cheese and smoked salmon; a tub of black olives; oatcakes with crumbly Cheddar, ripe Brie and black grapes; and then strawberries, clotted cream and what looked like very buttery shortbread.

There were bottles of sparkling water, a Thermos which she guessed was filled with coffee, and there was also a tiny bottle of champagne.

'I thought you might like some bubbly to go with your fireworks,' Roland said.

Given what she knew about the tragedy in his past, she felt awkward. 'Are you sure about this?'

He smiled at her. 'I did say I'm fine about other people drinking.'

'Then thank you. This is the perfect size for a treat. Plus it means I won't wake up with a monumental hangover or ask you to make me some banana porridge when we get home,' she said with a smile.

Then she realised what she'd said. *Home.* But the house in Docklands wasn't her home; it was his. She really hoped he hadn't noticed her gaffe.

But he seemed happy enough as he shared the picnic with her.

'So what do women expect to talk about on a date?' he asked.

'I'm probably not the best person to ask, given that I haven't dated that much apart from Howard and...' She let the sentence trail off and grimaced. 'Sorry. I'm not living up to my part of the deal. Let me start again. I guess it's about finding out about each other, and what we've got in common.'

'How do you do that?'

She was pretty sure he already knew that. There was absolutely nothing wrong with his social skills. But she'd go with it for now. 'I guess it's the same as you'd do with any new friendship or even a business relationship—you start with where you are and work from there. If you'd met your date at a swimming pool, you'd ask her how often she came for a swim, or whether she preferred swimming in the pool to swimming in the sea, or where was the nicest place she'd ever been swimming. That sort of thing.'

He smiled. 'So, as we're at a musical event, this is where I ask what sort of music you like? Even though actually I already know that you like popular classical music, and you sing along to the radio.'

She smiled back. 'And then I ask you what you like, even though you already told me yesterday that you like loud pop punk.'

'I do.' He thought about it. 'I like popular classical music as well as indie rock. And I've never been to the opera, but I've been to a few good gigs in my time. Especially since Hugh set up Insurgo.' He paused. 'So that's covered what we listen to. If I extend that to actually playing music—I did about a term's worth of violin lessons before my parents gave in and begged me to stop. What about you?'

'Apart from singing Christmas carols at the infant school nativity play—oh, and playing the triangle for "Twinkle, Twinkle, Little Star" one year and doing it in completely the wrong place—no,' she said. 'None of my friends are musical, either.'

'Some of mine are.' He shrugged. 'But you already know that my best friends own an indie recording label and Hugh's an amazing producer. And your sister gave him his music back. It's great to see him with his heart and soul back in place.'

'I think Hugh and Bella are good for each other,' she said. 'Which reminds me—today's Bellagram.'

Roland burst out laughing when he saw the photograph of Hugh by the railings on Fisherman's Wharf, posing like a sea lion clapping its front feet together, with a crowd of sea lions behind him. 'That's priceless.' He looked at Grace. 'Are you sending her Bellagrams back?'

Grace shook her head. 'If I did, she'd start asking questions—and our deal is just between us.'

'True.' He paused. 'OK. That's music done. What next? I know you can cook, and you know I don't bother. We both like good food.'

'And, even though you might not cook something yourself, you make great choices. This cheese is amazing,' she said, helping herself to another slice of the Cheddar with an oatcake.

'Food, music. Next topic.' He looked thoughtful. 'Travel?'

'I haven't travelled that much,' she admitted.

Because she was scared of flying? Or had she just never had the chance to travel?

If it was the latter, Roland thought, this was a definite sweeping-off-feet opportunity. The perfect way to end their time together, even. He knew exactly where he was going to take her. He'd book it later tonight.

'Do you have a passport?' he checked.

She nodded.

Good, he thought. That was the biggest barrier out of the way. Then he remembered that she'd called off her wedding very recently and grimaced. 'Sorry. Did I just put my foot in it? Had you booked an amazing honeymoon in Hawaii or something?'

She shook her head. 'Howard wasn't really one for long-haul flights—or even short-haul, really. We were going to drive down to the south of France. Cynthia had asked a couple of her friends to lend us their flat.'

Who on earth organised their son's honeymoon, unless it was a special surprise and something that the happy couple couldn't afford to do for themselves? Roland wondered. And although a borrowed flat in the South of France would be very nice for a short break, he didn't understand why a qualified accountant who worked for the family firm—and therefore had to be on a pretty decent salary—couldn't afford to book something a little more special for his honeymoon. So either Howard and his family were very mean with money, or his mother was a control freak who refused to let her son make his own decisions. Either way, it sounded as if Grace had had a lucky escape.

'The South of France is nice,' he said carefully.

'But not where you'd choose for a honeymoon?' she asked, picking up on his hesitation.

'No,' he admitted. 'And definitely not a borrowed flat if I could afford to pay for somewhere myself.'

'Where did you and Lynette go?' she asked. Then she bit her lip. 'Sorry. That was nosey. I didn't mean to bring up memories.'

'They're good memories,' he said. And, surprisingly, it didn't hurt to talk about Lynette to Grace. It was actually nice to remember the times when they'd been happy. Before the baby-making project had put so much pressure on them both and their marriage had started to crack under the strain. 'We went to the rainforest in Brazil and stayed in a treetop hotel.'

'That sounds amazing,' she said wistfully.

'It was a kind of private oasis,' he said. 'We could sit out on the balcony and watch the monkeys and hear the macaws. There were wooden catwalks through the canopy of trees, so walking between our suite and the dining room was amazing. There was even a treetop swimming pool.'

'That's really exotic,' she said.

'I've never been anywhere like it—swimming with all these tropical birds flying just over your heads. And the food was great; every night we had fresh grilled fish, beans and rice and amazing bread, and exotic fruit. The day I remember most was when we took a boat trip on the Amazon and swam with the pink freshwater dolphins.'

'That sounds perfect,' Grace said wistfully.

'It was the trip of a lifetime,' he said. 'We'd both always wanted to see the rainforest, and it more than lived up to our expectations. I'm not sure whether I liked the sunrise or the sunset most, or just looking up into the sky and seeing a different set of stars, so bright against the darkness of the sky and so very different from London.' He paused. 'So what about you? What's your dream trip?' The one that her ex-fiancé hadn't made come true.

'It's a bit nerdy.'

He smiled. He'd expect nothing less from Grace. 'Nerdy's good. Tell me.'

'I'd love to go on the Orient Express,' she said, 'all the way from Paris to Istanbul.' She shrugged. 'But that particular trip is only scheduled once a year.'

If Roland had been planning to get married to Grace, he would've arranged their wedding so they could start their honeymoon with the train journey from Paris to Istanbul before venturing further afield. Why hadn't Howard done that? Didn't he like trains? Or had he never bothered to find out what made his fiancée tick?

Not that it was any of Roland's business. And he wasn't planning to get married any time soon. This was practice dating, he reminded himself. Talking to his date and finding out more about her. 'Where else would you like to go?'

'Do you mean my fantasy travel wish-list—the really wild stuff that I know I'm never actually going to do?' she asked. At his nod, she continued, 'I'd like to go to Australia and see the stars in the outback, and to Alaska to see the glaciers and the whales, and maybe the Antarctic to see the penguins, and to walk along some of the Great Wall of China.' She paused. 'How about you?'

'Actually, I like the sound of all of those.' He was faintly shocked by how much their tastes dovetailed. Only a few days ago, he would've said that they had nothing in common. But it looked as if some of her dreams were very similar to his own.

'You haven't already done them?' She looked surprised.

'No. Lyn really liked city breaks, so I've been to all the big cities in Europe,' he explained, 'plus New York, Boston, San Francisco and LA. And I've travelled pretty extensively on business, with conferences and the like; I always try to spend a day looking round wherever I'm based.'

'So where would you go for your fantasy travel list?' she asked.

'I'd like to see the Victoria Falls, and swim in the Blue Lagoon in Iceland,' he said. 'And visit Yosemite, to see the hot springs and waterfalls.'

'So it's water that draws you?'

'I've never thought about it that way, but yes, I suppose it is,' he said, surprised. 'Venice is one of my favourite places ever, and I love the sea. There's nothing better than walking on the cliffs with the waves crashing below and sending spray everywhere. Or strolling on a flat sandy beach in the moonlight with the sea all calm and just lapping at the shore.'

'Plus you live right on the Thames,' she pointed out.

'And you could never keep me off the lake as a boy.'

'Would this lake be at one of the chateaux?' she asked.

'No. At my family home in Kent,' he admitted.

'You had a lake?' She blinked. 'So are you telling me that you grew up somewhere like this?' She gestured to the stately home in front of them.

He squirmed. This felt like bragging—and that wasn't who he was. 'It's not as big as this. But, um…yes, I guess it's this sort of thing. Though it's been in the family for generations, and the roof is a total money pit, to the point where Dad's opened the gardens to the public, and we're turning the boathouse at the lake into a café.'

'And would I be right in guessing that his favourite architect,' she asked with a grin, 'is going to suggest having a glass wall all along the side of the building that faces the lake?'

'You are.' He smiled back at her. 'Though I guess that was obvious.'

'Not necessarily. Do you have another brother or sister who's an architect?'

He shook his head. 'Will's the oldest, so he's pretty much involved with the estate because he'll take over from Dad. Actually, he's already doing his own projects—he's sorting out a licence so we can hold wedding ceremonies. I'm the middle child, and I get hauled in to look at the roof from time to time and give my professional opinion on any renovation work that crops up.

And Philly's the baby—she basically adopted the head gardener as her honorary uncle when she was a toddler and moved up to nagging him to let her have a corner of the greenhouse all to herself by the time she was ten. So it was always obvious that she'd end up being either a landscape gardener or a florist. And she's brilliant. Really gifted.'

'You sound close to your family,' she said.

'I am.' He smiled. 'And you're close to yours.'

'I'm lucky,' she said simply.

He could tell that Grace was thinking about her almost-in-laws. What he didn't understand was why on earth her ex-fiancé's family hadn't liked her. She was sensible, kind and tactful. And, once you got past her shyness, she was fun. Yes, she had a nerdy streak, but that meant she looked at things from a different viewpoint—and in turn that made him look at things differently, too.

Though this dating thing was a temporary deal. And she'd just come out of a long relationship; she'd made it clear that she didn't want to rush into anything new. He didn't want to rush into anything, either. So he needed to keep these burgeoning feelings firmly under control, because they just weren't appropriate.

The orchestra began playing on stage, so he was saved from further conversation. But every so often he sneaked a glance at Grace to check that she was enjoying herself. And once or twice he caught her sneaking a glance at him, too. In the darkening evening, her cornflower-blue eyes were almost navy. Hypnotic.

As the fireworks began, he found himself sliding an arm across the back of her chair. If she asked, he'd say it was because he was worried she might be cold—English summer evenings weren't that warm. He certainly wouldn't tell her that it was because he wanted to be close to her. 'OK?' he asked.

'Very OK,' she said with a smile. 'This is absolutely gorgeous—the music, the fireworks and the reflections. It's the perfect combination. Thank you so much for bringing me.'

'My pleasure,' he said, meaning it. He couldn't remember when he'd relaxed so much, just enjoying his surroundings and chilling out. And he knew it was all down to Grace. Her quiet calmness made him feel grounded.

Maybe, he thought, he should suggest turning this from a practice run to a real relationship. See where it took them. But would she say yes? Or would she back away?

He managed to keep his thoughts under control during the fireworks, and driving home in the dark meant that he needed to concentrate and didn't have the headspace for thinking. But once they were back in Docklands he found the question buzzing through his head again.

Should he ask her?

Or should he do the sensible thing and back away?

In the end, Grace made the decision for him, by kissing him on the cheek. 'Thank you for tonight, Roland. It was every bit as fabulous as I dreamed it would be. And it was even nicer because it was a total surprise.'

'My pleasure,' he said automatically. She'd kissed his cheek, not his mouth. Meaning that he needed to back off.

Before he could suggest making a drink so he could linger in her company just that little bit longer, she said, 'I'll see you in the morning, then. Good night.'

'Good night,' he said. 'Sleep well.'

Though he had a feeling that he wouldn't. Grace was stirring feelings in him that he thought were long buried. And, even though he was usually so sure about what he was doing, right now he felt as if he was walking blind-fold along a path littered with lumps and bumps and holes, having to feel his way to make sure he stayed on his feet.

Maybe he'd manage to get his common sense back into place overnight.

Maybe.

CHAPTER SIX

GRACE'S MOUTH WAS soft and sweet, and Roland couldn't get enough of it. Yet he wanted a deeper intimacy, too. He'd just unzipped her dress when he heard something banging.

Then he realised it was the door.

His bedroom door.

And he was completely alone in bed. It was Sunday morning, and he'd been dreaming about making love with Grace. Heat rushed through his cheeks.

'Roland? Can I come in?' a voice called.

Grace.

The heat in his face intensified. No way did he want her to have any idea what he'd just been thinking about. On the other hand, he didn't have a valid excuse to tell her to go away. 'Uh—yeah,' he mumbled, hoping that he'd be able to think on his feet, and sat up.

She walked in carrying a tray. 'No sweet peas, I'm afraid. But I hope you'll like this.' Then she looked at his bare chest and blushed. 'Um. Sorry. I didn't realise...'

'I'm wearing pyjama bottoms,' he said hastily. But he was very glad that the duvet was piled in his lap and hid his arousal. He didn't want to embarrass either of them.

When she handed him the tray, he realised that she'd

brought him coffee and Eggs Benedict. It looked and smelled amazing.

'Is that home-made Hollandaise sauce?' he asked.

'Yes.'

'If you ever get tired of working with numbers,' he said, 'I guarantee you'd have a fantastic career if you opened your own restaurant.' He still didn't get why she wasn't using her talent. Why she was hiding behind numbers.

'I like cooking for fun,' she said. 'Cooking as a business would be a totally different ballgame. And it'd be sad if something I really enjoy doing turned out to be something I felt I was forced to do. Not to mention the unsociable hours I'd need to work; I wouldn't get to see enough of my parents and Bella.'

'I guess,' he said. And it was a logical explanation, one he couldn't argue with.

'It's my turn to organise things today,' she said. 'That is, if you'd like to do something with me and you don't have to work?'

Maybe he should grab this opportunity to put a little distance between them.

Except his mouth wasn't working from the same script as his head and using his usual cast-iron excuse of working on some architectural design or other, because he found himself saying, 'I'd like to do something with you.'

'Great. Maybe we can be ready to leave in an hour?' she suggested.

'I can be ready before that. What are we doing?'

'Something immensely nerdy, but I hope you'll enjoy it,' she said with a smile. 'See you later.'

He watched her walk out of the room, noting the sway of her hips. He was definitely going to need a cold shower after breakfast. And it had been a while since he'd had such a graphic dream.

So did that mean that he was ready to start to move on? With Grace?

But she'd only just come out of a long relationship where she hadn't been happy. And although she'd said that she'd wanted to be swept off her feet, the Grace he was beginning to get to know liked structure and organisation. She was very far from being the sort to rush into things. He needed to be careful with her.

Which meant not giving in to the urge to sweep her off her feet, literally, and carrying her to his bed.

The cold shower was enough to restore some of his common sense. He shaved, got dressed, and found her in the kitchen doing a number puzzle in a magazine.

He smiled. 'Would this be your Sunday morning guilty pleasure?'

'Busted,' she said ruefully.

He glanced over her shoulder at the page. 'That doesn't look like the kind of thing you see in the newspaper supplements.'

'I suppose it's for people who like, um, really nerdy puzzles. My parents buy me a subscription to this magazine every Christmas,' she admitted.

'Don't hide your light under a bushel,' he said. 'Most people couldn't do these sorts of puzzles. Be proud of yourself because you can.' And why was she so diffident about her abilities? That was really bugging him. He'd actually met her family and liked them. They weren't the sort who'd do someone down to boost their own ego. So who had made Grace feel bad about herself and hide who she was? 'Would I be right in guessing that your ex didn't like you doing them?'

'No.'

But she looked away, and he guessed that yet again her ex's disapproving mother had been the sticking point.

'Not everyone likes puzzles,' she said, still not meeting his eye.

'Which doesn't mean you should take away the fun from those who do.' And it made him wonder why Grace's ex had put up with the situation. If his own mother had been difficult with Lyn, he would've taken his mother to one side and gently explained that he'd made his life choice and he'd prefer her to respect that and treat his partner with a bit more courtesy—even if they couldn't be close friends, they could still be civil to each other. Though Roland's mother wasn't the cold, judgemental type who placed importance upon appearances above all else, and he knew that his whole family would adore Grace. She would adore them, too.

Not that he intended to introduce them to each other. This was way, way too soon.

She closed her magazine. 'I'll just do the washing u—' she began.

'No,' Roland said, and put everything from his tray in the dishwasher before she could argue. 'Didn't you say you wanted to leave soon?'

'Yes. And it's my trip, so we're going in my car.'

'Yes, ma'am,' he teased.

As he'd expected, Grace turned out to be a very competent driver, but he didn't have a clue where they were going until she turned off at Bletchley Park. 'I should've guessed you'd plan to visit somewhere like this,' he said.

'Why?'

The expression on her face was fleeting, but he'd noticed it. Expecting that she'd be judged—and judged harshly. Although Roland didn't believe that violence solved anything, he would've liked to shake Howard's mother until her teeth rattled. Grace had been engaged to Howard for four years, so they'd probably dated for a year or so before then—meaning that the woman had had five years to crush Grace's confidence. And how. The fact that Grace had still had the guts to walk away from the situation was a testimony to her strength. 'You like numbers, so this place must be fascinating for you,' he said. 'If you'd been alive in those times, I think they would've asked you to work here, given that you're good at puzzles.'

'And if you'd been alive in those times, you might've been working on the architecture for the Mulberry harbour or something like that,' she said.

'Or working with the guy who was trying to find an alternative material to build the Mosquito planes when there was a shortage of balsa wood,' he said thoughtfully. 'There was a chemist who was working on making a foam from seaweed that dried into planks that would be as strong as wood.'

She glanced at him. 'A plane made from seaweed? I assume you're teasing me?'

'No, I'm serious,' he said. 'I read an article about it in a professional journal. Apparently one of the seaweed "planks" is in the Science Museum in London.'

'What an amazing story,' she said. 'I'm going to have to go to the Science Museum now to see it for myself.'

'Maybe we can go together.' The words were out before he could stop them. This was dangerous. He wasn't supposed to be finding shared points of interest for the future. They'd agreed to help each other out, not fall for each other.

'Maybe we can go next weekend, or on one of the evenings when they open late.' She gave him another of those shy smiles, then parked the car. 'We don't need to queue, by the way. I bought tickets online while you were in the shower this morning, and I've already downloaded the multimedia guide to my phone,' she said.

Typical Grace, being organised and thorough. 'Sounds good.' He took her hand and they wandered round, enjoying the sunshine and exploring the different code-breaking huts.

'I love the way they've done this so you can actually feel what it was like to work here—even down to the sounds and smells,' he said.

'Me, too,' she said. 'I hoped you'd like this—you said you liked museums and buildings, and this is... Well.'

'It's brilliant. And I'm going to be totally boring when we get to the displays about how they restored the buildings.' He kissed her to reassure her that he was happy with her choice of date, but kept it swift so he could keep his feelings in control.

They lingered in the display about the Enigma machines, and the Bombe machine that finally cracked the code. He could see how interested she was, and how her eyes lit up. If he was honest with himself, she fascinated him as much as this place fascinated her. He hadn't met anyone quite like her before. Lyn had been outgoing and confident—at least, until the baby-making plan had gone wrong—and Grace was quiet and shy and kept a lot of herself hidden. Yet something about her drew him. He wanted to take down all her barriers and let her shine.

They stopped for lunch in the site's café. 'So when did you know you wanted to work with numbers?' he asked.

She shrugged. 'I just always liked numbers. Dad found

me trying to do the number puzzles in the Sunday supplements, so he started buying me puzzle magazines. My favourite ones were where you have to fit a list of numbers instead of words into a grid. Then I moved up to logic puzzles and Sudoku. I, um, won a competition at school for being the fastest at solving them,' she added shyly.

'And you never thought about going to university to study maths?'

'One of my teachers tried to get me to apply to Oxford,' she said, 'but I don't think I was cut out to be a teacher. It seemed a bit pointless spending three years studying and getting into debt when I could've been learning on the job and making progress in my professional exams.'

Sensible and measured and reliable: that was Grace. Though he wondered what would've happened if she'd let herself have the chance to work with the more abstract branches of mathematics—how far she would've soared.

'And that's where you met Howard, when you were training?'

She shook her head. 'I qualified in a different firm, then moved to Sutton's because there was an opportunity for promotion. I never expected to fall for the boss's son, but we worked together on an audit when I'd been there for six months and he asked me out.'

Roland had the feeling that Grace had concentrated on her studies rather than on partying. He wouldn't be surprised if Howard had been her first serious boyfriend.

'And you liked him?' he asked.

She nodded. 'He was sweet and kind—and I guess I was a bit naive because I thought that his parents would eventually warm to me. I'm not a gold-digger.'

'Of course you're not,' he said. But clearly Howard's

parents had treated her as if she was. It made Roland understand where her insistence on being independent and doing her fair share came from. Clearly she'd had to prove herself over and over and over again. But why hadn't her ex stood up for her? And why had it taken her so long to realise that she was worth more than the way his family treated her?

'How about you?' she asked. 'How did you meet Lynette?'

'We worked together,' he said. 'I was an architect and she was a PA at the practice. We danced together at an office Christmas party, and that was it.'

'So you knew straight away that she was The One?'

'I guess.' He nodded. 'We moved in together fairly quickly, but she insisted on a long engagement when I asked her to marry me.'

'But not four years?' Grace asked wryly.

Roland smiled. 'Just one. And that was long enough. Though I guess she was right; it gave us time to get to know each other properly and be really sure we were doing the right thing. And we were happy.' Until that last year of their marriage, when Lyn's friends all seemed to fall pregnant the very first month they started trying, while he had to comfort his wife every month when her period arrived. The doctors had all said they were young and it was too early to think about fertility treatment, and advised them both just to relax and keep trying; but sex in those last six months had been all about making a baby and not at all about expressing their love for each other. Lyn had charts and ovulation kits everywhere, and every time they'd made love it had been carefully timed rather than simply because they wanted each other.

Roland had started taking every opportunity to work

away, or to give a paper at a conference, just to take the pressure off and make him feel less like a machine. And that was why he'd bought the house at the maltings—something that would take over his head completely. Something he could escape to.

Not that he'd told anyone about it. Not his family and not his closest friends. How could he tell them that he'd felt a failure as a husband, that he'd let Lyn down every single month?

And the cruellest irony of all had been when the doctor at the hospital had told him...

He dragged in a breath. Not now. He wasn't going to think of that now.

She laid her hand against his cheek. 'I'm sorry, Roland. I didn't mean to bring back bad memories for you.'

Yeah. They must've shown on his face. But he didn't have the words to tell anyone about the worst bit. He hadn't even told Lyn's parents. Which made him a seriously bad person, because he really shouldn't have kept it from them. Or maybe it had been kinder not to tell them. 'It's OK. But I could do with changing the subject,' he admitted. He still found it hard to handle the guilt. Although he knew it wasn't his fault that the drunken driver had crashed into Lyn's car, and it was entirely possible that the crash could've happened even if he'd been at home, he still couldn't forgive himself for not being there at the end—or handle that last, unkindest cut of all.

'Let's go and look round a bit more,' she said.

And funny how comforting he found it when her hand curled round his as they walked round the site. She didn't push him to talk; she was just there, offering quiet support and kindness.

If he wanted to make this thing between them real,

he'd have to tell her the truth. All of it. Including the
stuff he didn't let himself think about. He didn't think
she'd pity him, and she definitely wouldn't judge him.
But he still wasn't ready to talk, and he wasn't sure if he
ever would be. Maybe brushing up his dating skills was
a bad idea. Or maybe he'd work out some way to move
things forward between them without opening up that
world of hurt.

On Monday morning, Grace picked up a text from Roland during her break.

Can you get Wednesday to Friday off this week?

Why? she texted back.

Sweeping-off-feet stuff was the response. Which told
her nothing.

I'll see what I can do, she said.

Possibly because it was still June, before the summer holiday season started in earnest, the office where
she was working was happy for her to take the time off.

'Excellent,' Roland said when she told him the news.

She coughed. '"Sweeping-off-feet stuff" is all very
well, but if we're going away somewhere I need to know
what to pack.'

'A couple of nice dresses and something for walking
about in,' he said.

'Walking about—do you mean walking boots, water-
proofs and insect repellent?' she asked.

'Nope. Smart casual.'

'So it's urban and not country, then?'

He sighed. 'Grace, I can hardly sweep you off your
feet if you know all the details.'

'But if I don't know enough, I'll need three suitcases so I can be prepared for every eventuality,' she countered.

He smiled. 'Minimal luggage would be better. OK. It's urban. I'm not planning to make you walk along most of Hadrian's Wall—though,' he added, 'if you're up for that…'

Grace pushed away the thought that she'd go anywhere with him. Because this thing between them wasn't permanent. 'Uh-huh,' she said, hoping that she sounded polite enough but not committing herself to anything. 'Got it. Minimal luggage, a couple of smart dresses, and smart casual stuff with shoes I can walk in.' Quite what he had in mind, she had no idea.

'And your passport,' he said.

'My passport? Bu—'

He silenced her protest by the simple act of kissing her. 'It's sweeping-off-feet stuff,' he reminded her gently. 'And my bank balance can definitely take it, before you start protesting or feeling guilty. It's a place I'd like to show you, so please just give in…' He laughed. 'I would say gracefully, but, given your name, doing something "Gracefully" means asserting your independence and being stroppy.'

She nodded, simply because that kiss had wiped out anything she'd intended to say. And he just smiled and kissed her again. 'Sweeping you off your feet. That was the deal,' he said.

And how.

CHAPTER SEVEN

'REMIND ME NEVER to play poker with you,' Grace grumbled as they got on the Tube. 'You have to be the most...' She shook her head, unable to think of the words.

'Poker-faced?' Roland teased.

'Annoying,' she retorted.

Roland just laughed. 'If I told you where we were going, then I wouldn't be sweeping you off your feet. Trust me. It'll be worth it.'

Grace wasn't so sure—until he led her to a platform at Victoria station and she realised what was standing in front of them. An old-fashioned train, with the staff all lined up in front of it, wearing posh livery.

'This is the London starting point of the Orient Express.' She caught her breath. He couldn't mean this— could he? 'We're going on this? Now? Really?'

He looked utterly pleased with himself. 'Yup. I was paying attention when we talked at the fireworks, you know.'

And how. This was something she'd dreamed about doing for years and years, and never thought she'd ever actually do. When she'd mentioned it to Howard, he'd clearly discussed it with his mother because he'd told her the next day that it was way too extravagant and there were much better, cheaper and more efficient ways of going to Paris than the Orient Express.

Not that she'd ever been to Paris. Since she'd been dating Howard, they'd always been too busy at work to take off more than a couple of days at a time, which they usually spent in a cottage somewhere in England—even though Paris was only two hours away from London on the Eurostar.

And now Roland was taking her on her dream trip. Although they weren't going all the way to Istanbul—because that particular journey was only scheduled for once a year, and even Roland couldn't change that—they were still taking a slow train to Paris, the City of Light. The most romantic place in Europe.

He was really sweeping her off her feet.

She realised that he was waiting for her to say something, but right now she was so overwhelmed that she couldn't think straight, let alone string a proper sentence together. 'Roland, I don't know what to say.'

'"Thank you, Roland, it's nice to tick something off my bucket list" would do,' he teased.

'It is, and it's fabulous, and I'm stunned because I never expected you to do anything like this, but—'

As if he guessed she was about to protest about the cost, he cut off her words by kissing her.

'Grace, I wouldn't have booked this if I couldn't afford it,' he said, 'and I'm actually quite enjoying sweeping you off your feet. Do you have any idea how good it makes me feel, knowing that I'm able to make one of your dreams come true?'

It was something she knew she'd like to do for him, too. Except Roland hadn't really shared his dreams with her, so she had no idea what she could do to make him feel this same surge of delight. She took a deep breath. 'OK. Brattish protesting about the cost all swept to one side. This is really fantastic and I'm utterly thrilled. I can't believe you've done something so amazing and lovely for me, but I'm really glad you have.' And she meant that, from the bottom of her heart. 'Thank you so much. This is the best treat ever.'

'I'm glad you're enjoying it.' He took her hand. 'Let me escort you to our seat, *mademoiselle*.'

Roland had said that there was a French branch of his family, and given that his surname sounded French she could entirely believe it; but this was the first time she'd ever heard him speak the language. Admittedly, it was only one word, but it was amazing how much sexier he sounded in French.

And then she made the mistake of telling him that.

He grinned and launched into a rapid stream of French.

She coughed. 'My French is limited to schoolgirl stuff, and that's pretty rusty. I understood maybe one word in ten out of that. Even if you said it all again at half the speed, I still wouldn't understand much more.'

'Maybe,' he said, 'I'll show you later instead.'

And, oh, the pictures that put in her head. Heat rushed through her and her face felt as if it had turned a vivid shade of beetroot.

He simply gave her the most wicked and sultry smile.

Not only was Grace feeling swept off her feet, she was in severe danger of losing her head as well. And, even though she was loving every second of this, part of her felt way out of her depth. So she'd just have to remind herself that she was sensible and this was two weeks of sheer fun—he didn't expect her to fit into this environment permanently.

When they got to their carriage, it was nothing like the trains she normally used outside London. There was plenty of space, and the plush, comfortable seats were placed opposite each other in pairs, with the small table in between covered by a white damask cloth.

'I forgot to ask if you get travel sick,' Roland said, suddenly looking horrified. 'Sorry. Would you prefer to face the direction we're travelling?'

'I don't get sick, exactly,' she said, 'but yes, please—if that's OK with you?'

'Of course it is.'

But the luxury didn't stop at their seats. The waiter came to serve them their drinks—freshly squeezed orange juice for Roland, and a Bellini for Grace.

'This is so decadent,' Grace said with delight, giving herself up to the pleasure of being pampered.

Brunch was even nicer—fresh fruit salad, followed by crumpets with smoked salmon, caviar and scrambled eggs, then pastries and coffee. And everything was slow and unhurried, as if they had all the time in the world. So very different from the usual rush of a working life in London.

At Folkestone, they were met by a band serenading them, and then took the bus through the Eurotunnel to Calais. At the station, they were met by another band playing; and on the platform where the vintage blue and gold train was waiting, the staff were lined up in their smart blue uniforms and peaked hats. The restaurant staff were clad in white jackets with gold braid, black trousers and white gloves.

'I feel like a princess,' Grace whispered.

'Good. That's the idea.' Roland squeezed her hand.

'Now for the real thing,' he said with a smile. 'The Orient Express over mainland Europe.'

One of the uniformed staff took them to their cabin; it was cosy yet beautifully presented, and Grace had never seen anything so luxurious in her life.

Again, the pace was slow and unhurried. If they'd taken the express train from St Pancras, they would've been in Paris already; but the slow journey through the French countryside was so much nicer, giving them time to look at their surroundings.

'So tell me about the French side of your family,' she said. 'Didn't you say they have vineyards?'

He nodded. 'They're all in the Burgundy area. One branch of the family produces Chablis, and the other produces Côtes de Nuits.' He grinned. 'They're horribly competitive—but luckily because one specialises in white wine and one specialises in red, they're not in competition with each other. But there's a kind of race every year about how many awards and glowing reviews they can get.'

'But I bet they're the only ones allowed to be rude about each other, right?'

His eyes glittered with amusement. 'Right.'

'So do you see them very often?'

'Not as often as I'd like,' he admitted. 'It's very pretty in Dijon, with all the old narrow streets and houses built of honey-coloured stone. The whole area is lovely and the views from the chateaux are amazing. Actually, I really ought to go and visit them soon, because I've been getting pleading emails about difficult roofs and I did promise to go and have a look.'

'Do all old buildings have problematic roofs?' she

asked, remembering what he'd said about the roof in his family home.

'It's not just that—there's damp, dry rot, death watch beetle, subsidence...' He spread his hands. 'And if some-one hasn't been careful enough to use the right materials when working on an old house—using modern plaster instead of lime, for example, or replacing a wooden floor with concrete—it can create more problems than it solves.' He smiled. 'But I'm not going to drone on about restoration work.'

'Or glass?' she teased.

'There's one glass building I'm definitely taking you to see in Paris,' he said. 'But don't ask me what. It's a surprise.'

'No asking. I promise,' she said.

'One thing I was wondering about you, though,' he said. 'Why do you worry about the cost of things so much?'

She grimaced. 'This stays with you? You're not going to say a word to Bella?'

'It stays with me,' he promised.

'I guess it stems from when I was little,' she said. 'My father wasn't just unreliable about time—he wasn't very good with money, either. I can remember the bailiffs coming round when I was about three, and it was pretty scary. I remember my mum crying her heart out when she thought I was asleep. I don't ever want to be in that situation again.' She shrugged. 'Which is why I'm always very careful with money. I'm being sensible.'

'I wasn't accusing you of being a Scrooge,' he said swiftly. 'But don't you ever feel you've missed out, some-times?'

'No.' But her denial was too swift, and she could see in

his expression that he thought so, too. And, yes, she knew she'd missed out on things in the past because she'd been too sensible and too careful. Just as she would've missed out on this trip today if she hadn't for once thrown caution to the wind and agreed to his suggestion of helping each other out. 'Can we change the subject?' she asked, feeling antsy and cross with herself because she was ruining the mood.

'Sure.'

'Tell me about Paris,' she said. 'The first time you went there and what you really loved.'

'That's easy,' he said. 'My parents took all three of us, on the way down to Bordeaux. I must've been about five. It was Christmas, and we went to the Galeries Lafayette. The Christmas tree there was the tallest one I've ever seen in my life—before or since—and it was covered in lights and shiny red apples. And we went to a café for hot chocolate that had a cinnamon stick in it—something I'd never really seen in England—and we all had a slice of chocolate cake from the *bûche de Noël*. And my mum bought poinsettias.' He smiled. 'Philly of course loved the fact they're called *étoile de Noël* because the leaves are star-shaped and red, gold and green are the colours of Christmas in France. She always does them up the French way in her shop at Christmas.'

Grace relaxed again as Roland chatted easily with her about Paris and Christmas and how his family mixed both French and English traditions.

'It's nice to include both bits of your heritage, though—the English and the French.'

'Yes, it is,' he agreed.

They dressed up for an early dinner in the dining car—Grace was really glad she'd bought a new cocktail dress during her lunch break the previous day—and every course was sumptuous and exquisitely presented, from the lobster to the tournedos Rossini, the platter of French cheeses, and then a cone of coconut sorbet with a delicate slice of fresh pineapple that had been caramelised.

'This is beyond what I dreamed it would be like on the Orient Express,' she said to Roland when their coffee arrived. 'Thank you so much.'

'Je t'en prie,' he said.

'Um—I don't remember what that means.'

'You're welcome,' he said. 'And we haven't reached Paris yet. I hope you'll like what I've planned.'

'If it's even one per cent as fabulous as this,' she said, 'I'll love it.'

Roland had arranged for a plush car to meet them at the station and take them to the centre of the city. Grace drank in their surroundings in total silence as they drove through the centre of Paris, not wanting to break the spell; she'd had no idea just how pretty the city was. The wide boulevards, the pretty buildings, the light and airy feel of the place.

The outside of their hotel was beautiful, a five-storey white building with long narrow windows and wrought iron balconies—just what she'd imagined a Parisian hotel to look like. Inside, it was even better: the lobby was all white walls with gilt-framed pictures, red and white marble chequered flooring and wrought iron chandeliers. At the end was a marble staircase with a wrought iron and gilded balustrade. She'd never seen anything so glittering and gorgeous.

When the concierge took them up to their floor, her pulse speeded up. So this was it. Sharing a room with Roland.

As if he'd guessed her sudden nervousness, he said, 'We have a suite. There are two bedrooms and two bathrooms. I'm not taking anything for granted.'

So he wasn't expecting her to sleep with him. 'Thank you,' she said.

But, even though they hadn't known each other for very long and they weren't in a permanent relationship— and weren't planning to be in one, either—Grace knew that if he asked her to make love with him while they were in Paris, her answer would be yes. How could she resist him in the most romantic city in the world?

Her bedroom was gorgeous, with a pale blue carpet, cream walls, and tall windows that opened onto a balcony with an amazing view of the Eiffel Tower. Her bed was wide, with plenty of deep, fluffy pillows; and the bathroom was all cream marble and gilding. When she came back into the living room between the bedrooms, she noticed that there were comfortable chairs and sofas upholstered in old gold, and there was a vase of fresh flowers on the coffee table.

'This is amazing, Roland,' she said.

He smiled. 'Yes, it's pretty good.'

Had he stayed here before? Did this bring back memories of his late wife? But she didn't want to hurt him by asking.

He didn't seem to notice her awkwardness, because he said, 'And now we have an evening in Paris.'

An evening in Paris. It sounded incredibly romantic. And he said he'd planned things. 'What do you have in mind?' she asked.

'Come with me,' he said.

He'd retained the plush car from before. 'It would take us an hour to walk where I'm taking you, and the Métro journey means a lot of messing about, so that's why we're taking a car now,' he explained. 'We can walk through the city and explore tomorrow.'

'OK,' she said.

They ended up at what he told her was the fifth *arrondissement*. 'This is Quai St Bernard,' he said, 'and it's the perfect place for a summer evening.'

There was a mini amphitheatre on the side of the Seine. People were sitting on the side of the river, picnicking or drinking wine and listening to the DJ playing what sounded like tango music; and there was a crowd of people dancing.

'Tangoing in Paris?' she asked. 'Roland—this is fabulous, but I'm afraid I don't know how to tango. Though I'm very happy to watch the dancing,' she added swiftly, not wanting him to think she was ungrateful. 'I can still soak up the atmosphere and enjoy it.'

'I know you do dance aerobics with Bella, so you can follow a routine,' he said. 'Don't worry that you've never danced a tango before. You'll pick it up. Just follow my lead.'

And what could she do but give in to the steady, hypnotic beat and dance with him? He held her really close, sliding one thigh between hers and spinning her round, and it was his nearness rather than the dancing that took her breath away.

When he bent her back over his arm, his mouth skimmed the curve of her throat and she went hot all over. If there hadn't been so many strangers dancing around them—if he'd danced with her like this in the privacy of their hotel suite—she knew this would've been the prelude to a much deeper intimacy. She could see from the expression in Roland's dark eyes that right now he felt exactly the same way. And although part of her felt shy about it, part of her revelled in it. In being totally swept off her feet, dancing the tango by the river in Paris at night.

The music changed to a salsa—something she did know, from her aerobics classes—and Roland smiled as she segued into the step-ball-change routine, side to side and back to front.

'What?' she asked, aware that he was watching her.

'It's lovely to see you letting go,' he said.

'Are you saying I'm uptight?'

'No. More that you hide yourself. But tonight you're *la belle étoile.*'

Her schoolgirl French was enough to let her translate: he thought she was a beautiful star?

She realised she'd spoken aloud when he stole a kiss. 'Right now you're shining. And you're beautiful.'

Tears pricked her eyelids. 'Thank you. *Merci beaucoup.*'

'*Je t'en prie,*' he said, and spun her round so they could salsa together, holding her close enough at times so she could feel his arousal pressing against her, and at others standing facing her and shimmying along with her.

The DJ changed to playing slower, sultrier music, and they ended up swaying together, dancing cheek to cheek. Grace felt cherished and adored—something she wasn't used to, and something she had a nasty feeling she could find addictive.

She really had to keep it in mind that this wasn't real. Roland saw this as dating practice, nothing more. Wishing it could be otherwise was the quickest route to heartache. She needed to remember her fall-back position: being sensible, the way she always was.

When the music finally ended, they took the car back to their hotel.

'That was fantastic,' she said. 'I enjoyed that so much.'

'Me, too.'

'Obviously you know the city well.' She swallowed hard. Time for a reality check. 'I assume you've done that before?'

He shook his head. 'I've been to Paris a few times with Lynette, yes—but we didn't stay at the hotel where we are tonight and I'm not retracing our footsteps.'

Which made her feel a bit better; and she was impressed that he realised she'd been worrying about that. 'So how did you know about the dancing?'

'You want the truth?' he asked. At her nod, he laughed. 'The Internet is a wonderful thing. I looked up romantic things to do in Paris. And that one struck me as being a lot of fun.'

'It was.' And she loved the fact that he'd gone to that much trouble for her. 'Your dating skills really don't need any practice, Roland. That's absolutely the way to melt someone's heart. To think about what they might like and surprise them.'

His fingers tightened around hers. 'That's what these couple of days are about. Exploring and having fun. I'm not trying to recreate the past. This is just you and me.'

As they pulled up at the hotel, he gestured across the river. 'Look.'

'The Eiffel Tower's sparkling!' she said in delight. 'I had no idea it did that at night.'

'It sparkles on the hour,' he said.

Grace was so tempted to take a photograph of the Eiffel Tower on her phone and send it to Bella—but then her sister would call her and ask why she was in Paris, and it would get too complicated. Pushing back the wistfulness and disappointment that she couldn't share this with the one person she knew would understand how much she was enjoying the chance to travel, she said, 'This is just like I imagined Paris to be. The City of Light.'

'I'll show you more tomorrow,' he promised.

Despite what he'd said on their arrival, Grace wondered if Roland expected her to share his room that night. But he kissed her at her bedroom door. 'Good night, sweet Grace.'

It took the pressure off; but, at the same time, she felt disappointment swooping in her stomach. She lay awake, wondering if she had the nerve to walk into his room. If she did, would he open his arms to her? Or would he reject her? In the end, she didn't quite have the nerve, and she fell asleep full of regret.

The next morning, she felt a bit shy with him; but he was relaxed and easy. 'Are you up for a lot of walking?' he asked.

She nodded. 'Bring it on.'

After a breakfast of excellent coffee and the best croissants she'd ever had in her life, he took her to the Tuileries and they wandered through the pretty gardens. 'I know this is a bit touristy, but we can't miss it.'

'With you being a glass fiend, you're going to show me the pyramid at the Louvre, right?' she guessed.

He laughed. 'Not just the one everyone knows about in the courtyard. This is a bit of a whistlestop tour. I hope you don't mind.'

'No. It's fabulous,' she said, meaning it.

They walked through the museum itself, and Grace was stunned to come across pieces of art she'd known about for years, just casually dotted through the building. It didn't seem quite real, and she pinched herself surreptitiously.

And then Roland took her to the other pyramid.

'And this is what I love, here. The perfect symmetry of glass,' he said with a grin, and took a selfie of the two of them on his phone, standing under the inverted pyramid with a rainbow of light shining across their faces.

'You and your glass,' she teased.

From the Louvre, they walked to the Place des Vosges. 'It's the oldest planned square in the city,' he told her. 'Victor Hugo lived here when he wrote *Les Misérables*.'

It was utterly beautiful: a terrace of redbrick houses with tall windows and blue-tiled roofs, and little arcades running along the bottom storey. Grace was enchanted, and even more so when they wandered through more of the Marais district. 'This is lovely,' she said. 'All cobbled streets and medieval crooked lanes.'

'It's how Paris was before Napoleon razed most of it and built all the wide avenues and huge squares,' Roland said. 'What I like about it is the way you've got old-fashioned *boulangeries* mixed in with art galleries and wine shops and jewellery designers.'

'You could just lose yourself here,' she said.

He nodded. 'It's the best way to explore.'

They ended up at Place du Marché-Ste-Catherine, a cobblestoned square with pretty plane trees and lots of cream-coloured four-storey eighteenth-century houses. On three sides of the square there were little cafés with parasols and sunshades on; there were wrought iron benches in the centre, and a couple of buskers playing Bach on the violin.

'Time for lunch,' Grace said. 'And I'm going to order

for us. Even though it's a long time since I've spoken French.'

'Sure you don't want me to help?'

'Nope. I'm going outside my comfort zone,' she said. 'And I've got you to thank for making me that brave.'

'OK,' he said. *'Allons-y.'*

Grace's schoolgirl French was just about up to ordering two coffees and quiche, though she had to resort to sign language and a lot of smiling to order the lamb's lettuce salad, and Roland couldn't help smiling. Grace was oh, so sweet. And wandering through one of the prettiest districts of Paris with her had soothed his soul.

He'd called her a beautiful star, the night before. And even in the daytime she seemed lit up. He loved the fact that she was throwing herself into the whole Parisian experience, enjoying every single moment and sharing his delight in the glorious architecture. And a corner of his heart that he'd thought would stay heavy for ever suddenly seemed lighter, just because she was with him. But he knew she wanted someone who wouldn't let her down. His track record wasn't good enough. Falling in love with Grace Faraday wouldn't be fair to either of them.

That evening, they had dinner in the Michelin-starred hotel restaurant—another treat he knew she'd enjoy as much as he did—and then he took her to the Eiffel Tower. 'This is the best way to see Paris by night,' he said, 'with all the streets lit up.'

He showed her the broad boulevards radiating outwards; the River Seine was like a black silk ribbon with its bridges lit up. 'This is the Champ de Mars,' he said, showing her the south side of the tower, 'with the military school at the end.' He pointed out the shiny gold dome of the Hôtel des Invalides, and the Trocadéro gardens.

'This is amazing,' she said. And, to his shock, she threw her arms round him and kissed him.

Time seemed to stop.

And although there were plenty of other tourists enjoying the view from the platform, he felt as if the two of them were alone in a little bubble of time and space.

When Roland finally broke the kiss, he felt almost giddy and had to keep holding her tightly. And then he recovered his customary aplomb and told her more about the tower and pointed out more of the landmarks in the city. Just because if he kept talking, then he'd be able to stop himself kissing her stupid.

Back at the hotel, he had to damp down the urge to carry her across the threshold and straight to his bed. That wasn't the deal. And, even though he was pretty sure she wouldn't say no, it wouldn't be fair to her. So he kissed her good night at the doorway to her room—making very sure he kept the kiss short enough so it didn't play havoc with his self-control—and went to bed alone.

And he spent the next couple of hours lying awake, thinking of Grace.

What if she was the one who really could make him live again?

But the biggest question was, what did she want? And, if they did try to make a go of things, would their relationship splinter in the same way that his marriage had? Would she want children, to the point where nothing else mattered?

It was a risk. And he wasn't sure he had the strength left to take that risk.

So he'd stick to the rules.

Despite the fact that he really wanted to break them.

CHAPTER EIGHT

How DID YOU sweep someone off their feet without losing your own head in the process? Roland still didn't have any clearer ideas the next morning. But after breakfast he took Grace to Montmartre. As he expected, she was charmed by the gorgeous Art Deco Métro signs, loved the beautiful church and the amazing views over the city, and enjoyed walking through the crowded square where the artists sold their wares and did charcoal portraits of tourists. He got her to pose on the steps next to the funicular railway and took a photograph of her; when a passing couple offered to take a photograph of them together, he enjoyed the excuse to wrap his arm round her shoulders and for her to wrap her arm round his waist.

They stopped at one of the street vendors for a cinnamon crêpe, then wandered further through Montmartre, looking for the plaques to show where the famous turn-of-the-century artists had once lived or painted.

'Bella would love it here,' Grace said.

And for a moment Roland could imagine the two of them coming here with Hugh and Bella, Tarquin and Rupert, lingering at a table outside one of the cafés and talking and laughing until the early hours of the morning.

He shook himself. That wasn't going to happen. His

next step was dating again, not finding his true love. And who was to say that he would find The One? Maybe one chance was all you got, and he'd already had that with Lynette. Wanting a second chance was greedy. And he had to look at it from Grace's point of view, too; even if he wanted to try making a go of things with her, she wasn't ready to rush into another long-term relationship.

So he kept it light and fun and did touristy things with her for the rest of the afternoon until it was time to catch the Eurostar back to London. This time their journey was swift and businesslike rather than slow and romantic, the way the Orient Express had been. Which was a good thing, because the brisk and businesslike feeling would stop him doing something stupid.

'Thank you, Roland,' she said when they were back in Docklands. 'I've had the nicest time ever.'

'My pleasure,' he said, meaning it.

He used the excuse of catching up with work for Friday evening and the whole of Saturday, in an attempt to cool his head again; but on Sunday afternoon, when she diffidently suggested that maybe they could go to the Science Museum in search of the seaweed 'plank', he found himself agreeing. And again he ended up holding hands with her as they walked round.

Disappointingly, they couldn't find the plank.

'Let's go next door,' he said.

'Because you want to see the dinosaurs? Or because it's one of the most gorgeous buildings in London and you want to drool over the architecture?' she asked.

He loved it when she teased him like this. Grace really seemed to get who he was and what made him tick. 'Both?' he suggested.

'Pfft. It's the brickwork all the way, with you,' she said

with a grin. 'But let's go and see the dinosaurs as well, because I loved those when I was a child.'

'And I bet you used to count the bones,' he teased back.

'Absolutely. And I could always talk Dad into getting a dinosaur head on a stick for Bella and me—you know, the sort with a trigger on the end so you can make the mouth snap shut. We used to pretend to be T-Rexes and chase each other round the garden. Bellasaurus and Graciesaurus, that was us.'

Grace, all young and carefree and letting herself shine. When had that stopped? he wondered. He'd really, really liked the carefree Grace who'd danced the salsa with him on the banks of the Seine. Could she be that Grace back in London? And could she take a risk with him?

When they queued up to see the dinosaurs, the little girl in front of them was scared when one of the large animatronic dinosaurs roared unexpectedly, and burst into tears. Her father immediately swung her up in his arms to comfort her.

'Poor little lass,' Grace said.

Roland gave her a sidelong look. Was he being oversensitive and paranoid, or did she have the same kind of broody expression that he'd seen permanently on Lynette in that last year?

'Do you want children?' The question was out before he could stop it.

She stared at him and blinked. 'That's a bit abrupt. Why do you ask?'

'Just wondering.' Stupid, stupid. Why hadn't he kept his mouth shut?

'I don't know,' she said.

'But you were engaged to Howard for four years. Surely you talked about having a family?' He knew he should shut up and leave the subject well alone, but his mouth was running away with him. Big time.

'Actually, no,' she said. 'We didn't. What about you? Did you and Lynette…?'

The question made him flinch inwardly, but he knew it was his own fault. He'd been the one to raise the subject. 'I was still getting my business off the ground.' That was true. Up to a point. But oh, yes, Lynette had wanted a baby. More than anything.

'But did you want to have children when the business was more settl—?' She stopped herself. 'Sorry. I'm probably bringing back difficult stuff for you.'

Yes, she was, but not in the way she thought. Roland had never spoken to anyone about the way he and Lyn had struggled and struggled, and how their love had got lost somewhere under her desperate need for a child. Or about the shock news the doctor had given him at the hospital. 'It's OK,' he said. Even though it wasn't and it hurt like hell.

'Sorry, anyway,' she said, and squeezed his hand.

Change the subject. Change it now, he told himself.

But it was like prodding a bruise to see if it was getting better yet. And the words just spilled out before he could stop them. 'I can imagine you as a mum.' She'd bring her child somewhere like here, to point out the wonders of the big blue whale and the dinosaurs and the fossilised lightning and the beautiful colours of the gemstones. And he had a sudden vision of himself at the seaside, building sandcastles with a little girl who had her mother's earnest blue eyes and shy smile.

'I think I'd like to be a mum,' she said.

And that was the sticking point.

Roland had wanted to be a dad—but not at the expense

of his marriage. He'd wanted their life to grow and expand, not for some of it to be excluded.

'But there are no guarantees,' she said.

It was the last thing he'd expected her to say and it surprised him into asking, 'What do you mean, no guarantees?'

'Apart from the fact that I'd need to find someone I wanted to have a family with in the first place, not everyone can have children. I've got friends who couldn't, even after several rounds of IVF,' she said.

That figured. Grace would take the sensible, measured point of view. But then again, he'd thought that Lyn would take that point of view, too, and maybe look at alternative options when things hadn't gone to plan. But, once her biological clock had started ticking, Lyn's views had changed. She'd become obsessive, almost. And, instead of running away and hiding in work, he should've done more to help her. He should've found a middle way that worked for both of them.

'Not everyone can,' he said, and hoped that Grace couldn't hear the crack in his voice, the way that he could.

She didn't comment on the fact he was quiet for the rest of the afternoon, but she bought him an ice cream in the museum café, and she got him talking about the amazing architecture of the Natural History Museum.

Funny how she understood him so well and knew what was balm to his soul.

'I never thought to look it up,' she said, 'but is there a museum of architecture?'

'Actually, there's something really amazing here in London,' he said. 'It's the house of Sir John Soane—the architect who designed the Bank of England, and the Royal Hospital in Chelsea. He arranged for the house to become a museum for students and people who loved architecture, after his death. They do candlelit tours in the evening so you get the feel of what life was like there, nearly two hundred years ago.' He smiled at her. 'Actually, if there's one next week, would you like to go?'

'Yes, but haven't you been there already?'

'Several times,' he said, 'but I see something new every time I go. It's a total maze of rooms with all these hidden compartments and corridors. The collection's arranged by pattern and symmetry rather than by period, and it's a total magpie's nest—everything from Egyptian relics to old clocks and period furniture and incredible art.' And it would be nice to share it with someone. Someone who understood what made him tick.

She smiled back. 'Sold.'

'Great.'

They visited the shop on the way out; Roland used the excuse that he wanted to pick up something for his five-year-old niece, but when Grace wasn't looking he secretly bought one of the dinosaur heads on a stick she'd told him about. Later that evening, he wrote a note on the outside of the paper bag and sneaked it into her briefcase, hoping she'd enjoy it when she found it.

On Monday morning, Grace opened her briefcase at her desk and discovered an unfamiliar paper bag resting on the top of her things.

In Roland's precise handwriting was a note.

Saw this and thought of you. Rrrr.

Intrigued, she opened the bag, and she burst out laughing when she saw the dinosaur head on a stick.

It was the last thing she would've expected from the man she'd met at Bella's wedding. But the Roland she'd got to know over the last few days had a keen sense of humour—and he made her feel more light-hearted and carefree than anyone she'd ever met. Like the teenager she'd never really been, because she'd always been the serious type.

Roland made her feel different.

And she liked that feeling.

Smiling, she texted him.

Thanks for the T-Rex. Am sure it will scare the numbers into behaving.

On impulse, she added a kiss to the end of the message, and sent it before she could chicken out.

Pleasure, came the immediate response.

Checked and is candlelit evening at museum tomorrow. Entry limited to first two hundred so we need to be there by five p.m. latest. Can you make it? R x

The fact that he'd sent her a kiss at the end of his own text made her heart flutter. It would be so easy to lose her heart to him. But that wasn't what he was looking for, and she needed to remember that. This was their last week together. They'd just enjoy it, and part as...well, hopefully, friends.

On Tuesday evening, Roland met Grace at Lincoln's Inn Fields and they joined the queue—early enough to guarantee their admission, to his relief.

He took her to the catacombs in the crypt, so she could see the sarcophagus by candlelight; there was lots of dramatic up-lighting. 'This is the spooky bit,' he said. 'It always feels like being in the middle of a gothic novel.'

'Your architect liked drama, then,' she said. 'I can't believe this is all a private collection. Imagine living here with this in your basement.'

'And this is probably how he would've lit it,' he said. She shivered. 'It's a little bit too spooky for me.'

'Come and see my favourite bit,' he said, and took her to the model room.

'Oh, I can see why you love this,' she said with a smile.

'My favourite one is the Pantheon. I loved the model, when I was a child—and then, when I visited the real thing in Rome, I was totally blown away by it. I think it's my favourite building in the whole world.'

'So what is it about it that grabs you most?' she asked.

'The dome. It still amazes me how they constructed that dome nearly two thousand years ago, without all the modern equipment we have now. It's the most incredible feat of engineering.'

'It's impressive,' she agreed.

'I used to come here a lot when I was a student,' he said. 'Soane used to open these rooms up to his students before and after lectures, so they could get more of a feel for the subject. I could just imagine being taught architecture here with these models.' He guided her round to see the miniature Parthenon. 'These models are incredible. Even the acanthus leaves on the Corinthian capitals here are accurate copies of the real thing. It's like being on a mini Grand Tour.'

'Have you actually done the Grand Tour?' she asked.

'I did think about doing it, the year I graduated,' he admitted, 'but a real Grand Tour could last anything from several months to several years. That wasn't really an option if I wanted to get my career up and running, so I did the whistlestop version, concentrating on Italian architecture and pretty much missing out the art and sculpture.'

'What was your favourite building? After the Pantheon, that is,' she added.

'The Coliseum's a close second,' he said, 'and the Duomo in Florence is something else, especially if you go inside the dome.'

'So would you think about building something with a dome?'

'Maybe.' He smiled at her. 'I guess I could pitch to Dad and Will that we ought to have a folly—as in a mini Pantheon—in the grounds, but I have a feeling they'd both laugh until they collapsed.'

'I thought your family supported your architecture?'

'The serious stuff, they do. A mini Pantheon is pure fantasy.' He laughed. 'And if they actually let me do it, in two hundred years' time people would point at it and refer to me as Roland "the Mad Architect" Devereux. Though I guess it'd make us stand out from the crowd if we could offer weddings held in the English Pantheon.'

'I have a nasty feeling that I could be a bad influence on you,' she said.

He tightened his fingers around hers. 'And that's probably a good thing.'

They'd planned to go to the cinema the following evening; but at lunchtime Grace found a text on her phone from Roland.

Sorry, something's come up at work. I need to sort it out. Going to be late home. Can we take a rain check on the movie?

Sure, she texted back, burying her disappointment. She knew he wouldn't cancel without a good reason, and he'd given her as much notice as he could.

She texted him just before she left the office.

Have makings of stir-fry in fridge, so if you don't get time to eat I can cook you something in five minutes flat tonight.

It was a while before he replied to thank her, and he didn't get home until almost nine.

'Sit down and I'll make you a drink. Have you eaten?' she asked.

'No. I'm too tired to eat,' he admitted.

'You need to eat,' she said, and ushered him to the kitchen table. 'Give me five minutes.'

As she'd promised, five minutes later, there was a plate of chicken, stir-fry veg, sweet chilli sauce and noodles in front of him.

'Thank you. This is good,' he said after the first mouthful.

'You're very welcome. Did you manage to get your problem sorted out?' she asked.

He sighed. 'We're getting there. It's a problem with an eco extension we're doing. The team started digging foundations this morning and it turns out there's an old well shaft right in the middle of the new build site. It wasn't on any of the plans of the area, so we need to talk to the building regs inspector and the planning department about how we're going to deal with it. We can cap it and build over it, or we can make a feature of it say with a partial glass floor, but either way it's going to affect how we deal with the foundations.' He grimaced.

'I'm probably going to be tied up dealing with this until the weekend, and it means I'll be working late as well. Sorry, Grace. It isn't what we agreed and I feel bad that I'm letting you down.'

'It's not your fault,' she said, 'and it's clearly not something you can delegate so it's fine. I can amuse myself.'

'Thank you.' He reached over to take her hand and squeezed it. 'I really appreciate you being so understanding. And don't worry about cooking for me for the rest of the week. I'll grab something with the team.'

'If there's anything you need, just tell me,' she said.

The rest of the week dragged. Grace was shocked to realise how quickly she'd come to look forward to her dates with Roland. So maybe his problem at work was a good thing; it would bring her common sense back and stop her making a fool of herself by falling for him.

On Friday evening, she went to the flat after work to see how things were going and pick up any post, and discovered there was a letter waiting for her. The job she'd been interviewed for on the day of the flood was hers, and they wanted her to start the week after next.

Given that she'd resigned herself to having to keep looking for a job, she was thrilled by the news. She texted Bella swiftly.

Got the job. Celebrate when you get back. Love you lots. x

And then she called her parents.

'Oh, darling, that's wonderful,' her mother said. 'I'm so pleased for you.'

'Can I take you and Dad out to dinner tonight to celebrate?' she asked.

'That's so lovely of you,' her mother said, 'but your dad's booked us a surprise break and we're heading out to the airport in about ten minutes. But we'll take you out the day we get back.'

'OK. That'll be lovely,' Grace said, swallowing her disappointment. 'Hey. I'd better let you go and finish getting ready. Have a great time, and text me to let me know you arrived safely.'

'We will. Love you, Gracie,' her mother said. 'And I'm so proud of you.'

'Love you, too, Mum,' Grace said.

She tried calling her three closest friends, just in case any of them might be free to celebrate her news with her, but their phones were all switched through to voicemail. By the time she got back to Docklands, Grace was feeling just a bit flat; she had some seriously good news, but nobody to celebrate with. For the first time since she'd broken up with Howard, she felt really alone.

And it made her question all her decisions. Had she done the right thing in cancelling her wedding? Should she have settled for a man who was kind but made her feel like part of the furniture?

She shook herself. No. Of course not. She'd done the right thing for both of them. She and Howard hadn't loved each other enough, and eventually they would've made each other miserable. She just had to get used to her new life. And she had a new job to look forward to—a challenge to meet. Everything was going to be just fine.

'Nothing fazes a Faraday girl,' she reminded herself out loud.

She knew Roland was busy, but texted the news to him

anyway. He didn't reply, and she was cross with herself for being disappointed that he hadn't even had time to text her back saying 'congrats'. Talk about being an ungrateful, needy brat. 'Get a grip,' she told herself crossly, 'and stop being so selfish.'

Half an hour later, the doorbell rang. A woman stood on the doorstep, holding a gorgeous hand-tied floral arrangement and three helium balloons.

'Grace Faraday?' she asked.

Grace blinked. 'Yes.'

'These are for you.' The woman—who looked strangely familiar, even though Grace knew they hadn't met before—handed her the flowers and balloons. She opened the card to find a message from Roland saying, *Well done! Congrats. R x.*

'That's amazing,' she said. 'How can he arrange something as gorgeous as this at such short notice—especially as practically everywhere is shut at this time of night?'

The delivery woman said drily, 'Because if your sister's a florist, you can talk her into doing things out of hours.' She looked Grace straight in the eye. 'He's kept you very quiet. I had no idea he was even seeing someone, let alone *living* with someone.'

This was Roland's little sister? 'You're Philly?' Grace asked, shocked.

'Phyllida Devereux of Philly's Flowers,' she confirmed.

Now Grace realised why the woman had looked familiar. Because she looked like Roland; she had the same dark eyes and the same gorgeous smile.

And Philly thought that Grace was living with Roland? Oh, help. She needed to do some damage limitation. Fast. 'We're not living together. This isn't what you think.'

Philly tipped her head to one side. 'Care to try me with an explanation?'

Roland wasn't here but, from the way he'd spoken about Philly, Grace was pretty sure they were close. 'Look, if you're not already on your way somewhere, come in for coffee and I'll explain.'

'All right.' Philly followed her inside.

Grace played for time while she made coffee. 'Have you eaten yet tonight?'

'No.'

'Then, if you're free, why don't you stay and have dinner with me?' She rummaged in the fridge. 'Do you like gnocchi with tomato and mascarpone sauce? I apologise in advance that it's shop-bought rather than home-made.'

Philly smiled. 'It sounds lovely—and Ro never cooks anyway. If I come here, either he orders something in or he makes me cook for us.'

'And I guess at least this is quick.'

'Is there anything I can do?' Philly asked.

'Lay the table?' Grace suggested, pretty sure that Roland's sister knew her way around the kitchen.

'Deal,' Philly said.

Ten minutes later, they were sitting at Roland's kitchen table with dinner in front of them.

'All righty. I'm not living with Roland—I'm staying in his guest room,' Grace said. 'I'm Bella's sister. There was a burst pipe in my flat—which used to be hers—and Bel left me Roland's number in case of emergency. He said if something like that had happened to you, he knew Hugh and Tarq would look after you, so he was going to do the same for me, as I'm Hugh's sister-in-law. And he offered me a place to store my stuff and stay until my flat dries out.'

'I get that's why you're staying here, but what I *don't* get is why he's sending you flowers.' Philly flapped a dismissive hand. 'Well, obviously as he asked for helium balloons that said "New Job" and "Congratulations" and I wrote the message on the card, I realise you've just got a new job. But this is my brother we're talking about and he hasn't sent a woman flowers since—' She stopped and narrowed her eyes. 'I assume you *know*?'

'About what happened to Lynette? Yes, he told me,' Grace said.

Philly looked thoughtful. 'And it's something he doesn't talk about very much. So are you seeing each other?'

How could she explain? 'It's complicated,' Grace prevaricated.

Philly folded her arms. 'Which tells me nothing. Spill, or I'll make his life a misery until you do—and, trust me, only little sisters can be that annoying.'

Grace smiled. 'Mine isn't annoying. She's lovely.'

'I can be lovely. But I'm definitely the annoying variety,' Philly said. 'Explain complicated.'

'We're helping each other out for a few weeks. Which are practically at an end.'

Philly frowned. 'What do you mean by helping each other out? And why is there a time limit?'

Grace knew that this was going to sound bad. 'He's practising his dating skills on me.'

Philly looked suspicious. 'And what do you get out of it?'

'Being swept off my feet.'

'And what happens at the end of these few weeks? You're going to be just good friends?' Philly added quote marks with her fingers round the last phrase.

Grace felt herself blush. 'Yes.'

'And you'd swear that in court?'

'I'd swear that he doesn't think of me romantically.'

Bad move. Because Philly honed straight in on what Grace hadn't said. 'But *you* think of *him* that way.'

'It's not going to happen,' Grace said. 'I went into this with my eyes open. To be honest, although he says he wants to start dating again, I think he's still in love with Lynette. But if I can help him take those first steps into coming back unto the world, then I'm glad I can do that.'

'You're in love with him,' Philly said.

'We barely know each other. We only met briefly at Hugh's wedding and we've known each other a little over two weeks,' Grace protested. But she had a nasty feeling that Philly was right. Even though it wasn't the sensible thing to do, she'd let herself fall for Roland. A man who wasn't available. Which was as stupid as it got.

'A little over two weeks is long enough.' Philly paused. 'He's seemed different whenever I've talked to him recently. Now I know why. I think you might be good for him.'

'It's not going to happen,' Grace repeated. 'I'm not what he's looking for.' And, even though a part of her really wished that she could be what Roland was looking for, she was sensible enough to know that she didn't fit into his world. She wasn't glamorous and exciting; she was sensible and slightly dull.

Philly had left by the time Roland returned, that evening.

'Thank you for the flowers and balloons,' Grace said.

'My pleasure.' He inspected them. 'Philly did a good job.'

'I like your sister.' Grace paused. 'I hope you don't mind, but she stayed for dinner.'

'And interrogated you?' he asked wryly.

'To be fair, she was delivering flowers to a woman at your house. If I'd been in her shoes, I would've been asking questions, too.' She smiled. 'Philly's nice.'

'Yeah, she is.' He paused. 'What did you tell her?'

'That you're putting me up while the flat dries out.'

'And she didn't ask anything else?' He looked sceptical.

Best to admit the truth, Grace thought. 'She did. So I told her about our deal.'

'Uh-huh.'

She wasn't going to tell him about what Philly had guessed. Because that was way outside the terms of their deal and he didn't need to know about that. 'She gets it. I think she's glad you're...' She grimaced. 'Sorry. That's not tactful.'

'Planning to get back in the land of the living,' he said. 'It's fine. I'm sorry I was working and couldn't take you out tonight to celebrate your new job. The flowers were sort of an apology as well as a congratulations.'

'The flowers are absolutely lovely,' she said.

'And Bella's away, so you couldn't celebrate with her.'

'And my parents are going on holiday; they're on their way to the airport now. Plus my friends are all busy. So, actually, I was pretty glad that your sister came round,' she admitted. 'It stopped me feeling completely like Billy-No-Mates.'

'I intend to make this up to you tomorrow—that is, if it's not going to mess up any plans you've made?' he asked.

She shook her head. 'We agreed to keep ourselves

free until Hugh and Bella got back, so I haven't made any plans.'

'Good. It's going to be an early start, so can you be ready for six?'

'Sure.'

'Pack for a night away. Nothing bigger than a case you can take in the cabin of a plane. Shoes you can walk in, something dressy, a hat, sunglasses and your passport. And don't ask where we're going.'

'Because you're not going to tell me.'

'Humour me. I want to see your face when we get there.' He wrapped his arms round her. 'Congrats again. I knew you'd do it.'

'Thank you.' She hugged him back. Funny how the world felt all right again when he was this close to her. But she'd have to get used to being on her own from next week onwards. So she needed to start putting that little bit of distance between them from now on.

CHAPTER NINE

THE NEXT MORNING, Grace was ready to leave at six. And Roland refused to tell her anything about where they were going until they were at the airport and their flight was called.

'We're going to Venice?' Her eyes grew wide in wonder. 'You're taking me to Venice just for the *day*?'

'And night,' he corrected. 'We fly back to London late tomorrow afternoon.'

'Venice,' she said again, seeming unable to quite take it in.

'It's my favourite place in the world,' he said.

Then he saw the wariness creep into her expression. He could guess why. 'Yes, I've been there a few times with Lyn,' he said, 'but you're not going to be following in her footsteps. This is just you and me. We're celebrating your new job.'

The beginning of her new life. And ending their deal on a high note. He didn't say it, but he was pretty sure she was thinking it, too. He was sticking to the plan. Sweeping her off her feet—and then saying goodbye.

Venice.

Who else but Roland would think about going to Venice just for one night? Grace thought.

And she had a feeling that he'd planned this right from the beginning, when she'd first told him that she hadn't travelled much. It would be the perfect end to their perfect few weeks together.

She was very aware that tomorrow was the last day of their agreement. And, as soon as Bella came back from honeymoon and discovered what had happened with the burst pipe, no doubt she'd insist that Grace came to stay with her and Hugh until the flat was habitable again. There was no reason for Grace to remain at Roland's house.

Unless he asked her to stay.

Somehow, she didn't think that was going to happen. Roland's job meant that he was used to planning in advance and working to a schedule. This was no different, really. It had been a short-term project to brush up his dating skills and sweep her off her feet. Mission accomplished, just before the deadline.

So she'd just enjoy this weekend for what it was.

The end.

Roland held her hand all the way on the plane, and when he walked with her to the end of the jetty at the airport. 'I thought we could take a water taxi into the city,' he said. 'It's the best way to see Venice for the first time.'

Once they were on the lagoon, Grace understood why he'd suggested bringing a hat and sunglasses. The reflections of the sun on the water were so bright that she would've been squinting without them. 'Right now, I feel like a princess,' she said.

'That's the idea,' he said. 'Watch the horizon.'

The water was pure turquoise and she couldn't make anything out at first. But then she saw rooflines, all spires and domes. As they drew closer, she could see that there were houses packed in tightly along the shoreline, with bridges arching over the entrances to the waterways running through the city.

'Venice rising from the water—this is one of the most beautiful things I've ever seen,' she whispered.

Roland's fingers tightened around hers. 'And it gets better. Watch.'

As they grew closer, she could see the architecture more clearly. There were shutters at the windows of the houses; plaster peeled away from some of the brickwork, while other houses looked as if they'd been recently restored.

Their driver took them under a bridge, and now they were really in Venice.

'I've never been in a city without any traffic noise, before,' she said. And it was odd to hear the swish of the waves and hear people talking where she'd usually expect to hear engines revving and horns blasting.

'What's that building?' she asked. 'All that latticed plaster reminds me of the icing on a wedding cake.'

'That's the Palazzo Ducale—the Doge's Palace,' he said. 'And that tall tower opposite—the one with the red bricks and green roof—is Galileo's Tower.' He smiled at her. 'We'll walk through St Mark's Square later, so you can have a closer look at them.'

'Thank you,' she said. Coming here was a treat— but coming here with someone who knew the place and could help her to find all the most interesting bits was better still. And the fact that that someone was Roland...

When their driver moored at the jetty, Roland helped her from the boat.

'I still can't get over this,' she said. 'I've seen documentaries and photographs of Venice in magazines, but the real thing is beyond anything I'd dreamed about. I think,' she added shyly, 'I like this even more than Paris.'

He looked pleased. 'I hoped you'd like this. Let's check in, and then we can go exploring.'

The hotel was part of an old palazzo; the decor was all cream and navy and gold, with marble flooring and a fountain in the reception area. Roland had booked them a suite with two rooms. Because they were only staying for one night, Grace managed to unpack her overnight case very swiftly.

The streets outside were crowded, yet at the same time it was so much quieter than she was used to in London, without the traffic noises. Gondolas and small rowing boats glided through the narrow canals; there were bridges everywhere, with the sunlight reflecting off the water and dappling the undersides of the bridges.

Shops crowded against each other, offering glass and Venetian masks and marbled paper; tourists posed for photographs on the bridges and in the little squares. 'All the signs seem to point either to the Rialto or San Marco,' she said in surprise.

'In this part of the city, they're the two main destinations and all the streets lead to them—though sometimes it's the long way round,' he said with a smile. 'Let's start at the Rialto. There's a gorgeous view of the Grand Canal from the bridge.'

The marble on the bridge had been worn shiny by countless hands skimming across it; and Grace leaned against the bridge to watch the traffic on the canal go by. When they finished crossing the bridge to go into the marketplace itself, she discovered that it was a sheer delight, full of colour—selling everything from fresh seafood glistening in the sunlight through to tiny wild strawberries and fragrant herbs sold by the handful.

'This is amazing,' she said.

He glanced at his watch. 'Wait a second.'

And then suddenly bells were pealing all over the city.

'Is it a special occasion, or does this happen every day?' she asked.

'Every day. In the summer it's like aural sunlight; in the winter, especially if it's foggy, it's a little spooky,' he said.

'I can see why Venice is one of your favourite places,' she said. 'It's amazing.'

They walked hand in hand through the narrow streets, enjoying all the bustle around them and stopping to buy a *piadina* from one of the street vendors to keep them going over lunchtime. Grace stopped to take photographs of the figures outside some of the mask shops—the terrifying plague doctor with his hooked beak, and the pretty harlequin—and took a selfie of Roland and herself standing on a bridge with a gondola gliding behind them. 'Do you mind me being horribly touristy?' she asked.

'Not a bit.' He smiled. 'Actually, I'm enjoying seeing how much you like Venice.'

'It's gorgeous,' she said. 'I know I keep saying it, but it's like… Venice is just like nowhere else I've ever been.'

'If you don't mind us doing a whistlestop tour,' he said, 'we can go take a look at the basilica and the Doge's Palace.'

'But you've seen it all before,' she said.

He shrugged. 'You know I never pass up the opportunity to look at architecture. And besides, you can't come to Venice and not see the *quadriga*—the four horses. They've been in Venice for more than eight hundred years.'

Grace thoroughly enjoyed their tour of the cathedral and the palace, especially as Roland turned out to be a mine of information about the buildings. And she loved the fact that he took a selfie of them on the loggia of the basilica, next to the replicas of the four bronze horses.

Right now, she thought wistfully, this felt like a honeymoon. Though she knew she was being ridiculous. Roland hadn't given her any signals that he wanted their relationship to continue past their agreement, let alone anything more. They'd known each other for only a few weeks; it was way, way too soon to fall in love.

Stop being greedy, she reminded herself. Just enjoy every second of this and stop wishing for something you're not going to get.

'I thought we'd have dinner early,' he said, 'because there's something else you absolutely have to do in Venice.'

'Bring it on,' Grace said with a smile.

Roland found a little tucked away restaurant. 'My Italian's a bit scrappy,' he said, 'but I can get by. What would you like to eat?'

'A Venetian speciality,' she said.

'Let's ask the waiter what he recommends,' he said. 'But for pudding I'd say it has to be tiramisu in the area where it was invented.'

The waiter recommended *sarde in saor*—sardines in a sweet and sour sauce—followed by *polenta e schie*—tiny Venetian shrimps on a bed of white polenta. And the tiramisu was the best Grace had ever, ever tasted.

'This is perfect,' she said. 'Thank you so much.'

But the best was what Roland had arranged for after coffee.

'I wanted to eat early,' he said, 'so we'd get to see the sunset.'

And then she discovered where he'd planned their viewpoint to be: from the seat of a gondola.

Their gondolier wore the traditional black trousers, striped jersey and straw hat; he guided them through the narrow waterways, using his pole to propel them and pushing his body against it to help them turn the odd corner. To Grace's delight he actually serenaded them in a mellow tenor voice.

The sunset itself was the most romantic thing she'd ever seen: the sun sinking, the sky turning shades of orange and apricot with the domes and towers of the city silhouetted against it, and the turquoise waters of the Grand Canal changing to reflect the deep tones of the sky.

She was too moved to say a word; she leaned her head against Roland's shoulder, drinking in the view and enjoying his nearness. He held her close, and again this felt so much like a honeymoon.

The gondolier took them through the narrow waterways again, which had turned almost inky to reflect the darkened sky; reflections from little globe-shaped lamps flickered on the water. 'This is so pretty,' she said. 'Thank you so much.'

'My pleasure,' he said, and stole a kiss.

They lapsed back into companionable silence; then, as a covered walkway rose in front of them, Roland said, 'This is the Bridge of Sighs. It's traditional to kiss underneath it.'

What else could she do but kiss him as the gondola glided underneath the bridge?

'This was the perfect end to a perfect evening,' she

said as the gondolier tied up the boat at the jetty by St Mark's Square and helped them off the gondola.

'We haven't finished quite yet,' Roland said. 'Remember tangoing by the Seine? Now we're going to do the same in St Mark's Square. Well, not necessarily dance the tango—it depends what they're playing.'

As they walked into the square, lit by more of the pretty globe-shaped lights, Grace realised what he meant. There were tables and chairs outside Florian's and Quadri's, the two oldest *caffès* in the city, and a couple of small bands played on stages underneath gazebos.

Roland spun her into his arms and began to dance with her. Other couples were doing the same, she noticed, so instead of protesting that they were going to make a spectacle of themselves, she relaxed and gave herself up to the sheer pleasure of being held by Roland.

Grace looked so beautiful in the soft light of the square, Roland thought. Tonight, she was really shining—relaxed, happy, enjoying the music and the dancing and the sheer romance that was Venice.

And he, too, was being seduced by the place. To the point that when they got back to the hotel and he'd unlocked the door to their suite, he actually picked her up and carried her across the threshold.

Then he realised what he was doing, and set her back down on her feet. 'Sorry. I got a bit carried away.'

She smiled and reached up to stroke his face. 'I think you were doing the carrying. Literally. And the answer's yes.'

He sucked in a breath. Was she saying…? 'But—'

She pressed a finger lightly against his lips. 'No

strings,' she said. 'That's what we agreed. And tonight's just you and me and Venice.'

'Are you sure about this?' he asked.

Her eyes were almost navy in the low light. 'I'm very sure.'

'Grace, you don't owe me anything. I didn't bring you here expecting you to sleep with me in exchange for the trip.'

'I know, and that's not why I'm saying yes.' She took a deep breath. 'It's because I want to. I know there are no strings and this is just temporary between you and me—but you've swept me off my feet this far, so let's go the whole way.'

He needed no further encouragement. He picked her up and carried her across the threshold to his bedroom.

And then he got to live out the dream he'd had the previous weekend. Unzipping her dress, sliding it off her shoulders, kissing every centimetre of skin he revealed—and finally losing himself in her warm sweet depths.

That night he fell asleep with his arms wrapped round her and her arms wrapped round him, feeling more at peace with himself than he had in way too long.

The next morning, Roland woke first. Guilt flooded through him. He really had let the romance of Venice carry off his common sense, last night. Even though Grace had told him that she was sure, he shouldn't have let things go this far.

So what now? Would her feelings have changed this morning? Would she regret it? Would she want things to be different? Or would they both be able to blame it on the romance of the sunset and the music?

She was shy with him when she woke, and he knew he had to break the ice.

'I'm sorry,' he said. 'I, um…I guess last night shouldn't have happened. I apologise.'

'Don't apologise. It was just as much my idea as yours,' she said. 'It wasn't part of our deal. We got carried away by—well, by Venice. So we can pretend it didn't happen.'

If she'd wanted last night to be the start of something more, now was the perfect time to say so. The fact that she hadn't made it clear to him that she intended to stick to the terms of their arrangement.

So today was their very last day together.

This was going to be goodbye.

As far as he knew, the landlord hadn't contacted her any more about the situation with the flat, so she might still need to be his house guest for a while. But Bella and Hugh were due back from their honeymoon tomorrow, and it was more than likely that as soon as Bella learned what had happened, she would insist on Grace moving in with her.

And then he and Grace would be polite and distant strangers.

That was what they'd agreed, so why did it make him feel so antsy?

'I, um— There was something I wanted to show you this morning,' he said. 'Shall we go exploring straight after breakfast?'

'That sounds good,' she agreed.

A shower helped him get some of his equilibrium back. Strong Italian coffee helped even more.

And then, with the help of a map, he found the Sotoportego dei Preti. 'This is what I wanted to show you,' he said. 'It's the *cuore in mattone*—the heart in the brick.'

'I should've guessed it would be something architectural,' she said with a smile, looking at the brick just below the lintel. 'A heart-shaped brick is very appropriate for Venice. What's the story behind it?'

'You're meant to touch it and make a wish—so the legend goes, if your wish is respectful and harms no one, it will be answered within the year,' he said.

'So have you known about this for years, or was this like the tangoing in Paris?'

'Like the tangoing. I looked it up on the Internet,' he admitted. 'Shall we?'

They touched the brick together and made a wish. Roland couldn't help asking, 'So what did you wish for?'

'I imagine it's like the wish you make on a star or when you blow out the candles on your birthday cake,' she said. 'So I can't tell you, or it won't come true.'

'I guess.' And that meant he didn't have to tell her what he'd wished for, either.

For love to fill his life again. For this thing between them to become real.

They took the water bus over to Murano to see all the pretty painted cottages and to see a glass-blowing demonstration.

'You and your glass,' she teased afterwards.

He spread his hands. 'You can't come to Venice without seeing glass being blown or lace-making.'

'I guess. And it was pretty spectacular—I've never seen anything like that before. Do you mind if I take a quick look round the shop?'

'Sure. Though shopping's not really my thing, so I'm going to sit in the sun while you're looking round. Don't rush,' he added. 'Just come and find me when you're ready.'

* * *

Grace was glad that Roland wasn't planning to shadow her in the shop, because she'd hoped to find a gift for him to thank him for taking her to Venice. And there was a beautiful modern paperweight that was absolutely perfect. Better still, the sales assistant wrapped it beautifully for her, so he wouldn't have a clue about it.

Roland found a little *osteria* that sold *cicheti*—Venetian tapas—for lunch, and the choice was breathtaking: tiny *polpette*, stuffed olives, tomato bruschetta, white asparagus wrapped in pancetta, baby octopus in lemon, slices of grilled polenta with salami, *arancini*, spider crab, *zucchini* stuffed with tomatoes and cheese, and marinated artichokes. Between them, they tried a little of everything, sharing a plate and feeding each other little morsels; again, it felt like being on a honeymoon, and Grace had to remind herself to keep her feet on the ground. To go back to being sensible, quiet Grace.

But on the flight back to England, Roland went quiet on her.

And that in turn gave her time to think. Today was the last day of their arrangement. Their last day together. Grace and Roland had agreed that once Bella and Hugh returned tomorrow, from then on they'd be polite strangers.

A few weeks ago, that had seemed perfectly reasonable. But, last night, they'd made love. So would he still want to stick to their original deal, or would he suggest that they try to make a go of things?

She knew what she wanted. She'd wished on the heart-shaped brick that things would be different—that this thing between them could turn out to be real. But she wasn't quite brave enough to bring it up. This morning, she'd woken to find him looking full of panic, clearly having second thoughts. What else could she have done but pretend everything was just fine and let him off the hook?

It was pretty clear that her feelings were one-sided. Last night, they'd simply got carried away with the romance of Venice, the gondola and dancing through St Mark's Square. It hadn't been real.

So it was better to leave this situation with her dignity intact.

And she'd get over this.

She would.

Back in the airport at London, she switched on her phone to find that it was dead. 'I must've left an app on that drained the battery,' she said.

'You can use my phone if you need to,' Roland offered.

'Thanks, but I didn't tell my family I was away so they won't be worrying. It can wait,' she said.

Back at Roland's house, there was a pile of post. He set his coffee machine working, then sat at the kitchen table to go through his mail, while Grace plugged in her phone and waited for it to charge for long enough that she could switch it on again, then checked the messages that came through.

She was about to tell Roland the good news when she noticed that his face had blanched. 'Is everything OK?' she asked instead, concerned.

'Sure.' But he didn't move. He just sat there, staring at the table.

She finished making the coffee and brought his mug over to the table. 'You don't look sure,' she said gently.

'I...' He sighed and gestured to one of the envelopes. 'This came from Mindy, Lyn's best friend from school.

They're moving house and she found these photos and thought I might like them.'

'That was kind of her,' Grace said. Or was it? He looked as if someone had ripped his heart out. Roland had clearly loved his wife deeply. Despite the fact that he'd said he was ready to move on, from his reaction to getting those photographs Grace didn't think he was. Was he feeling guilty that he'd taken her to Venice— as if he'd betrayed Lyn's memory? Though asking him would be like stomping over still-fresh wounds, and she didn't know what to say.

In the end she reached over to squeeze his hand. 'I didn't know Lyn, but you said that she wouldn't want you to be sad. Why don't you look at the photos and re-member the good times?'

'I...' His voice sounded thick with emotion. 'But you...'

'We had a deal,' she said. 'It finishes today. And I'd like to think that we've become friends.' More than that—they'd been lovers, and it had shown Grace ex-actly what she'd been missing in her life. How wrong she'd been when she'd thought she could settle for nice enough instead of the real thing.

Roland could so easily have been her real thing.

But she knew that he wasn't ready to move on, and she wasn't sure if he ever would be.

'Friends,' he said.

'I'd like to see the photos,' she said. 'Talk to me, Ro-land. Tell me about Lyn. Tell me about the good times.'

Roland knew he ought to tell Grace the truth. About the bad times. But he didn't want her to think badly of Lyn. Or of him.

He took the photographs out of the envelope. 'They're from years ago. Just a weekend at the beach with friends.'

'She looks nice,' Grace said. 'As if she was fun. And you both look so happy.'

They had been. Once.

'Yeah.' His voice cracked.

Grace pushed her chair back and walked round the table to wrap her arms round him. 'Don't focus on the fact that she's gone. Focus on the fact that you were together and you loved each other.'

And it hadn't been enough. But how could he explain?

'Grace, I wish…'

As if her thoughts were totally in tune with his, she held him just that little bit tighter. 'Roland, these past few weeks have been amazing. You've swept me off my feet—but, better still, you've shown me that I don't have to settle for being sensible all the time. That it's OK to dream and to reach for those dreams. And your dating skills are just fine—but I don't think you're ready to move on. Not yet.'

No. Because his guilt still held him back, making him feel that he didn't deserve a second chance. Not when he'd messed up so badly. 'I guess,' he said.

But, even if they could get over that hurdle, there was another sticking point. The one that had cracked his marriage. He and Lyn had had trouble conceiving, and he didn't know if the problem had lain with him. What if Grace wanted children—and, just like it had happened with Lyn, their love got bogged down in the problems of conception? He couldn't bear to go through that nightmare again. And, even though he knew Grace was sensible and down to earth, even the most sensible person could be sideswiped by emotions.

He had to let this go. For her sake as well as for his own. He had to get out of her way and let her find the happiness she deserved. Even if it was with someone else.

'Those messages that came through—one was from my landlord,' she said. 'Thanks to your restoration expert sucking up the water and putting a dehumidifier in early, the flat's all dried out now. It seemed they don't need to strip the plaster back after all, so I can move my stuff back whenever I like. Which is perfect timing,' she said brightly.

Meaning she was going to walk out of his life. Roland didn't want her to go—but he knew she was right. He wasn't ready to move on. It wasn't fair to ask her to wait indefinitely.

'I'll get a couple of the guys to move the heavy stuff for you in the morning if you don't mind lending me your key,' he said.

'Thank you.'

'No problem,' he said. 'And thank you. You've helped me, too, these last few weeks.'

But not enough, Grace thought. Not enough for him to be able to move on from the sadness of his past and ask her to stay.

'Great,' she said. 'I guess I'd better start getting my stuff together—and let you get on.'

'Uh-huh.' He gave her an awkward smile. 'Let me know if you need anything.'

She did. She needed him. But it wasn't fair to put that extra burden on him. 'Sure,' she said.

'I'd better check my emails,' he said.

'Yes. So life goes back to normal tomorrow for both

of us,' she said. 'You get your space back. And I get to stand on my own two feet again.'

'Well—good night.'

'Good night. And thanks for everything.' This time, she didn't hug him—because it would hurt way too much to let him go. Instead, she had to go back to the fall-back position. Sensible Grace.

If only it could've been otherwise.

CHAPTER TEN

GRACE SPENT THE morning moving her things back to the flat. Just as Roland had promised, he'd sent a van and two of his workmen to move the heavy stuff for her, and she'd bought them both a case of beer to thank them for their help.

When she'd put the last of her things in the car, she took the gift-wrapped paperweight she'd bought in Venice from her bag and went into Roland's office. She put the parcel in the top drawer of his desk, along with the card she'd written earlier, and closed the drawer again.

Once he'd finished grieving for Lynette, he'd make someone a wonderful partner.

If only it could've been her.

But he wasn't ready to move on; and she was still up in the air after her break-up with Howard. Being the one who'd called everything off didn't mean that she'd escaped any feelings of hurt and loss. She still needed to work out what she really wanted from life.

Besides, it was way too fast for her to have fallen in love with Roland. She'd just responded to the way he'd swept her off her feet, that was all. She couldn't possibly be in love with him.

She set the alarm and locked the door behind her, then

posted his door key through the letterbox. Have locked up and left your key, she texted.

Back in her own flat, she spent her time cleaning the place from top to bottom and then moving everything back into its rightful place. She called in to see Bella and Hugh with a bottle of champagne, and thought she'd managed to fool Bella into thinking that everything was fine; though the next evening her sister turned up unexpectedly, bearing a seriously good walnut cake from her local bakery.

'Spill,' Bella demanded.

Just like Roland's sister had demanded last week, Grace thought wryly.

'There's nothing to tell,' she said, giving her best fake smile.

Bella coughed. 'You look worse now than when Mrs Concrete Hair used to do a hatchet job on your confidence with her sly little insinuations. So what's happened? Has Howard had an epiphany and asked you to go back to him, and Mama Dearest has stuck her oar in?'

'No to both,' Grace said. 'And I'm not going back to Howard. We wouldn't make each other happy. And he's a nice guy, Bel. He deserves to be happy.'

'And he needs to grow a backbone, but OK,' Bella said. 'So if it's not Howard, it's someone else. You might as well tell me, Gracie, because you know I won't shut up until you do.' Bella cut them both a large piece of cake.

Grace knew that her sister meant it, so she gave in and told Bella about her deal with Roland. 'And it's fine,' she said. 'We both did what we promised. He swept me off my feet and I helped him with his dating skills. End of story. If we see each other again, we'll be polite but distant strangers.'

'Which obviously isn't what you want.'

Grace denied it, though she knew full well that Bella wasn't going to believe her.

'Just call him,' Bella said, rolling her eyes. 'Tell him how you feel. What have you got to lose?'

'Bel, he's still in love with Lynette. I can't compete with a memory,' Grace said. 'And don't get any bright ideas about inviting us both to dinner and trying to fix us up. It'll just be embarrassing. I'll be fine. I've got my new job to look forward to, and that'll keep me busy.'

And if she kept telling herself that, eventually she'd believe it.

Over the next couple of days, Roland threw himself into work and refused to admit to himself how much he missed Grace. How empty the whole place felt without Grace around.

She thought he couldn't move on because he was still in love with Lyn. It wasn't true. But he'd let her go because he came with baggage and he hadn't wanted to drag her down with it.

Had he made a mistake?

If he'd opened up to her properly, told her the whole truth instead of just parting, would she have understood? Could she have helped him start his life all over again—give him a second chance?

He shook himself. No. He was being selfish. He'd done the right thing—even though it hurt.

He tried distracting himself with a magazine. On one page, he saw a photograph of the heart-shaped brick he and Grace found in Venice. According to the paragraph beneath the photograph, Roland had got the legend completely wrong. It wasn't about wishes coming true. Allegedly, if you pressed the brick you fell in love immediately; if you pressed it together, you'd be devoted for ever.

And he and Grace had touched the brick at the same time.

A pretty story. That was all it was. He tried to put it out of his head and started on some preliminary sketches from his latest design brief. When the point of his pencil snapped, he opened his desk drawer to grab a new lead; but there was something he didn't recognise in the drawer. A wrapped parcel, next to a card. The handwriting on the envelope was Grace's. When he opened it, the card showed a picture of Venice at sunset, very similar to the one they'd seen on the gondola. Inside, she'd written, *Thank you for sweeping me off my feet.*

The parcel contained a beautiful paperweight in shades of turquoise and blue. The sort of thing he would've chosen for himself. He handled the smooth glass thoughtfully. She'd thanked him for sweeping her off her feet and she'd bought him the most perfect present.

She understood him.

Would she understand if he told her the rest? And would she be prepared to take a risk on him?

There was only one way to find out. He called her. Her phone went through to voicemail, so he assumed that she was busy. 'Grace, it's Roland. Please call me when you get this message.' He left his number, just in case she'd mislaid it.

And now it was up to her.

Why was Roland calling her? Grace wondered.

Maybe she'd left something behind and he'd just discovered it. Of course he wasn't calling her to say he'd changed his mind about the terms of their deal. It was ridiculous to hope.

When she was quite sure that she wasn't going to make a fool of herself and blurt out something inappropriate, she returned his call.

He answered on the second ring. 'Roland Devereux.' He sounded as cool and impassive as he'd been the first time she'd called him. When she'd mistakenly thought he was her landlord. And now...

'It's Grace,' she said. 'Returning your call.'

'Thank you.'

'What did you want? Did I leave something behind?' Despite her best intentions, hope flickered in her heart.

'Yes.'

The hope sputtered and died. 'Sorry. Let me know when it's convenient to come and pick it up.'

'I'll come over.'

'I can't put you to all that trouble,' she protested.

'It's no trouble. I'll be in the area anyway.'

Why? Work? But it wasn't her place to ask. 'OK. Thank you. Let me know when, and I'll make sure I'm here.'

'Now,' he suggested.

Now? As in...right *now*? Then she realised he was waiting for her answer. 'I—um, yes, sure. I guess at least this time you won't be helping me shift furniture out of a flooded flat.'

'Indeed. See you soon.'

It took all of ninety seconds for her to tidy the flat.

And then what? Would he stay for coffee? Was this the beginning of them becoming friends? *Could* they be friends, after their fling? Or would the memories always get in the way?

When the doorbell rang, her heart leapt. She took a deep breath and reminded herself to act cool, calm and collected. 'Hello, Roland,' she said as she opened the door. Then she noticed that he wasn't carrying anything. She frowned. 'I thought you said I left something behind?'

'You did.' He paused. 'Me.'

'What?' She couldn't quite process this. 'I don't understand.'

'We need to talk.'

She frowned again. 'But I thought we'd already said it all. We had an agreement. You swept me off my feet and I can rubber stamp your dating skills. And now it's all done and dusted.'

'There's a lot more to say,' he said, 'but I don't want to do it on your doorstep.'

Her head was in a whirl. 'Sorry. I'm being rude. Come in. Can I get you a drink or something?'

He shook his head. 'I just want to talk.'

She gestured to the sofa. There wasn't anywhere else to sit, unless she opted for one of the metal dining chairs at the small table in the kitchen part of the flat, so she sat next to him.

'I don't know where to start,' he admitted.

'Try the beginning,' she said. 'Or wherever you feel like starting and you can go back and forth.'

'Then I'm going to tell you something I've never told anyone—not even my family or my best friends.' He took a deep breath. 'It's about Lyn. Everyone thinks I've been mourning her for the last two years.'

'And you haven't?' she asked, surprised. But Lynette had been the love of Roland's life and he'd lost her in horrible circumstances. Of course he'd been mourning her. He didn't even have any of the wedding photographs on display in his house because it clearly hurt too much. And the way he'd reacted to the photographs Lyn's friend had sent had signalled very clearly that he was still in love with Lyn.

'More like nearly three,' he said.

He'd mourned her for a year before she'd died? But why? Grace bit her lip. 'Was she ill but you hadn't told anyone?'

'Sort of.' He sighed. 'She wanted a baby.'

Which wasn't remotely the same as being ill. Or did he mean a different sort of problem? But Roland hadn't seemed the selfish type. She didn't understand. 'I take it from that, you didn't want a baby?' Grace guessed.

'No, I did,' he said, 'but I always thought love would expand along with my family. With Lyn, it narrowed. Right from the moment we first talked about it and started trying, she changed. All her friends who started trying fell pregnant the very first month, which made it even harder for her when she didn't.'

'Did you talk to a doctor about it?'

He nodded. 'He said we were both young and they wouldn't even consider offering us fertility treatment until we'd tried for at least another year. And it broke her, Grace. Every month when her period started, it was like the end of the world. And every time we made love, it was timed by her ovulation chart. I tried taking her away for the weekend and being spontaneous to take her mind off things, but nothing worked. She was driven. It was as if our relationship was only there for the sole purpose of having a baby, and I hated that I was letting her down all the time.'

She took his hand. 'Hey. You tried. You were there for her.'

'Not enough,' he admitted, 'and that's the really shameful bit. I don't like myself very much, Grace.'

'Hey. We all have things that make us feel that way,' she said gently. 'I'm not squeaky clean, either. I broke off my engagement three weeks before the wedding day, remember?'

'Which was the right thing to do,' he said. 'Whereas I...' He sighed. 'We stopped seeing my family. Will and Susie have a little girl, Matilda, and when Lyn couldn't get pregnant she couldn't handle being around children. It made her feel a failure, even though I tried to tell her that she wasn't a failure and nobody was ever going to judge her. But I couldn't exactly explain to everyone why Lyn didn't want to be anywhere near Tilda, not without telling people the truth—and she'd sworn me to secrecy because she didn't want anyone pitying her or judging her. So we used my work as an excuse, saying I was too busy for us to see people.' He grimaced. 'My mum even rang me to say she was worried about us—she said that I was neglecting Lyn for work and she asked if she could do anything to help. I hated having to lie to my family.'

'But you weren't neglecting Lyn—you were trying to protect her,' Grace protested.

He shook his head. 'Actually, my mum was right. Because it got to the point where I was glad to have an excuse to be away. I did end up neglecting Lyn. I accepted invitations to give lectures abroad so I didn't have to face all that pain. And that's why I was away when the accident happened.'

'The accident wasn't your fault, Roland.'

'I know,' he said. 'And I keep telling myself that, even

if I had been in London, the accident might still have happened. But at least then I would have been there to say goodbye to her before she died, instead of being thousands of miles away.'

'I'm sure Lyn knew that you loved her.'

He nodded. 'And I did, even though our marriage was cracking at the seams. But the very worst bit was what the doctor told me, something I couldn't bear to tell anyone because it was just so...' He caught his breath.

She squeezed his hand. 'Roland, you don't have to talk about this. And it's understandable that you're still in love with Lyn.'

'I'm not,' he said. 'I miss her. But I missed her for a year before she died. I missed the closeness of being with someone. And it's taken me a while to work through all the guilt and misery I've been feeling. I wasn't sure that I'd ever be ready to put my life back together again, but...' He drew her hand up to his mouth and kissed the backs of her fingers. 'I've worked out for myself that the only way to finally get past the pain and heal again is to talk about it. I don't want to have any secrets from you, Grace.' He closed his eyes for a moment, and her heart bled for him. He'd been through so much. 'I haven't been able to say this to anyone, because—well, I know what Lyn meant about not being able to face all the pity. I've been there. But I know you won't pity me.'

'I won't pity you,' she promised. 'But I do reserve the right to give you a hug.'

'OK.' He dragged in a breath. 'Lyn was pregnant when she died. It was so early on that she probably didn't even know. But how different things might've been,' he finished wistfully.

Roland would've been a father and Lyn would've had

the baby she'd longed for so badly. And his marriage might have healed. But the driver who'd crashed into Lyn had taken away all those possibilities. No wonder Roland had locked himself away. 'I'm so sorry,' she said, still holding his hand.

'And that's partly why I haven't really dated since she died. Part of me wants to move on, because I can't spend the rest of my life in mourning. The Lyn I married wouldn't have wanted me to do that—just as I wouldn't have wanted her to be on her own if I'd been the one who was killed and she was the one left behind,' he said. 'But it went sour for us because she wanted a family so desperately. And that's what's stopped me moving on. I don't want to go through that again, to lose the woman I love a little more each day and know I can't do anything to help.'

'I can understand that,' Grace said.

'But then I realised something,' he said. 'These last few days I've been running away again, burying myself in work so I didn't have to think or face things—but I'm ready to face them now.'

'Face what?' she asked.

'The fact that…' He took a deep breath. 'I love you, Grace. And I want to be with you. And I should've told you that as soon as we got back from Venice, instead of letting you come back here on your own.'

'I don't get it,' she said.

'You don't believe I love you?'

'I don't get why you're saying this to me now. Nothing's changed since we came back from Venice.'

'Oh, but it has,' he corrected. 'I've had time to think. Time to miss you. And what finally made me realise was when I found the paperweight—and you thanked me for sweeping you off your feet.'

So did that mean…? The hope she'd ruthlessly squashed earlier flickered back into life.

'And I think you swept me off my feet, too,' he said. 'In just over two weeks, you taught me to have fun again. You taught me how to reconnect.'

'But I didn't really do anything,' she said. 'You're the one who did all the big romantic stuff and took me to places I'd always wanted to see. I don't even know what your dreams are, so I couldn't even begin to start making any of them come true.'

'I didn't know what my dreams were, either, but I do now,' he said. 'I want to live, really live, with the woman I love. A woman who's brave and funny and sweet.'

He couldn't possibly be describing her. 'But I'm not brave. Or funny. I'm just *ordinary*.'

'You're quiet and sensible and grounded,' he said, 'which is all good. But there's more to you than that. There's also a part of you that shines. The woman I danced with on the bank of the Seine, and who was brave enough to order lunch in Paris in schoolgirl French. The woman who likes to plan everything but who put herself out of her comfort zone for a few weeks. The woman who makes my world so much brighter just by being there. And I want you in my life for good, Grace. As my wife.'

But he'd been there before and it had all gone wrong. She couldn't just sweep that under the carpet. 'What about children?' she asked.

'Yet more proof that you're brave,' he said wryly, 'since you're not scared of dealing with a subject that would make most people shy away. Especially because you're the only other person in the world who knows the whole truth about Lyn and me.' He looked at her. 'I admit, part of me is scared to death about it. I've had one marriage go sour on me—and it's something I can't really talk about, because Lyn can't speak up for herself now and I don't want people to think badly of her.'

'Absolutely,' she agreed. 'And, just so you know, I don't think badly of her either.'

'Thank you.' He took a deep breath. 'I'm not confusing you with Lyn. I'm not seeing you as her replacement—I'm seeing you as you. But, even though I want to be with you, it scares me that I might end up repeating the same pattern.'

'How?' she asked.

'I don't want to see you get hurt and bogged down,' he said. 'When I asked you in the museum if you wanted children, you said there were no guarantees.'

'Because there aren't,' she said.

'I don't know if the problem was with Lyn or with me,' he said. 'If it was with me, then you and I might not be able to conceive. I hate the idea of going through all that again, knowing month after month that I've let you down. But,' he said, 'if having children is really important to you, I'll take that risk. I just need to know that...' He stopped. 'I'm making a mess of this.'

'You need to know that our relationship is about more than just having children,' Grace said. 'I get it.' She paused. 'Do you want children, Roland?'

He nodded. 'But not at the cost of my marriage. I love you, Grace, and I want to marry you. But wanting everything is greedy.'

'You taught me something,' she said. 'You taught me that it's OK not to settle for things, not to stick rigidly to my fall-back position of being sensible. It's OK to dream. But you need to balance it with real life and you need to keep it in perspective. If having children naturally doesn't work for us, we can look at other options. Being a biological parent is no guarantee of being a good one. Ed isn't related to me by blood, but he's the best dad I could ever have asked for.'

'I agree with you. OK. So what happened to me and Lyn—that won't happen to us,' he said.

'Definitely not,' she confirmed. 'We won't let it.'

'You know when we touched that heart-shaped brick in Venice?'

She nodded.

'What did you wish for?'

'You asked me that before—and if you tell a wish it doesn't come true,' she reminded him.

'Actually, I got the legend wrong. Apparently, the real one is that if you touch the brick, you fall in love. If you touch the brick at the same time as someone else, you'll be devoted to each other for the rest of your days.' He paused. 'We touched the brick at the same time, Grace. I remember that very clearly.'

She felt the colour heating her cheeks. 'Yes.'

'And I fell in love with you. I think I fell in love with you before then, but that was when it hit me.' He raised an eyebrow. 'Do you want to know what I wished?'

'What did you wish?' Her words were a whisper.

'I wished that our arrangement was more than that. That it could be real. And carry on for the rest of our lives.'

Exactly the same as her own wish.

'So will you marry me, Grace?' he asked. 'Will you make my dreams come true?'

Every nerve in her body was urging her to say yes. To go for her dream. But her common sense still held her back. 'We've known each other only a few weeks, and you really think we can make a go of it?' She shook her head. 'But I'd known Howard for eighteen months before he proposed—six months as a colleague and a year as my boyfriend.'

'So you don't want to marry me?' His face went inscrutable.

'My heart's telling me to rush in and say yes,' she admitted, 'but I'm still scared. Like you, I've been there before and it's gone wrong. I was engaged to Howard for four years, Roland.'

'And you still hadn't bought your wedding dress, three weeks before the big day—when I know you're the super-organised type who likes planning things in advance,' he pointed out. 'So maybe you knew deep down that marriage wasn't the right thing for you and Howard, and you let it go as slowly as you could.'

'Maybe.'

Again, he lifted her hand to his mouth and kissed the backs of her fingers. 'His parents didn't like you, and they made you feel as if you were a worthless gold-digger. So I'm guessing that you're worried my family will feel that same way about you, too.'

She swallowed hard. 'Yes.'

'My family isn't like Howard's,' he said. 'They're not judgemental. They're eccentric and they have bossy tendencies—well, you've met Philly so you already know that bit for yourself—but they're warm and they'll love you to bits as soon as they meet you. And I definitely like everyone I've met in your family.'

'Uh-huh.' She bit her lip. 'Roland, I'm not very good about being spontaneous. And I know you're good at sweeping me off my feet, but that wouldn't be right—not for this. Can I have some time to think about it? Time to sort my head out?'

'Yes,' he said, 'but I'm not giving you time to worry about things. Come and meet my family tomorrow, so you can see for yourself that it'll be fine.'

She looked at him, horrified. 'That's not giving them much notice.'

He smiled. 'Are you telling me you wouldn't ring Bella or your parents on the spur of the moment and ask if you could drop in for a cup of tea? Or that they wouldn't drop in on you unexpectedly?'

'They're my family. That's what families do.'

'Exactly. And it's the same for me. So you'll come and meet them tomorrow?'

She didn't have any arguments left. And she knew she was right: the only way to get over her fears was to meet them. 'OK.'

'Good.'

'But I need you to know that I'll never come between you and your family. If they don't like me, then I'll fade out of your life,' she warned.

'Deal,' he said. 'And I need you to know that I'm absolutely certain that won't happen. They'll love you, Grace. They'll see you for who you are and they'll love you.' He kissed her lingeringly. 'More to the point, *I* love you.'

'I love you, too,' she said shyly.

'But you're worried that the past is going to repeat itself and you need to be sure it won't. I get that.' He smiled. 'And I'll wait until you're ready to give me an answer.'

CHAPTER ELEVEN

THE NEXT MORNING, Grace woke in Roland's arms. She lay there for a moment, just enjoying being close to him; but gradually she grew antsy.

Today was the day she was going to meet his family.

He'd said it would be light and easy. Just coffee. And he was sure they'd love her.

But what if they didn't? Howard's parents had never thought she was good enough for their son. And Roland's background was very different from her own.

She knew that if she lay there, she'd get more and more miserable, and she'd start fidgeting. She needed to be active; but she also didn't want to wake Roland and start whining at him.

When life gives you lemons, she thought, you make lemon drizzle cake.

And maybe that would be a good way to break the ice with Roland's family. She could take them some home-made lemon drizzle cake to go with the coffee.

Gently, she extracted herself from Roland's arms, shrugged on her dressing gown, crept out of the bedroom and quietly closed the door.

She'd just finished putting the hot lemon and sugar solution on the cake, letting it sink in, when Roland walked out of the bedroom.

'Sorry—did I wake you with all the noise?' she asked.

'No. But something smells amazing.'

'I thought I could take some cake with us,' she said.

He wrapped his arms round her and kissed the top of her head. 'Stop worrying. It'll be fine. But cake is good. You didn't make any spare, by any chance?'

'You'd eat cake for breakfast?'

'French family rules,' he said.

She laughed. 'Made-up rules, more like.'

'Busted.' He held her close. 'Grace, it's going to be fine. I promise.'

He took her mind off things by having a shower with her.

But her nerves returned, doubled, when he drove them to his family home and she could see the enormous house at the end of the long drive.

'Roland—this is a stately home!'

'It's not open to the public. Well, the gardens will be and we're going to do teas and weddings, but...' He shrugged. 'It's not a big deal.'

Yes, it was. She bit her lip. 'Roland, I come from a very ordinary background—and I'm not like Bel. I'm not all bubbly and bouncy and easy to love.'

'Your background is absolutely not an issue—and you're not ordinary, you're the woman I love,' he said firmly. 'Yes, I know you're a bit shy and it takes time to get to know you—but you're more than worth getting to know, and my family's perceptive. They'll see that straight away.'

Grace, remembering Cynthia Sutton's judgemental sneer and her habit of muttering disapproving comments behind the swing of her perfect bob, wasn't so sure. By the time Roland opened the front door, she was feeling physically sick.

But then two dogs came romping down the hallway, barking madly, with their tails wagging nineteen to the dozen.

'Morning, beasties. Coco's the poodle, after Chanel, and Napoleon's the basset hound,' Roland explained. 'French dogs, French names, yada-yada-yada.'

Grace made a fuss of the dogs, who insisted on licking every bit of her they could reach.

'Paws off the cake, beasties,' Roland said with a grin. 'Most of that is mine.'

And then the hall was full of people. Roland introduced them swiftly.

'Grace, these are my parents, Henry and Joanna; my brother Will and sister-in-law Susie; my sister Philly you've already met; and this is my niece, Matilda.'

'Hello,' Grace said shyly, holding out a hand.

But, to her shock, instead of shaking her hand, they all hugged her in turn; and that included little Matilda.

This was so very different from Howard's family; and so much more like her own.

'Coffee's ready,' Joanna said. 'Would you prefer to sit in the drawing room or the kitchen, Grace?'

Grace looked to Roland for an answer, but his face was impassive.

'The kitchen, please,' she said. 'And, um, I made you some cake. I hope that's OK.' She handed the plastic box to Joanna.

'Told you she was a keeper,' Philly said in a stage whisper.

'Shut up, Philly,' Roland said, in the same stage whisper. 'Sorry, Grace. But you've already met my sister. You know she's bossy.'

'Runs in the family,' Philly retorted, and put her arm round Grace. 'What kind of cake is it?'

'Lemon drizzle.'

'Yes! That makes you my new best friend,' Philly said with a grin.

'Actually,' Joanna said, 'I think the men should go and sit in the drawing room while we go and sort out cake and coffee in the kitchen.'

'Good idea,' Susie said with a smile.

'Hang on,' Roland began, his eyes widening. 'No interrog…'

But it was too late. Joanna swept Grace off to the kitchen along with Philly, Susie and Matilda. When Roland came in to try and rescue her, his mother just waved him away and said, 'This is a girls-only chat. Off you go, and close the door behind you.'

Roland gave Grace a helpless look, mouthed 'sorry', and did as he was told.

'We really are glad to meet you, Grace,' Joanna said, putting the cake on a plate. 'And this smells gorgeous. Did you make it this morning?'

'Yes. I, um—when I'm nervous, I bake,' Grace admitted.

'And meeting all of us for the first time is pretty scary,' Susie said. 'I remember what it feels like.'

'Though it's not all of us for the first time. You already know me,' Philly pointed out.

'And we feel we know you,' Joanna said, 'because Philly's told us about you.'

'There isn't actually that much to say about me,' Grace said. 'I'm very ordinary.'

'Tell us about you in your own words,' Susie invited.

This felt like a job interview, but she also knew that it was the most important interview she'd ever have in her life. If Roland's family couldn't accept her, then she'd fade out of his life—for his sake. 'I'm an accountant, I have a clean driving licence and I like cooking,' Grace said. 'I think that covers it.'

'I think there's something quite important you forgot to say,' Joanna said quietly. 'You've put the smile back into Roland's eyes. And to do that takes someone very out of the ordinary.'

'Seconded,' Philly said promptly.

'Thirded,' Susie added.

'Fourthed,' Matilda said, beaming at her. 'Can you make cupcakes, Grace? They're my favourite.'

'Chocolate or vanilla?' Grace asked.

Matilda thought about it. 'Both.'

Grace laughed. 'Good choice. Yes.'

'Are you going to marry Uncle Roland?'

Susie swept her daughter up and plonked her on her lap. 'We're not supposed to ask that, sweet-pea.'

'Why not? I like Grace. So does Coco. I think she should marry Uncle Roland and then I can be the flower girl at the wedding,' Matilda said.

Susie groaned. 'I'm so sorry, Grace. She's obsessed with being a flower girl.'

'My best friend's been a flower girl three times already,' Matilda confided, 'and she's got a tiara with sparkly butterflies on it.'

'That sounds lovely,' Grace said, smiling.

'I think you should go and tell Daddy the cake's coming soon, Tilda,' Susie said, and Matilda slid off her lap and scampered out of the kitchen. 'I really am sorry about that,' she said to Grace.

'It's fine. Really,' Grace said.

'Out of the mouths of babes,' Philly said with a grin.

Then it hit Grace. This wasn't anything like her first meeting with the Suttons. Roland was right. She hadn't been judged and found wanting. His family was eccentric and bossy—and utterly lovely. And it felt as if they'd already taken her to their hearts.

'This,' she said, 'feels exactly like my parents' kitchen would if I had a brother who'd brought a girlfriend home to meet them for the first time.'

'Is that a good thing?' Joanna asked carefully.

Grace nodded. 'Because, although I don't have a brother, I do have a mother and a sister I love very much. And the best stepfather in the world.'

'That sounds good to me.' Joanna lifted her mug of coffee in a toast. 'We really are pleased to meet you, Grace. And I'm sorry for the interrogation.'

'No, we're not,' Philly admitted, not looking in the slightest bit abashed.

'Of course you're not,' Grace said, laughing back. 'Just as I wouldn't be in your shoes.'

'If it's any consolation, they did it to me, too,' Susie said, giving her a hug. 'And they're all right, this Devereux lot.'

The ice was well and truly broken then—especially when they re-joined the others in the drawing room and everyone tasted Grace's cake. 'You're officially in charge of cake from now on,' Will said. 'And we are so going to pick your brains for tea room suggestions.'

'Yes—Roland ought to show you the boathouse after

lunch and tell you what he's planned,' Henry added. 'He can explain them better than any of us can.'

'Actually, I have new plans,' Roland said. 'I know exactly how we can make ourselves stand out for the wedding business.'

Grace had a feeling she knew what was coming next, and hid a smile.

'We could,' he suggested, 'build a folly. A mini-Pantheon.'

Merciless teasing followed.

'This lot has no vision,' he sighed theatrically. 'Grace, tell them you think it's a great idea.'

'I think I'll stick with what you said originally,' she said. 'In two hundred years' time, visitors to the house will be told that you were Roland the Mad Architect.'

'She's got your number, little brother,' Will said with a grin.

After lunch—and after Grace had absolutely insisted on being allowed to help with the washing up—Roland took Grace out to the boathouse and explained what they were planning to do.

'It's got the perfect outlook,' she said. 'And you're right. That wall of glass will give a spectacular view of the lake.'

On the way back to the house, he took her on a detour into the rose garden.

'Oh, now this is pretty,' she said in delight. 'And I've never smelled anything so lovely.'

'You'd need Philly to talk you through all the names and their history,' he said. 'But.' He paused by the sundial. 'You've met my family now.'

'Yes.'

'Do you like them?'

She smiled. 'They're lovely. And they remind me a lot of my family.'

'Good.' He paused. 'I know I said I'd give you time to think—but I really hate waiting. I'm sure that my life with you will be good. And, now you've met my family, I hope all your fears are set to rest, too.'

'They are,' she said.

He took something from his pocket and dropped to one knee. 'Grace. I love you. Will you marry me?' He opened the box and held it out to her.

Set on a bed of purple velvet was the prettiest ring she'd ever seen: a solitaire diamond set in a star-shaped mount.

'A star,' he said, 'because you're *ma belle étoile*. And I really, really love you.'

Grace swallowed hard.

She'd asked him for time. But she didn't need it any more. 'I love you, too. Yes,' she whispered.

He slid the engagement ring onto her finger, then stood up, picked her up, whirled her round, and then kissed her until she was dizzy.

'I hope you're prepared for what happens next, because my family have a really bad habit of taking over,' he said.

'I'm with you, so I can be brave.' She smiled. 'Bring it on.'

It took Matilda all of five seconds to spot the difference when they walked in. 'Your hand—it's all sparkly!' she said in delight. 'Oh—it's a ring. And it's like a star!'

And Roland slid his arm round Grace's shoulders, clearly enjoying the spectacle of seeing his closest family stunned into silence. 'This has to be a first,' he said, laughing.

Everything suddenly went high-octane, with everyone talking at once.

'So when's the wedding? And it has to be here—every Devereux gets married here,' Will said.

'I have a friend who makes amazing dresses,' Susie said.

'*Croquembouche.* We need a proper *croquembouche* wedding cake,' Henry said. 'With sparklers. Lots of sparklers.'

'The flowers are mine, all mine,' Philly said, rubbing her hands together. 'I can't wait to make you the most beautiful bridal bouquet in the world.'

'And I can be the flower girl and have a sparkly tiara with butterflies!' Matilda crowed happily.

'Wait,' Joanna said, walking into the middle of the room and holding her hands up for silence, for all the world like a headmistress in the middle of a noisy assembly hall.

Grace felt her stomach drop. Had she made the wrong decision? Would Joanna feel the same way that Cynthia had—that Grace wasn't good enough for her son?

'Listen, you lot. I know this is the best news ever, but we have to remember that it's Grace and Roland's day,' Joanna said quietly. '*They're* the ones who make the decisions, not us. And we are absolutely not talking wedding plans without Grace's family being part of those discussions.'

So very unlike the way the Suttons had seen things, Grace thought with relief.

'OK. We'll have a planning meeting tomorrow—or as soon as Grace's family can get here,' Will said.

Roland coughed. 'Did you not hear what Mum said? And I agree. It's Grace's choice.'

Everyone stopped and looked at her.

They all wanted to be involved in her wedding, Grace

realised. Not because they wanted to take over, the way that Howard's family had, but because they wanted to be part of it and make her and Roland's day truly special.

She knew without a doubt that, unlike Cynthia, they'd be more than happy for Bella to be her bridesmaid. Just as Grace would be very happy to ask Philly and Susie to be her bridesmaids and Matilda to be the flower girl—complete with her sparkly butterfly tiara. And butterfly wings, if she wanted them.

'My parents are in Italy right now,' she said, 'but they're due home next weekend. A planning meeting sounds good to me. And your house is beautiful. I can't think of anywhere nicer to get married.'

'In our private church,' Will said. 'Or in the house—I'm doing the paperwork to get licensed to hold weddings right now, and I'm sure I can rush it through if you need me to.'

'Or I could build the mini-Pantheon in the grounds,' Roland suggested. 'That'd be a really spectacular wedding venue.'

Everyone groaned. 'Roland. *No!*'

'Spoilsports,' Roland grumbled. But he was laughing.

'And, whatever anyone suggests, Grace gets the casting vote,' Henry added.

Coco and Napoleon barked, as if agreeing.

They were all on her side.

And Grace knew that this time everything was going to be just fine.

EPILOGUE

Three months later

ON A PERFECT Saturday afternoon in September, Grace got out of the car at the gates leading to Roland's ancestral home, and let her stepfather help her up into the old-fashioned coach pulled by four perfect white horses.

'You look beautiful, Gracie,' Ed said. 'Like a princess.'

'Thank you,' she said shyly.

'I know I'm not your real dad, but I'm so proud of you.'

She squeezed his hand. 'You're not my *biological* dad,' she corrected, 'but as far as I'm concerned you're my real dad and you have been ever since you came into my life. I'm a Faraday girl through and through. And you're the only person I would ever consider asking to walk me down the aisle.'

Moisture glittered in his eyes. 'Oh, Gracie.'

'Don't cry, Dad,' she warned, 'or I'll cry too, and Bella took ages doing my make-up—she'll kill us both if it smudges.'

'I love you,' he said, 'and I'm so glad you're marrying someone who loves you and will always back you.'

This was so very different from what she'd planned before. And even making the plans had been different this time, too: because both families had arranged things together.

The horses pulled the coach up the long driveway. Grace's mother, the bridesmaids and the photographer were waiting outside the little private church where every member of Roland's family had been married for the last three hundred years.

The photographer took shots of her in the coach with Ed; then Ed helped her out and her mother made last minute adjustments to her veil and dress.

'You look wonderful,' she said. 'Now go and marry the love of your life, with all our love and blessings.'

Grace's smile felt a mile wide as she entered the church.

The string quartet—Hugh's latest signing—struck up the first movement of Karl Jenkins's *Palladio* as Grace walked down the aisle on Ed's arm. The chapel was filled with old-fashioned roses chosen by Philly from the formal gardens at the house, and the arrangements were echoed in the simple but elegant bouquets carried by Grace and her bridesmaids. Matilda walked in front of them, wearing her sparkly butterfly tiara and scattering rose petals. Grace could see Roland waiting for her at the aisle, and saw his brother Will nudge him and whisper something just before he looked round.

As he saw her walking down the aisle towards him, he smiled and mouthed, 'I love you,' and the whole world felt as if it had just lit up.

She couldn't stop smiling through the whole service. Finally, the vicar said, 'You may now kiss the bride.' And Roland did so lingeringly.

There were more photographs outside the church and in the rose garden; then they finally walked down to the lake, where the boathouse was newly renovated and ready to host its first ever wedding breakfast. The wall overlooking the lake was completely glass, giving perfect views across the lake; and as they looked out they could see swans gliding across the water.

'This is so perfect,' Grace whispered.

Roland kissed her. 'It certainly is.'

The tables were set with more beautiful arrangements of roses and the last of the sweet peas. 'Like the first flowers you ever bought me,' she said to Roland with a smile. 'Philly's really done us proud.'

Everything was perfect, from the meal to the speeches and the music from Hugh's quartet. And Grace knew that it was going to get even better; they had a band for the evening reception, and Roland had planned a display of fireworks just behind the lake.

And there were fireworks indoors, too: because to Henry's pleasure they'd gone with his suggestion of using a tradition from the French side of the family, and instead of a tiered wedding cake they had a *croquembouche* with a spiral of white chocolate roses curled round it. At the top of the cone, instead of a sugar crown there was an array of indoor sparklers; as soon as they were lit, everyone oohed and aahed.

'It's magical,' Grace said.

'Absolutely. And that's how it's going to be for the rest of our life,' Roland agreed. 'With our whole family behind us, helping us to make our dreams come true.'

She raised her glass of sparkling elderflower cordial to toast him. 'For the rest of our life.' She paused. 'Roland, do you think we can sneak out for a moment without anyone noticing?'

'Why?'

'Because…' She needed to tell him something, but she wanted to tell him in private, and so far she just hadn't found the right moment. 'I need a moment with you. Alone.'

'And you want us to sneak out, given that all eyes are on the bride and groom?' He grinned. 'Well, hey. We're a team. We can do anything.' He put her glass down on a nearby table, and waltzed with her over to the corner of the room, then quietly danced with her until they were at a side door. 'Righty. Let's slip out.'

Once they were outside, he found them a quiet spot by the lake. 'OK. From the look on your face, it's not just because you want to be on your own with your new husband. What's wrong?'

'Nothing's wrong. But… What you were saying about us being a team. A team means more than two, or it can mean a pair.'

'You're splitting hairs, but OK,' he said. 'You and me. Two. We're a pair, then.'

She coughed. 'I'm trying to tell you something. We're a *team*.'

'You just said we were a pair.'

'But,' she said, 'we went to Venice just over three months ago. We made love for the first time.'

'Ye—es.' He frowned. 'You're talking in riddles, Gracie.'

'No, I'm not.' She stroked his face. 'I thought architects were good with figures? And have an eye for detail?'

'We do.'

'So did you notice that I toasted you in elderflower cordial, not champagne?' she asked. 'And alcohol is off the menu for me for the next six months. Along with soft cheese and lightly cooked eggs.'

She saw the second that the penny dropped. 'Are you telling me…?' he asked, hope brightening his face.

'I know we didn't plan it, but we're definitely Team Devereux,' she said. 'I didn't want to tell you until I was completely sure—and I wanted you to be the very first to know. I thought I might be a bit late just because I've been rushing about sorting out wedding stuff. Not because I was stressed, because our joint family is brilliant, but just because…it's a wedding.' She spread her hands. 'And it's not that. Because I did a test this morning.'

'And it was positive?'

'It was positive,' she confirmed.

'I don't care that we didn't plan having a baby. It's the best wedding present ever,' he said, picking her up and whirling her round. 'I love you—both of you.' He set her back down on the ground and cupped his hand protectively over her abdomen. 'Team Devereux. You, me, and a baby that's going to have the best family in the world.'

'The best family in the world,' she echoed.

* * * * *

LET'S TALK
Romance

For exclusive extracts, competitions
and special offers, find us online:

[f] facebook.com/millsandboon

[Twitter] @MillsandBoon

[Instagram] @MillsandBoonUK

Get in touch on 01413 063232

For all the latest titles coming soon, visit
millsandboon.co.uk/nextmonth

MILLS & BOON

THE HEART OF ROMANCE

A ROMANCE FOR EVERY READER

MODERN

Prepare to be swept off your feet by sophisticated, sexy and seductive heroes, in some of the world's most glamourous and romantic locations, where power and passion collide.

HISTORICAL

Escape with historical heroes from time gone by. Whether your passion is for wicked Regency Rakes, muscled Vikings or rugged Highlanders, awaken the romance of the past.

MEDICAL

Set your pulse racing with dedicated, delectable doctors in the high-pressure world of medicine, where emotions run high and passion, comfort and love are the best medicine.

True Love

Celebrate true love with tender stories of heartfelt romance, from the rush of falling in love to the joy a new baby can bring, and a focus on the emotional heart of a relationship.

Desire

Indulge in secrets and scandal, intense drama and plenty of sizzling hot action with powerful and passionate heroes who have it all: wealth, status, good looks…everything but the right woman.

HEROES

Experience all the excitement of a gripping thriller, with an intense romance at its heart. Resourceful, true-to-life women and strong, fearless men face danger and desire - a killer combination!

To see which titles are coming soon, please visit

millsandboon.co.uk/nextmonth

might just be true love...